MW01102647

Jeds' World

A Novel

Author

Larry Danek

Title # 4788523

ISBN-13: 978-1499368802

Table of Content

Acknowledgements

Prologue

ACKNOWLEDGEMENTS

This book is dedicated to my wife Donna for her love and assistance along with her patience in putting up with me over the long period that this book took to complete. She allowed me the freedom to work on it when I probably should have been doing something else. She also spent some of her precious time editing my poor spelling and grammar.

This book is a complete fabrication from the deepest parts of my mind. I have always been a "day dreamer" with lots of ideas about writing them down. I wasted way too many years working for a living and not finishing the dozen or so stories that I had started. I can only hope that the readers of this book find it as interesting as I found in writing it.

Reference material was gleaned from the following: Primitiveways.com, Paleotechnics.com, Wildernesscollege.com and Wikipedia.org. I also used the Webster's Dictionary for those hard to spell words.

A special thanks to Steve Hughett, a fellow writer, for his guidance and assistance. When I met him at the post office in Nine Mile Falls, he told me he was a writer. I didn't tell him at that time that I aspired to be the same. I never had anything published before and didn't know if I could get this one done. When I finally told him, he encouraged me to keep at it. I will be eternally grateful for that.

JEDS' WORLD

Prologue

George (Jed) Martin is an aging twentieth century man, living in the twenty-first century. He hates progress and fights the thought of the internet and cell phones. He recently lost his wife to cancer and is depressed and expects to die soon to join her.

Instead he gets transported back in time to something akin to the Stone Age. In the process he gets a new and younger body. He finds himself completely nude with a Neanderthal like appearance.

He is now living in a time that requires the making of tools and learning to start a fire. He has to deal with the hazards associated with wildlife and Mother Nature. He spends a considerable amount of time trying to find his way back to the twenty-first century but to no avail.

He sets up camp on the river and stays there while learning to survive and make shelter and clothing. George finds himself fighting wild animals and eating raw fish. His Boy Scout skills are no match for the new environment.

He is then forced to move on with his new life. He thinks that a gray fox has adopted him as it follows him everywhere he goes.

He wonders why he didn't die of old age and who is responsible for what has happened to him. He spends months alone before finding out that there are other people that he will have to associate with.

His old memories with the new body seem to combine to make him a much more complete person.

The discovery of an amulet leads him into a world of mystic powers.

He must find a way to save the people of this world from their own destruction.

Chapter one

The Change

I need to explain this as best I can so that you understand what happened to me. I doubt that you will believe me but it probably won't matter as I can't seem to get back to tell you about it. This has been and is the most harrowing and awesome experience anyone could possibly have.

It was early afternoon and I was having a tough time concentrating on anything that might have some significance to it. One of these days I have to get the car in for service and I may need a lawyer to clean up the paperwork on name changes. I don't know about any of it at this time. Maybe tomorrow I can sit down and work through some of it. It had been a small service and over quickly but for me it seemed to take a life time and then some. Now I just need to get out and clear my mind a little. I'll just go to the state park and do some walking and try not to think too much.

I parked the car and remembered to put the parking tag in the window. The sun's not so hot today and I shouldn't need anything to drink. I never was much for drinking anyway. In any case I forgot to bring a bottle of water with me. I locked the car and checked around to see if anyone else was out and although there were cars in the lot, I didn't see another person. I had always carried a camera and binoculars on these walks before but didn't think to bring either of them today.

It was a sunny day but not short sleeve type of weather, just a regular shirt and slacks would be just fine. I'll have to watch where I walk as someone had horses out here earlier and didn't clean up after them. As I walked along, caught up in my recent loss, I didn't notice that the scenery around me was changing. The blacktop path through the park was getting narrower and the trees on both sides were closing in on me. I was in a sour mood and knew that depression can cause this sensation. My thoughts were for the time, not long ago, when I had walked this way with my wife and how she seemed to see so many things around us. She had commented constantly about what she saw and heard. I was never the observant type and this had bothered me some because I wanted the solitude and serenity of the surroundings to help me feel at peace. Now I wished she were here to enjoy this walk with me. We had walked here a lot as she liked it and I needed the exercise. Her death had left me cold. She had been the one that had seemed healthy while I was sick off and on for most of my life. She had been my strength, taking care of me during those times. I never thought I would feel this way, but then again I thought I would die first.

I was angry at her for dying and now was feeling sorry for myself and knew it was a part of the grieving process. If I managed to get through the stages, I would be able to go on almost like normal. Then I wondered what normal could possibly be like for someone my age and alone. It nearly brought me to tears as my eyes blurred with the thought. I scolded myself under my breath; there was no need for self pity. I had lived a long time and knew that I would be joining her soon enough.

I felt oddly, stronger now and more energetic than I had for some time and picked up the pace. The blacktop was gone now and the graveled path was turning to dirt. Walking faster, without thinking about where I was, I had to just keep going. It would help me forget the things that waited for me at home. I was going downhill now on what must be one of the trails that the horseback riders use to get to the river, but it even seemed small for a horse to pass along. It probably hadn't been used much lately.

I slowed my pace to keep from sliding on the pine needles that covered the path. It wasn't a conscious thought, just years of knowing my own condition. Were I to fall down this steep hill, something would surely break. The medicine I had been taking for years now had caused the loss of bone density and the fear of breaking some bones had been with me for a long time. Being careful had become a way of life.

As I reached the river, I began to pay more attention to my surroundings. The water in the river was lower than I thought it should be. Maybe the power company was holding it back behind the upriver dams to create more electricity. It was noisy here but not the kind of sound that I was familiar with. Not the loud city type noise but almost like the noise you would hear on a farm. The insects were thick in the air and making loud buzzing sounds. The ducks and geese had noticed my arrival and wanted to let me know with their cacophony chorus that I was being watched. I could feel the mud on my feet and looked to see the numerous animal and bird tracks. Small and large and many in between that I did not recognize because they were overlapping. Some were much deeper than others but of course animals of all kinds would come here to drink. Not a surprise for that but why hadn't I seen any of these tracks before or the animals that belong to them.

Then the real shock set in, I didn't have any shoes on my feet or anything else on for that matter. I was completely nude and covered with a fine hair, though not so thick that you couldn't see the skin under it. I reeled from the thought and tried to sit down. The touch of the mud on my backside caused me to jerk upright and move forward into the river a step or two. It was shallow here and the water wasn't moving very fast, so I had no fear of it. I wanted to wash off the mud and wondered what had happened to my clothes. Looking around to see if anyone was watching me, and seeing no one, I began to rinse myself off. Feeling thirsty, I got down to take a little drink of the water. I never got that far. The reflection in the water was not my face but of some stranger of odd decent.

The shock of what I saw caused me to jump with fear and I started to run away from it as fast as I could go. Still in the water and getting deeper, I slipped on some rocks and fell head first. I reached for the bottom and grabbed on to the thing that was under my hands. It tried to squirm away but I just tightened my grip as I struggled to my feet. I stood up in water just over waist deep and holding the largest fish I had ever seen, I was shell shocked. I had never been the observant type in all my years but now I seemed to feel my surroundings more than just see them. The fish was trying desperately to get away and I instinctively dropped it. The sound of the fish hitting the water seemed to bring me back from that wild fear. I would have thought of it as reality but there was nothing real about what had just happened to me. There was no way to make sense of it but I would

[11]

have to gather what I could of the situation and try to get back home. I had left many things undone and there would be a price to pay for that. Closing my eyes and trying to get a picture in my head of what had just transpired. It seemed to be more than anyone in their right mind could expect to grasp. What should I do first?

I knew that I had no clothes on and that the face in the water had been the one that belonged to this body. I now gathered myself as I needed to look again at the face in the water and the body it was attached to. Raising my hands up to eye level, I slowly opened both eyes and stared at them. They were huge and rough and very strong looking, covered with fine hair over the back of the fingers. The good news was that the numbers added up to what I had started out with, four fingers and a thumb on both hands. Quickly looking over the rest of the body answered all I would need to know about it. The appearance was different in that most of the parts I could see were covered with a fine hair, not very thick and dark brown in color, almost black. It was definitely a male body of immense size and obvious strength. Except for the coloring I could have been the Incredible Hulk or an ogre like Shrek. This body was like a Neanderthal or early Homo sapiens or maybe a mix of both. I wasn't sure what either of those looked like but knew it wasn't a comfortable fit for me.

Not knowing how to comprehend what had happed to me, and knowing that I had to get home, I turned in a circle to see if I could find out where I started from. The panic that set me off scrambled my sense of direction. I was in the middle of the river and both sides looked the same. How can I know which way I went, I thought? I had gone in the water to wash the mud off and get a drink. Common sense would be that I would be facing upstream when I tried to get a drink as the mud on my feet would be going downstream. Ha, I said out loud, my brain is still working. I will just go downstream and the muddy path will be on my left. Another thought occurred to me before I could get started. What if I turned to run away from the image in the water, then I would have been running downstream and now need to go the other way.

It didn't matter, I hadn't gone far enough to get lost and retracing my steps would just require a few minutes in each direction. I could look for the muddy spot with the big footprints in it.

I started downstream, along the left bank, looking for the spot that would indicate my entry point in the river. A hundred yards or so was far enough and I switched sides of the river and went the other way. The water never got deep enough that I would have to swim. Thinking that I covered about two hundred yards and not found my starting point, I now waded over to the opposite side and headed back down. The current was pushing me around a rocky outcropping when I noticed a shallower area with a sand bar. There was the muddy entry into the river just beyond it and what I had been looking for. It was at the very end of the sandbar and made a very convenient place for animals to come and get a drink.

I hurried over the sandbar and skirted the mud on the bank, looking at all the tracks there. I could identify some of them and saw the ones that I had made on my way down. I started back up the trail hoping to retrace my steps and get back home. I didn't even think about what might happen if I got home looking like this. There was one exception, of course, I couldn't go back stark naked. I looked around for something to use for a covering and the only thing available was some bulrushes at the river's edge. I quickly assembled a hula skirt from them but not one that would pass inspection in Hawaii.

I then followed the trail as it meandered uphill among some very big pine trees. Some of them must have been five feet in diameter and well over a hundred feet high. It had gotten late in the day and the sun was about to go down and I hadn't found the top of this trail yet. Thinking that I might have some luck seeing where to go if I climbed one of the bigger trees before it got dark, I looked around and noticed that most of the trees didn't have limbs low enough to climb on.

As I continued up the trail it seemed to run into a cliff and since I hadn't come down a ridge like that I stopped to look around again. One of the biggest trees was growing right next to the rock wall and I could see a branch that was low enough to climb on. From there I could see the limbs almost like stair steps going up the tree. The sun was now below the horizon and the area under the trees was getting dark. I grabbed the lowest limb and started to climb. By the time I got high enough for a good view it was too dark to see anything. I thought about climbing down and trying to find a place to bed down for the night but realized for the first time that the insects that had been pestering me were gone. I located a double branch that was quite heavy and close together. It had a single limb, growing upward on one side. I stretched out on them, placed my feet against the trunk and rapped one arm around the upward growing limb. I listened for a few minutes and was surprised at how quiet it had become. I then fell fast asleep as if nothing in the world had happened.

I woke with a start in the predawn morning, cold and confused. It took a couple seconds to focus on where I was and what had happened. Being thirty feet in the air would make for a hard landing if I tried to move too fast. I had no idea why I even thought to stay up in the tree and sleep. Something made it seem like a natural occurrence. I rolled to a sitting position and held onto the upright branch to secure my balance.

The sunshine was coming through the tops of the trees and would soon warm me up. As I waited for this to happen, I noticed some slight movement below. It was still dark at the foot of the tree and my eyes seemed to adjust a little to compensate for it. The dark brown, four legged critters, were moving down the trail I had come up the night before. I knew that they were deer and they were probably going to get a drink and browse by the river. I seemed to know these things instinctively and wondered at it. How I came to be here and naked as a blue jay, was another thing indeed. I would ponder that for a long time and never get the answer I was looking for.

For now I would seek to get home and worry about the rest later. I climbed the tree, limb after limb, to the very top. It swayed under my weight. I looked around but could not find a point of reference that would help me get home. The cliff that I discovered last night was still there and was higher than the trees. There was another one on the other side of the river. I was determined to get to the top of this ridge and see what was up

[14]

there. It might have some answers for me. Climbing down from the tree and seeing that the deer had moved on down the trail, I started up it. At first I thought it would go just to the cliff face and around the end of it. Now as I reached it I could see that it had a path that worked its way along to the right and up the front of the ridge. The deer must have come down this way to get to the river. It would mean that there was either no water or food for them up on top. It didn't matter to me; I just wanted to see if there was a place to start back to home. Looking up, the trail wandered through rocks and open areas and got lost from sight at various locations.

What was that old quote? "Every journey begins with one step" and I stepped out, putting one foot ahead of the other on my way up. I hadn't gone far before I started to get nervous. I stopped and crouched down, something or someone was watching me and I didn't know how I knew that. Without moving a muscle, just my eyes, I scanned the path and rocks ahead. Not sure what to look for, just anything different or standing out.

I didn't see it at first but after a second scan of the path it was there. Its color made it easier to see than I thought it would. The tawny coat of the cougar contrasted with the darker lava rocks all along the path. There would be no way to get away from it so I would have to find a way to get it to go in the other direction. Moving only my hand, I slid it along the side of the path feeling for a sizeable rock. There would be no nice smooth, round ones like on the river. I felt a sharp edged stone that was about the right size to get a good grip on. The big cat seemed to anticipate my move and rose up from its crouching position. I rose up also, cocking my arm as I stood. If the cat charged at me I would try to hit it in the face or as close to the nose as possible.

To my surprise the animal jumped sideways and straight down the cliff wall. My reaction had been instinctive and I threw the rock on an intersecting course with the cat. I wasn't sure how I knew where and when to throw the stone but it was very accurate and hit the cat in the front shoulder and caused it to go tumbling down the rocks. It rolled into the trees below. I looked on in amazement for a few seconds after the thing scrambled into the trees and disappeared. Now I knew I could be in grave danger and needed some kind of weapon to protect myself with. I wouldn't find anything but rocks along this path so I started picking some up as I went along. I discarded one after another as I found a better one. They would make a clattering sound as I dropped them off the side of the path. I would make sure that the next one fit my hand and felt good for balance. With one in each hand, I continued up the path, giving little thought to what happened to the cougar.

The trail was quite steep and had some places where it wouldn't be safe to walk without checking where you put your feet. I hurried now, wanting to get to the top before another creature started down and blocked my way. The path was well worn and showed years of use but the weather had caused some erosion. Those places could be tricky to cross and I had to watch each step then. I did not encounter anything else on my way up and didn't realize that the noise from the rocks I discarded would warn most animals to stay away. Reaching the top I had a quick look around to insure safety and then walked a little ways out onto the open plain. It was almost barren here, the grasses were brown and dry and the shrubs showed little sign of life. It must not have rained here for some time.

The plain stretched out ahead of me for what looked like miles. I turned in a complete circle, taking in the view. The river had gouged its way through the plain to create this deep gorge. Looking across to the far side, I could see that it was the same over there. I couldn't see the start or end of the ravine as they disappeared into the horizon. However, I could see the mountains that the water was coming from but they seemed to be a very long way off.

None of this was familiar to me and didn't indicate that I could find what I was looking for. I started off toward the mountains and had only gone a few steps when I stopped to look around again. The path up from the canyon was not visible from this angle and I realized that if I were to go back down it I would have to mark it someway or other. There were no landmarks or obvious ways to recognize it. Some of the animal tracks would lead to it but there were tracks all over the place and looked mostly like those left by the deer.

I would worry about the other tracks later but now I had to find a way to mark the trail. If I got too far from it, I might never get home. I circled the area and could find nothing that would work as a marker. Going back to the trail and looking down didn't seem to help. I could go all the way back to the tree line and get some sticks to make a marker but that might take more time than I wanted to spend. There were many loose rocks along the trail I could use. I would only need a dozen or so to make a stone pyramid. Once I had figured that out, it only took a few minutes to gather enough to make the locator that I knew was important for my search. One trip down to where the lava flow started and in no time I had an arm full and returned to the top of the ridge. I placed them in a small circle and stacked them up till they were three high in the middle forming a pyramid. I had made sure that they were away from the path enough that the animals using the trail would not find them of any interest. Now I could start out and feel very sure that I would find my way back here.

As I started out, I looked at the sky. The sun wasn't half way up yet, so I knew it wasn't noon. The morning was going fast though and I would have to hurry to make some progress today. Keeping the canyon on my left and walking east, I could set a good pace and put some distance between myself and the trail. A couple hours into it, I began to feel tired. I knew what tired felt like in my old body but this tired was new to me. I pushed on anyway, knowing that I would have to get somewhere before night fall. I just didn't know where that would be. I was still pushing my body hard when the sun reached the horizon and started to create those long evening shadows.

There would be no traveling at night and rest would be very important. I found a small depression after a short search of the area. It had some dried grass in the bottom and would provide some protection. I tried to gather more grass to make bedding with but just couldn't get the energy up to do that. I lay down and tried to sleep but my body was now complaining bitterly. As soon as I stopped moving, my legs began to cramp up and my stomach indicated that it was empty. I was getting cold also and knew that the lack of clothing was going to be a real problem. I hadn't eaten anything for at least two days and couldn't remember my last drink of water. I must have gotten a drink yesterday when I was in the river. Was it only yesterday?

So much has happened in so short a time. Now I became acutely aware of my bodily functions. I hadn't passed water at all today let along anything else. That would be a bad thing and the reason I was not doing so well now. I also knew that water was more important than food or anything else. I would have to get down to the river as soon as possible. I hadn't crossed another path leading to the edge. Should I go back or look for another way down. I decided to rest tonight and make my decision in the morning. I didn't have a lot of choice in the matter.

It was a long night for me. The cold and cramping made it seem like morning would never come. I forced my mind to concentrate on relaxing my body. I managed to cat nap off and on though out the night. When it got light enough to see I got up and started back the way I came. There was no sense in going on now. No way to know if I would find a new trail down the rocky cliff. I had just started to move when the fingers of my left hand released the rock I had been carrying since yesterday morning.

As it fell to the ground and I watched it, something moved in the grass that I had used for a bed. I knew that it was a grasshopper and while picking up the chunk of sharp lava rock it jumped again. It crawled under some of the flatted vegetation and was out of sight in an instant. I saw where it had gone and stood there for a minute watching for it. The ground was cold enough that the hopper wasn't going very far or fast but thinking it was out of sight, sat still. Now I remembered something about the grasshoppers being used for food. People had covered them with chocolate and fried them in butter. They had fixed them in many ways and would eat them like any other food source. I placed both the stones down on the ground and put a hand over the grass that the hopper was hiding under. I then slid my other hand under the grass and grabbed the bug before it could get away. "Tag, your it" I said to the bug and popped it in my mouth.

[18]

I crushed it between my teeth and forced it down my throat nearly retching from the thought. I found that the taste wasn't so bad and I needed something for nourishment and with nothing else available this would have to do. I had seen quite a few of the hoppers yesterday and knew that there would be more along the way back. I searched around the immediate area and managed to find five more of them.

I was about to congratulate myself for finding food when I was startled but the flight of two partridges that flew up from almost under my feet. I instinctively cocked my arm but had nothing I could throw except the grasshoppers. The birds were out of reach before I could retrieve the lava stones that I had been carrying. Instinct told me to watch them go. I might get another chance at them yet today. No way, they were going further onto the prairie and away from the direction I had to go. I popped another hopper into my mouth and watched the birds spread their wings to descend. Before they reached the ground, something jumped up and grabbed for one of them but missed. They gained a little altitude and flew even farther away.

The distance wasn't so great that I couldn't tell what appeared to jump but I had to compute in my mind how big it was. It was doggish in appearance but way too small to be a wolf or maybe even a coyote. It had to be a fox and a grey one at that. What was a grey fox doing out here? How long had it been there? That little itch I had in the back of my head all day yesterday, could it have been following me? I knew now that was possible and I just hadn't recognized it. This was another lesson learned, and I would have to pay more attention. I thought about the fox for a couple minutes. It must have miss timed its jump to not catch the bird. Maybe it was just a kit or an older fellow that had lost some of its skills. It could have been just dumb luck on the bird's part. Any way, it was no biggie for now. I would just keep an eye out for the rascal on my way back.

I picked up one of the stones and looked at it and the other one on the ground. With the grasshoppers in one hand and the stone in the other I would have to make a decision. How to make sure I had enough protection and still have some food. I had no pockets or pack to carry anything in and felt the need to have that extra stone. What to do. I took the quick answer and ate the hoppers. Now with my other hand free I could pick up the stone that had remained on the ground. I would just have to keep track of where I dropped the stone while catching more grasshoppers. I would also have to keep one stone ready in case more birds flew up or some other critter showed its face. I hadn't seen anything I could use as a weapon so far, either today or yesterday. For that I was determined to hang on to the two stones.

With the hunger partly taken care of, the thirst was getting harder to handle. I remembered hearing that if you were thirsty you could use something in your mouth to make it draw saliva. There were no small pebbles or stones I could find there but maybe a stick would do. Most of the shrubbery was dry and leafless now and those that had leaves were way too dry to work. I didn't see any cactus type plants even though it seemed dry enough for them. The prairie was covered with straw grass with a few plants here and there. Most of those were sagebrush and they were on their way to becoming tumbleweeds. I would keep going and watch for something to use along the way.

It wasn't long before I saw a bush that stuck up just a little bit higher than the grass but had heavier branches. Most of the leaves were dead or gone but that didn't matter as I just wanted the stock to chew on. Breaking off a piece wasn't easy as it wanted to shred when I pulled on it. I took one of the stones, the one with the sharpest edges, and sawed off the biggest part of the plant. I stuck it in my mouth and bit down on it. It didn't have much of a taste to it. Thinking back to when I was a kid and chewed on bark, the taste was about the same. The plant had a little liquid in it and now my mouth began to supply some more. It was a minute or two before I had enough to swallow and it felt good going down. I didn't have time to stand around now and headed back toward the trail.

I thought I might be getting close to the trailhead so I walked over to the edge of an outcrop. I could see the river and lots of trees. Looking along the cliff I was able to see the path where it came out of the pines and worked its way up the high wall. There on the path was a small herd of deer. They seemed to be looking for something lower down in the trees. I couldn't see anything and let it go at that. I needed to get down there and headed toward the trail as fast as I could go. At this point it wasn't fast at all but fast enough. I saw the little pile of stones that I left as a marker and felt some relief.

However, that didn't last long. The deer and I arrived at the trailhead at the same time causing quite a bit of excitement. The deer had been so interested in what was behind them that they didn't see me until the very last minute. The lead deer jumped backward when it saw me and bumped into the following deer. Then as they jumped forward, directly at me, I moved out of the way to let them get by. During the quick movements of the heard, one of the young deer got bumped off the trail. I could hear its hooves scratching for traction just for a second or two then it was gone. I looked over the edge and saw the spike buck tumbling down the rock face. I turned to watch the rest of the heard charging across the plain. I didn't bother to watch them out of sight but turned back to the path to start down. Just then I got to see the worst and the best of the animal world. The young buck had broken something in its fall and couldn't get up. It would suffer a horrible death if left like that but Mother Nature has a way with things that we sometimes find offensive.

"Along came the spider" I thought, as the tawny coat of the cougar showed through the trees. I forgot about the drink of water for a couple minutes as I watched the events unfold. Something about this sort of thing makes it hard to turn away. The big cat had watched the deer fall and was ready for it but came out of the trees slowly as if very cautious. The deer couldn't escape and the cat knew it, so speed didn't seem to be necessary. The behavior of the cougar seemed odd at first but made more sense as things unfolded. There was a problem with its right front leg or foot that caused it to limp. Still it got to the deer and put an end to its misery fast enough. Grabbing it by the neck and crushing its vertebra.

Now the roar of objection broke the silence that was engulfing the scene. The reason the deer herd was nervous in the first place now showed itself. Down near the foot of the path stood a huge brown bear and it

[21]

wasn't happy to lose the game it had been after. The bear charged along the tree line and the cougar dragged the deer down out of sight. The encounter would not go well for the big cat since it was already wounded having probably injured itself when it tumbled down the cliff. Soon, both combatants were out of site.

I ignored the noisy fight between the cougar and the bear and started down the trail again. I was startled by the grey fox as it jumped past me and raced ahead of me down the trail. The fox would be looking for a meal while the two combatants kept each other busy. I was about half way there when the fighting stopped. For a second I wondered which one was the winner but recognized the roar of the bear claiming its territorial rights. It must have driven off the cougar and taken over the kill. That would not have been a surprise as the bear seemed in good health and must have weighed twice as much as the cat. I continued down the trail as the bear kept sounding its anger about something or other. That fox was probably causing the bear some irritation.

When I reached the river, I dropped the stones I had been carrying and splashed right in. I dropped down to get a drink, knowing I needed to get something to eat but right now the water was more important than anything else. I stayed in the water for awhile, even though it was cold. Remembering the fish I caught when I fell the first time I was in the river caused me to think about food again. If I caught a fish could I eat it raw or would I have to cook it first? I didn't know if I could wait for the fish to cook if I had to first start a fire. I wasn't sure if I could do that or not.

While I thought about that, I started to get the itch in the back of my head again. Only this time it seemed more urgent. Instinct told me that the fox didn't cause that much of a distraction. This had to be more of a threat than he would be. Turning my head slowly to the shore and trying not to move anything else brought the realization that I was in some kind of trouble. The big cat had made it to the water's edge and now seemed to want to take out its pain and loss on me. The bear had done a considerable amount of damage to the cat. Its face was tore on the left side and the eye on that side was missing. The front legs seemed as if they could hardly support it. I let my fingers rap around a stone on the river bed as I watched the big cat start to set itself to jump.

Although the movements were at hyper speed, I saw it all in slow motion. The cat sprang, I rose up and threw the rock and dove off to the side. I hit the cat in the good eye, causing it to swerve to its left and miss me. However, as it went by its rear feet came down on me and the claws cut into my backside. The water probably saved me from some real damage as the big paws pushed me down in the water on their way past. The water turned red around me and I thought that the worst had happened. The sharp pain diminished almost at once as the cold water filled the groves that the claws had cut into me.

Now instinct took over and I knew that the big cat wasn't done with me yet. Grabbing a rock from the bottom and spinning around to face the cat I saw that it was trying to focus on where I was. I knew instantly that it was blind now, as I had taken out its good eye but it was still very dangerous. Its ears twitched to locate the noise I was making in the water and as it started its next leap I dove out further into the river. I thought the water depth would give me a slight advantage and I needed all the help I could get. I set my feet and threw the rock as the cougar tried to locate me. It bounced off its head and didn't seem to have any effect. Reaching and grabbing another rock made enough noise that the cat zeroed in on me. I moved to my left this time and the cat missed by mere inches and got hit in the head again for its trouble. This time though, I made sure I located the blow on the right ear and it almost tore it off.

The cougar had sustained so much damage and lost so much blood that it now was having trouble just getting turned around to face me. I moved with it as it turned and kept off to one side for the next couple of minutes. I now had a chance to finish the cat off and wasn't going to pass it up. I was getting one stone after another and making sure I hit its head with every one of them. Several minutes passed as the cat tried to keep its head above water but the damage the bear had done took its toll. The rocks I hurled at it only hasted the end. I wouldn't have been much of a match for the cat if it were healthy. Once again I felt the fear of not having some kind

[23]

of weapon for protection. I would have to find some way to make a bow or spear.

Not having anything to eat but grasshoppers for the last two days and having to fight the cougar had drained me of all energy. I sat down in the middle of the river and watched the big cat drift away. The pain in my backside caused me to lean to one side as I remembered the damage the cats claws did to my buttocks. The gravel river bottom was grinding against my bottom and sort of opening up those claw marks.

I saw some fish moving in the water as I got up and my hunger returned with a vengeance. The fight had taken me downstream so now I had to work my way back up to the sandbar. I moved closer to the shore and could move more easily there. I was watching for fish as I walked, hoping to be able to grab one or splash it out of the water. They moved away from me as I walked. When I got near the sandbar most of the fish were smaller and they stayed close to the shore. At first I didn't know why but soon guessed that the bigger fish would eat the little ones if they could reach them. It was that thought that slammed home the need to eat something. The little fish would have to do if I could find a way to trap or catch some of them.

At the top end of the sandbar was a small inlet no more than two feet across and less than a foot deep. I could try to push the smaller fish into it and then maybe catch some of them. I moved around the end of the sandbar while swirling the water with my hands and feet. The fish tried to stay ahead of me and where forced to go into the inlet. I was surprised to see that three bigger fish also swam in. I pushed sand across the opening and closed it off. I pushed more sand into the inlet to reduce the size and make it easier to catch the fish. Now I only had to splash the water and fish up on the bank to get my dinner. I went after the bigger fish first but in doing so only managed to get a couple small ones out of the water. I picked up one of them and put it in my mouth, deciding to swallow it instead of chewing like I did the grasshoppers. It went down easy enough so I did the same with the other one. The rest of the fish were still trapped there and I needed something to work with to get them out, especially the bigger ones.

I tore the limb off a small sapling that had lots of little branches on it and used it to push the fish to one end of the inlet. I was able to scoop and splash the fish out of the water now that they were all crowded together. This time I got one of the bigger fish out along with three small ones. Grabbing the larger one before it could work its way back into the water, I tossed it higher up in the bank. I thought it was a trout but couldn't remember how to tell. Maybe it was the color or stripping on its sides. I had never been much of a fisherman and hadn't cared all that much about eating them either. Now it looked like that was going to be my main diet at least until I could make something better than throwing stones.

I started back to get the rest of the fish when I saw a grey blur dash across my peripheral vision. I swore when I looked up in time to see the fox grab the fish and dart off with it. While this was going on, the three small fish had flipped around enough to get back in the water. I felt the urge to hurry now and grabbed the branch and pushed the fish up to the end again. This time when I scooped at them I was able to get five little fish but the big ones managed to evade me. It was then that I noticed it was getting dark and that the sun had gone down. I grabbed the five little fish and swallowed them one at a time. Now I needed some place to sleep and the only thing I could think of was to get back up the tree I spent the first night in.

I patted some mud onto my back side to cover the scratches made by the cougar's claws. I hoped it would keep the insects away from them. Then heading up the path in the dark turned out to be easier than I expected as memory took over. My night vision wasn't as good as an owl but I was able to get past all the obstacles without stubbing my toes. Climbing the tree I had the feeling that none of this was real and then the fact that it was cold and I was naked left me with some strange thoughts as I settled down for the night. Sleep came quickly again but I would be bothered while I slept by all the things that had happened. I dreamed that I was in a fish bowl with no way out, just going around in circles. My partners in this were strange also; the bear, the cougar, and the fox seemed to be alone or along for the ride. I wasn't sure if this dream meant anything or if it was indeed what was happening.

I woke with a start in the morning. I was so cold and stiff I could hardly move and that may have been a good thing. Being thirty feet up in the air, without having a good mental hold on anything, wasn't such a wonderful place to be. Before I could move I realized that my bladder had filled up overnight from the water I had sucked down the evening before. I didn't feel the mixture of grasshoppers and fish had worked their way down far enough yet but was sure that would happen sometime soon. I lay there for a few more seconds before I came to know what had awakened me. The deer were under the tree again and moving down the path to the river. I envied them their fur coats and thought about how to get something to wear. I was cold because I had the sweats last night and now I stunk to high heaven. I would have to get over not having a hot shower whenever I wanted one and maybe use to the odor also. It had been three days now and it seemed like a lifetime already. The deer had moved on down the trail and out of sight. I climbed down from the tree and walked a little ways into the woods to drain my bladder and kind of get my bearings back.

The time had come for me to make some decisions about what to do next. Knowing I could not keep eating grasshoppers and raw fish caused me to mentally count off the things I had to do. First and foremost I would have to start a fire and prepare a way to cook the fish I caught. Second I would need some clothing or body cover. Third I needed some way to carry food and water. Fourth I would need some tools and or weapons. They didn't all have to come in that order but knowing there would be other things I would need, those would have to wait. Fire was the most important and I would work on that down by the river this morning.

I worked my way down to the river slowly to allow the deer time to drink and browse a little. I made some extra noise on my way down in order for the deer to have time to move away from the area of the sandbar. The deer had moved upriver, knowing that the bear was probably on the downriver side of the trail and it would try to protect what was left of the deer kill from yesterday. I didn't think the bear would have left much to guard, considering the size of the bear compared to the deer. I hadn't gotten to the river before the bear started complaining again. Something was bothering it and maybe it hadn't finished off the deer after all. The fox

[26]

wasn't around this morning, so maybe it was causing the bear some grief. Ignoring the bear and avoiding the deer, I started downstream in search of a good spot to start a fire. I wanted to be far enough away from the trail to keep from scaring off the wildlife, some of which I would be looking for as food and clothing later on.

I found it easier to wade downstream in the river than pushing through the brush and around the wood piles that had accumulated along the bank. One particularly large pile of debris would give me lots of fire wood but still be a problem to get around. It extended out into the river and back up the bank into the trees. I waded further out in the water and stepped into a rather deep hole. I was in over my head in an instant and was forced to swim. I now remembered that I never was a good swimmer and still had to struggle to get out of the deep area back to where my feet touched bottom. I didn't have any fear of what happened but would keep that in mind for a later try. If you live on the river you should know how to swim and I did but I wasn't very good at it.

I got my feet on the bottom and pushed to get around the logjam. A surprise met me as I looked toward the shore. The way the water swirled around the logjam and the deep water hole caused many floating things to accumulate. Mr. Cougar had found its way there and was patiently waiting for me to drag it out of the water. It would have to wait though as I hadn't located a good place to set a fire. I went about a hundred yards or so to where the river turned sharply to the right. This may have been the cause of the logjam. The river ran in that direction for a short stretch before it ran into the far bank and turned back toward the middle of the canyon. The logjam extended down into the corner but had been pushed up the bank for a few yards. That allowed some space between the water and the pile of debris. This looked like a good spot and I set about clearing the weeds and setting a fire pit. I was aware that some rocks were better than others for use with a fire but I would just have to get by with what was on hand.

I broke off a dead limb and used it to dig out the grasses. Making a large circle first and then carrying stones up from the river, placed them all around the outside. The next thing I needed was the fire starter material.

That would be a straight smooth stick, some bark and a little shredded grass. I gathered them up quickly and then broke off some small branches and placed them off to one side. I had a pile of dead grass set to the other side to help as a fire starter. Now the "How to" from Boy Scout one-oh-one came into play. Spin the stick on the bark fast enough and when it starts to smoke add the shredded grass and a little bit of blowing and walla, we have fire. I built up the fire with the small sticks and then added some larger ones till I had a nice size blaze going. I then pulled one of the straighter sticks out of the fire after it had burned off one end. I rubbed it on the flattest stone I could find and made a point on the burnt end. Now it was time to go spear fishing.

I thought that getting some fish would be easy but that wasn't happening. I had been lucky at the sandbar but here the fish just swam under the logjam and out of sight. I stabbed at a couple as they swam past but missed them badly. Somewhere in my head were the instructions on how to do this and I knelt down to where only my head and shoulders were out of the water. I waited for the first fish to swim by. I knew that if I were still they would forget about me and sure enough they did. I lunged with my spear but again missed badly. It took me a couple more tries before I remembered the visual deflection caused by the water. Just then a larger fish swam by. I knew it was a salmon but didn't know what kind. It didn't matter as it would turn out to be dinner. This time I got the angle right and came away with the salmon. I lugged the fish out of the water and instinctively looked for the grey fox. It was nowhere to be seen, not surprising as I was blocked off from the forest area by the logjam. I guessed the weight of the fish to be about ten pounds but wasn't sure as things here seemed so different from my life before.

The fire had died down by the time I got back to it so I had to put some more fuel on it before I could do anything with the salmon. It was easy getting enough wood to keep the fire burning. I just had to break off chunks of the logjam into the size best suited for cooking. Next I needed to make a spit of some kind to hold the fish over the fire. I didn't have a knife to gut the fish with so the sharp stones from the trail would have to do. I had not gone anywhere without them since the encounter with the big cat.

That was the reminder to go fetch the cougar and get it out of the water. I did that as soon as the fish was on the spit and cooking. I was going to miss the Skippers Tartar sauce or even some butter. I was so hungry that it wouldn't matter anyway. I wouldn't be able to eat the whole salmon and wondered if I could let it set over the hot coals and dry out, like you would if you were smoking it.

I dragged the carcass of the cougar up past the fire and hung it over some of the driftwood. I hadn't looked at it before now but had some time while my dinner was cooking. The big cat had lots of damage to its face and I was responsible for some of it. Both of its eyes were useless as the left one was hanging out and the right one was crushed from the stone I had hit it with. The bear had done more harm to the cat than I did as its belly was tore open and some of the guts were hanging out. Now I knew where all the blood in the water had come from. Just then my back side started to itch as a reminder of what the big cat had done to me. I then noticed the right front shoulder had some rock pieces stuck in it and realized that is where I hit the cat. I had met the cat on the trail, was that two days ago or three? Time was becoming blurred for me now. So many things were happening that they ran together and I lost track of when but not where.

I sat there munching on the fish and trying to sort out all that had gone on in the short time I had been stuck in this time warp. I had slept in the tree twice and on the plateau once, so this is the fourth day. It wasn't going to make much difference anymore as I couldn't explain any of this to the people back home. That is if I was ever to get back home. With that thought in mind, I began working on a plan to go up and down the river looking for another way out. I had managed to start a fire and spear a fish. I now needed to make some tools and or weapons. A hammer should be easy, once I got something to use as rope or twine. Making a bow and arrows was probably out of the question for now but something to think about for the future. I would make some more spears and get some good throwing rocks.

Getting some clothing would be more difficult and I wondered if the cougar hide would work for that. How much work would it be to skin the cat and clean the hide enough to wear it? I decided to work on that for the rest of the day using the sharp stones from the trail. How I wished for that Boy Scout knife I had left at home in the dresser drawer. It would have been a little small for this kind of work but a lot better that the shards I was using. The cougar pelt took a lot more time and effort than I wanted to spend but knew I didn't have a lot of choices. I couldn't run down to Walmart and buy a jacket, cap, and gloves or even socks. I was just thinking about the things that I had gotten use to doing over the seventy years or so that I had lived.

I removed the intestines and washed them out the best I could. I wouldn't need them for this trip but might latter on. I then hid them under some rocks in the water hoping they would be undamaged there and safe from roving animals. I thought only raccoons would be good at finding these things and I hadn't seen any of those around.

I wasn't able to make any real clothing out of the pelt but instead made a loincloth and used the tail hide for a belt. I tried to make sure not to cut too much away from the hide as I would use the biggest part as a blanket. I could use it as a shoulder rap while traveling and sleep on it or under it at night. I could tell that it was going to be "a work in progress" for me to learn all the intricacies of caveman life. I laughed at the thought, since I didn't have a cave to work out of.

All the clichés of my past kept popping up in a haunting way as I went along just trying to survive. Sometimes I would get lost in thoughts of how easy life had been before, although not as simple as this. I could just drive down the street to a store, go in and buy a loaf of bread and a jug of wine, then be off to meet my "Thou" at some rendezvous. Now I was "Thou-less" and missing the other two items also. I never experimented with wine making in my "other" life so there probably wouldn't be any in this one either. On top of which, I couldn't find anything that looked like grapes around here or anything else that would work as a replacement for them.

I slowly gathered up the things that I would take with me and let my mind wonder a little too much. I had left things undone at home and now

[30]

worried that someone else would get stuck cleaning up the me
bills that got paid were the automatic withdraws from my checking ⌣
I knew it was fruitless to think about these things but sometimes I was overcome but the enormity of it all. I had become more and more emotional as I got older and now I was trying to shed that just so I could survive. It would be better if I just worked on getting ready to go and making sure I had what I needed. I decided to go upstream first and see if it led to anything or place. I had not seen anything in the river to indicate that someone could be up that way but if you had to flip a coin, up was as good as down in this case. I would go two days upriver or further if something looked promising and I would camp along the way to fish or find food and check for tool making material. I would stay on one side of the river while going up and return on the other side. If I saw something on the opposite side I would cross over and look at it.

I would be looking for a way out of the canyon and for any type of food supply that might be there. If I could find crayfish or frogs to supplement my diet, that would be good. Even a turtle or two would be a welcome guest at dinner. I felt sure that I could knock off a duck or goose with the stones I had available to me. That would give me a nice change also. Then there was the prospect of fruit of some kind, maybe berries or something like that. Even some plants or their roots could be edible, especially if stuffed into one of those ducks. I would have to remember to save some of the feathers or down from those birds as I might use it later for something. I had no idea how much good any of this was going to do but I was starting to look on it as an adventure. That would be really nice if it produced some things of interest. Just the thought of something besides fish to eat made me want to hurry on my way.

Chapter two

The Bear

e better part of two weeks going up and down the river. The ... e was blocked by a high waterfall and extremely steep rock on both sides. The way up looked too dangerous to try at this time. Maybe I would get around to it later if the downriver side had nothing to show. I searched the banks of the river looking for a way out but didn't find any.

I worked both sides for any option that I might use. I was looking for a path or animal tracks but all I found was nesting areas for the ducks and geese that were well past the nesting stage now. I did manage to supplement my diet with duck meat a couple times but mostly ate fish. The cougar pelt came in handy as the nights seemed to be getting colder.

All along the way, I had been working with the bark of different trees and shrubs to see what use they could be to me. One of them was stringy enough to work into a rope if I braided enough of it together. I used it to carry some extra fish and a duck back to the site where I built the first fire.

I didn't want to leave the area that might have the hidden means to get back home. I would search the whole area to see if I missed something that would lead to the path back. Then I would start downriver again after that and see if I could make it to the ocean or lake that the river emptied into. Surely there would be someone close to the end of the river or on the water somewhere. The isolation and loneliness were getting to me and I longed for companionship.

I was now able to make a fire quickly using the stringy bark and a small bow to spin a starter stick. I had a lot of bark and soft grasses to work with all along the river and never had to work hard at getting the material together for a fire.

I had noticed that the drift wood and log jams were very high up on the banks of the river in some places, especially where the river walls were

[32]

close in. I thought that the spring floods must be dramatic to do so much damage and move so many logs that high up. It was something to keep in mind since I was sitting in what must be the spring flood plains. I didn't think I would have to worry about it now as it seemed to be going into winter, making spring a long term problem. I didn't expect to be here then because I was going to find my way out.

I surprised myself at times with the detail I was noticing around the area. The small things I wouldn't have seen before were becoming more and more obvious. There were lots of birds and insects to be seen all along the river but none of the small animals that I expected to be there. I remembered the tracks in the mud and now thought about them a little more. They varied in size and depth but most of them belonged to the animals and birds that I had already encountered.

There should have been mice and small to midsized animals like raccoons and opossum and porcupines and the like. Maybe even skunks could have been here but I didn't see any trace of them. There were some squirrels around but not as many as I thought could be supported by the number of trees here. The strangeness of the situation was making me nervous and I vowed to look for another path out of there in the morning.

I went to look for the cougars internal organs that I had hid in the river but they were gone. Something had managed to find them and spoiled my plan to use them to carry water in. I checked the bank and surrounding area for tracks to see if I could determine which animal had gotten to them. I didn't have any luck there, whatever it was had probably been in the river and not gone up on the shore. On the other hand my tracking skills might not be good enough to trace the culprit.

I got up early the next morning and restarted the fire. It had gone out over night and I was cold even though I had the cougar pelt for cover. The thin grass bedding I had slept on didn't keep the ground temperature from cooling me off. I had eaten the duck last night and cooked the fish this morning, and now I had to start looking for another route out of here. Not wanting to go back into the water, I sought to climb over the logjam and go into the forested area. I loaded some good throwing stones into the small

[33]

bag I had made out of one of the cougar leg hides and left the sharp lava stones there. I made sure I knew where I placed them so as not to do without if need be. I took the stringy bark rope and three short spears and started over the pile. It was unsteady and dangerous but I took my time and made sure each footstep was secure before going on. There would be no 9-1-1 calls from this location.

The far side of the logjam was up at the tree line and away from the grass and shrubs that grew along the river. I knew that the rock wall to my right would stop me and the side to my left had no path up the rock wall except the one I had taken before. That didn't stop me from looking as I knew I got here somehow and maybe could find the same way out.

I started with the shorter side first going to my right through the trees. It was easy walking because there were no lower branches on the trees. It only took me a couple minutes to find out what had made the bear so mad after it ran the cougar off. There in one of the trees was the spike buck. The big cat had managed to get the deer up into the tree and hook its head between two limbs. I wasn't sure why the cat didn't stay up in the tree and avoid the fight. Something must have happened that I couldn't guess at. Just then I got that itch in the back of my head again and decided to get out of there. It was that bear again and I climbed the next tree to get away from it.

I wondered if I could still use some of the hide off the deer but knew the meat would be no good by now. The bear hung around for a while and tried several times to climb up after me. I tried to discourage it with one of my spears each time it made an attempt. When it gave up trying, it headed down toward the river, maybe to fish for some of the salmon that had been so prominent lately. I continued my search but didn't have any luck finding a way out on either side and it turned out to be a smaller area than I first thought it to be. I had one more encounter with the bear and fortunately, it had the same results.

I hit it with a couple of the throwing stones when the spear didn't cause it to leave. The rocks just seemed to bounce off the thing as if they were puff balls. The bear didn't seem amused at the effect and let me know with a threatening growl. It left after that to find other things to torment.

I worked my way back over the logjam and set about spearing some more fish. I had a lot of thinking to do as I settled down to eat my fish. The sun was gone and the clouds had moved in with the first threat of bad weather. I built up the fire and set some stones close to heat them up. I would place them on the ground where I intended to sleep that night and see if that made any difference against the cold. It did seem to help as I slept better that night and I would remember to do that a lot over the next few months.

When I awoke in the morning the ground was covered with a light coating of snow. I brushed the snow away from the fire pit and tried to start a fire. It took a lot longer now with most of my bark and grasses a little damp. Keeping that in mind would be a good idea as I could cover most of what I needed to keep it dry.

It had become obvious that I wasn't going to find a way back to the twenty first century any time soon. Winter was starting to set in and the coming snows would make it difficult to find adequate warmth and shelter. I knew it was time to start preparing for the worst. There was no way to tell how long the cold would be here on the river but it was cold enough now to freeze the edges of it.

I had gone up and down the river on both sides and not found anyplace better to set up a camp. There were no caves or natural shelter areas I could use. The land on the bluffs was flat and open. Down here among the trees I would be out of the wind and get some shelter from the snow. The river would supply fish and the deer that come down off the prairie would supply the rest. I would continue to search for tool making and weapon materials. I had done well with the spears so far but they were not going to be of use against the bear or other large predators or game.

The biting insects that had been so bad just a week ago were now just about all gone. The migratory birds had been leaving in small and large groups and could no longer be seen on this part of the river. I had watched them leave and wondered about the direction they took. There had been many more of them coming from the upriver side. Mostly they seemed to be going west or down the river and not south as I would have expected. Maybe there was a feeding ground in that direction before they had to turn south. It was just one more thing to ponder in the long list I was creating in my mind. The fish hawks and eagles were still here but would be leaving soon. The dead and soon to be dead salmon would be frozen in place with the cold weather, robbing them of any food source. I was sure that the river would freeze over as it just didn't have enough speed or volume to keep open.

I decided that I would build my camp at the base of a large tree, down river from the sandbar and just up from the logjam. I had climbed trees a couple times now to get a better view of the area. This tree, like many others, had no lower limbs. I remembered seeing loggers use a rope to climb a tree or pole. It turned out to be a simple trick if you had a rope. I used the bark of a tree, cutting it into strips and hammering it to get the strands out. I then braided the strands and offset them to get the makings of a rope. I didn't know what kind of tree it was but I thought of it as willow because it grew next to the river. I had to be careful though as this was not the best material for holding my weight. I would have to find better material for that and to hold other things together. This would do for now and I probably would need some deer hide to make a stronger one.

I had all these memories of how to do things. I had been a Boy Scout, had read books, watched TV shows, and had gone hunting, fishing and trapping but to no real extent. I had done these things as a boy and was certainly no expert. The experiences and memories were going to keep me alive until I found a way out of this place.

A lean-to would be easy to build against the tree, using some of the drift wood and newer pine branches. I could keep a small fire going in the coldest days. There was an abundance of wood in the logjam and along the banks on both sides of the river. I had already accumulated some to work with. The spears had been the easiest tool to make, just requiring a straight stick or limb. There had been many of those along the river that had already been debarked by Mother Nature. I just had to make a point on one end by setting it in the fire and rubbing that end on one of the larger flat stones at the river's edge to make a point. The fire would harden the wood somewhat and I had used them to spear fish.

I also poked the bear in the nose several times when it tried to climb the tree I was in. I was glad it was a brown bear, they don't climb very well. Maybe their size was a hindrance to that, I didn't know. I did know however, that if that bear came after me again I would aim for its eyes instead of the nose. I should have learned that lesson from the cougar that I killed because it couldn't see me.

The logjam turned out to be the source of all the wood I needed to build my lean-to and gather fire wood. I would keep getting the bark of the willow type trees to make rope and string to tie things together. I gathered up a lot of the bark over the next couple days, knowing that if it froze, it would be harder to get and work with. The strands in the bark ran vertically so I would cut into it with the sharp lava stone and slice it down the trunk or limb. I tried to get as long a strip as possible to keep the rope from having too many breaks in it.

The hammer I made from a forked stick and a good egg shaped stone. I chipped notches in the stone to let it fit in the forked part of the stick and I tied it in place with the string from the willow bark. I started to make a path through the logjam to the river, using the hammer and a lot of muscle. I didn't get very far with this project the first day, before it got dark.

I scraped out a fire pit and built a small fire, making sure it would not spread. I didn't want to lose my living quarters before I even had any living quarters. I raked a large pile of pine needles together with my hands and made a bed near the fire. I placed a log across the far side of the fire to reflect the heat toward myself. This arrangement would work until I was able to get the lean-to built.

It took me four days to break through the logjam and clear a path to the river. In doing so, I managed to find some really good framework pieces for my lean-to. During this time the grey fox had started to hang around, showing up whenever I had a fish on the fire. I took to tossing the parts of the fish I didn't eat out to where the fox could get it without getting close. This of course has cause and effect, "where every good deed deserves a bad result", one should plan on it. The smell of the fire had kept most of the animals at the other end of the canyon, but now the smell of fish cooking was attracting an unwanted guest.

I had just finished eating and was going back down to the river. I had a clear path now and wanted to strip some bark off the willow trees to make some more rope. I intended to tie the framework together and then get some pine boughs to cover everything with. I almost missed the feeling in the back of my head when the fox let out a yelp. I looked up just in time to see the fox disappearing into the trees.

Big old Mr. Bear had made its entrance and came looking for the fish that had been recently cooked. Now it was eyeing me for a possible bigger meal. It didn't have any fear of me but knew about the pointy stick to the nose thing. I retreated into the water as the bear started after me. I didn't have time to go for the spears or the sharp stones.

The bear didn't seem to be in a hurry but didn't stop its advance, following me into the water. Now the bear had a huge advantage as it could move faster in the water than I could. I went upstream to try to get around the logjam and hoping to get out of the water before the bear could catch me. I knew that even that made no sense as the bear could easily out run me on land as well as in the water.

The bear had almost caught up to me when I reached the deep spot in the river. I grabbed a lung full of air as I went down, diving for the bottom. The bear on the other hand just waited for me to come up for air. The water was extremely cold but crystal clear and I could see the bear on the surface. I knew my options were slim and decided that the best defense was going to be a good offense. I groped around on the bottom for something to throw at the bear and found two really good stones. I drifted under the bear to get in behind it and set myself to launch up to the surface.

The bear was almost motionless as it held itself against the current. I made sure I was far enough behind the bear to have time to dive again as soon as I had thrown the rocks. The movement of the water alerted the bear of my coming and it started to turn around. I had pushed so hard off the bottom that I almost came out of the water but in doing so had time to throw both rocks at the bear. I hit it on the head but couldn't tell if I did any damage or not as I fell back into the water and dove to the bottom again. I did this twice more and then from the bottom I could see the water was turning pink from blood near the bears head. I got ready to launch again but the bear had guessed that it wasn't a battle it could win outright and swam to the opposite shore. I watched the bear shake off the water and look back at me as if to say "I'll get you next time". As it ambled away going up river, I had the feeling that one of us wasn't going to make it through the winter. I started to think of ways to end it in my favor.

I was almost numb from the water but felt cleaner than I had since I got into this strange world. It was then that I realized that the cold didn't bother me like it use to. I was cold but not enough to shiver and quake. There was something about this body's metabolism that kept me from slowing down with the cold.

As I thought back over the last few weeks and listed the times I did something different than I would have in my other life. I began to see that the will to live was stronger here than back there. I wasn't sure if I could have swallowed the fish or eaten the grasshoppers before. It seemed that the survival instinct was so strong that I might be doing things without actually thinking about them. The fight with both the cougar and the bear took place in the river where I really shouldn't have had the advantage. Somehow I had made instinctive moves in both cases that let me survive and stop the others.

I hadn't intentionally gone to the deep water hole or at least I didn't think I did. What was it that guided me to make the right choices so far? I would have to keep these things in mind but also keep my guard up. I didn't want to forget that the bear could still be a problem for me. Anyway the cougar was gone and I now had a fur blanket for my trouble.

[39]

I had done well with the cougar kill. It had taken some time to skin, scrape and then dry the hide. I had to work with it every day for a while to keep it from getting stiff. I had rubbed it with sand and pounded it with a rock on the inside and that seemed to soften it up somewhat. It didn't turn out to be soft like the tanneries did it but it still was a warm cover when I needed one.

Now that the bear was off tending its wounds maybe I could try to skin the deer that was hanging in the tree. I thought about that for a minute or two and decided that the sharp lava stones were too far gone to keep using. I would have to get some more of them off the trail. I took the hammer, two of the longest spears and the cougar leg pouch making sure I had it full of good throwing stones. I knew it would be too late in the day to go up the trail but I could get an early start in the morning.

I planned on sleeping in the tree up by the trail and trying to judge the time of day the deer came and went. I was almost too late as they were on their way up when I got to the tree. I watched them disappear over the top before I climbed the tree and settled down for the night. I managed to get the cougar skin around my shoulders before going to sleep and thinking this would be the last time I would do this. I didn't normally dream much or remember them if I did, but this night was one to make me think a lot. I dreamed of my youth and things I did as a young boy and at the same time of another youngster growing up wild and free. They seemed to be one and the same but very different also. I had no memory of the second boy but recognized him anyway. That one made me feel very close but very much alone.

When I awoke in the morning, I had the dreams of the night still stuck in my head. I couldn't forget the other boy or the feeling of not having anyone around. Something had happened and I didn't have any idea what it was but knew it was very bad for this youngster to not want to remember it.

I sat on the limb of the tree some thirty feet in the air and waited for the deer to come down the trail. The sun came up but the deer were a no show for some reason. I hadn't been watching them so had just

[40]

assumed that they came down every day to drink and browse. Well I wasn't going to wait all day for them. I had to do some rock mining and get that dead buck skinned. After that I would be busy working on the lean-to and gathering fire starter material. If I could make the lean-to big enough I could even store some of the wood in there to keep it dry.

I went up the trail to about the half way point where I could see the layer of crystallized rock from the volcano. There were a lot of small pieces lying on or near the trail but I wanted as many big ones as I could get. The trail ran diagonally through the seam of rock and that meant I could only reach a small portion of it. I worked slowly and with lots of patience to get the biggest pieces out that I could. I would stop frequently because I kept getting that little tingly feeling in the back of my head. I would look around and search for the cause both up the trail and down into the woods. Whatever it was stayed hidden from sight and I hoped it was the fox but didn't know. It didn't seem urgent but the feeling was that something was watching him. Going back to work I would break away the rock over and under the seam before trying to get the glassy rock out. I knew that the bigger the pieces were the longer they would last and that at some point in time I wouldn't be able to get any more.

I wondered if there was a place where I could get flint instead of the stuff I was working on now. That would likely be up the river near or in the mountains but I was planning on going the other way. It would only make sense that if there were people around that they would choose to be closer to the ocean or whatever this river emptied into. I kept gathering the volcanic rock until I had trouble reaching any more. I bundled up what I had in the cougar hide and sat on the trail for a couple minutes.

I hadn't gotten over the feeling that I was being watched and was a little nervous about heading back down into the woods. I decided to go up on top first and watch the trail to see if something followed me up. I remembered the outcropping where I could see the trail but maybe not be seen from down below. I stopped several times on my way up just to make sure whatever was down there wouldn't start up before I could get to the outcrop. I was still getting the tingle feeling and it seemed to be more urgent now but still nothing showed up on the trail.

I placed my bundle of new stones near the rock marker I had made on my first trip up here. Then I headed toward the outcropping to see if I could get a view of the bottom of the trail but something caught my attention. The ground at this point was torn up pretty bad with lots of blood and fur around. I had seen some bigger birds overhead and failed to make a connection with them and the itch in the back of my head. Now I noticed that they were buzzards or vultures, I didn't know one from the other. They could be Turkey Vultures but they should have gone south by now. I remembered that they were black with no feathers on their head. I didn't know anything about buzzards except that they look a lot like vultures. These must be hanging around today because of the recent kill that happened here. Was this why the deer never came down this morning? Did the bear find its way up here?

I moved slowly back to the trail while keeping my eyes open for any type of movement. I checked the trail and saw nothing there. The area here on the prairie was really flat and I could see a long way but nothing was moving. There were some landscape features that might hide a predator but the bear was too big for that and probably not inclined to hide. Holding a spear in one hand and taking the pouch with the throwing rocks, I walked back to the where the deer was killed. I guessed that it was a deer because the fur looked similar to their hide. The vultures seemed to be waiting for me to leave before they landed but I needed to check the area first to see if I could tell what actually happened.

I looked carefully at the location as I knew it held the answers I wanted, but would have to make sure I got it right. I guessed that it hadn't been the bear or it might still be around and I didn't think it would have gone up the trail in the night. I had slept near the bottom of the trail and saw the deer go up just at sunset. If the bear had been waiting for them at the top then they would have come back down or so it seemed. So what had caused this carnage?

As I checked the ground, I could see tracks of different animals. There were deer tracks, bird tracks and large paw tracks. The latter ones were made by some kind of canine from the looks of them, way too large to be from the fox. I put my hand down to measure them and then looked again at my hand. I didn't know how to guess at the size of my own hand now, let alone the footprint of the animal that left the tracks. I did know that the tracks were much bigger than the foxes would be and smaller than the bears. I had seen enough of those to get a good idea of size and as I looked around at these tracks I could see that some were bigger than others. That would mean that more than one animal had been there. My best guess here was this was done by a pack of wolves. Then I thought it was just one more thing to complicate my new life. What to do if the wolves come down into the canyon?

That itchy tingling feeling I had was now a fading memory. The wolves must have been going away but in what direction I didn't know. Were they following the rest of the deer herd or just moving ahead of the oncoming winter. Anyway, they were gone for now and I needed to get back to my "would be" camp. I decided to go after the deer hide in the morning as I spent more time getting the new rocks out than I expected to. I picked up my treasure trove of glass rocks and started back down the trail. I saw the flash of a grey tail in the woods and knew my companion was still around. That fox wouldn't live long if the wolves made it down here.

I got back to camp without running into the bear and tried to think of some way to get the best of it. I expected the bear to tree me again but I needed to know which tree that would be. I guessed that the best bet would be the tree at my camp site as I would be there most of the time. I had so much to do before it got any colder but I would have to be very aware of my surroundings. I couldn't let the bear sneak up on me again. I went through my normal routine of starting a fire and spearing a fish, then cooking and eating it and throwing the excess to the fox. I then let the feeling in the back of my head tell me if I would have company or not. With that taken care of I set about making a ladder to get up the tree with.

The thought of a ladder instead of a rope made more sense and was a faster escape method. It would also make it easier to set a trap for the bear. I hadn't seen or heard from the bear today and wondered if it would be hibernating over the winter. It hadn't shown any signs of that yet but it was a possibility. I would prepare as if it would be coming for me regardless of the weather.

It didn't take me long to build the ladder as most of the materials were real handy there at the logjam. I just had to assemble them in a fashion that would make them strong enough to hold my weight but not strong enough to hold the bear. I thought that the bear must weigh four or five times as much as I did, but again I didn't have much of a reference point to go by. I had to break some pieces down to make the rungs for the ladder and used up most of my rope to tie it all together. The day had slipped away while I worked and now it was dark. I built up the fire for the night and made sure it wouldn't spread. I lay down on the pine needles and covered with the cougar pelt and went to sleep.

I woke before it was fully light and gathered my gear together. This time I added the ladder knowing that I would have to climb the tree the deer was hanging from. The sun was making its appearance as I reached the tree and it only took a minute to set the ladder and get up into it. I looked over the deer carcass and wasn't sure if it would be worth the effort. It had deteriorated badly over all the time it hung there. It had bloated and burst out its bottom and became infected with insects. The smell wasn't very appealing either. If I could just get some of the hide off the back area that didn't seem to be rotting yet, maybe I could use that to make strips to tie my stuff together with.

I dropped the deer down out of the tree and started to work on it immediately. I cut as much of the hide off the back as I could and then cut the head off. I didn't know what to do with the head yet but thought the antlers and teeth might come in handy at some point. I kept interrupting my work to make sure the bear wasn't in the neighborhood. While I was thinking about the bear and what to do about it, a plan started to develop that made some kind of sense. First I would have to get back to camp and see if I had the right setup in the tree for it to work. There was going to be a great risk in attacking the bear but the reward should be even greater if I was successful and I had to succeed.

I started on my project as soon as I got back to the camp site. I climbed into the tree using the ladder and surveyed the lower limbs. Two of those were spaced just about right even though one was a bit higher than the other. I set about carrying up some logs to make a platform to work off. Then I dug through the logjam for just the right piece. I broke off the excess limbs and left a couple stubs sticking out about half way down. I placed the bottom end in the fire as I had done with the smaller spears I had made. I then went down to the river and retrieved some big rocks, not too heavy to carry but too big to throw.

I had used up the rest of my rope on the platform, making sure it was secured to the tree and would hold my weight along with the items from this project. I then carried the rocks up to the platform being careful not to put too much weight on the ladder rungs. I spaced them out to distribute the weight and allow room for me on the platform. The wood piece wasn't ready yet and looked like it would be awhile before it was. I decided to take a break and get something to eat while I waited. And besides the fox had been hanging around trying to get at the deer head and hide pieces that I had put up high on the logjam. I retrieved them and put them on the platform for now, then went to get a fish or two. Mr. Fox would have to wait for his dinner.

I kept rotating the log end that was in the fire and burned it down to a semi point. I had done this while cooking and eating the fish I had just speared and at the same time I worked on making more rope. I was getting fairly good at working the willow bark down to strands and then weaving them together. I would have to keep working constantly now to get everything done before it got too cold.

I wondered why it hadn't snowed any more even though the sky was cloudy most of the days now. When the log end was shaped a little like the spears I had made, I continued to work on the pointed end to make it as sharp as possible. I then put the other end in the fire and started to burn it

[45]

down also. This end I would make flatter instead of pointed. I had made sure this piece was long enough to reach from the ground to the lowest branches of the tree my platform was on. Once it was done I hoisted it up to the platform and tied it to the tree trunk.

I was now ready for the bear but didn't know how to attract it without getting in too much trouble myself. I was sure the bear would visit the site where the deer had been hanging in the tree. That should give me a chance to set up some kind of bait to get its attention. I thought about it for a while and guessed that the bear had found my stash in the river. That would take a good nose for finding and following scent. Maybe I could use the deer head to attract it to my tree. It hadn't come looking for it so far but that might be just coincidence.

In the morning I gathered up some of the same things I had been carrying around and added the deer head and some more rope. I went straight to the site of the deer kill and checked to see if anything had been there. There was nothing left of the deer carcass but the ground was torn up were it had been. Something had either eaten or removed the deer and didn't leave anything for me to find. I wondered if the bear could handle the rotten meat or if something else had been there. Checking the ground where the deer had been, I saw claw marks indicating that the bear must have left them. That didn't relate to a positive match for what ate the deer but it was close enough for me. I hadn't seen or heard any other predators in this little canyon, so one and one should equal two. That would be the bear and nothing else. At this point I decided to set the bait out for Mr. Bear and see if I could coax it down to my tree.

I looped the rope around the antlers of the deer head and dragged it through the area were the rest of its body had been. Then I started back to the camp site and the tree which held the surprise package for the bear. It was then that my instinctive itch kicked in and I tried to hurry away from there. The deer antlers kept digging into the ground and I would have to slow down to keep from breaking the rope.

The bear had reached the area where the dead deer had been and seemed to recognize the fact that something else had happened since it was there last. It knew that I had been there with the deer head and started to follow the scent. About that time one of the spike antlers dug into the ground and hooked under a root. I had to move fast to dislodge the head before the bear could catch up to me. I ran to it and kicked it loose and ducked behind a tree. The bear saw the movement and stopped to sniff the air. I jerked the rope to one side and flipped the deer head away from me and let go of it. The bear saw it rolling and started after it. This gave me a chance to go the other way while keeping the tree between me and the bear. Now that I had some space to work with, I started to run for the camp and my tree.

It didn't take the bear long to get the scent of me and see that I was making a break for it. It ignored the deer head and started after me. Bears can run faster that even the best sprinters, and with so much distance to cover, I just wasn't going to make it to the tree before the bear caught up to me. I reached into the rock bag and pulled out two nice sized throwing stones. I had to slow the bear down somehow.

As I stopped to throw the first stone, I saw a flash of grey dash behind the bear and off again. The bear stopped to see what had done that and got hit on the head by the first stone. Before it could start after me again the fox made another run at it, just enough to keep it occupied as the second rock was on its way. With that, I took off again headed for the tree. I didn't even look to see if the second stone had hit its target, but I knew that it did by the sound it made when it landed. As I ran I hoped that the fox had enough sense to get away from the bear.

I got to the tree just ahead of the bear and launched myself up the ladder. I grabbed the first limb and swung up as the bear hit the ladder and knocked it down. I scrambled onto the platform as the bear tried to climb up to get me. I stepped out a little ways onto a limb, trying to attract the attention of the bear. When the bear looked up at me, I retrieved a rock from the platform and hurled it down on its head.

Up till now the many hits to the head had not seemed to affect the bear but this rock was much bigger and it had more of a chance to do some damage. I didn't see the immediate effect of the rock and quickly grabbed another one. The bear didn't seem as stable now but still held its ground. The second rock made more of an impression as the bear now seemed to sway back and forth. I wasn't about to stop at this point and hurled the third rock down causing the bear to drop to all fours. I then hit it with the remaining two rocks to make sure it wasn't going anywhere.

I untied the pointed log and set about aiming for the middle of its back. I would try to hit that hump between the shoulder blades and drive it on through. I lifted it up and pushed it down to get some momentum going and then jumped on board to ride it down. I had left two limb studs sticking out to put my feet on and grabbed the flat end with both hands. My aim would have been good but the bear moved a little to one side and I hit the right shoulder instead. This caused a major problem for me as both the log and I fell away to the side and I was sent sprawling.

I realized that I wasn't hurt and the bear was, but the problem being that the bear didn't know it was hurt to the extent that it was. The bear lunged toward me but its right front leg couldn't support it and down it went. This gave me enough time to get up and moving, using the trees to block the bears view I was able to get around behind it. I grabbed the pointed log and placed the flat end against the tree. I had seen this done in the movies but wasn't sure it would work in real life. The bear seemed to be confused, probably caused by the numerous hits to its head and the broken shoulder, and it was slow to react to where I was. This gave me time to set up the final trap.

I retrieved the ladder and took the rope that had held the log to the tree. I tied it to the log and climbed up to the platform. I tested the rope and it felt like it would hold, then I started making noises to attract the bear. This time the bear leaned hard on its left side as it started to charge but never got there as it collapsed and lay still. I didn't know if it was dead or not and decided to stay in the tree for awhile. I had been sitting there for some time when I saw the grey shadow moving between the trees. The fox came to check on the results of the combat and declare a winner. Mr. Fox spent a few minutes walking around the corpse and then grabbed an ear and pulled on it.

[48]

When the bear didn't move the fox lifted a leg and pissed on its head then trotted off. I felt it was safe enough now to come down and take a closer look at it. The bears head was crushed enough that it probably was the cause of death. I was checking for damage when I noticed that a couple teeth were broken. Probably from the previous encounter in the river.

The bear looked pretty healthy other than that and must have been putting on weight for the winter months, as if for hibernation. I would have to remember to check for a den to see if the bear had dug in somewhere. I knew that there were no natural spots that would work for an animal that size, but in the meantime I would have to work on getting the hide off this thing and cutting up some of the meat. I knew that with the ladder and my tree I would be able to protect some of the meat for a long time. Most of it would have to be cut into strips and dried over the fire for a while to make jerky out of it. I had to think about the size of the bear and how to cut the pelt off to make the most use of it.

I went through my collection of sharp lava stones and decided on the biggest one there. I then looked over the river rocks I had and grabbed one that I could use for a hammer stone. Working quickly, I was able to make a sharp edge on the glassy stone. I would use this to cut the bear open and gut it out.

I had to make sure to save as much of the intestines and organs as possible for further use. I knew that some of the organs were edible so I took the heart and set it on a spit over the fire. I didn't intend to cook it as much as heat it up and keep it away from the fox while I worked on the rest of the intestines. Those would have to be washed out and put up high enough that the fox wouldn't steal them. The timing couldn't have been any better for this as the cold weather had killed most of the insects that would have infected the hide and meat.

As I was working on the bear, I would cut off small pieces and toss them off to one side so the fox could get them. I didn't need the fox sneaking in and trying to steal something as there seemed to be enough for both of us here. The bear had stored quiet a lot of fat and that would come in handy during the cold and darkest part of the winter. I stuffed it into

[49]

sections of the intestines and tied both ends shut. I put that and the meat I was cutting up on the log jam, as high up as I could reach. I didn't know of any other animals that might be interested in getting at it but I wanted to make sure. It could be a long winter and I just might need most of this to last.

I cooked some of the meat and would take a break every so often to eat and sleep. The sleep part was more like catnaps than anything else but it was enough to keep me going. It took three days for me to finish with everything and by then I was getting tired of bear meat. I had cut the leg skins off and turned them inside out. They would make arm and leg covers for me while I tried to make a coat from some of the hide.

I moved all the food items up into the tree and hung them to let them air. I wasn't sure if that was a good idea or not but I hoped they would freeze and be edible all winter. I would continue to work on the bear hide to try to soften it up and make it more pliable. In the meantime I speared a couple fish just to change my diet a little. It seemed the fox appreciated the change in food also and now seemed to be coming closer almost daily. We might become companions but of course we would never be friends.

Chapter three

The Camp

After I finished up with the bear hide and meat, it was time to start on the lean-to. I dug four holes and set the corner post with the two longer ones in the front and the shorter ones in the back. I tried to align the short ones up with the tree trunk to use it for the back of the shelter. There was enough wood in the logjam to make a hundred or more lean-tos, so I had my pick of the best pieces to use. The second thing I did was lay four logs down to form the floor base. I would be able to fill that in with pine needles and grasses to create a good bedding area to sleep on. The walls and roof went up easy enough and I covered them with pine boughs. I made it wide enough to stretch out in and still have room for some dry fire starter material.

The whole time I worked at this I kept thinking about my youth and the Boy Scout training I had. Some of the things I did come from that but others seemed to just be a part of my makeup. I wondered about that when I had the time but mostly I just kept working. I would have plenty of time to mull over the circumstance that led to this later on. For now I had things to do and I was busy doing them.

When I finished with the lean-to, I worked on setting up a heat reflector behind the fire pit. I needed to have the heat from the fire transferred into the lean-to. I dragged the biggest logs I could get to the fire pit area and placed them across from the lean-to. Stacking them four high I then placed two smaller poles on each end, standing them straight up and burying the ends into the ground. By putting two on the inside and two on the outside it would keep the big logs from rolling in either direction. I worried about it a little because it cut off my view of the river when I was lying down.

I had been a very cautious person by nature and now was finding that I still was, but with some exceptions. Then there was that thing with the bear, where I dropped out of the tree on the log. That was not like me at all. I couldn't explain it or even understand why I did it. Now as I was building up my camp site I had to take into consideration the fact that I needed to protect myself and at the same time find aggressive ways to survive in this time period.

Those were just some of the things I would wonder and worry about over the coming months. I just knew that for now I had to survive and that would require hard work and patience. The hard work part of that would be ongoing and started with fire wood. I pulled out logs from the jam and separated them by size and stacked them to the upriver side of my lean-to. The wind seemed to be coming from that direction most of the time and I would use the stacks to shelter from it.

With each piece of wood that I pulled out, I would check it to see if it may have a use as some kind of tool. I would need hammers, and spears and maybe one or two of those throwing sticks to launch the spears with. Some of the wood could be shaped for use and I would set those aside and put the others in the burn stacks.

I collected dry grass and bark and small twigs for fire starters and placed them in the lean-to to keep them dry. I again wondered why it hadn't snowed yet and checked the sky for clouds. It was always cloudy now and there was frost on the ground every morning. The river was starting to freeze over and I had to break ice along the edge of it to get drinking water and a chance to spear a fish or two.

I sat there by the fire eating away at a piece of fish and thinking. What would I need to do this winter to get by? I would surely forget something and be surprised by something else but I wanted to get as much done as I could imagine. Although I couldn't write them down and catalog them, I knew most of it would remain in my memory in the order I placed them. The biggest things now would be food and warmth, since the shelter was done. I might have to find a way to take down a couple deer before the winter was over. I would need the meat and the hide for clothing. I was gradually learning how to scrape the inside of the pelts to keep from cutting holes in them. When I dried, wet and pounded on them they became softer and easier to work with.

[52]

I was thinking about that stuff, when I remembered the deer head and started out to get it back. I couldn't find it and wondered what could have happened to it. As I checks around for where I thought it should be, I saw slight traces of scraped areas. Those places indicated that something had been dragged across the pine needles and disturbed them. I could see where I had dragged it and where it landed when I flipped it to the side. My rope would still be tied to it and between the head and the rope I now could see a track though the trees.

My elementary tracking skills from the Boy Scouts would not have helped here but something I wasn't aware of made the line of scattered needles look very obvious. I walked along, following the marks and misplaced pine needles. They were leading down toward the river but not to my camp. This would be more downriver from there. The trail became harder to follow as I got closer to the logjam and the river. It seemed as if something had scattered more of the pine needles in this one area as if there may have been a fight or an effort to hide something.

I looked closely at the area in question and noticed that it appeared to be round in a circle. It was almost a perfect circle at that. In the center of the area was a small shrub that had grown up here under the big pine trees. I studied the small shrub closely and saw that it had been chewed and had several branches broken off or bent. I walked around to the far side of the circle and noticed that the trail continued from that point on down toward the river again.

Before I got to the logjam, I started to hear faint noises and animal sounds. Using my best stealth mode, I crept toward the noise. I used the trees for a buffer and moved in as close as I could get without warning the animal. I watched for a couple minutes as the animal, hidden by the logs, worked furiously, trying to get the deer head under the pile. The spike antlers were caught on the outermost log with the deer head was facing out and that made it look like the deer was stuck under the logs and was trying to escape.

I took a stone out of the bag of rock and prepared to throw it at the animal if it came out. The rope had trailed the head and was lying in a

[53]

straight line away from the deer. I found it hard to keep from laughing at the sight as the deer head kept moving. I approached the scene with some caution, holding the stone in one hand and a spear in the other.

The thief must not have noticed me at this point as I put down the spear and picked up the end of the rope. I was sure I knew how hard I could pull it without it breaking so I gave it a yank. It came away just as the animal was changing its bite grip on it. I burst out laughing at the site of the little grey fox racing after the head and rolling over the top of it when it stopped. The antlers had dug into the ground just as the fox reached it causing the funny display of antics. The fox, however, was not so amused and bared its teeth as it backed away.

I watched the fox enter its den and disappear from sight. I put the stone back in the bag then pickup up the deer head, rope and my spear and started back to camp. I thought back to see what I could learn from the recent incident. When I got to the site where the deer had been hung, I saw the marks left by the bear but had ignored them. That had registered but since I knew what it was I let it go. I had seen the place where the fox had run behind the bear and nipped at it, leaving some pine needles disturbed. I was going over this in my head because I knew I might have to track something one day and I wanted to know that I could.

When the fox grabbed the head and started away with it, part of the head or antlers and all of the rope dragged some pine needles with it. This caused the trail of needles to aim in the direction the fox took. When I thought about the disturbed circle I had to guess as to what the fox did to cause the problem. Somehow it caught the rope in the bush and had a tough time getting it out. It must have been a site to see and I wondered why the fox hadn't chewed the rope off at that time, as it is there didn't seem to be any sign that it tried to chew on it anywhere. That seemed odd since it chewed on the bush instead of the rope.

When I arrived back at camp, I was still thinking about the odd things that seemed to happen here. The fox and the rope may have been stranger than some of the other things but there were plenty of those also. My train of thought was broken by the chatter of a squirrel. I had seen

[54]

several of them around but this was as close as I had gotten to them. There were two of them and they were trying to get at the bear meat that I had hung up in the tree. I put everything down and fished a stone out of the bag I had been carrying. My aim was good again and the first squirrel fell from the tree. If it wasn't dead it would soon be.

Before I could target the second one it took to the higher branches and out of sight. I was sure that the second one was going to cause me some problems if I didn't dispatch it also. Now here is where the patience comes in, as I set about readying the first squirrel for my dinner. I wasn't sure what to do with the pelt but I would save it for now and see if I could use it later. The first thing I thought of was that I didn't have a car antenna to hang the tail off. Anyway, that was a fox tail thing and nobody had done that for years and newer cars didn't even have antennas any more, at least not the kind that stuck up in the air out of your front fender.

I kept a couple stones handy while waiting for the number one squirrel to cook and I didn't wait in vain. The number two squirrel worked its way down the tree to the meat stash and was trying to get at the bear grease tubes. The rock caught it clean and knocked it several feet through the air. I got up to retrieve it when a grey flash whipped in and out again but with the squirrel in its teeth. In an instinctive reaction, I let fly the other stone and knocked the fox for a loop. The fox dropped the squirrel, rolled over several times and lay still. I thought it was dead and went to pick it up but got bite for my trouble. The fox got lucky because it was running away and got hit with a glancing blow. It still would take a couple minutes for it to recover completely.

It was a hard lesson but the fox would be much more careful the next time it tries to steal anything from me. It did confuse the situation for the fox, which had been getting its food thrown to it on a regular basis and it must have looked like the squirrel had been thrown in its direction. I munched on squirrel meat while skinning out the second one. I worried a little about the fox as it was the only companion I had and was likely to have any time soon. I put the second squirrel on the spit and tossed the remains of the first to where the fox could get it. The fox had left the area and did not return for the offering.

I wondered about the attachment to the fox and decided that it wasn't that big a deal. I didn't have any emotional feeling for it but if it died I would miss its accompaniment. Being alone always has a price to pay and I was becoming acutely aware of that. I had checked the bite mark on my hand and knew that it wasn't very deep. It had drawn some blood but very little and by tomorrow I wouldn't even notice it. The thing I would notice though was the fox was staying out of sight. I wouldn't see it again for several days. It probably was nursing a headache as well as a grudge.

I went about my daily routine now getting everything in order so as to be able to survive the harshest part of the year. Winter has a way of pushing you to the limit and if you take too much time off you'll pay dearly for it. The gap in the logjam kept getting wider as I removed more and more of the logs and smaller pieces from it. I continued to stack logs on the upriver side of my camp to create a bigger and bigger wind break. I had to make some mud caulking for the heat reflector as it wanted to catch on fire. I mixed mud and grass to make a paste and lathered it over the logs and in the cracks between them. The grass that stuck out of the mixture would singe off and the remaining material would dry as hard as stone masonry.

The days continued to get shorter as the sun came up later and went down earlier. I only knew that because it was the time of daylight and night. I hadn't actually seen the sun for days now or was it weeks. I was again loosing track of time in that sense. Anyway, if the sun were to shine I might not see it because of the depth of the canyon I was in. It created an artificial horizon that the sun would stay below.

The lack of sunshine, the long night hours, and the low level of the camp location added to the falling temperature, or is that subtracting to the falling temps, I mused. It was nice to know I still had a sense of humor as I thought back to the antics of the fox with the deer head. With the temp falling so was the water level in the river. I had to break the ice every day now and the water would be down a little below it. I didn't think it was an inch a day but it could have been. The fish were starting to gather in the

[56]

deep hole where I fought the bear and that made it easier to spear my dinner. I made sure to only take out enough to eat and between the fish and the bear meat I had plenty. That didn't help with the clothing I needed and a change of diet might do me some good.

I had been paying attention to the deer herd lately and noticed that they weren't going back up on the prairie. They must have known that the bear was gone and they expected to be safe. That should make it easy to bag a buck or two over the winter months and make some clothing suitable for this weather. I was now experimenting with a throwing stick, I was sure there was a name for it but I didn't know what that would be. It was three feet long and had a notch at the end. I would set the short spears in the notch and launch it from that. It would go further and faster than I could send it by hand. Now all I had to do was get the deer to hold still while I threw spears at them. As it turned out they didn't want to cooperate with my idea. I followed them around for a couple days, making them nervous until they finally left and went up on the prairie.

I knew they wouldn't stay up there for long and now made plans to catch them when they came back down. I headed back to camp to gather up some things to work with. I took two long poles and tied two short cross poles to them at one end. I again knew there was a name for this kind of thing but would just call it a pull-along until I could come up with it. I loaded everything up and started back up to the trail.

When I got back to the tree at the bottom of the trail I unloaded my supplies and checked the tree for good support limbs. Using my ladder, I carried several short logs up and laid them across two of the branches and tied them in place. I then carried two big rocks up and placed them on the small platform that I just made. This should work a little like the first one I made to kill the bear but I would have to make sure the deer were not spooked by what I was setting up. I knew that they wouldn't come looking for me like the bear did but would avoid me if at all possible. I decided to leave the supplies there for a couple days and then see if the deer would accept them or even if they would notice them up there. I left two short spears, several throwing stones and of course the two big rocks. The ladder was left standing against the back of the tree so it would not be so noticeable. The pull-along would have to be hidden somewhere else and I hauled it to the upriver side of the canyon. When I no longer could see the trail, I propped the thing up against the wall.

I knew that this was a shorter section of the canyon but I really hadn't covered it very well in my travels. Now I looked around and could see the rocky outcropping that I had stood on top of earlier. It was the same one I had to get past when I walked the river, the one that had hid the path and sandbar from my view. I walked into the corner where the hill jutted out and looked at the bushes and trees that were growing there. The big pines had thinned out and the smaller plants had room to grow. It was closer to the river and might have supplied more water for those to set roots.

I noticed a mound of dirt in among the bushes and up against the rock wall. I had found the bears den by accident and checked it out to see how deep it was. It was shallow but probably big enough to handle the bear. It looked like the bear had just dug enough of a hole to fit its body in. I had been hoping for a cave or something like that. It would have made a better place to winter if any really bad storms came in. As it was, I would have to settle for my lean-to.

I looked more closely at the bushes and small tree that were growing there and thought some of them may have had fruit at one time. They were bare now but had signs of having grown something on them. I thought the bear and maybe the birds had cleaned them off before I got there. I wished I had known about them earlier. "A day late and a dollar behind again" I laughed. Maybe next spring I would see what kind of berries they were. "Ugh" the thought of being here that long was just revolting. I needed to plan on being out of here before then. However, some of the saplings looked interesting; maybe I could do something with them. There seemed to be three different kinds of trees here and I had to work some to get them broken off at ground level. I intended to take them back to camp and see if they had a use or not.

I walked back to camp via the river route, staying along the bank to pick up some dry grasses and check for edible roots. I had found some root bulbs before but hadn't tried them yet. Now I saw that the deer had pawed the ground up to get at some of them. That should be a good indication that they were safe to eat. I was able to dig up a dozen or so with the stems attached, and that would allow me to hang them in my tree for safe keeping. I could then roast them with some of the bear meat or deer if I managed to get one. I wiped the mud off one of the bulbs and took a bite but didn't swallow it. Just letting it sit in my mouth for a few minutes to see if I had any reaction to it. It didn't taste bad and wasn't burning my tongue. I then chewed it up and swallowed it. I would wait to see what happened before eating any more of it.

I passed by the sandbar and muddy path on my way back, looking for anything different than I had seen before. I checked for foot prints in the mud again and determined that there were no new ones. The deer were the most common ones and I saw that the fox had been there recently. The bear tracks were the most obvious but I could tell they were older now. I kept in mind the need for food, tools and any more of the little trees that had the string bark. I knew that I would need more of it as the winter continued.

At one point I picked up some egg shaped stones that looked good for use as hammers or even throwing. They were a little different from what I had in my bag of rocks. This trip was proving to be better than just setting up to get a deer or two. I would be after them in a day or so and in the meantime I had some new stuff to work with. I also could make some more string or rope to use with the upcoming project I had in mind.

When I arrived back at camp, I was surprised to again hear the sound of a squirrel chirping at me. I didn't think that there were that many of them in the canyon to keep locating my food stash. I was a little careless on my throw and missed the squirrel entirely. It even surprised me as I had been very accurate up till now. The animal of course, fled to the upper branches of the tree and continued to chatter at me. I would contend with the squirrel later, for now I needed to restart the fire and fix something to eat. There would be no TV dinner in the microwave tonight so I had to settle for something over the fire. It could have been the squirrel but for the errant throw.

I better check on the bear meat and see if the damned animal had gotten into any of it. As I climbed up to the platform, the squirrel took off for the next tree over and kept going. I used the rope to get into the tree as I had left the ladder up by the trail. I could see that it had indeed been into one of the hanging chunks of meat and left way too many teeth marks. I thought that I would have to keep an eye out for that one and any others that might be around. Did these things hibernate when it gets cold enough or stay active all winter long? I wasn't sure about that but thought they may just slow down during the coldest part of winter.

I took down the piece of meat that the squirrel had chewed on and cut away the area of teeth marks. I then split the meat down the middle, cut one of the tubers up and put that inside the meat. I pulled the meat halves together and fixed it with small sticks to hold it in place. I then put the thing on a spit and over the fire. It would cook for a while and I could look for the squirrel and retrieve my stone. I also took the cut away meat and dropped it off near the fox den. The fox was still in hiding and probably trying to get over its headache. I was unable to find the squirrel for now but knew it would be back for more and I could wait it out.

I went back to play with my new toys and wait for my dinner to cook. I had wondered if I could make a bow out of one of the saplings I brought back. All three seem to be flexible enough but at what point would they break. I worked with them very carefully, removing the bark and slowly checking for the bending limit. Listening to the wood on each one of them, I could tell their breaking point or very close to it. How I knew that, I wasn't sure.

I set everything aside and sat down to eat and wait for the squirrel to come back. Maybe it would bring some friends along and make a couple meals for me. I wondered about their population and then decided that the reason they were so few probably had to do with the raptors that were there all summer. I had only thought of the birds as fish eaters but some of them may have liked the change of diet also. Then there was the bear, cougar, and fox if the squirrels came down to the ground.

This squirrel hadn't come back yet but would surely show up in the next day or two. Between the deer and the squirrel, if all goes well, I should have a few busy days ahead. My nights though would become routine as I would do basically the same thing every night for most of the winter months. I would check the caulking on the heat reflector wall, then place some hot rocks in the bedding of the lean-to, bank the fire to make sure it stayed lit all night, and last but not least I would make sure nothing could catch fire while I slept. There would be some things I could do while working by the light of the fire but most of it would require daylight. One of the things I could do was to make more string and rope. I didn't really have to see, as it didn't take much of anything but feel.

I wondered about the problem of light during the night hours. Could I make a torch with the grease from the bear fat? Could it be dangerous and drip burning grease? Everything here was so dry that a small fire might get out of hand in a hurry and I couldn't call 911 for a fire truck. The reason I was so careful with my fire was to prevent it from spreading. If I limited the size of the torch and the amount of grease, maybe it would supply a little light to work around with. It was something to think about for now but would have to wait. I had other irons in the fire now and needed to keep everything moving in the right direction if I was going to get out of here before spring came.

I put the torch thing on the back burner and went to making some more rope. I was running out of the bark for this and knew I would have to use hide if I was to finish my project. I planned on giving the deer another day before going after them. I had to work harder with the rope as the pieces were getting shorter now and causing me to work more and more of them into the length I needed. I had taken to holding the end of it in my mouth to keep it tight while I spliced in the short strings. I worked on it for some time and then decided to turn in for the night.

I awoke in the middle of the night as sick as a dog. I had diarrhea and was throwing up and my head hurt real bad. I was having trouble thinking but knew enough to get some water into my system. Maybe I could flush it out if I drank enough but I had no idea what had caused the problem at this point. It was the first time I had felt ill since this whole thing started. For the next two days it was all I could do to keep the fire going and get to the river for some water. I would pass out for hours at a time and have terrible dreams about my past and someone else's.

I knew that the squirrel had come back and was into my food supply but I couldn't hit it with the stones I threw. I had enough trouble just seeing it. The fox had come back and sat by the fire laughing at me. The bear and the cougar danced around the fire and poked claws at me. I dreamed that they put me on a spit and roasted me over the fire. One minute I was so cold I thought I would freeze to death and the next I was sweating bullets. Then there was the stork, flashing in and out with a bundle for me but I couldn't see what it contained. It looked like a FEDEX or UPS package with lots of strings attached.

The thing that scared me the most was the sight of people dying. People I should have known were being killed because they were different. I didn't know who they were but still they looked familiar in some way. I would wake up and go get some more water and stoke the fire then fall back into a restless sleep. I would cover up with the bear skin and when I woke up the next time it would be off to the side again. I would crash back down again and see someone running for their life, being pursued by the same people that did the killings.

By the end of the second day, I was starting to get control of the situation. I knew I was dehydrated and that I would need to eat something soon. There would be no chicken soup and I would have to settle for something more mundane. I was too weak to climb the tree and now really missed the ladder I had left at the trail head. Try as I might, I just couldn't hit that damn squirrel and I was going to have to go pick up all the rocks I had thrown at it. I was going to have to spear a fish and hope I didn't fall in on top of it.

The ice was harder than ever over top of the deep hole and I worked at breaking out big chunks of it. The smaller slivers I would put in my mouth and scoot the larger pieces off down the river. I was surprised by the fish coming to me as they were running out of oxygen. After I had two of them I whipped the water with my spear to put some oxygen back in it and make it more suitable for the fish to live. I would have to come down and keep the water open on a more regular basis or lose my main food supply. As it was I couldn't tell how many fish were still alive in there.

That silly thought about the chicken soup got me to thinking about a bowl to put it in. I had made the muddy lather to protect the reflection wall from fire, now I wondered if I could make a bowl out of the same stuff. I didn't know why I hadn't thought of that sooner but had to file it away for the night. The mud wasn't exactly clay but maybe there was some mixed in and in the next day or two I would try to find out. Anyway, I just needed to get some more sleep and finish the recovery process I was on.

I had another restless night with wild dreams and scary things going on. This time the fish were chasing me and I had to put the big soup bowl on my head to keep from getting it crushed. The bear, cougar and fox were up in the stands, clapping and hollering to encourage the fish. The fish were swinging long poles at me and I had to keep ducking away to keep from getting hit. When I finally escaped, I saw a village with people dying and everything on fire. I ran and ran to get away from it but the faster I ran the closer it seems to come.

I woke with a start and knew that this last dream would keep coming back. I lay still for a couple minutes to gather my thoughts and gently feel around to see if I was alright. These dreams were so real that I couldn't get them out of my head. It was the first morning that I wasn't thinking about getting home because I was home, at least in part. The transformation wasn't complete but it did seem to make a difference in my attitude. I now needed to know why I was here and what I was supposed to do while at this place and time. If the opportunity came to go back, I would jump at it, but I was becoming sure that it may never happen. The thought that my previous life was ending and the present one was just beginning persisted all day.

I had tossed the tail ends of the fish off to the side last night and today they were gone. Maybe now I would begin to feel like this was normal. The fox must have forgiven me for the hit it took and now was coming back to get my leavings. I was a day or two late going after the deer but I was sure the deer didn't mind. They were having trouble getting water also now that the river was frozen over every place but where I had broken through. This now presented an opportunity that had not existed before. The deer had to get out on the ice to get a drink from the hole I cut and would find that the traction wasn't very good for hoofed feet. I decided to keep away from them for awhile and just walk around in the woods as they browsed along the bank of the river. I would take my time going after them. I had another food item to get off my grocery list, that being the pesky squirrel.

I was really getting ticked off at the squirrel and let my anger take over a little of my conscious mind. I would need that food this winter and it was going to pay for the trouble it was causing. I was still collecting the stones that I had thrown before when the little creature started to scold me again. That did it and without a thought to what I was doing, let fly the rock I had in my hand. The rock and squirrel traveled a good twenty paces past the tree and I grinned in satisfaction. "Hang em, it'll teach em a lesson" I thought, as I went to pick up my quarry. I would fix dinner with some tuber packed in it but I sure did miss the salt and pepper or some other spices.

I put the squirrel on the spit and went to look for some of that muddy mixture I used on the reflector wall. I would try to make a bowl while my dinner cooked. The mud was frozen and I had to work some loose with a spear to get enough for a bowl. I gathered it up and warmed it by the fire then felt the texture to see if I could determine if it had clay in it. It was kind of slimy and slippery but still had some sand in it. I mixed some grasses with it and set the lump down near the fire to dry a little. I would have to work it while it was still wet but take some of the moisture out a little at a time. I didn't have a kiln to bake the thing in but hoped it would get hard enough to hold water.

I worked on it off and on while I ate dinner and got it shaped a little like a bowl. I then placed it over a rock that I had heated up by the fire and let it harden. I forgot to flatten the bottom before it got hard and so it wouldn't sit even to the ground. It would work better for getting a drink than the way I had been doing it with my hands. I was sure I couldn't cook anything in it but I could keep cooked items warm in it while I was eating.

I planned on giving the deer another day before going after one of them. I was still recovering from whatever had attacked my insides and that made me stop to think about it for awhile. Then it only took me a minute or so to put it all together. None of the animals would touch the rope that I was making and I had held it in my mouth the night I got sick. It did have a slight bitter taste to it but I had ignored that to get the rope made. I must have swallowed some of the residue from the bark.

Then I thought back to when I was up on the plateau and put the stick in my mouth to draw moisture. "Dumb luck" or what? I kept thinking that something was wrong with this picture but how could it be. If I had gotten one of those sticks to chew on I would be dead.

I just learned a valuable lesson again. I had worried about the tubers but never thought about the tree bark as a possible poison. I registered that in the back of my mind adding it to the many things I had just recently discovered. I wondered if I had been poisoning myself all along, as I handled the rope and then drank water or ate and never washed my hands. It may have been accumulative and just hadn't registered with my system or mind up to that point. I would be more careful from now on.

I knew that the recovery was still going on because as soon as the sky darkened for night I just wanted to go to sleep. I made sure I drank lots of water before going through my normal routine for the night. I rolled up the cougar pelt for a pillow and pulled the bear hide up under my chin and fell fast asleep.

The night was not going to let me alone though as the strange dreams and night mares came back to haunt me. The village was on fire again and I was running away from it while things were being thrown at me.

I saw a young boy, running, jumping, swimming and throwing stones and knew who it was until I awoke. I was cold because I had thrown the bear hide off and the fire had died down. I got up and put some more wood on the fire, drank some water and went back to sleep.

This time I slept longer and without the haunting dreams. I was sure they would be back but for now I was just glad to have had some real sleep. The poison had taken a lot out of me and I had trouble getting the energy up to do much of anything. The deer would wait for another day and I went up through the woods to retrieve my ladder. I would just cook some bear meat for the next day or two and hope that I was able to recover my strength.

I tried not to touch the rope with my bare hands anymore in case I was picking it up through the skin. I used one of the squirrel hides to hold the rope as I took down the bear meat. I would cut away the meat that had been touching the rope and burn it in the fire. I didn't want to poison the fox either, so none of it would get left on the ground. I didn't know if it was a strong poison or just accumulative. I had been exposing myself to it for a while now and would have to make sure to stay away from it. Now I was going to need the deer hide to replace the rope I had already made.

I checked all the bear meat and stored fat and found that the squirrel hadn't done as much damage as I first thought. I decided to work on the torch idea I had earlier. It wouldn't require much effort and I could see if it was going to work. I put some of the bear fat in the new bowl and set it by the fire to warm up as it was frozen along with everything else here.

Most of the bear meat was overly fatty and the piece I was cooking kept dripping into the fire. This tended to kick up some ash and I tried to remember what I had heard that the ash could be used for. I knew that you mixed it with something and used it for something else but the answer kept eluding me. If it was important enough I would eventually remember or discover its use.

I cleared my mind and got back to the torch. I dipped some reed like grasses in the bowl of bear grease and wrapped it around the end of a short pole threading the ends underneath the previous wrap. I hoped that would keep it from falling off while on fire. So many of the things I had to do were just experiments at this point in time. I hadn't watched enough of the survival shows on TV or the Native American lore on how to do's. I was now into the DIYS mode with no help in sight.

I set the unlit torch aside to cool and went to munching on the bear meat. I would have preferred a prime cut of beef to this any day but there weren't many head of beef running around here. I wouldn't say that the taste of bear meat was bad but it didn't have the kind of flavor I enjoyed. It did have one essential thing going for it though and that was its availability.

My little squirrel thief had come into view but was staying a lot further back than it had before getting hit. You couldn't call it entirely stupid for that as self preservation is a great instinct amount most animals. This one had figured out how to stay alive and where its meal ticket was. I had saved a couple small pieces that the squirrel had chewed on just for this occasion. I tossed the first one out but the fox took off like a shot when it saw the arm movement and was slow to come back. It was waiting to see if I did anything else or just stayed put. After a minute or two it crept up to the chunk of meat and grabbed it on the run. It would get to trusting me again but not today.

I was still in recovery mode and spent the rest of the day just keeping up the camp chores and the fire. I did make a point of going to the river and stirring the water in the hole to keep it from freezing over. I noticed that the fox would come out from behind the logjam on the river to get a drink at the water hole, and wondered how it managed to get to the other side like that. I wasn't curious enough to go look now but maybe later when I felt better. I settled down for the night, trying to get some rest.

It had been four days since I experienced the poisoning and I was feeling much better. It would be a week or more before I was fully charged up but for now I didn't have any problem dealing with it. It was well past time to start the big winter project I had planned so I surveyed the logjam

[67]

all the way into the corner where the river turned. I was able to find a couple long pieces to start with and hauled them back to camp. It wasn't going to do much good though, until I got some deer skin to make bindings with. I went to check on the deer and they seemed to know where I was and stayed away from me.

Going back to the river I opened the hole a little bit more and cleaned up the edges. The water had dropped another inch or two below the ice and that would make this work even better. It would wait till tomorrow and I speared a fish for my dinner. I spent the rest of the day keeping the deer away from the water in order to make them thirsty.

I broke another hole in the ice where the deer had been coming to the water then lit my new torch and set the base of it in the hole. Making sure it was far enough from the bank to keep from starting a fire. This took care of two things at once, keeping the deer away and seeing how long the torch would burn. Both worked out to my satisfaction.

It was dark by the time the torch finally burned out and I had finished my dinner. The fox had ventured in again for its meal but still stayed back from where it had been stopping. This time it did not run when I tossed the fish head in its direction. "We're making progress" I thought, but it sure was slow. That statement could have been for both the fox and the project I wanted to complete before spring came. Now I just had to wait till morning and see if the deer cooperated with my plans. As I bedded down for the night I had the odd feeling that something was wrong but couldn't put my finger on it. There didn't seem to be a hint of danger, just maybe I forgot something or just didn't know it. I double checked the fire just in case and then went to sleep.

This time the dreams came fast and furious and they were the same ones but rotating though at a faster clip. It was the bear, cougar, fox and now the wolves, all carrying torches and making me run. There were village fires and people screaming, blood was everywhere and I was running away again. It didn't look like me but I knew it was and I was so young too. I was hiding in a dirty rocky place that smelled bad and the animals ran past with their torches, lighting everything on fire. I covered myself with dirt and hid

[68]

my eyes from the sight of such horror. When it was all over, I stayed hiding and finally fell asleep and now sleep felt good.

When I woke up, I didn't know what to make of the dreams. They seemed so real and personal but nothing like the life I had lived, so where did they come from? It didn't matter as I had things to do and they couldn't wait for me to guess at what the dreams had meant. The deer would be coming for the water and I had to be there to make sure I got one of them. I wanted to get more than that but taking care of two or more at once could be problematic. With the proper tools it might not be so bad but I didn't have those to work with.

I got to the river and removed what was left of my torch, it had burned all the grass and grease off and very little down the stick. This was a good sign as it hadn't dripped and gave me the chance to make more without the worry. I checked to make sure the water hole was open and the edges hadn't formed a crust. I ran my hammer around it to clear any loose pieces and then left the area to give the deer time to get on the ice. I saw them standing further up in the woods and again wondered what could have happened to the lower branches of the trees. It was as if Mother Nature designed them to grow high before putting out any limbs.

The deer didn't seem to be in a hurry to get to the river so I returned to camp and made sure everything there was in order. I stood behind the windbreak and watched the area that the deer would have to come through to get to the water. The deer came down to the river and stopped just short of getting on the ice. They began munching on the grasses there and I waited to see which one would be the first to try it. One of the younger bucks started onto the ice, just as the little grey fox came trotting up the river from the logjam. This spooked the deer and they all ran off. I cursed the fox but knew better than to do anything about it. I knew the deer would be back and I would get another chance at them.

To assuage my anger, I picked up a stone and threw it against the pile of rocks I used to heat the bedding. The stone broke apart and I thought I saw sparks fly off it. I thought it was hot ashes from the fire and went back to watching the fox and looking for the deer.

[69]

The fox was busy lapping up some water and keeping an eye on the surrounding area and for good reason. The big buck that seemed to be the leader of this heard was making its way down to the river. It looked like it was going to attack the fox for interfering with their chance at the water hole. With its head lowered and making some snorting sounds, it started to go after the fox.

The fox wasn't in any trouble on the ice and knew it as it danced away from the buck. The fox had enough water and gave ground to the deer, moving back down river with its head in the air. It must have thought it won that battle and now it was time to go home. The buck snorted after it as if to say it was the winner here. The rest of the deer started for the river and I ducked out the back side of camp.

I took two spears and my bag of rocks with me as I circled around to come back to the river. All the deer were on the ice now and though they had watched me moving through the trees, I must have seemed far enough away. The big buck moved to the edge of the ice as if to confront me, lowering its head and snorting. I walked slowly as if just wandering through the woods and making sure the deer didn't panic yet. When I got exactly even with them I stopped for a second, then raising my spears over my head and yelling, I ran straight at them.

Now the deer did panic and since they were on the ice and bunched up, they went skidding in all directions. This, of course, brought on the exact thing I had hoped for, as two of the deer fell through the hole in the ice. The rest of them, skidding, sliding and crawling, managed to get to the other side of the river and escape. I didn't know if this would work a second time but if I could get them on the ice again I would have a good chance.

For now though, I sat down on the bank to wait. The deer in the water would get tired and become easy targets for me. As I watched, I noticed that one was much smaller than the other and may have been a yearling that had been born late. I would let that one go if I could get it out of the water without hurting it. The other one wasn't going to be so lucky. Neither one of them had antlers but I couldn't tell if the smaller one was male or female. I would liked to have had the big buck for the simple

[70]

reason it had more meat and hide than the doe did. "Beggars can't be choosers" I said under my breath.

I ended up having to kill both deer as I couldn't get the smaller one out and I wasn't going in the water after it. Once they were dead I just had to drag them over the icy edge of the hole and get them to dry land. I was going to be busy for the next couple days, working the meat and hides. The fox had come back through the woods and was watching the whole affair. The rest of the deer herd crossed the river upstream at its narrowest point and headed up to the plateau.

I didn't worry about the deer herd being on the prairie as there wasn't much for them to eat up there and certainly no water. They would be back and now I was going to be ignoring them for a week or more. They might forget about the cause of all the excitement they just had and I still had that other trick up my sleeve that could work. Before I went to work on the deer I had to find a way to preserve it. I wasn't going to tie it up with string again, that had already caused too much trouble for me. I settled on just freezing it and expanded the platform in the tree and lined it with bark.

I cut the meat into meal sized pieces, put each on a spit, seared it over the fire and then set it on the bark. It should freeze before going bad and with no insects around to infect it, it should be ok. When I wanted to eat any of it, I would just have to set it over the fire again and let it finish cooking. I dressed out the doe first and stretched the hide on the back wall of the lean-to. When I did the yearling, I cut the meat in the smallest strips I could and set them over the fire to dry, hoping to make jerky out of them.

All this took the best part of two days and made my fingers hurt. I was going to make sure I only got one deer next time. My best friend in the whole world kept coming in closer and closer, as if to remind me that we hadn't eaten in two days. That, of course, only affected the fox, as I had been nibbling on deer meat off and on but forgot about my companion. "Some friend you are" I said of myself while throwing a rib bone out to where the fox could get it. It still had some meat on it and the fox was quick to grab it and run. It was only then that I realized that the fox was entirely dependent on me. There wasn't anything here for it to eat unless it went back to chasing partridges.

With the most important things taken care of, it was now time to get some rest. I went about my night time routine after getting all the meat up in the tree. I would start scraping the hides tomorrow, now that I had them hanging up. I went through my normal routine before going to sleep but had it disrupted when I got the heated rocks for my bed. There, next to the fire where the rocks were heating, was a shard of stone unlike any I had seen since I got here. I picked it up and looked it over very carefully. It had the same appearance as the lava stones that I used for cutting but had a different feel to it. I set it aside, put the heated rocks under my bedding and went to sleep.

This night my dreams were different and less stressful. None of the animals showed up and the kid just hunted for food and a place to sleep. Many of the things that were missing here were in this dream. The small rodents and the amphibians and bats, seemed to be all around. He didn't have any trouble catching some of them to eat and slept in a small cave with the bats hanging from the ceiling. It smelled terrible but it felt safe.

When I awoke in the morning, I felt refreshed and better than I had in months. It may have been the best night of sleep I had since getting there. It also, may not have been but I couldn't remember a better one. The odd thing about it though, was the smell from the dream stayed with me. It didn't make me worry but I wouldn't forget it any time soon. As I started to put the rocks back near the fire to reheat them, I remembered the stone shard from the night before. What was that thing made of and where did it come from?

Chapter four

The Sled

I rekindled the fire and put a chunk of deer meat on a spit to cook for breakfast, one big enough for me and the fox. I now knew that I could rotate my menu from bear to deer to fish and not get so tired of the same thing for every meal. So today would be deer meat and I could see that the fox liked the idea also. While it was cooking, I took care of all the morning essentials and then picked up the stone shard from the night before.

My mind worked quickly now as I thought back to where I found the round stones in the river bed. I had brought several of them back but had mixed them in with the other river rocks and had tossed them at the squirrels. Now where could they be hiding? If I could find them, it might work out to just make my day, week or month, whichever came first.

I found the one I had tossed aside the other night and could see where the shard had chipped off it. It was showing a nice shiny surface where it had cracked and I guessed or hoped that it was flint. The kind you make arrow heads out of, as well as other things. I didn't know how to knap flint but thought I could learn if I had enough time to work on it.

I had been thinking about the glassy rock I was using to cut and scrap with and was aware that it could be knapped to a sharp edge. However, the pieces I had were already sharp and too small to work down. I had tried and just managed to keep an edge on some of them but most would break. I had been trying to remember the name of that stuff and thought it was "ob" something or other.

Maybe I would remember it now that I had some flint; then again memory is such a fleeting thing. I was thinking about the tools I would need in order to knap the flint and I was sure now that it was flint. Then the word for the glassy rock popped into my head, obsidian was formed from volcanic activity but I didn't know how that happened. Flint was also a product of the same process and I wondered why I would even care. On the other hand I hoped there were no active volcanoes in the area.

Right now I needed a scraper stone and this flint rock was bigger that any of the obsidians I had. I knew that to make an edge on the flint, I would have to pound the piece at some kind of angle to get it breaking in the right direction. I worked slowly at first, using a river rock that was shaped like a pear with one end more pointed than the other. I managed to get in a rhythm of chipping one side then the other to work the stone to a reasonable edge. That would do for now and I would later try to make a sharper piece for cutting with. This stone had a better gripping surface and my fingers wouldn't get so beat up and sore.

I dampened down the deer hide and started to scrape the inside. It went better with the new scraper and my hands and fingers didn't hurt as much. That was the easy side of the pelt and when I wanted to get the fur off the outside that would be harder. I didn't know how to make it work so I had to experiment with it. I rubbed in dirt, sand and ashes in small areas and scraped against the grain to see what might work.

At first I didn't see any difference but slowly the area with the ashes produced better results. I mixed water and ashes in the bowl and spread small amounts on the area I was working and soon had a good feel for it. I only did this to the larger of the hides and kept the smaller one wet in hopes that it wouldn't crack as it dried. I would scrape the inside of that one when I was done with the bigger of the two.

I threw the last piece of deer meat to the fox and checked to make sure the water hole was still open. I then rinsed the bowl out and got a drink, thinking that I needed to make some more bowls of different sizes. How much trouble would it be to make jugs to carry water in? If I was going to trek out of here before spring came, I would need food that wouldn't spoil and water.

On the river I might not need the water but finding food along the way could be problematic. The only way I knew to preserve my food was to dry it, as in smoked or jerky and I wondered if I could build a smoker without burning everything up. With each item on my list of needs, the time table kept getting longer and longer. My main project would have to be the priority and the rest would fit in as time and material allowed. I needed to cut the deer skin into strips for rawhide before I could do anything else.

I had decided on a sled, loosely based on the type of dog sleds I had seen in the past. It didn't have to be that big and I didn't think I could get the fox to pull it either. If I made it so the weight was further back and a little like the pull-along, I might not need a real long harness. That would save some of the deer hide for other things. I might even tie a push/pull bar across the front and not even need a harness. Without a computer CAD program I would have to do the calculating in my head. Then that was probably how they did it in the old days anyway.

I would need to keep the sled as light as possible and still strong enough to handle the weight I would be putting on it, which of course I had no idea of at this point. So much of what I would be taking might not actually be in camp yet.

Building a sled just might be harder than I thought as the tie points or straps could not be below the runners. The cross pieces would hold the hide flooring and all that would tie together without much trouble. I might have to notch or drill the runners and that would be a problem. I would have to think about that for a while and get back to working on the rawhide strips.

I had to find a way to make a good edge on the flint and the hammer stone I was using to shape it wouldn't do. Maybe one of the deer antlers would do for that. It was the one thing I had that was pointed and just might be strong enough to withstand the pounding. It had been a spike buck and the horns were just a little longer that my fingers. I did have a hard time breaking them loose from the skull as I tried not to damage them. I had guessed that the grain of the flint stone ran in the direction of the first chip it produced and used that as a guide for putting the edge on it.

I used the hammer stone to create an arched cutting surface and then the antler to fine tune the edge. I used sandstone from the river to even out the face a little and put more of an edge on it. I was surprised at how well it went and how sharp I managed to get it. I hadn't found the other flint stones yet and was thinking about that while getting this one ready. I may have hit the last squirrel with one and that stone would be out about two trees away. I took a break from working on the flint and walked over to where the other one should have landed. When I had picked up the squirrel I didn't bother with the stone but did know about where it would be.

My sense of direction was pretty good and I found that stone right away. The other two or three might be harder to locate but I wouldn't need them for a while and let it go at that. I took the second stone and hit it with the hammer stone to see if I could locate the grain line in it. It split in half and didn't indicate which way it would chip if I tried to form something out of it. I would have to be more careful with it and the rest of them from now on. I just got lucky with the first one and learned another lesson.

Cutting the deer hide into strips as thin as shoestrings was going to be a work in progress. I stretched the hide over a log and set to carving at it. I cut the first one wide so as to get a relatively straight line to work the rest of them from. The edges of the hide were jagged and rough from the initial skinning and once that was removed the next cuts should be a lot easier to line up. Of course, should be's, could be's and would be's don't always turn out that way as I shortly found out.

It was very hard to cut a straight line and I had to work slowly to keep from slicing the rawhide into short little pieces. I had to wonder how the Native Americans were so good at it but knew it was just three things, practice, practice and more practice. Then of course, having a sharp cutting tool would help and I had to keep working on the flint stone to keep an edge on it.

It took some time to get the hang of it but I was able to cut most of the pelt into strips thin enough to use. I lacked for clothing also and tried saving enough of the hide to make a pair of moccasins. But I had guessed

[76]

wrong on the amount of material needed to make them and was left with just some smaller pieces I would have to use for something else. I would save them for now to use as a pattern on the next hide, but add some extra size to it. I didn't want to cut up the smaller deer hide for moccasins; instead I decided to make a vest out of it. I turned it inside out and punched holes in the front edges for tie points. I used the shortest pieces of cut rawhide to make the ties. The vest turned out a little short and left an opening across my chest but covered my back and shoulders. I was beginning to create a wardrobe now with the leg and arm covers, loin cloth and the vest. I would have to work on the moccasins next time as I would need them out on the ice.

For now the sled would be my main objective and require most of my time. I started with the runners and thought that if I used a reverse notch in the bottom of each one I could tie the cross bars in place. With the notch cut from back to front, it should pull easily across the ice and might even work for breaking if the thing slid backwards. This of course was all conjecture for me as I had never seen anything like it before and did not have the experience needed to justify the work. I took my time with the runners and lined them up so that the notches were as close to even with each other as I could get them.

The flint stone I was using wasn't like any tool I had ever handled before and it took a little getting used to. It was one thing to cut the hide with and another to chop into the wood without damaging the wood or the stone. I then chopped a small notch on the top side directly above the bottom one and set the cross piece in before tying it in place. The cross piece overlapped the outside a little so it could be tied both inside and out of the runners.

There wouldn't be much ground clearance but on the ice I didn't think it would be necessary. I knew that weight could be a problem and with each added member I would lift it for feel. Pulling it would require some effort and I wasn't sure how far I would get before running out of the frozen part of the river. Even worse, I might have to leave the river to get around some obstacles or objects, meaning that it would have to be light enough to carry when unloaded.

I now needed two more items to make the sled workable and that would be a deer hide and a pull/push bar. Depending on the size of the deer, I might have to use the entire hide for the bed of the sled. The pull/push bar just needed to be a three piece frame that would tie into the cross bars and extend out the front far enough that I could walk between them without the bed hitting the back of my legs. The third piece would tie the two side ones together and give me something to push against. I could hold the two side arms to pull with and put my chest against the other one to push. That way I wouldn't need a harness.

The frame was set up a little like a large "A" without the front end touching. I worried about the weight and if that would be a problem. Then I needed to make sure the pull/push bar was high enough so I wasn't bent over trying to move the sled. I started a search through the log jam for two limbs that were turned up at one end and fairly long but not very big. They would have to be very close in size to make this work. There were many pieces of wood in the logjam that were bent or malformed in one way or another but I was having trouble finding any that would serve the purpose I was looking for. This was going to take a little more time than I expected and I wondered how many of them I may have burned up without knowing it. It had always been easier to take the lighter long limbs than to drag the bigger heavy ones to the fire pit.

While I was climbing around on the wood pile, I notice that the air seemed to be colder now than just a day or two ago. The sun had not come out for so long a time and I began to worry about that also. I had been so busy with the sled that I hadn't checked on the deer until now and couldn't find them anywhere. They must have gone up on the prairie for some reason and I would have to check on that if I was going to get another hide or two.

The hole in the ice was almost completely frozen over now and I worked on getting it opened up again. The fish population had been dropping and now I wondered if I would have any left before I broke camp and headed down stream. I might have to check for other deep spots but not now as the wind was picking up and I thought I could feel some snowflakes starting to land on me.

I returned to camp without any luck on anything this time. I hadn't found any wood pieces for the sled, the deer were gone, and I hadn't gotten any fish. I also noticed that the fox had not come out to see what I was doing either. I began to think that whatever had brought me to this point was in the midst of testing me one more time. I had tried hard to concentrate on just doing the tasks at hand and more or less keeping a tunnel vision going. Now however, I was looking at just buttoning up for the coming storm and that would give me time to think about what I was doing here in this place.

The animals must have known that the storm was coming in long before I did and taken shelter as I now would do. I checked off all the items in camp to make sure I would be able to survive. The list wasn't very long and I settled down in the lean-to to wait it out. The heated stones would make the grass bedding warm to start with and the bear hide would keep me that way for some time. I had some deer jerky and had put ice chips in the bowl for water.

The last thing I checked on was the fire starting material to make sure it would remain dry. If the fire went out during the storm I would be able to start a new one right away. I then crawled under the bear hide and watched as the wind swirled the ashes from the fire and sped up the burning process. The snow continued to fall and started to accumulate but not to the extent that I expected it to. The wind would blow for the next two days but the snow never amounted to much.

It didn't seem like a proper storm without a lot of snow but as the wind died down the temperature continued to drop. I could hear the sound of trees splitting from the sap freezing solid. I restarted the fire, making it bigger than normal to get some heat into the lean-to. I reheated the bed rocks and a little bit of deer meat then went back to waiting.

I had slept through most of the first two days and now sat wrapped up in the blanket. The dreams had come back while I slept and now I had time to think about them. They had become more confusing than ever as I seemed to be two people at the same time, both watching the other go through some very trying times. There didn't seem to be the fear in these dreams like had occurred in the others. Now I was more of an observer than a participant but there was still plenty of violence and bloodshed. The attackers seemed less like animals and more like people but not recognizable.

I could see myself, sitting in my car and looking through the windshield at a drive-in movie screen, watching the action going on. There was no speaker to let me hear the noise but I knew it was loud with screaming, yelling and burning. Much of my recent past was on full display also, with the death of my wife and the depression afterwards. It was a dark time and I had fought it hard when I felt it winning. The emotions of it all drained me and I fell asleep again to more dreams.

There was that little boy again in the cave with bats hanging from the ceiling. It was now very quiet and he wanted to see if it was ok to go out. The entrance was extremely small and covered with vines so he had to crawl and push the vines aside. When he did this he came nose to nose with a wolf that was as shocked as he was. Then the scene changed and he was looking at the burned out village.

The carrion eaters were all around, crows and vultures and large and small predators. He couldn't watch them eating and turned and ran away again. He wanted to go back to his cave but the wolf was there and so he wandered down to the river and swam to the other side. He had to get away from all the trouble.

The dream came back to me then and there was the check from the insurance company. It had been enough to pay for the funeral costs but didn't cover anything else. I had some money in the bank but would eventually have to move in with someone. There were just too many bills and not enough income to keep up with them. I hadn't planned well enough for this kind of future. The medical bills had eaten up most of the money I had put away for retirement and now I was basically broke. This didn't look like a wild dream but more like the real thing. Was I just recalling my past or was it something else that I needed to see?

There I was again but this time I was running. Not running away from something but chasing after someone. It was the little boy I was trying to catch and the shock of it woke me up. I sat there thinking about it for a while and then noticed that the fire had gone out again. The ashes were still hot so I put some more wood over them and with a few puffs of air was able to get it going again.

I chewed on a piece of jerky and sucked on a chunk of ice and thought about the dreams. They seemed so real and I felt as if something or someone was pushing me along as if I were a puppet. I had always hoped that there was life after death and now wondered if I was dead and stuck in some strange afterlife. I had experienced pain and sickness, hunger and thirst, anger and fear, heat and cold, so what was the reason for being here and what did it have to do with the little boy? Why didn't I just go to heaven like the bible said or could I be in hell instead?

I, George Martin, sat there staring at the fire and hoping things would change or the light would go on or the angel of death would show up. Anything would be better than not knowing and the frustration was taking hold of me. I even wondered if I was supposed to wonder about all of this. It seemed like such a setup as I thought about the things that had happened. It couldn't be a coincidence that I was meeting these challenges one at a time. How could I be able to even compete with animals that were bigger, faster, and stronger than me? I thought again about the fights with the cougar and bear and felt the scars on my butt. They were real enough and the fear had been real and I had the hides to prove it. I pulled the bear skin tight around me and stopped to listen for any sign of life.

There was nothing I could hear except the wood burning in the fire. The smoke from it was rising straight up and now the silence was like the bear skin over the whole valley. I was startled by a slight movement off to my left and I hadn't felt the little itch in the back of my head. I had been too engrossed with my thoughts. It was my little gray buddy looking for a hand out and waiting patiently for any sign of life.

I took this as an omen and rustled up some grub for the furry tailed creature that seemed to be sent to awaken my spirit. I had been brooding and I knew it, feeling sorry again for my situation. I couldn't change what had happened to me and the Lord knew I had tried. I would have to live with whatever was going to be put on me even if I never found out by whom or why that was.

The fox waited for each of the little chunks of jerky that was sent its way and quickly gobbled them up. It seemed to have lost all fear of being hit again and paced back and forth in between the pieces of deer meat that it was getting. When it knew that there would be no more at this time, it headed back to its den to wait for warmer weather. Having the fox show up when it did had the effect of motivating me into activity and I had needed that badly. My somber mood was now changed by the intrusion of the fox. This caused a welling up of energy and changed my outlook to a more positive one.

I roused myself enough to go looking for the other flint stones. It might be too cold to do anything else but I sure could be working on scrapers and spearheads and maybe an ax head if one of the stones was big enough. The stone that had broken in half could be used to make two spear heads. I could work on the bow too but the arrows might be another problem. I had kept some feathers from the ducks I got off the river but making arrow heads might just be a little much for my ability.

I didn't want to start on the flint until they warmed up a bit but made sure I didn't get them too close to the fire. I knew that if overheated they might just slip or crack apart. So far I had been lucky in picking stones to heat that didn't blow up when they got hot and I could see that happening to the flint. I managed to find three more of them and that seemed to be about right. I knew I wouldn't get any more of them as they were in the riverbed and now encased in ice.

The cold spell lasted for the better part of a week more and gave me time to work on the flint. I took my time and worked the stones very carefully so as not to damage anymore of them. I made the two spearheads first and I thought they looked pretty good for someone with so little experience at this sort of thing. I carved a slot in the end of two spears and fitted and tied the heads in place. I used a little bear grease on the rawhide ties to make them more pliable and get them stretched tight. With the throwing stick and these spears I would now have a weapon that could work better than anything I had before.

The next flint stone seemed as if it was meant to be an axe head and I started to work on it with that in mind. I might even use it as a scraper until I could find a handle for it. It turned out to be better than I imagined and I was almost ready to claim myself a pro at this sort of thing. Then the thought occurred to me that I might not be that good and something else was bringing out this latent talent. I didn't know who to blame for my being there and now who was responsible for my doing so well with the flint stones. I couldn't even remember seeing an un-napped stone before now and what made me think that the deer horn could be used to put an edge on these pieces.

I left the other two stones for future use and picked up the branch I was going to make a bow out of. I had been forcing it between the tree trunk and the lean-to to get it bent a little and wetting it down every once in a while. That seemed to work as it was holding the bow shape for now. The rawhide wasn't going to work for a bow string and I could only use the strands from the tree bark that I knew were poisonous. I knew that if I used the bark string I could not put my fingers in my mouth and I needed to cover my fingers with rawhide when pulling the string to launch an arrow. I didn't have any arrows yet so that wouldn't be a problem for a while.

Attaching the string to the bow required some dexterity and a little bit of notching without cutting too much away. It took several tries to get the string the right length while leaving a loop on each end. It had to be braided to keep from slipping and once it was right I just had to put it together and see if it would work. With a couple minor adjustments I was

[83]

able to make it into a working bow. I looked at it knowing that the wood would dry out and crack, so I needed something to reinforce it. Somehow I was aware of the fact that bows always break close to the middle or where you hold it to stretch the bow string. Then I thought about the sinew or tendons from the deer. I hadn't paid much attention to them while cutting up the deer and ended up with just short pieces. I was going to use them for the bow string but none were long enough. I would be more careful with the next deer on several things but that one more so than any others.

I put some ice in the bowl and set it by the fire to melt. Once it was warm, I would put the sinew pieces in it to soak and become more pliable. Then I would wrap the more stressed parts of the bow with it and let it dry. Now, I thought, the arrows might not be too far behind as I had saved some nice straight tree branches for that propose. I just wasn't sure how to go about making them into useable arrows. All in good time as I looked for something else to do while waiting for the weather to warm up a little. It didn't seem as cloudy now as it had been but the sun hadn't broken out yet.

I stepped out of the lean-to and looked up at the sky; the tops of the trees seemed to be brighter now than before. I wondered if the river was now causing a fog down in the valley area and maybe the sun was out up on the prairie. I needed to check on that and see if I could find out what had happened to the deer herd. I gathered up some food and ice along with my normal rocks, spears and other equipment, and then headed up the trail to see if it might just be warmer up on top. I thought I had a lot to carry as I wrapped myself in the bear skin.

I made a quick survey of the valley before heading out but still didn't see any deer or even signs that they had been there recently. I had nearly reached the top of the trail when I looked back and saw my little gray friend sitting at the bottom. I hollered down to it. "Come on up, I won't hurt you." The fox decided to wait anyway just in case. I wondered how the fox knew I was leaving; maybe it just has really good ears.

As soon as I reached the top I headed straight for the outcropping to get a view of the valley and see how far the fog reached. It was not exactly clear there but much worse down below. I looked to see if the fox was on its way up or not but couldn't see it anywhere. The fog at the bottom might be hiding it or some other option had taken place. The fox was fast enough that it could already be up on the prairie or it may have drifted back to the camp to see what it could steal. I stood and took in the view for a little bit and marveled at how nice this would have been to camp here in my previous life, and I thought of that life as lost for good now. The wonderful equipment that had been available at all the sporting good stores would have made for a fun time here and how I wished for just one good ax or hunting knife. Wish in one hand and; oh never mind it's not worth the time or trouble.

I reminded myself to get on with this life and see what it had in store for me. I headed back to the trailhead and spotted the fox sitting there just watching me. It moved off into the brush as I approached and disappeared from sight. I marveled at the way it could hide so easily in such an open environment. I had come up to see if I could find out what had happened to the deer and so I began to search for scat and hoof prints. I questioned in my head if their feet were called hoofs or paws or something else again. No matter, I would look for the prints in the soil and try to get a direction from that.

The deer had left during or before the storm so there were very few marks in the soil that would indicate which direction they may have gone. I walked along the ridge going downriver to where the valley ended with the big logjam and found nothing. The fog was obscuring the river and most of the valley, and all I could see was the top of the taller trees sticking up through it. I had not seen any tracks here or in the other direction either when I had gone to the outcropping overlook. They must have headed out into the prairie but it was a big expanse and I would have to be cautious if I headed into it.

I returned to the trailhead and looked around to see if there was any way I could mark my path out into the wasteland. There were no trees or other visible land marks to use since the fog was obscuring the mountains to my left. I had marked the trailhead with a rock cairn but couldn't haul enough rocks to mark a path of any distance. I thought that I could use a spear to scratch a line every so often but that might cause me to split my concentration between where I was going and where I had been. If I was to come upon the deer herd I would have to move fast and could lose time finding my way back to the path I made.

Then I thought about the pull-along and the use it would be in this case especially if I managed to get a deer or two. Pulling it would leave a good track and I could keep my eyes on the area ahead. I hurried down the trail and retrieved it and carried it back up to the top. It was heavy and awkward but I managed to get it up there. I had brought enough supplies for about a week and now the pull-along would make it easier to haul it with me. I had dried fish, deer jerky and a couple chunks of frozen bear meat, along with water in the form of ice. I didn't think I would be starting any fires because of the lack of wood but brought some starter material anyway just in case. This time I wouldn't have to eat any grasshoppers and there wouldn't be any available anyway.

Before starting out I took a little time to look around and get a sense of where I was and what direction to go in. The sky was still shrouding the surrounding area with clouds or fog and though it now seemed warmer I could not see any land marks. The deer would have known their destination before leaving the valley and should have headed straight for it. My best bet would be to walk out about a day's journey and go left and right from there looking for some sign of a path or track that the deer might have used.

I was about to take the first step when I became aware of the fact that I had missed a thing or two very recently. I began to wonder why my memory was playing tricks on me and how I missed what should have been obvious. I knew which way the deer had gone and what to call the pile of rocks I made on my first trip up here. I still couldn't remember what to call the pull-along but was sure even that would come to me. The rock pile is called a cairn and used as a landmark. I saw the deer head-out after the bear ran them out of the valley, so that's how I knew which direction they had taken.

All critters are habitual and do the same things over and over again, not because they want to but because they have a certain comfort level in doing so. Being familiar with something makes it easy to do, so the deer probable would go to the same location every time. I just had to follow the line that they took when I encountered them at the trail head. With that in mind I wondered what habits I had that needed to be attended to. I knew the fox would be around me as long as it was getting food without working at it, so I would have to make it work for its' keep. I wasn't sure if there was a way to do that but I would find out while we went looking for the deer, besides maybe it was just nice to have it around.

I tried to visualize the scene again of the deer rushing past me and going to beat the band to the south west of where I stood. I had begun to think of the river as running west because the sun had moved down the sky on that side. I then would be looking south if I was at the trailhead facing away from the river. The sun was still obscured by the clouds but the sky was brighter in that direction. By now I had lost some time and needed to get going. I picked up the handles of the travois and realized that was the name for the pull-along I had built. "I'll bet I had that word a hundred times in crossword puzzles" I said out loud. The fox stuck its' head up as if to see who I was talking to and then vanished again just that quickly.

I hadn't taken more than a couple steps when a partridge took flight just in front of me. I guessed the second one would be right behind it and dropped the handles and grabbed a stone to throw. When the bird didn't fly, I ran forward a few steps and it launched into the air. It only hung there for a second before the stone caught up to it and down it went. I charged after it in order to beat the fox to it and to make sure it was not going to run away with just a broken wing. It wasn't moving when I got to it and the fox had gone further out after the first bird flew up. During the process I managed to keep one eye on where the first bird landed and decided that it wasn't much out of my way. I would alter my course to see about getting the second partridge before continuing after the deer herd.

The fox seemed to be miffed at not being close enough to have a chance at the second bird and now it wasn't going to let me get further than a few quick jumps ahead of it. At the same time it now had a great interest in what was on the travois. "Stay away from my bird" I shouted at the fox. "If you're lucky you'll get a piece of it when it's been cooked". I just wasn't sure when I would get a chance to cook it or anything else for that matter. The fox seemed to know that getting too close to the food source might not be too healthy, but it wasn't going to let it get to far away either. We moved on and the fox couldn't hide so easy now and be close to the travois. It didn't take very long for us to get to where the first bird landed but now the real problem began. If I walked out to flush the partridge, I would leave the other one unguarded with Mr. Fuzzy Tail hanging around. The bird took care of that. It tried to run around us and head back the way it came. It had inadvertently run into the fox on its way and was greeted with open jaws. It didn't make it easy for the fox and almost got away before finally being hauled down. I almost threw a rock at it but wasn't sure which one I would hit and having hit the fox once I didn't want to do that again.

I left the fox to its kill and moved on in the direction the deer had taken. The fox would catch up in a day or so and now my food would be safe for awhile.

I put some effort into making up the lost ground from the detour and slow start to the day. I had to move fast while the sun was up even if I couldn't see it. I needed the daylight and the direction to keep going. I hadn't paid any attention to the stars for location but with the clouds it wouldn't have helped anyway. That would be something else I should keep in mind if I was to be traipsing all over the map.

I would look back every so often to make sure I had been going in a relatively straight line. The sun was setting when I came upon some heavier brush and decided that I should spend the night there. I hoped there was enough wood in the bushes to make a fire and cook the bird. I still wasn't sure what kind of bird it was, so a partridge it would remain. I was sure no one was going to correct me for it. It didn't take long to get a fire going, skin the bird and get it on a spit to cook.

It took longer to collect enough wood from the brush than anything else. The fire wouldn't last long and might not be hot enough to cook the

[88]

bird all the way through. I could eat the parts that did cook and give the rest to the fox if it showed up yet tonight, otherwise it might be breakfast. I managed to keep the fire going long enough to cook the bird and I didn't leave much for the fox. I tossed the remains out a ways and rolled up in the bear skin. I was fast asleep in no time but the dreams reminded me of my past and present problems.

It seemed that the more stress I was under the worse the dreams were. When I was relaxed and willing to accept my circumstance then the dreams were mild or forgettable. Otherwise they would get more troublesome and painfully clear. I had been worrying about leaving the valley and if I would find the deer and what if this and what if that. I could get lost with visions of the broom tailed dog in The Wizard of Oz brushing away my trail or was that Alice in Wonderland. It didn't matter as I was never big on movies anyway. I even worried that the fox wouldn't catch up to me, which of course was really dumb as I knew the fox wasn't about to lose its food source.

This time the dreams were more about me and what I had been through. The bear and cougar fights were running through the whole theme of this nightmares episode. Even the fight between the two of them as if I was there to see it. Then the deer, the fox, and salmon kept popping up along with a few ducks and now the partridge was getting added in.

Something else occurred in this dream that hadn't happened before. I could see someone working with a dead animal, doing the things I had been working on. It appeared to be a woman from the way she was dressed but the features where undistinguishable. She skinned the animal and cut it up for the meat but saved some parts for what I didn't know. The animal may have been an elk or very large deer but it also was not discernible as I never saw its head. She hung up long strings of something to dry. I thought that it might be the sinew or tendons from the back or legs. Maybe it was meant as a metaphoric slur on my skinning of the deer. I didn't think dreams did that sort of thing or it could be a lesson to be learned. She then put some of the meat into a thatch smoker and put some leaves on the fire to add flavor. I put most of that in my memory bank as the dreams faded away.

I awoke up with a start as something unusual was going on and my sense of dread kicked in hard. I was instantly alert but did not move even one muscle except for my eyes. The fox was crouched down very close to me with its ears laid back and looking out into the night. I waited to see what had caused the fox to come this close to me and clutched one of the spears under the bear skin. Nothing happened and after a little while the fox gradually eased up its ears and twitched them back and forth. It seemed to have noticed that I was breathing differently and slowly moved away from me while constantly monitoring the night for some sound or smell. I had no idea what had just happened to make the fox react like it did but it must have been serious and maybe even life threatening for it. That itch I had in the back of my head was now dissipating and I felt as if I could go back to sleep, however the fox didn't appear to be in any hurry to call it a night as its ears kept moving rapidly back and forth. Something was out there somewhere and causing the fox to be very nervous.

I wasn't able to get back to sleep like I had earlier but instead just catnapped for the rest of the night. I would eye the fox ever so often and see that it wasn't relaxing much. The only good thing to come of the night was that I didn't have any more dreams or if I did, I didn't remember them. In the morning I gathered up my belongings and set out again to find the deer. The sun of course was still not visible but it did seem brighter than yesterday and made for a little earlier start. The fox had moved off a little to allow me room without getting too far away or even out of sight. I did survey the area before leaving just in case something or someone was hanging around. Not seeing anything that would peak my interest was a good thing and I didn't need to have more to worry about. The fox now looked like a lost puppy as it followed me along at a discreet distance.

I judged that I had been going uphill for most of the time now as the second day was coming to a close. I had gone nonstop all day and now seemed to have reached a high spot in the terrain. This day had seemed warmer than yesterday but I wasn't quite sure as I had been traveling hard and there was no breeze at all. The ground was relatively bare here and there would be no camp fire but I felt that it provided the best location to start from in the morning. I should have a better view of the area when the sun came up than I had now as it was going down. I had been careful to protect my food and water supplies and would continue to do so. I set up the travois as a back drop and smoothed out a place to lie down for the night, making sure my supplies would be hard to get to for any of the possible night creatures. For my own safety I had taken to placing the two spears under the bear hide where I could grab them quickly, making sure that they were pointing in the opposite direction of each other.

Nothing of great interest happened that night and my dreams had been more or less common to what I had been getting for some time. I would try to decipher them during the day as I traveled but I was glad that they didn't contain any of the violence that I sometimes had. I saw that the fox had again moved in close but not nearly as close as the night before and it seemed to have slept a little better this time. Whatever had bothered it the other night must have stayed away this time. I had the nagging sensation that the fox had a bigger purpose for being there than to just beg for food. I almost hoped that I would never find out if that was true or not but somehow it would be revealed to me and then what would I do.

I waited on this high spot for the light of day to get a better look at the area ahead. I felt as if I should be seeing something different and more telling as far as direction goes. I looked to my right and left and noticed that I was on a ridge line that seemed to go on for a great distance. From here I would be going downhill a little but not steeply. The shrouded sky made everything seem darker out in front of me but still there were no discernible landmarks.

This ridge had to be crossed by the deer and other animals that were headed in this direction and there probably would be a trail or path to indicate it. It had to be the one place where some sign of their passing could be found and I had to look for it. The problem would be in which direction I should start. I had been going in a southwest heading and using the sun for a guide but the clouds made that a little sketchy at best. I had a fifty/fifty chance of getting it right no matter which way I went and so I said "flip a coin". I spit on one side of a throwing stone and tossed it spinning into the air. "Dry left, wet right" I said as it tumbled to the ground. The wet side came up and I headed to the right in hopes of finding some sign that the deer had crossed the ridge.

I hadn't gone very far before finding a trail that seemed to have been in use for some time, though maybe not recently. It wasn't very wide and the ground so dry that I could not distinguish any foot prints. I looked back toward the north and saw that the trail gradually turned to the west as if going away from the mountains. The other direction had the trail going south with little or no deviation. There was absolutely no cover in any direction as far as the eye could see but again the clouds or fog hid a lot of the surrounding area. I studied the terrain for a moment or two. I knew that if the fox could disappear in this open ground then some other animals might be just as good at it also. I not only didn't see anything, I couldn't feel any presence either. That is except for the fox, which I was getting use to being there all the time now. The trail was slightly depressed, which indicated heavy use but whatever had been using it must have gone single file. That seemed to be rather odd as the area was so open. Maybe the type of animal that used the trail was prone to follow the leader. I thought about that and didn't think deer reacted that way but in this new environment maybe they did.

"Hitch up the sleigh and get moving Jack" I said as I started off, not knowing how far I would have to travel on this day. I kept a rock handy in case another partridge or two should get spooked and take to wing. I didn't have any luck with that and the further I went the darker the day seemed to get. If it was due to fog then there must be a water source around somewhere and I was beginning to feel as if there were more animals nearby than just the fox. I didn't have that itch in the back of my head that would indicate trouble but something was out there and I hoped it was the deer I had been looking for.

The travois I was pulling was making enough noise to alert any animals that I was coming and I knew they would move away to avoid me. I couldn't do much about that or the strong male odor I had either. I was only three days out of camp and hoped the deer would just think of me as part of the environment. I had the throwing stick and two flint tipped spears that I expected to use to my great advantage but first I would have to find something to throw them at.

I had been traveling all day and though I hadn't seen much of the fox, I knew it would be close by. I had been dropping some bits of jerky on the path as I went along, knowing they would be picked up almost immediately. There had been no hint of trouble even though I was able to sense something else was out there. The fox had been hanging around close enough that it tended to make me nervous and more cautious than ever. The fox had been more active and roaming around before the incident of the other night. Now it was just following me and making sure not to get left behind.

The area continued to be fogged in and with the day coming to an end, visibility was dropping even more. I stopped and closed my eyes and tried to sense the area around me. There was an odd smell in the air that I had a little trouble recognizing but it seemed to be more of a chemical odor instead of natural animal or plant scent. There was no hint of a breeze, so being downwind or not wouldn't have much effect on where it may have come from. It was getting dark so I set the travois as a backdrop just off the path and settled down for the night. I sensed the fox moving closer as it came in behind the travois. It would sleep there all night unless something unusual happened to upset it.

The thought that the fox was so close seemed to bring me a little comfort and I drifted off to sleep. The dreams came back again but seemed to create more questions than answers. The fox in my dream had risked its life by distracting the bear but in this dream the fox was bigger than the bear and chased it away. It tried to tell me something but I couldn't understand the language it spoke. It pranced around and pointed as if it wanted me to go somewhere but I still didn't understand. What could the fox want that was so important?

The fox faded from sight and the little boy came back, hiding in the cave again and crying for something or someone. The boy was scratching something on the side walls of the cave that looked like hieroglyphics. It could have even been stick figures but they were not easy to decipher. The carvings grew in size as if I had a magnifying glass to look at them with but instead of getting plainer they got harder to read.

What did the boy want me to see? First it was the fox, now the boy, what was I missing here? There must be some clues that I needed to find. Why was this getting so complicated and what was the purpose? Then the fox reappeared and came into the cave. It told the boy something and he scratched it on the wall. It took a long time as the boy carved the symbols and the fox told more and more of its story. The stone knife that the boy was using made his hand bleed but he didn't stop. When the fox left, the bear showed up and the boy carved its story in the wall as well. Next it was the cougars turn and the wall was getting filled up with all the carvings. Then the boy took his bloody hand and put it against the wall to make hand prints as if to sign his work. Did he think this was art or was it just so he would not forget it? Why did he mix their memories together?

I watched as the boy, tired from the work, curled up and went to sleep. The boy seemed to have found some peace now that the stories of the animals were done and they had left. The bats didn't bother him either as he slept but the smell was really strong so he had to put up with it. That smell was strong enough that it made me wake up and I would take note of it. What had happened during the night to cause such an occurrence? The wind must have come up a little and now I knew what the odor was but not where it came from.

Chapter five

The Park

I had to wait for morning to see where to go but I knew the cause of the smell would be fairly close. It wasn't windy enough to have it very far away and it was strong. The caustic smell of sulfur in the air could only mean one thing and that would be a hot spring of some kind. I remembered the visit to Yellowstone Park and the hot springs there had the very same smell to them. It was something you just didn't forget. I had visited hot springs in other locations and most of them didn't have that odor to them. The hot springs in Yellow Stone could boil eggs and I didn't think I was going to jump in this one without testing it.

As the day got lighter and the view to the south didn't, I began to realize that I was seeing trees and a lot of them. "Almost like the Black Hills of South Dakota" I said knowing that I had come within a short walk of a forested area. Maybe that's what the fox in my dreams had tried to tell me. As I walked up to the wooded area, I noticed that the trees had a similarly appearance as the ones back at the valley. Most of the lower branches were gone and there were little or no small trees around. I hadn't questioned that enough back there and now I took notice of it in a big way. Trees don't grow like that so something or someone had to have caused this to happen.

I planned to get back to that thought but first I had to locate the hot spring and then the deer. I followed the path through the woods, which gradually thinned out and stopped short of the water hole. Steam was rising from the water and it was bubbling away in the middle. It wasn't a very big pool but ran away to the left or east to another one and another one. I started to count the number of pools that this fed but couldn't see the end of them as they ran down hill one after another, hidden by the steam caused fog.

The ground here wasn't as flat as the rest of the area had been and sloped to the east causing the water to run over small waterfalls on its way to the next pool. I checked the area for possible signs of a geyser so as not to be caught by one if it should erupt. There were no immediate signs of any as the ground was dry all the way around it. It was not much of a surprise to me that I just couldn't tell but guessed that it was possible and left it at that. To the west of the pool was a mud mound that kept popping up blobs of mud and splattering them on the surrounding ground. This indicated to me that the hot spot was moving away from the mountains and had been for some time. Why it wasn't building up was odd as the whole area seemed to be sunken and more so to the east. My knowledge of volcanoes and hot spots just wasn't good enough to understand some of the things that were going on under ground. I knew that I had to concentrate on the above ground things like finding the deer and getting some fire wood and maybe getting back to the valley.

The fire wood looked like an easy pick as I walked past the mud pot, making sure to stay out of reach of the splatters. The trees at this end were showing signs that the hot spot was getting close to them. Many of them were dead or dying from the sulfur gas and the heated ground; they would supply lots of dead wood for my fire. Several of the dead branches were hanging low enough for me to get hold of and I broke a couple off to take with me further down the park. I packed them on the travois and headed east to see if there was a good spot to set up my day camp and a tree I could put my supplies in. As I was walking away from the hot spot, I realized that I had just named the area The Park. It would be my way of keeping track of it and The Valley.

I had no idea how far the park ran. I knew that if there were animals near they would not be at this end. They would stay away from the sulfur and hot water so they must be somewhere closer to the other end. There were no tracks here even though the path I had followed came directly to this spot. The ground was hard and maybe even baked as I didn't leave any footprints either but the travois managed to scratch the surface. Not that it mattered much, as I wouldn't need to follow them back to the path and didn't think anyone else would ever notice. I had no evidence that there had been any people around but I was beginning to think that it was a possibility. I looked at the trees as I walked past and paid more attention to the lower area of each one. It seemed as if they had lower branches at some time and that they had been removed. Some of the trees had burls on them and that could have been where the original branches had grown before being removed. Thinking back to the valley, I now recalled that some trees had the same type of formation on their trunks.

I had passed about six of the hot pools and thought that it might be time to check one of them to see how hot it was. This was the seventh one and like all the rest it was putting out some steam. The air being as cold as it was made it hard to tell if the water had cooled much or it the ground under it was still heating it up. I felt the ground near the pool before testing the water itself. I then took a quick slap at the water to make sure it was safe and I didn't get scalded by it. This pool was still hot but not to the place where I would get burnt if I fell in. It was now evident that the water was cooling as it went from one pool to the next. Now I wondered if it could be getting to the place where I could drink it at the far end of this chain of small lakes.

I wasn't sure if they could be called lakes or just ponds or pools. How big would it have to be to be a lake? It was a stupid question at this point as no one with that knowledge would be anywhere close enough to answer it. I would keep an eye open for signs of life near or in the water as I walked along. I still couldn't see the end of The Park due to the fog from the steam but I knew that things were changing in this direction. For one thing the line of trees now seemed to be closer to the water than before, although they were still some twenty paces back from the edge.

I stopped at the tenth pool and felt the water there and it gave me the feeling that it would be the Goldilocks pool for a bath. I had stopped there because I saw a tree that would make a perfect place to put my supplies while I wandered through the rest of The Park. I used my climbing technique to reach the lowest limbs and the two branches that I got off the dead tree to make a quick platform. I then moved my food and water supplies up there and secured them in place. I hadn't seen any animals that might try to steal my food but hadn't forgotten about the fox. I could still tell it was around but staying out of sight for now. It probably didn't like the smell of the sulfur in the air or the hot water and that would be common to all animals. Now with my food secured, I took the time to look around and check for any possible problems. I managed to spy the fox moving between trees farther away from the water and remembered to toss a bit of jerky out for it. I then wondered if the presence of the fox might make it harder to get close to the deer if I ever found them. The way to find out of course meant locating them first then seeing how close I could get. With that in mind I set off again for the far end of The Park.

I had been counting the pools as I went along but not thinking about them. It was more or less a subconscious effort, probably from a long ago experience that was like a mental exercise. I knew that when I reached the last one it was the twenty second in the chain. The bad news was that I hadn't seen any deer or other animals around and the good news was that I now saw lots of tracks in the now softer dirt around the pools. To my great relief, they were mostly deer tracks but mixed in with as yet undetermined tracks of some other animals. I was the only one making the man like prints there and felt a little bit of remorse for that. Man wasn't meant to be a solitary mammal. I had every intention of trying to follow the deer tracks to see where they went but the thought of a hot bath was nagging at my conscious mind.

First I needed to check around this area and make sure there were no surprises in store for me later. I could see that the forested area continued on toward the east and got somewhat thicker as it went. Exploring that would have to wait. There didn't seem to be a direct path to it so the animals were coming and going in every direction. That could make locating the deer even harder but so far nothing was coming easy. I was still sure I would be able to find them.

The layout of the last pool was different than the rest, it was smaller and the water drained into a hole at the far end. It looked almost like a bath tub with the water going out. I tried to imagine the process of the water being recycled by the way it went from one end to the other. It was a little too much for me to get my head around so I left it at that. I could still smell the sulfur in the air but didn't know if it came from this pool or just floated in from further up the chain. I scooped up a little water with my hand and tasted it. It was not very pleasant and I spit it out. I then scooped up some more and smelled it, the sulfur scent wasn't strong enough to cause the bad taste but it sure wasn't fit to drink. There must have been some other chemicals dissolved in it. What were the deer and other animals drinking if the water was so bad? I would have to look around for a fresh water spring or just watch the animals to see how they were getting enough of it. The deer had been leaving this area and going to the river so maybe there wasn't enough good water here for them. I guessed that I would find out but not till tomorrow and I was headed back to the goldilocks pool for my bath.

I checked on my supplies and walked back to the mud pot to get some more fire wood. I needed to get some things ready before jumping in the water. I wouldn't want to miss out on the deer or other animals if the opportunity arose and I would have to dry off after getting out of the water. I managed to bring down two whole trees that the roots had rotted off due to the sulfur in the ground under them. The limbs broke away easily and I soon had more wood than I could carry. I used the tree with the most limbs still on it and loaded the other branches on top of that and dragged the whole thing back to camp. I was always slow to recognize the fact that now I was so strong. These trees were not as big as the ones down by the river but I would never have been able to lift one end of this one, let along drag it any distance. There seemed to be a dichotomy of thought going on in my head as I never stopped to think that pulling the trees down and pulling them to the camp required the use of the same basic muscles.

I got the wood to the camp site, and then went about creating a fire pit. It had to be away from the trees far enough as to not catch any on fire. I got a fire started and set a bear roast over it to cook. It was close enough to the water hole that I could watch it while I relaxed. I made a circle around the area and checked on everything. I made sure to take my throwing stones down to the water's edge along with one spear. I didn't want any surprises while skinny dipping. I stuck a toe in the pool first to make sure I didn't get the water temperature wrong and then proceeded to ease the rest of me in.

The steamy water felt good on my body as I tried to clean off months of grime and soot. My hair was exceptionally greasy and though I would wash it, it would stay that way. "What I wouldn't do for a bar of soap" I said to no one in particular. The fox sat on the edge of the barren ground, next to the tree with my food in it, and watched me intently; not knowing why any creature would enter into water you couldn't even drink. It seemed to be the most curious of creatures and it baffled me to understand how or why it was here. Most wild animals prefer to avoid humans as much as possible but this one must have been the exception to the rule. It must have been following me from the minute I stepped into this weird world, as if I was its adopted changeling. So many things have happened that were not the way you expect them to be. Not only the fox but the other animals and the lack of some made it hard to understand. This chance to relax was giving me too much time to think and I'm not sure that's a good thing now. I just don't know if there ever will be a good time to do any of that. Maybe I should just get back to scrubbing off the dirt.

I lay back in the water and thought that the salt content must be very high as I tended to float to the surface. I looked for the salt ring around the outside of the pool and didn't see any. Maybe it wasn't the salt that was causing my buoyancy. I guess it didn't matter either as chemistry was not one of my better subjects. I was sure that there wouldn't be a class held on it anytime soon, at least not in this neck of the woods. Anyway it wasn't like the river at all, as I never experienced this floating sensation in that water. As a matter of fact it seemed to be just the opposite of what was going on here. I didn't have any trouble sinking to the bottom while fighting with the bear or the first time I stepped into the deep hole. I sank like a rock and had to swim to get out of it.

I raked my hand along the bottom to pick up some sand to use in place of soap and rubbed it over some of the more obvious parts of my body. It was then that I noticed the scars on my buttocks had healed completely and no longer bothered me. I could still feel the three rows of scratches that the big cat had made and guessed that they would work for war wounds.

[100]

I really hadn't paid much attention to this body before and now did a thorough inspection of it. The first thing I noticed was that the hair on my body wasn't as thick as I thought it was and my face lacked any hair in the form a beard. The hair from my head, hung down to my shoulders and I could have passed for a hairy-chested he-man. The face was square with heavy ridge brows and more teeth than normal but only by one more set. Did I forget about the wisdom teeth being pulled and that would make the same amount of them? The ears stuck out a little more and that could be for better hearing over longer distances. The jaw stuck out some but didn't create an overbite. The shoulders were broad and supported a thick neck. The arms might be a bit longer and the hands and fingers were powerful. The back, abdomen and leg muscles seemed to be built more for strength than speed. The feet would have been called a good foundation back where I came from. With the construction of this body I knew that I could walk all day without it having an effect on me, that is as long as I provide food and water for it. I wasn't about to forget the thing with the grasshoppers.

I poured some sand over my head and rubbed it into the hair, hoping to get as much of the grease out as possible. Then by doing the same to both arms and legs I noticed that some of the fine hair seemed to be coming off with the sand as I rubbed it in. Not enough of it came off to make a real difference but it probably would have clogged the tub back at home. I didn't know if that would be caused by the matting or was seasonal or just a normal situation. It could have been caused by the hot water or some of the chemicals in it. At this time it wasn't going to be a big concern to me as I just wanted the months of grime gone.

I made a quick run to the fire pit to put some more wood on it and make sure the roast was going to finish cooking. I then did another quick look around to make sure everything was alright.

Then I headed back to the pool for more soaking and to finish scrubbing down. I now felt as clean as I had since leaving the house so many months ago. I lay back in the water and tried to relax but the memories came flooding back. I wondered if someone had taken care of all the things I never got around to doing. I wasn't feeling sorry for myself as much as just curious now about the events that lead up to this. I was interrupted in mid thought as the fox let out a yelp and went racing across the barren area and jumped the rivulet between the pools and disappeared into the woods on the far side. The itch in the back of my head let me know that something big this way cometh. I was worried that it might be another bear and I was ill prepared to deal with something that size. I jumped from the pool and raced to the fire pit and grabbed a burning stick to brandish at whatever was coming. I was well aware that most animals fear fire and would not come close to it. Whatever it was must have caught the scent of the smoke and stayed back just out of visual range. I guessed that it had better eyes and ears than I had and already knew I was there. Since the fox was in such a hurry to leave, this thing must have been a real threat to it.

Nothing like ruining a guy's bath as I then tried to dry off and get some cover on my exposed areas. It was still cold enough that I could feel my hair getting stiff with ice. I built up the fire a little more and kept an eye out for anything unusual. The fox made it back into the open and had its head on a swivel. It must have known that whatever was around wasn't staying in one place. The fog was giving cover to any movement around the pools and into the tree line so whatever was out there and moving could stay out of sight. I felt safe with the fire now burning a little bit higher and made sure the roast I had cooking was not getting burnt. I got a chunk of ice down from my supplies along with the bowl and set it by the fire to melt. I didn't know if the fox would be coming in for dinner or not but would make sure I saved it some of the bear meat.

I pulled the travois over by the fire and used it to sit on while I ate. I cut off little chunks of the roast from the outside as I knew that would be done but not sure if the middle had been over the fire long enough to even thaw out. I knew that if I cut the bottom parts of the meat away that the top would rotate down of its own weight. That would allow the meat to cook all the way around and I could eat a little at a time while keeping a watchful eye out for our predator. I guessed that it probably wasn't a bear as it wouldn't have bothered to stay out of sight but maybe another cougar. They tend to be more secretive than most other animals and less inclined to move about in the open. Whatever it was could be a problem for me as it would no doubt be interested in the same deer that I was after.

By the time I had finished eating my share of the roast, the sky was beginning to darken for the night. I took what was left of the meat and tossed it over to the other side of the pool and watched the fox run in to get it. It ran off with it but not very far. I thought how it would have been back at the valley where it had a den to hide in. I then started to get ready for the night by banking the fire and making sure it wouldn't spread. I made sure to have my weapons handy just in case and rolled up in the bear skin. I was glad I hadn't cut it up when I was working with it and it now came in real handy for keeping me warm. It was soft enough and I wasn't sleeping directly on the ground. I had positioned myself so that I could see the far side of the pool and the location that the fox was in. That way if anything unusual came up I should be able to see its reaction to it. I hadn't had a particularly bad day so I wasn't very tired but had in mind to keep a vigil for a little while before going to sleep. The best laid plans.

I woke with a start and a ruckus of noise and this intense itch in the back of my head. I was instantly alert and grabbed my spear in one hand and a rock in the other. Just then five deer raced past me quickly followed by a couple wolves. I interrupted the chase when my spear hit the second wolf in the neck and it went down. It wasn't dead but also wasn't going anywhere. The first wolf broke off the chase and darted away into the woods. I grabbed the other spear and waited to see if any more would show up. After a couple minutes, I went and finished off the wolf. Now I knew what had bothered the fox earlier in the day. I then looked for the fox and it was nowhere in sight. This time it took off without warning me with its little yelp. I may never forgive it for that but I certainly hoped it was alright. "Timing is everything" I said and looked around to make sure nothing more was going to happen this night. My timing was bad in getting to The Park about the same time the wolves did. I might say that the wolf I just killed ran into a timing problem also. In my case, I thought that the deer were not going to be hanging around any longer now that these predators had made their entrance. If there were only the two of them that would make it a little easier to deal with but in most cases, wolves run in packs and not in pairs. However, a stray pair would be less of a challenge for me and the deer.

I put some more wood on the fire as it was dying down now. I would just leave the wolf till morning when I would have more light. The wolf hide might make a good coat as it was big enough to fit over my upper body. That would be better than having to wrap myself in the bearskin every time I got away from the fire. I then set the dead wolf up to look like it was a sentry guarding the camp. I felt sure nothing was going to come around again this night as I propped the wolf's head up with a stick. I wasn't sure the fox would feel the same way I did over this but that would be its problem. I determined to just cat nap for the rest of the night, just in case the other wolf came back to see what happened to its partner. The couple hours of sleep I got before the chase occurred seemed to be enough to get me through the night and I just sat by the fire resting and waiting. I soon found out that I wouldn't have been able to sleep anyway as the howling started not long after I sat down. There were more than one of them out there, baying at the moon. I guess that's just a saying as I couldn't see the moon and neither could they.

In the morning, I set about skinning the wolf and thinking about the problems that these newcomers were causing me. The work on the wolf hide would take up to two days and that would be lost time chasing down the deer. Then again the deer may not be in the park anymore now that the wolf pack had made its presence known. I wasn't sure if this pack of animals had ever seen a human before and what kind of reaction they might have to encountering me. From the reaction of the wolf that ran away I was hoping that they would keep their distance from me, although with pack animals its' always hard to tell. I also wondered if this was the same pack that killed the deer near the valley. I had already guessed that they stayed away from there because the bear scent was pretty strong and they may not have wanted to deal with it. If I kept the bear hide close at hand then they might find that to be more than they liked. There were so many variables here that I had to deal with and still didn't understand. The only animals that I had seen in any numbers at all were the deer and now the wolves. I wasn't going to count the geese and ducks as I knew why they were on the river. I then reminded myself to pay attention to the wolf hide or I would have it full of holes.

I was scrapping the inside of the wolf's hide and thinking about the odd conditions that I had encountered so far. Most of the animals seemed to be out of place in this environment. The lack of small rodents which should be in the food chain for the likes of the fox, cougar, and wolves had me worried. The deer herd didn't really belong in an area that didn't have proper vegetation. The bear could get by on the fish in the river and maybe some of the berries that I was too late to get. It would also have an occasional deer that was slow or injured and maybe duck eggs or their young. The fox was the biggest question mark as I could only guess as to how it survived before I got here. Maybe it got here at the same time. The fox family usually works the small rodents and birds and is not commonly found around people. There doesn't seem to be a food item on its menu except what I give it. It managed to catch that one partridge after I spooked it up but that's it. With the bear, cougar, and wolves feeding off the deer, they should have eliminated the herd in no time at all but that didn't happen. The thing about the wolves was pretty strange also as they disappeared after killing the one deer over by the valley. Where could they have gone and what did they do for food in the meantime. I have to quit thinking like this. It gives me a headache to know I'm at the top of the food chain and can't find the bottom of it.

I sat there and thought about the food I had consumed and if I would run out of edibles sometime in the not too distant future. The deer herd didn't seem to be very big any of the time I saw them and the partridge pair could have been just that. I only saw the three squirrels and now they were gone. If I made it to the spring the ducks and geese would be back and maybe the fish also. I needed to get out of here and find a better place to live. I guess that means I won't be going home anytime soon. Was I meant to eliminate the competition for the food? What was I suppose to do here? Was I sent or put here for a reason? Should I go out and hunt down the wolf pack? What if they decide I was in their way and come looking for me? How do I answer any of these questions and still keep my sanity?

Get back to the world your living in Mr. and leave the what-ifs to a higher power. I wasn't much on religion before and this wasn't helping any. I was supposed to be dead by now but this body has a real will-to-live in it. Maybe my old body was dead and buried by now. It didn't seem to matter anymore and I didn't feel any loss over it either. I hadn't felt the itch in the back of my head since the howling stopped last night. Now did that mean the wolves had moved on or just shut down for the day? I dragged the wolf carcass back away from the pool and dug a small trench to bury it in. I didn't know if anything would be around to dig it up or not but at least I tried to keep it from rotting and causing a stink. I had thought about dumping it in the mud pool or burning it up in a pyre but didn't think either of those would be such a good idea. Maybe this way had something to do with the thought I just had of what became of my old body.

I decided to call it a night and get some rest. The last couple nights had me on pins and needles and sleep was hard to come by. I went through the routine with the fire and checking supplies and making sure I had the spear and rocks handy just in case. The fox hadn't come back yet either and I wandered if it had anything to do with the smell of wolf all over the area now.

I sat by the fire for a little while before rolling up in the bear skin for the night. I needed to make some kind of plan for the coming days if I was to have any success here. The wolves may have put a damper on my hunting trip but I still had to make the rounds and see if anything could be salvaged from it. The wooded area at the far end of the park must have something going for it or the deer wouldn't be here in the first place. That should be my first goal in the morning, finding out what could be there and if the deer were still in the area or if the wolves drove them away. I curled up for the night thinking that I should explore the far reaches of the forest and see what I could see. I fell asleep thinking about deer.

The dreams were back again and not so nice. People with wolf heads were chasing me and trying to beat me with clubs. People with deer heads just stood back and laughed as I tried to get away. They all ran after me and threw rocks and spears at me and I ran and hid in the cave again.

[106]

Was I the little boy this time? Why was I getting the two confused? Where was this cave? Did I need to find it? There is so much confusion in these dreams and I don't understand the meaning of them. I awoke with a start and a great feeling of dread.

I came up instantly with a spear in my right hand and a rock in the left. The fire had died down to just embers and although it was still dark I could see the wolves across the pond from me. There were six of them and they didn't look too friendly. I took my time and slowly rekindled the fire, while keeping one eye on them and the other on what I was doing. Two of the wolves were pacing back and forth and the other four just stood and watched. They seemed to be well aware of what fire was and not interested in coming any closer. I had the feeling I would have to deal with this pack before long but now wasn't the time. I had the advantage of the fire to keep them at bay and hoped to just get them to leave for now. I picked my biggest rock and heaved it across the pool without trying to hit any of them. They scattered and disappeared into the woods. The fog was heavy this morning and I lost sight of them almost instantly. The fear factor that woke me up was beginning to fade as the wolves moved farther away. They were headed west and my intent was to go east this morning, maybe that was a good thing.

The day was getting lighter as the sun came up, even if I couldn't see it. I packed my days worth of supplies and walked between the ninth and tenth pools, making sure to step carefully over the little rivulet that separated the two. I was trying not to get my feet wet, but that didn't make much sense as I had been walking barefoot all this time. It must have been something from my past life kicking in again. I picked up the rock that I had thrown to chase the wolves off and took a good look around. They had left their scent markings in several places before they departed.

I checked to see if the fox was near but couldn't feel it in my head. I hadn't seen it for a couple days now and hoped it was able to stay away from the wolf pack. I then headed toward the far end of the park. I needed to find the source of water that the animals were using. I then could check to see if the deer had left the area or just stayed away from the wolves. I was wrapped in the bear skin as I didn't think the wolf hide was dry enough yet. I was careful to keep an eye out for any trouble as I walked along the south side of the string of pools. I knew that something had made it possible for the trees to grow here despite the sulfur in the air and water. Maybe the spring rains were sufficient to overcome the acidic conditions. I was also looking for any form of life in or near the water. There hadn't been any sign of birds or rodents here and an ominous silence permeated the area. I hadn't realized that until now.

I got to the last pool with the water draining down to who knows where and spent a couple minutes just looking around to see if anything might be out of place or not where it should be. I may just be getting too worried about the strange things that have happened and still seem to be going on. Sometimes I feel like the snowman in the snow globe and wonder who could be watching me from the outside. With that in mind, I gave them a friendly wave and headed off in the direction of the woods. I had no idea how far it was to the end but I was determined to check for all the possibilities. The trees continued like before with the lower branches missing, making it easy to walk. The first thing I noticed was as soon as I got away from the pools the fog started to lift. This of course made it easier to see but the sky was still cloudy and though I could see the sun, it wasn't shining very bright. If I was in a snow globe, it was a very big one as I hadn't found the edges of it yet.

I had been walking for a while before I realized that I made a major mistake. I neglected to mark my trail and without a clear look at the sky I might have a problem getting back to where I started. I could be lost in the woods now as all the trees looked alike. I had thought that I was walking in a straight line but with trees in the road I had dodged them and now worried that they may have forced me to change course. I looked to see if I had left any tracks but the ground was covered in pine needles and they were thick enough that even the heaviest foot prints would be obscured. It wasn't helping that the canopy of the trees and the clouds continued to hide the sun. I could see about where it was but had no idea of the time or if I could use it to return to the park. It was still on my right which would

[108]

put it south but at what angle for the time of day. Why did my Boy Scout training fail me this time? How was I going to get back on track?

I decided to mark the nearest tree on all four sides and carve an arrow in the direction that I thought the park would be. If I encountered the tree again I would know if I had been walking in a circle or just returning the way I came. So far I hadn't seen any sign of the deer or the water that they would surely be using. I continued on my way but this time I would mark trees as I went, always on what I perceived to be the south side. I tried to line up a tree that was visible from the first marked tree in the general direction that I wanted to go. I would then do the same for each tree in turn, hoping that they would all line up before I managed to get any more lost. With this method I was able to line up the trees in a very consistent way and got a relatively straight line going. I began to realize that I would be spending the night out here as the forested area was larger than I first thought. About this time I began to notice the slight tingling in the back of my head that said I had company. Somewhere the fox had found me and joined the search for water and the deer. I hadn't seen it yet but just knew it was there and it made me feel a little more comfortable knowing that. Obviously it had been able to avoid the wolves and somehow determine the direction I was going in. I thought it would be nice if I could sense things that easily. But then again, maybe I could.

It was immediately after that thought that I became aware of the scent of water or at least the things that are often associated with water. I marked one more tree and headed in the direction that the odor was coming from. The flora of the area was quite strong and easy to follow to its' source. The fauna on the other hand kept moving and in this case much harder to find with the exception of the fox that kept finding me. I could hear it long before I could see it as the spring was almost like a fountain the way that it was bubbling up out of the ground. I almost wanted to run but thought better of it and knew that I should just slip in quietly and see if any of the locals would be at the water hole.

The first thing that I encountered was the plant growth, something that I hadn't dealt with anywhere else since I got into this mess. With the exception of where the bears den was, there had been little or no vegetation to deal with. This was a tangle of briars and shrubs that grew too thick to see through, but the smell of live plants was thick in the air. It seemed hard to imagine with the weather being as cold as it was that any of these plants would be actively growing. I pushed my way through looking for the source of the water that fed this stuff. I began to notice that some of the plants had been chewed on and the smaller limbs eaten away. The bark on some was torn off so that the scent was coming from the freshly eaten portions of the plants and not from them growing. This was a good sign as the only herbivores that I had seen were the deer and that meant they had been here recently.

I broke through the undergrowth to a beautiful lakeshore setting, with a babbling brook coming from a hillside stream. The stream was fed by a gushing spring that ran over what looked like lava rocks. There was a coating of ice on most of the water but where it came in was ice free. I must have made enough noise working my way through the brush to have frightened any animals away as the only one there was the fox. It stood next to the running stream with water dripping from its muzzle. I thought it was a good indication that the water was quite safe to drink. I just stared at the lake for a couple minutes and took it all in. I thought of it as a lake but it could have been a large pond and was bigger than the pools at the hot springs. There was plenty of vegetation around it and signs that many animals had been there. The deer tracks were the most obvious and the wolves had left some prints there also. I was not able to determine if other animals had been there as the tracks overlapped just as they had at the river. The newest ones were the most prominent and easiest to read. Even the fox had left a couple small prints in the mud, speaking of which, it decided not to protect the water from me and moved off a ways.

I tested the water before drinking any of it and sure enough it was as good as advertised by the fox. I may need to name that sucker as it keeps showing up in everything I do. I could call it Charlie or Sam but Foxy sounds too feminine for a male animal. Maybe I'll just call it Fred, though it aint no Flintstone that's for sure. OK that's enough about the fox; it's time to get on with what I came here for. I'll keep in mind that I need to break out

[110]

some of the ice later to take back with me. Now I need to look for a place to set up my overnight stays to get firewood and make a blind to keep the deer from seeing me. I wonder if the trick I pulled on the herd in the valley would work again. If I trap them against the water maybe one or two of them will go out on the ice and fall through. I'm not even sure that they are still around since the wolves have been here. The ground seemed to go uphill from the waterhole to the south. The trees and foggy mist had obscured the landscape and I hadn't notice the hillside before now. Think man, water doesn't run uphill or across flat land, it had to be coming down from somewhere. It seems as though I was still struggling to keep up with the obvious and missed some of the things that should stand out in a way that made sense. Then on the other hand not much of what had happened to me made any sense at all, but I did need to pay attention to these things. I left the lake area and moved up the hill in hopes of finding an adequate site to set up my camp. I still needed to survey the lake and surrounding area but that would wait till I had picked a site for my overnight stay. I reached a small plateau from where I could still see the lake and if I place some pine boughs down I couldn't be seen from below. There were some smaller pines growing on the hillside and it was easy to rip off some limbs to use for cover and also bedding. I raked up some of the pine needles for that also.

Again another clue to my surroundings, and I almost missed this one also. This is the first time I found small pine trees that didn't have their bottom limbs removed. Whoever had been chopping the branches off all the trees had left these alone. On top of which, there weren't a lot of small trees anywhere else that I had been. I hadn't seen any kind of recent activity that would indicate some form of human intervention. I would have to keep a keen eye out for just about anything that would show an unusual or permanent sign of usage. The path coming into the hot springs from the east was well worn but had no recent footprints except for mine and maybe Fred the fox. Whatever had created the path must have used it a lot or had a lot of individuals lined up one behind the other. It was not the kind of trail that one would expect a whole troop of people to take as they would have made it wider than that.

While I was thinking about all this stuff, I started the survey of the lake and had walked down past the spring. Fred had wondered off some place and now returned to see what I was up to. I might have to keep reminding myself that Fred was now the name of the fox and I wasn't sure if that meant that I had a closer bond with it or not. I still didn't feel any empathy for it. I swung around to the north side of the lake and noticed that the ice was much thicker on this side as it was further away from the spring and probably got less movement in the water on this side. The ice was crystal clear, which probably meant it had less impurities in it than the water on the river did. I could see the bottom of the lake and noticed that there were some fish swimming around in it. Because the water and ice were so clear, it was hard to determine the depth at any given point in the lake. I broke out a piece of ice to see how thick it was and then used my spear to check the depth. Even at the edge, it was a lot deeper than it appeared to be. I guessed that the spear was five feet long and less than a foot of it remained above the water line when I touched the bottom. The ice itself was a good three inches thick but again I had to guess at all the measurements as I had nothing to compare them with. I may have to go back to the old English measures of hand, foot, and arm lengths to have a chance to get it close enough to be understandable. As I walked away from the hole in the ice, Fred come over to smell around it and got a drink. I dropped a piece of jerky for him and continued on around the lake.

I had reached the west end of the lake when I noticed movement coming from my right. A big brown creature was making its way down to the lake and not making any noise. About that time I saw Fred make a bee-line for parts unknown and the new animal seemed to know that I was there but didn't bother to stop. As it came in closer it looked as if it had more legs than normal. It was the first moose I had seen in years and watched in fascination as it walked straight into the lake and broke through the ice as if it was tissue paper. It was then that I was able to see the reason for the extra legs. It was a cow with calf or should they be called cows and calves. Anyway, the cow had no antlers and used its powerful legs to bust up the ice in a large circle. Apparently she was trying to keep the calf in the center of it. The whole time she was looking back up the hill that they had just come down from. Something was making her very nervous as she continued to thrash around in the lake and break more and more ice away. I settled down at the east end of the lake to watch her. I knew that this was my meal ticket for the next month or so if I handled it right. But taking on a moose wasn't the same as going after a couple deer. This thing was very big and would not be afraid to come after me if I didn't do a good job getting it down. While it was in the water it would even be a bigger problem getting at or retrieving it. I was hoping to be able to find a way to turn it into food for the foreseeable future.

While I was trying to devise a plan to attack the momma moose, the reason she was in the water became all too apparent as the wolf pack came down the hill on the same line that she had. She was ignoring me to this point and would continue to do so until after the wolves were gone. That is if they decided to leave her and her calf alone, which didn't seem very likely. There were six of them and they seemed to be trying to figure out a way to get at her and the calf. They stayed off the ice for a little bit as they probably recognized the fact that the moose was up to her belly in water and if they fell in she would certainly have the advantage over them. Even as long as their legs were they wouldn't be touching bottom. The calf, on the other hand, was up to its neck and I wondered how long they could stay in the icy water while the wolves sat on the shore.

I hadn't moved but it only took a few seconds for one of the wolves to take notice of me. I hadn't brought my bearskin with me but did have one spear and four rocks. That seemed to be a little short of what I would need to run off the competition if it came to that. Instead it got worse as the wolf was now taking a big interest in me and with head down and ears back was slowly working its way in my direction. Two others of the pack had been watching the first one and now turned their attention to what was going on. The other three had not given up on the moose yet and while one of them walked back and forth along the edge of the lake the other two sat down to wait. I tried to think of a way to get out of there without using all my ammunition but knew I couldn't out run them. If I tried to fight them I probably would run out of tools before they ran out of wolves. But I did have a tool that I carried with me ever since I made it back in the valley. The hammer I had attached to the hide rope that kept my loin cloth on. I

[113]

decided to take the advice of the moose and go into the water. As I started to move the wolf stopped to see what I would do. It seemed confused about the type of animal I was and didn't seem to be in a hurry to get real close. The ice was thin at this end of the lake as some water weeds had grown up there and created weak areas. My first couple steps into the lake the ice gave way and I set my feet in the muddy bottom. I then needed the hammer to break the ice farther out. Once I was waist deep I proceeded to break a ring of ice away so that I could use that to word off the wolves if they came after me. It was at this point that the first wolf sat down as if to guard me and make sure I didn't interfere with what was going to happen with the moose. I wondered how long I could stay in the icy water before it became a problem. That's when things began to happen almost too fast to tell here.

I needed to distract the first wolf somehow to get a chance to get away or at least out of the water. That's when I saw the fish swimming around near the opening that I had created in the ice. I made a quick stab at the largest one I saw and got it on my spear. I then heaved the fish up on the bank as far as I could and not in the direction of the wolf but farther from the others. Number one wolf recognized the fish for what it was and immediately went after it. The other two that had lost interest earlier now saw what was going on and come running after the first one. That one grabbed the fish and took off running up the hill with the other two chasing it. I was now down to three wolves and those numbers looked a little better to work with. That's when Fred the fox came barreling out of the woods on the opposite side of the lake and onto the ice. It skidded across and almost into the hole the two moose were in and Mrs. Moose took a swipe at it with her front feet. It got him scrambling in my direction with feet slipping and sliding all over the place. It would have been quite funny except for the reason he was in such a hurry. It was smart enough to know that its only salvation now would be if I could protect it. The two wolves that had been chasing it didn't stop at the edge of the ice as the others had and they didn't seem to think I was going to be a problem for them. That turned out to be a big mistake on their part. They hit the ice on the run and headed straight for Fred who dove into the water next to me. I could see that one of the wolves was well ahead of the other and would slide directly into me and the water.

The things that happened in the next few seconds and minutes became a jumble of high speed action. With Fred trying to swim to the shore the first of the two wolves slid across the ice with its teeth bared and aiming right at me. I brought it to a halt when I slammed my spear up under its chin. The spear point must have gone all the way to the brain as the wolf lost all movement at the point. The action caused me to move backward from the sheer weight of the wolf. The second wolf couldn't stop and slid into the water at which time I dropped the first one on top of it and held it down. In its attempt to escape the weight of its raiding partner, it swam under the ice. My first instinct was to grab its tail to keep it from getting away. Then I had the proverbial tiger by the tail scenario. As I pulled it out from under the ice, it started snapping its jaws at me but I dropped the first wolf on top of it again and kept turning away from the toothy end as it swung back and forth trying to get at me. The whole time its head was under water or never out of it long enough to get a good gulp of air.

Now while this is going on, Fred had second ideas about going ashore as the other three wolves had become interested in the proceedings and come over to watch the show. I wasn't sure how I could handle those three if they entered the fray. The moose on seeing the wolves leaving now decided to get out of the water but that attracted the group of three and they started to return to their original location. In the mean time, Fred had been swimming around near the front end of the chomping teeth of the wolf I was trying to drown. With my help, we managed to keep those teeth from finding a piece of Fred. It took a while of holding on to the wolf's tail but he finally gave up the ghost and quit swimming. The moose went back into the deep end of the pool and the wolves stopped about half way in between. I tossed the two dead carcasses out on to the ice and Fred swam to the shore.

Fred looked worse than the dead wolves and seemed to have lost any ability to understand his predicament. He had used up all his energy running from the pair and swimming for his life. Now he just lay on the bare ground and waited his fate as the pack leader slowly approached him. I was tempted to just watch but knew that I had more important things to contend with. With the wolf distracted by Fred he seemed to forget about me for a few seconds. That was all I needed to get a stone out of my bag and into the air. He knew it was coming but couldn't react fast enough to get out of the way and the rock caught him on the side of the head. "I should have been a baseball pitcher" I said knowing the rock had reached the wolf at a real high rate of speed. I then dragged the two dead wolves off the ice and on past Fred and up onto the bank. I jerked the spear loose and used it to make sure the other one was not going to recover from his headache. Now with three of them down and three off chasing a dead fish, it left just the two remaining and they didn't look as if they were going to cause me any trouble. I picked up the rock and with the spear in the other hand, started toward them. They got the idea fast enough and quickly departed for the hills. I got the feeling that they wouldn't be interested in tangling with me again but it did leave five of them still roaming the area. I wandered how they divided the fish up and if the new arrivals would have anything to eat when they got there.

Now for the meat of the problem, the moose would have to feed me for much of the rest of the winter as it looked more and more as if the deer had abandoned the area. While the moose looked formidable enough I thought it would pay way to much attention to keeping the calf alive. That should make it easier for me but not real easy. That turned out to be an understatement. Before I could get to it the moose had exited the water and turned to face me with the calf behind it. While I had been tiring myself out fighting wolves, she had been resting in the lake recovering from having run away from them. I knew she would weigh in at half a ton or more but did not know how that would compute here and now. I did know that if she were to come after me I would be hard pressed to get away from her. The one advantage that I had was mobility and her need to stay close to the calf. I started by moving from tree to tree up the hill in order to cut off her retreat back into that area. If I could get her back in the water I would have the advantage with spear and rocks. She continually turned to face me and keep the calf behind her.

[116]

I had picked a location up the hill from her that had several trees growing close together. They were wide enough apart that I could fit between them but not the moose. As I maneuvered back and forth she would keep turning with me and the calf kept trying to stay behind her. When the calf made the mistake of turning sideways, it exposed its head on one side and its rump on the other side of its mother. I threw a rock at the rump side, hard enough to knock the calf off its feet and enrage the cow. She charged at me and gave me the one chance that I probably would get as I only had the one spear. I stepped back through the trees as she arrived at my location and she came around the side of the nearest tree. As soon as her head cleared the tree I launched the spear into her neck and doubled back through the same two trees. I knew instantly that I had missed my mark but by only a mere inch or two. Now it's going to take a lot longer than I had hoped. The spear had gone all the way through her neck and was sticking out the other side. It had not been the killing blow that I had tried to make. She kicked and bit at me as I jumped back and forth between the trees and I just managed to stay out of her reach. When she tried to get past two of the trees, she managed to get the ends of the spear caught just long enough for me to act. I used the hammer to great effect as I brought it down on her head directly between her eyes. At that point the spear ends came off the trees and she pulled back as if to look at how better to get at me. She then lost all focus and her back legs collapsed and she sat down on her rump. She was done and I knew it as she couldn't get back up on her feet but refused to give up. I stayed in the trees long enough to make sure of that. With the blood now gushing from her mouth, she finally keeled over. I again wondered at the fact that I felt nothing over the loss of life here.

While this was going on the calf saw this as its chance to escape and run uphill on the same path that they had come down. I knew that was a major mistake on its part but wasn't able to do anything to stop it. I really didn't have much interest in it anyway as I would be very busy for the next few days with skinning and scraping hides and reducing the moose into sizeable chunks to save for my food supply.

It wasn't long after the calf got out of site that the noises I heard were just the inevitable. The wolf pack, now consisting of five members, hadn't gone all that far and probably were interested in the results of the moose, man encounter. They would be eating well tonight and would wait around for the parts of the moose that I wouldn't have much need for. With their Alfa member dead, they wouldn't be marching into my camp to demand their share.

It was getting late in the day and I needed to get the carcasses up to the new camp site and set up a fire pit. I would need to find some wood to burn and everything else would wait till morning. I pulled the moose up first and then the wolves but it took two trips for them. Fred was nowhere in sight and I guessed that he had recovered by now and was in hiding. He better be careful as the five wolves would be roaming the area looking for a handout or anything else they could kill. I surveyed the ridge that I had picked for my bivouac area and decided to put the fire pit almost in the middle as there were no trees close and I could use the hill behind for some shelter. The pine needles had been particularly deep at this point and as I moved them around an unusual shape started to take place. With the first handful of needles moved I discovered a stone of rather large size. Then there was another one next to it and so on around in a circle. As I cleaned out the rest of the pine needles an old fire pit became visible. There were so many pine needles that I would have to burn some and use others for bedding.

I was still thinking in these terms when it hit me that the fire pit had been created by someone. It was not a natural occurrence. I knelt down to sniff the area for the tell-tale odor of fire. If there was any it was too faint to smell over the scent of pine. It had not been used for a very long time. As I looked at the depth of the pine needles it could have been many years since its last use. I had expected to have a fire, so had brought along my fire starter kit. Now all I needed was the wood for the fire and something to mount over the pit to hold my dinner. Also I would need something to cook.

I decided to start with the food item first before it got too dark to see and ran down to the lake. The area that the moose had been in was still open water and it was easy to see several fish swimming around in it. My knowledge of spear fishing had increased to the place where if I could see them they didn't have a chance. There were no large ones in site and I took two midsized ones in rapid succession. I returned to the ridge area and dropped the fish next to the moose carcass. I thought that getting fire wood now might be a problem. The sky was getting darker as it was going into night. I started up the hill behind the ridge and tripped on something under the pine needles. As I moved the needles out of the way I was rewarded with the site of old tree limbs stacked neatly. Someone had expected to be back here at some time and left the fire wood for future use. I could hardly believe my good luck or was something else at work here again. I could never get over that feeling of being under a microscope as if someone was playing with me. I didn't want to think about what had taken place today as I faced down a wolf pack and killed a moose and didn't even get a scratch.

I had a fire going in no time and used some green tree branches for a spit to put the fish on. The wood was so very dry that it burned hot and fast but didn't create any sparks. I would have to put out the fire before turning in for the night as the amount of pine needles in the area could create a huge problem if they caught on fire. I was really hungry and by the time the fish were ready also a bit sleepy. I needed to do something about the moose before I could get to sleep or our friends from the pack would be in over night to help themselves to my future dinners. I placed the three dead wolves on top of the moose and propped the Alphas head up to look alive. I had no idea if this would work or not but nothing ventured nothing gained. As it turned out the pack never bothered the moose and I have no idea why that was. I did a quick walk around the perimeter to make sure nothing unusual was going on that I might see or feel. It seemed calm enough and I arranged some pine needles for bedding next to the wood pile. I would have lots of work to do for the next couple days as I put out the fire.

It took a week to render the moose into hide and food packets and skin and scrape the wolves. The tools I had just weren't adequate for this type of work and my fingers hurt long before I was done. Except that done wasn't adequate either, as I had to haul all this stuff back to the hot springs where I had left the travois and the rest of my gear. It was too much to carry and I wasn't going to leave some to get at a later date.

I didn't plan on making another trip down here as I had detected a change in the weather. It was already starting to warm up and I would need to get back to the valley before the ice broke up. I just had to make another travois that was just big enough to carry the items I had accumulated. I selected a couple small pine trees for that and literally ripped them out of the ground. I set the root sections into the fire to burn them off and to harden them. This unit would be less complicated than the one I made earlier but would do the trick for the short haul up the line.

Earlier in the week the fox, Fred, had returned and I would sometimes awake to find him sleeping just a few feet from me. I assumed that the threat from the wolves was causing him great concern. They had been hanging around off and on, waiting for the parts Fred and I didn't want. I was even surprised that they dragged the fellow wolf carcasses away also. I wasn't sure if they ate them or not and I didn't care as long as I didn't have to take care of them myself.

I got up early to get a start on the day and for the first time in a long time, got to see the sunrise. It was a nice surprise and would help guide me back to the hot springs or so I thought. The sun shine was short lived as it must have heated the ground up and a heavy fog developed before I could get past the lake. I had stopped to get some ice to take along. I noticed the sky darkening as I was breaking up some of the lake surface. I packed the ice on top of the other items and headed to the end of the lake.

I had marked some trees on my way here and needed to find the first one on my way out. In my mind's eye I recreated the arrival of a week or so ago and checked to see where I would have been at that very moment. I walked to the location and turned back to see if the scene looked the same and it did. So turning one hundred and eighty degrees

[120]

would put me on a return course that should take me to the last tree I marked and in the correct direction to the hot springs. I knew that the skinned mark would be on the south side of the tree and to look for it there. As I started off, I checked to see my little grey companion close on my heels. He wasn't going to let me get out of sight while the wolves were still around and a threat to him. Poor Fred, I thought, he must be close to a nervous breakdown. He must have wondered if I would really protect him or not. I thought maybe it would be best if I did at this stage. We were becoming a pair, even if it wasn't going to be friendly. I had hit him with a rock and he bit me in return for that. I guess it was going to be that kind of relationship, a love hate affair.

I found the first marked tree without any problems and returning along that line went very well. That is until the marks stopped, then I had to rely on the hard to see sun as it ducked in and out of the pea soup fog. The going got a lot slower as I tried to keep a straight line going. Everyone who has ever been in the woods knows that trees don't grow in a straight line except where planted for some purpose. There was no rhyme or reason for the way these trees were growing. Sometimes I would have to walk around one tree or maybe a bunch of them, so straight, smate, I just had to guess at most of it and use the brighter part of the sky as my south. When I could smell the faint odor of sulfur I knew I was getting close and within a short time we broke out into the open. Fred had been very close to me the whole time and I had to think his senses were better that mine so the wolves were still around.

Chapter six

The Flood

I knew that I wanted to get another dunk in the hot springs before heading back to the valley but first things first. I had to make sure nothing had happed to the supplies I had stored in the tree and of course I would need to move the new stuff to the old travois, which was bigger and easier to pull. I would be leaving in the morning and hoped that I could get there without any further interruptions.

I could tell from the air that spring was coming and was afraid that I had taken too long here at the springs. I got a fire going and put a chunk of moose meat on a spit over it. I checked the fire to see that it was banked properly. I needed to make sure that the meat wouldn't burn but would cook nice and slow. I then climbed into the water, making sure to have one spear and a couple stones nearby. I didn't expect company but as in all cases, better safe than sorry. I did feel pretty safe at this time and for good reason. The only threat I encountered had been the wolves and I had almost cut their pack in half. I guess I hadn't thought of the moose as a threat but don't tell that to the moose. As I lay back in the goldilocks pool, I let my mind reach out to see if any unknowns were hanging around. Fred was the only active itch in my unconscious and I hoped it would stay that way for a while.

I shared my dinner with Fred and noticed that he didn't run away with the food as he had done all along. He didn't seem to want me out of his sight so the implication was that the wolves may have followed us down to this end of the park. I wasn't going to let that bother me and thought it was OK for Fred to hang around. I knew that the top predators always tried to reduce the number of competing animals in the food chain. It was hard to see how these two could be competing but I wasn't going to tell the wolves that, not that they would have listened anyway. I tried to make sure everything was buttoned up for the night and headed for dreamland.

I woke up in the morning feeling quite comfortable and realized that it was almost warm. The temperature had gone up over night and the fog wasn't as thick as it had been. I was sure the sun would be more visible than it had been for months now. I made a quick check of the camp and fire pit to make sure no hot embers could reignite. I had burned the green wood from the smaller travois last night and listened to the popping and watched the sparks go up like fire flies. It had been the best night I had since I got into this mess. I even got a laugh in when the wood first popped and Fred jumped up as if someone had shot at him. It took a while for him to get over the noise and fireworks. The best part of the night was that if I had any dreams I didn't remember them. It was almost like a blank slate.

I gathered my gear, loaded a little firewood on top of everything else and said good-by to the springs. The trek back to the Valley was going to take two days if I pushed it, longer if anything delayed us. Fred of course was going to be happy to get away from there but he didn't care how long it would take to get back. I just had to make sure he had enough to eat. At first he seemed confused as to what was going on and paced back and forth. Once we got to the trail and started north, he almost acted like a puppy, bouncing around and jumping out in front. I wondered if I let him lead, if he would take us straight to the valley. No, I couldn't trust him that much but it was a thought.

By the time we had made it though half the morning, he had settled down to just testing the air and looking for any thing he could chase. I tried to ignore him and kept plodding ahead. The trail slid a little to the west but I stayed with it until I got to the ridgeline, then I swung northeast. I knew that would take me toward the valley.

The day had been bright with the sun shining off and on. The clouds were breaking up and the temperature was rising. I stopped and made provisions for the night, setting a fire and cooking another chunk of moose meat. It cooled off quick as soon as the sun went down and I wrapped up in the bear hide and went to sleep. I woke up knowing I had dreamt during the night but it didn't stick with me. It must not have been very important and I felt better for that. I wished that they would all be like the previous night but somehow I knew that wouldn't happen.

I pulled out a couple pieces of jerky, kicked some dirt over the fires ashes and got underway. We had covered a lot of ground that first day and now I wanted to finish this off. Fred grabbed his chunk of jerky and in a second it was gone. He then looked to see if I was going to give him some more. "Sorry Fred, that's it till tonight" and he looked like I might have just kicked him. "You act too much like my old dog did" but he didn't pay any attention to me.

The second day out wasn't quite as pleasant and much slower. We weren't going to make it in two days and that became obvious not long after we started out. I began to feel that itch in the back of my head again that indicated something this way cometh. I tried to speed up to get some distance in before something unusual happened and we were making good time. "All good things must come to an end" because Fred was now becoming a nuisance as he moved in closer and closer until he was underfoot. When I nearly tripped on him, I knew it was time to do something about the possible threat. I hadn't seen anything yet but with the way Fred was acting, I guessed that it had to be the wolves again. Once the deer had left the hot springs, the wolf's food chain must have gone with it and now I was carrying a good portion of the rest. The pack must have picked a new Alfa to lead them and I was suspecting it would be the one that got the fish I had tossed to distract it at the lake. The other four seemed more like followers than leaders but as a group they could be real dangerous to me and of course to Fred.

We were out on the open prairie and I just couldn't believe it was so hard to see these predators. They were much bigger than Fred with longer legs and you would think they would stick out in the open here. Maybe they were further back than I thought but anyway I had to make some kind of stand to prevent them from causing more trouble. I was just hoping to chase them away for now. Anything else would seem to be too time consuming and I already lost way too much time with them. I scanned the trail behind to see if I needed to double back and intercept them but could not locate them anywhere.

"Think" I said out loud, if you were a wolf what would you be doing out here? They knew I wouldn't be safe to tangle with and even though I had a lot of food with me they would have to get past me to get it. So if they were human, they would think about stealing it at night or overwhelming me. Since they were wolves, they were born hunters and scavengers that tried to stay out of a heads-on fight but attack most animals that can't do any real damage to them. Not that they wouldn't do so but with what had happened back at the lake, they might think twice about attacking me.

I decided to do a perimeter check before continuing on to see if I could find out what they were up to. I walked out about a hundred steps or so and circled the area to no avail. The itch in the back of my head was getting less intense and I had the feeling that they had left the area to me and Fred. Speaking of Fred, he seemed to have lost a little of the fear he had as he now was out from under the travois. I thought it might be a good idea to stay put for a while to make sure the wolves had gone. "Dinner is early tonight, Fred" I said as I set about building a fire and getting something ready to cook. Maybe it would be lunch instead of dinner. I knew that Fred wouldn't care what I called it, as long as he got to eat something.

I had the thought that maybe we could travel by moonlight to make up for the lost distance but getting to the valley at night might not be the best idea I ever had. There was that old me again, overly cautious. The weather had been great so far and the sun was shining since early this morning. There would be a chance that the moon would be out but having not seen it for months on end now I had no idea what faze it would be in.

We had traveled a fair piece before stopping so I knew we would be at the valley sometime tomorrow. I decided to setup camp here for now and get an early start in the morning. The threat from the wolves kept diminishing and I became comfortable with the thought that tomorrow would be soon enough to get back. Fred seemed to like the idea also as he now began to roam out a little further, listening, and sniffing the air. I

[125]

watched as Fred stopped and cocked his head to one side. He looked like he was about to jump on something when two partridges bust into flight and his chance at them just flew away. They were flying due east and all of a sudden turned south as a much bigger dog like animal made a jump at them.

I now had a location of at least one of the wolves. Chances are the rest would be very close to the same location. I couldn't understand why they would be so far from where we were, especially since we would be downwind from them. I think that's right as the wind would be coming toward us from them instead of the other way around. There didn't seem to be much wind right now and maybe that's why Fred didn't react to it. It could be that they knew where we were and didn't much care about the rest of it. I sometimes think I have so much more to learn.

I spent the late afternoon and evening telling Fred all the trouble I have had, including some that he caused. It was more like going over the whole episode of my new life here and my old life there. Guess what, Fred didn't seem to care one iota about my life as long as he got his share of the food. I asked him about his life but he didn't want to talk about it. Some friend he turned out to be. I burned up the last of the fire wood I had brought along and as the sun went down the fire slowly died. There would be no more fires till we got back to the valley and with that I rolled up in the bearskin and went to sleep.

I was up before dawn and shooed Fred out of the way. I knew he was looking for something to eat but we needed to get moving and I would get out a bit of jerky later on. I took my heading as soon as it was light enough to see and started out. The night had been restless as the dream train came back and now haunted me. There must be more to these dreams than I can get a handle on as they keep coming back and disrupting my sleep. Most of the time they don't make any sense and I wish they would go away. I can still see the fires burning and the screaming and running and blood everywhere. Most of the time they end in the bat cave with the terrible smell.

I pushed hard to try to reach the valley as early as possible, maybe because of the dreams. I needed to make so many things happen if I was going to get down the river before the ice went out. Maybe I should have built a raft instead of a sled. I then thought about the logjam and decided that might not have been a good idea either. I stopped to get some jerky out before the sun was half way up and Fred almost came running to get his share. I think he's turning into a dog. I busted up a chunk of ice to share with him and then we were off again. The sun was on the downhill side when the far edge of the canyon came into view. That's when Fred started to act strange again.

I looked for land marks and it took a few minutes to recognize the location as we were a little west of the trail head. I had not bothered to follow the track from when we went out as it wasn't the shortest way to go and I was in a hurry. I turned east and headed up river. I had a good visual map in my head from the scouting I did early on. I could tell exactly what part of the river I was looking at. I wasn't off by much and the logjam at the lower end of the valley came into view in a matter of minutes. A short time later we were at the trailhead and the cairn I had built was now visible.

Fred was more nervous than ever and I was getting concerned about that. It would seem that the wolves had made it here before us and I would have to deal with them again. Otherwise I could not explain why Fred was acting so odd. I looked for signs that they were there and found some paw prints mixed in with the deer track at the top of the trail. They had already gone down into the valley and probably followed the deer. There would be no place to hide for the deer and the wolf pack could decimate them. Just then I heard something that caught my attention. It was hoof against stone and the deer were coming up the trail and in a big hurry. There were only three of them and I moved aside to let them get past. The wolves must have trapped or killed the rest of the herd. I waited to see if they would be following the deer up out of the valley or not. I could see the trail from where I was, but anything on the trail might not see me. Two of the wolves were on their way up and I readied myself to meet them. With a spear in both hands, I crouched down to make it even harder for them to see me until the last second. I put the first spear in the chest of

[127]

the lead one and the second spear in the neck of the next one. I managed to jump back and let them fight with the spears. The second wolf had not quite cleared the top of the trail and went tumbling down the rock wall.

The lead wolf recognized me as the cause of its pain and made a lunge for me. I moved sideways just enough to keep from getting seriously injured but he managed to rake my arm with his teeth. He didn't get any further than that as the spear had found it mark and he coughed up blood and he died. I made a quick check of my arm and saw that it wasn't damaged very much but again I would have another war wound.

I retrieved the spear from the dead wolf and looked down to see if the other was at the bottom. I didn't see it anywhere but knew it wouldn't be going far. That did leave the other three wolves in the valley and I didn't know how I was going to handle that situation. I did have the rocks to throw but now only one spear. I had left several more in the camp down below but wasn't sure if I would get that far as the current residents of the valley would want to protect their kill.

I was caught in a dilemma with the moose meat and hides on the travois and my other supplies down in the valley. It was going to be a challenge to protect my new assets and also drive the wolves out. The number of wolf kills was mounting but now I had a mark on my arm from the latest encounter. I had to wonder if I was getting careless or if the circumstance were just changing. It was getting late in the day and it would be best if I slept on it. The problem of course was where to sleep and what precautions to take. Fred had disappeared and I knew I wouldn't see him again till after the wolves were gone. I struggled with the thought of what to do. If I let the wolves come up the trail and get past me then I would have trouble protecting the supplies that were on the travois.

I decided to camp at the trailhead on top and keep the last spear handy along with all the stones I had in the bag. If they tried to get past me tonight, I would just have to stop them any way that I could. I would sleep on that.

I woke in the morning to an even warmer temperature and knew that time was running out for me to sled down the river. The wolves had not tried to come out of the valley and probably were lying around after having eaten their fill of deer meat. I checked again to see if the second wolf I speared yesterday was dead at the bottom of the cliff but I couldn't see it. I wanted that second spear and wished I had more. One spear might not be enough to handle the three remaining wolves.

The dreams last night had been rough again but I managed to sleep through them. I think they get worse when I have to deal with adversity and the wolves were a major concern. Now I needed to sneak down and find the dead wolf to get that spear back. I hoped I didn't wake the sleeping giant. I left the dead wolf up top to protect my gear and shifted to silent running mode. I wanted to have the advantage over the pack and needed to kill the Alfa before anything else happened. "The best laid plans of mice and men" I said as I started down the trail.

When I got to the bottom of the trail I stopped to listen but didn't hear anything unusual. I couldn't see any evidence of the disturbance that had to have taken place. I moved along the rock wall to the west as I was looking for the second dead wolf and where he would have fallen to. The spear must not have killed it outright and it would have tried to get away from where it landed. It should have left some sign as to the direction and I would need all my trailing instincts to follow it or so I thought. I could see the area where it hit the ground after its fall and where it had struggled to get up and move. Its trail was easier to follow than I thought as it was bleeding and dragging itself along. It hadn't gone far and the reason I hadn't seen it from above was that it got in behind a big pine tree.

I was retrieving the second spear when my sixth sense kicked in again and I managed to spin and trip over the dead wolf as the Alpha charged at me. I fell over backward just as the wolf leaped at my throat. The Alpha never saw the two spears as they hit their mark, one under the chin and the other into the chest. I launched the full weight of its body off me and jerked out the spears at the same time. The other two wolves had no stomach for battle and took off for the trail out.

I grabbed the bag of rocks and ran to the edge of the woods. With a clear look at the trail up I had the two wolves in site and managed to hit the first one hard enough that it bounced off the side wall and fell down into the trees. The next one got hit in the rear quarters and also tumbled down. That one was closer and I speared it and held it down till it quit moving. The other one was still alive and moving away. I started after it and found that it could still move faster than I could. I kept it in site till it got on the river ice and started downstream. It was leaving a trail of blood and I knew it wouldn't be going very far but I didn't think I had time to chase after it. It could go for a day or two at this rate and I needed all the time I could get. I heard the first sound of spring as a fly went buzzing past me.

The Ice broke at the edge as I was stepping off it and I could hear the sound of geese honking overhead. I didn't make it in time and now I knew it all too well. I checked on my supplies in the tree and found them to be exactly as I left them. It had been a harsh winter and the spring sunshine was starting to take its toll on the frozen earth.

For the first time in months I would now have to deal with mud, insects, noisy birds, and a plethora of strange things, most of which I wouldn't have had to deal with at any time in my previous life. I had learned a lot over the winter months and now I would try to put that to use. The clothing, backpack, weapons and tools would get separated from the food and water. Most of these items would go on the sled I had fashioned from various wood and hide pieces. I had planned on dragging it down the river while it was still frozen but couldn't finish it and get the rest of the stuff ready in time. Now that the ice was melting I would have to haul all of it up the cliff. It was the only way I could go with all my belongings. The roughest part would be tearing down the sled into small enough pieces to carry up to the trail head. The rest of the stuff I could haul on my back with the rack I had made. I would leave the sled till last and use the dead wolves to protect the food supplies. It all sounded good and I just hoped it would work out.

The first thing I did was to haul two of the dead wolves up the trail and place them with the other one around the travois. I then packed as much of the meat on the back rack I made to add that to the moose meat on the travois. I was hoping that the meat wouldn't thaw out right away. The next trip was getting the tools and other essentials up there. I then started to tear down the sled to get it up the trail. It was big enough that it wouldn't fit on the trail and would have been too clumsy to try to carry.

There was a loud booming sound like an explosion and followed by a roar and rush of air. The ground shook and I thought it must be an earthquake. I stopped what I was doing and raced to the top of the trail to see if I could determine what had happened. I could see a cloud of steam or dust rising from the riverbed way up near the mountains. The sound was continuing to build and the cloud was getting higher over the riverbed. Fred raced in from where ever he had been and then raced away again. I didn't know what to do but guessed that running away was not an option. The geese that had just landed on the river ice were now in the air and flying north. I thought that I must be on the wrong side of the river if they went the other way.

The sound kept getting louder and the cloud closer. I could see that something big was happening but this was beyond my control. I walked to the edge of the trail and looked down. From there I could see that the canyon was filling up fast and that if it overflowed I would be in big trouble. The prairie ran up hill a little bit from here but I couldn't see a higher land mark anyplace. My incursion to the south had proved that there was some high ground in that direction but it was two or three days away. There wasn't going to be even one days time to get out of this area.

The outcropping was a few feet higher than the rest of the prairie and I headed in that direction. The outcropping caused a fairly large eddy to appear and swirled all manner of flotsam and jetsam to come in close. I knew that the far end of the canyon would also serve as a whirlpool. That's where all the logjam material was from previous floods. This flood looked to be a lot bigger than the one that caused that logjam. I tried to identify the items that came flashing by that might not be future fire wood but the jumble was crowded with trees and large chunks of ice. Some furry

[131]

creatures were being pushed downstream but I could only identify the color and not the species.

When it became apparent that the water was going to stay in the river bed and not overflow, I began to think about rescuing some fire wood as the trees and other unidentified things came by. When a branch or tree got close enough I would grab it and pull it out of the water, but it seemed to be overly risky to do that. I thought the other end of the valley, above the logjam might work better and I started in that direction. Just then a pair of antlers showed up and I grabbed them and pulled out an elk. It was definitely dead and beat up but I could probably save most of the meat and some of the hide. I pulled some more future fire wood out and then started again for the far end. I was interrupted again as I saw what I thought was a cat on a large tree trunk and I could hear it crying. As it spun its way around, I was able to reach it with one of the tree limbs I had already retrieved. I pulled the tree toward shore and the cat jumped on to dry land, that's when I notice it didn't have a tail.

I was staring at the cat thing; I think it was a bobcat or lynx, when I heard the crying sound again. Now it seemed to have moved downriver a little. I couldn't imagine what it was, but since I was going that way I just ran a little faster. The whirlpool at this end was much bigger and more flotsam was gathering near to the shore. I started pulling out as much wood items as I could and again heard the crying noise. It seemed to be coming from the center of the pile and I tried to isolate the sound as I heard it again. I thought it might be another cat but it was off key for that. It was faint as it came again but this time it had drifted past and was on the other side. I couldn't determine what kind of animal it could be so let it go and tried to keep dragging wood and even some carcasses out.

When the sound came again it was on the shore side but even fainter this time when I saw what looked like an Indian papoose. It was half submerged and hooked under a tree branch. I caught the branch and tried to pull it in but the bank gave way and I fell in. I pulled myself up on the branch and got the papoose out of the water. I didn't know if we would survive as the current dragged us away from the shore and toward the torrent. I carried the child and worked my way over the top of the pile and out on a log that was headed in to the bank. When it got close enough I jumped for it, pushing the baby ahead of me. I hoped it didn't get hurt but I had problems of my own as the bank kept crumbling under me as I fought to get out of the water.

The bank crumbled at such an angle that I was able to crawl out. I grabbed the papoose and took it further from the water. I knew that I had to get this kid dry and warm or it would surely die. I didn't have any dry wood so a fire was not going to be possible. I got her (it's a girl) out of the wet material and wrapped her in the bear hide. I knew immediately that wouldn't work so pulled one of my bear hide sleeves off the travois and slid her into that. Then I wrapped her in the big hide. She was still breathing as I tried to hold her to add some warmth. I needed to pull more stuff out of the whirlpool and as soon as I felt she was going to make it, I went back to work. I saw many animals floating by but ignored most and went for the deer and elk.

I continued to pull in as much wood as I could get hold of as I knew there wouldn't be any left in the valley. Not that I would be able to get into the valley any more. I was sure that the trail would be wiped out as the bank on both sides of the river kept giving way and you could see the gap widening. I had to move all my stuff further back to keep from losing it. I checked on the baby a couple more times and she seemed to be breathing alright.

I wasn't shocked to see several bodies float past but they were badly mutilated from the pounding of the ice chunks and various tree parts. When I saw a woman float by I started to ignore her but the tree branch she was attached to would be easy to reach and I was still pulling in wood. When I dragged this piece in I notice that she wasn't as banged up as the others, so I separated her from the branch and dropped her off to the side. When I did that, water came out of her mouth and it sounded like she gasped. I didn't have a first aid badge but thought if she were to live I might have to help her. I pushed on her chest a couple times and turned her head to the side and she spit up more water and coughed. Her eyes came open and she passed out but was breathing.

You don't need first aid training if you live long enough to see how things are done. Now I was going to get to practice those things. This woman had been hit hard in the right side and both her arm and leg were broken. Maybe some ribs too but I didn't think I could do anything about the ribs. I made some quick splints from smaller tree branches and straightened out both the arm and leg. Once they were tied to keep them immobile, I moved her to the bearskin with the baby.

I checked on both of them and they were still too cold so I climbed in with them to provide body heat. I had been working hard so the break was good for me and my body was warm from the exercise. Within a short while they both began to warm up but I didn't know what I could do to feed the baby. As soon as I felt they would be warm without me being there, I got out and created a big fire pit. I knew that the wet wood would spark and pop, so I cleaned out a large area around it. While I was doing that I noticed that the cat-thing was taking way too much interest in the baby. I didn't save it to have it eating my relatives. I chased it away and when it saw me coming after it with a stick it left for greener pastures. I didn't know if it would come back or not but if it did I would have to think about the alternative to its survival.

I didn't have any trouble starting a fire but keeping it going with all the wet wood was turning in to a real problem. I picked through the wood for some that had been dead and just carried downstream with the rest of the flotsam. I put those close to the fire to let them dry out a little. I was a very busy boy for the rest of the day, pulling wood and dead animals out of the water. I concentrated on the wood later as I didn't think I would be able to convert enough of the animals into meat and hide before they went bad. The green wood burned with lots of noise and sparks but also helped dry the older pieces out and I was able to get a nice fire going late in the day. I used the bowl I had to heat up some bear grease and mixed in a little water. I put a chunk of moose meat on a spit and got it cooking before my newfound companions woke up.

When I saw the bear hide start to move I walked over to see if everything was alright. The woman must have been in terrible pain, as she opened her eyes and then passed out again. The baby was still sleeping; they must have used up all their energy just trying to stay alive in the flood. I will try to get the baby to take some of the bear grease and water for nourishment; I don't know what else to try. The baby started to move around and needed attention. I carried her to the fire pit and sat down close enough to get the warmth from it. I used my finger to test the mix in the bowl and put a little bit into her mouth. She sucked it off my finger and I kept doing that for a while. I knew she should still be getting milk, but the Safeway was closed so she would have to settle for what the locals had. After a while she went back to sleep and I sat there rocking her.

I heard the woman cough and didn't look at her; she would still have a little water in her lungs and would need to get it out. I thought if she needed anything she would say something. I didn't know if we spoke the same language or not but we would find out soon enough.

I no sooner thought that than she started to moan and tried to roll around. That cause more pain and she let out a yelp. I let her think that I wasn't going to come running and at this point considered the child to be more important. It was only a minute or two before I got up and carried the baby over to where the woman was. She was looking at me with big fearful eyes as if she knew that she should be dead and didn't know why not. When she saw the baby, everything changed. She tried to reach for it but her right arm caused her much pain and she slumped back. I placed the baby on her left side and let her put her arm around it. I knew that they would have to have names. I couldn't keep calling them baby and woman, although those wouldn't be the worst names they could have had. I went and cut off a couple pieces of moose meat and brought the bowl over to her. I took one of the chunks of meat and stuck it in my mouth and reached the second one to her and she took it. It was progress.

The baby wasn't hers and I could tell that by looking at them. She didn't act like a mother but more like a sister. She was pretty young too but I had no idea how young and I was never good at guessing age anyway. I gave her a sip from the bowl to see if she liked it and she drank all of it. I headed back to the fire to heat up some more and get more meat to eat as I was really hungry and it would be good for her to eat some more also. I tried to talk to her when I got back with the meat but she didn't seem to understand me.

I pointed to the meat and said "moose" and she repeated it. It sounded more like "mouse" when she said it. I thought that was close enough and let it go at that. She kept trying to move and grimacing with pain. I didn't know if she needed help or was just trying to reposition herself. I tried to ask but only got a blank stare back from her. She knew that I had removed her wet clothes and must have splinted her arm and leg. I could see she wanted me to take the baby from her and I obliged.

Then she tried to get up by herself but there was no way that was going to happen. I placed the baby down on the bearskin and put my hands under her arms and lifted her to her feet. She couldn't walk or stand or even put weight on her right leg, so I carried her a little ways out so she could relieve herself. She seemed so very embarrassed even though I had turned my head away. Bodily functions are a common occurrence and need not be something to be ashamed about, so I think it was more that she wasn't able to get there without help. I got her back to the bearskin and had her hold the baby again. It looked like they would be sleeping through the night. I would get up several times to check on them.

We could have many surprises, as I think it will be weeks before we can travel. I made a shelter from the logs and branches that I had pulled from the river. I talked constantly about what I was doing and the young lady listened carefully and would repeat some words. The ones that she recognized helped to get us going in a small way with the conversation. I made a crutch for her and after the second week she was able to move about a little on her own. She was really shocked when Fred showed up and demanded to be fed. He looked pretty bad, as if he had been on the run the whole time and hadn't eaten anything. I thought he would bite my hand off grabbing for the first piece of meat that I offered him. I melted some ice in the bowl for him and he drank the thing dry. It wasn't until he had his fill

[136]

that he paid any attention to the other two people in our camp. He went around and sniffed at everything, especially the baby, but didn't bother them after that.

During those first two weeks, the woman watched me closely and tried to say something or point to something as if to let me know I was doing it wrong. I wasn't surprised by that but since we didn't understand each other, there wasn't much I could do about it. After she was able to get on her feet, she would get more animated when I didn't do something the way she expected it to be done. I knew that I was ill prepared for life in the wild but she made me feel even less so at times. I could hardly wait for her to get fully mobile so she could do some of those things and I could learn from her.

I had been watching the water in the river bed gradually start to go down and the sound slowly subsided. It looked like it would last for months before it would be back to a normal run off. Then I wondered what that would look like. I had guessed that the river had been locked up in an ice dam many miles to the east. The result of the dam breaking would now let the water flow at its normal rate once it drained whatever lake there was behind it. I was still able to see some flotsam and jetsam going down the river. I would have thought that most of it would have been washed away before now but something's kept showing up. Most of those were trees or parts of them with an occasional animal.

It was about the end of that second week when I saw smoke far to the east of where we were. It was a calm day and fairly clear, so if it was a real fire then someone had to have started it. The likelihood of spontaneous combustion was highly unlikely. I pointed it out to the woman, who I have now been calling Mary, and she got real excited, pointing and hollering. While she watched I made a very smoky fire with some green wood and grasses. Then I threw a deer skin over it and caused a smoke signal to rise as I pulled it off. I did three then two then three more. I knew she wouldn't get the meaning and neither would they but I felt I had to try something. I then waited for a while and repeated the process several more times. To our surprise the smoke from the other fire stopped and did not restart again. I had to think that something was wrong but the possibilities were great. They could have run out of wood or not seen our signals or just didn't want anything to do with us. We could only wait to see if the smoke restarted or if the people that made the fire would show up.

I had been working furiously for the past two weeks and now had hides everywhere. They were deer and elk and couple of wolves. I had cut and dried as much meat as I could and the unused parts had to be tossed away. Mary tried to scrape the hides but she couldn't get her broken arm to hold them. I could see that she was right handed and that even made it harder for her to do anything. I had been working with my right hand a lot but seemed to be able to use both if I needed to. Mary and been chewing up pieces of meat and feeding tiny bits to the baby that I had started to call Ann. Woman and baby just didn't seem to roll off my tongue so very well. She didn't know why I called her Mary but she began to answer to it.

I pointed to myself and said George but what she said didn't sound like that at all. I guess I can live with whatever it is she just called me. It almost sounded like Jed and I thought of the Clampets. I don't think we will find any oil around here anywhere. Anyway, when it came to naming the two of them I stuck with simple instead of the harder to pronounce that had been getting common back home. As soon as I was able to work some leather into usable material, I made a skirt for Mary. We couldn't get her deerskin dress over her head with her arm splinted and so I put my vest on her for a little more warmth.

I pointed to her feet and to mine and motioned that they should have some kind of covers over them. I then laid out a deerskin and she drew an outline on it with a stick that we kept dark by putting it in the fire. She first had me put my foot down on it and she traced that, then doubled it and added some extra. When I looked at it I couldn't see how it would work but she showed me where to cut and where to punch holes in it. I then overlapped the pieces and ran rawhide through the holes and what do you know, we had a moccasin. I was surprised at how good it came out. It seemed easy then to make the other three and we now had our walking shoes. She pointed out the wolf hide and how to cut enough to make a sole

[138]

for each one to give better wear and softer feel. I was ecstatic. I had struggled so hard just to make a vest. Maybe I'll keep her around just for the knowledge.

The weather had been spring like with some rain, some wind and some sun. The temperature went up and down like a yoyo, so we never knew from day to day what to expect. The insects didn't seem as bad up here on the prairie as it had been down on the river. We started getting lots of grasshoppers as soon as the first rain hit. I suspect that there just weren't enough birds around to keep that population down. We never saw the deer again and I think they found a home at the Park, now that the wolf pack was gone. I never thought I would miss eating fish but it would have been nice to have some, even without the tartar sauce.

We were into the third week since the start of the flood and the wood pile was beginning to dwindle. I thought that we would have to start moving before long and began to make preparations for that. Mary took notice and acted as if she wanted to know where we would be going. I wasn't sure which way would be best so I just shrugged. I would have to think about that for a little as the flood would have changed almost everything in both directions. Then again the Park might be the best bet as I thought the deer would be over there. Mary wasn't going to give me the chance to pick as she kept pointing east. I thought that might be where her family would have been. They probably didn't survive but I didn't know how to tell her that. We still had a little time and I dropped the subject for now. She would be ready to walk a little in the next week or two and I thought I could stretch the wood for that long. I had made a bigger travois with some of the green wood and we burned the wood from the old one as it was really the driest stuff we had.

I was busy putting things together when Mary started screaming. I looked up quickly to see what it was and she was pointing across the river gorge. There on the other side were six men walking downriver and they hadn't seen us yet. The noise from the flood water was still high enough that our voices wouldn't carry that far. I quickly stoked the fire and put some green grasses on it to cause smoke. Then started the same sequence I

[139]

had used before with the three, two, and three smoke signal. They saw it almost immediately and started to wave back. They ran in both directions, looking to see if there was a way to cross. The canyon was a third to half full of rushing water with chunks of ice and trees still being pushed downstream. There would be no chance to get together any time soon if ever. I guessed that at this point the canyon may have been a half mile across. It would be hard to identify someone from that distance. I didn't know who they were and I was sure Mary couldn't tell either. The recent loss of family and friends might make all of us survivors and that might have been enough.

I guessed that they must have been a hunting party that was away from the river when the flood started. They were traveling light with only two of them carrying packs. There was no fire wood available to them and if they were the ones that had the previous fire then they must have used up all the wood there was. I tried to remember if it was two or three days ago that we saw the smoke, I think it was three. They must have been walking for that long to get this far and now couldn't get together with us. They appeared to be signaling us to go downriver and Mary kept trying to point upriver. They kept shaking her off as if to indicate there was nothing to go back too up that way. Mary sat down and cried for the loss and I knew she wanted to see for herself but I didn't think we could afford the time to do so. I let her cry by herself. I didn't know how to help her get over her loss any more than I knew how to get over mine.

The group on the other side of the river camped overnight and in the morning signaled that they were going to continue on downstream. I was sure they felt like they had no other option and we waved them good-bye. Mary would be ready to walk in two more days but even then it would be slow going. She seemed to have made some decision in her mind and now I would have to live with it. I've always be a sucker for a pretty girl so now she looked like she would prove it. I knew she wouldn't go downstream no matter what I did and I knew I couldn't let her try going anywhere alone. So while I made ready to leave I thought about the possibility that we would be gone from here forever. I had not wanted to change locations for a good reason but I guess I wasn't going home anyway.

I said good-bye to the twenty first century and would now face this one with everything I could muster. Whatever brought me into this world would have to live with me. My dreams had been convoluted lately and I had maybe gotten use to that. At some point they had became less violent but I still lacked understanding of them.

The next two days were a struggle for me as I had not felt any empathy for anything or anyone to this point and now I was finally getting some feelings back for someone. I may not have seen the animals and even the people here as real since I had trouble believing I was stuck here for good. Now it seemed as if I was growing attached to the people and even that one fox. I thought back to when I rescued the papoose and then Mary but I hadn't felt anything for them then. I just did it because it was the right thing to do and what I would have done in my previous life. I had watched other bodies float by and thought nothing of it. I had pulled the animals out because they represented food and clothing.

When the six men on the other side of the river pulled up stakes and departed, it triggered a reaction in Mary that made her sit down and bawl. I couldn't console her at the time as I didn't feel anything for the men leaving. However, while she was crying something inside me started to feel the pain she was going through. I didn't know if I would ever feel the same kind of emotions that she was having but I now wanted to help her as much as I could. We would see how far she wants to go and I will see how far I can take her.

I removed the last of the braces from Mary's arm and leg and gave her two days to get used to using them again. She would walk away for a while and I made sure she took a spear with her. I didn't even know if she knew how to use one but she took it as if she did. It was interesting that Fred would go out with her, maybe thinking she was going hunting. He wouldn't want to miss a possible meal. He had gotten use to the two of them and them of him. I didn't think he would make friends with them either; he seemed more self-centered than that. Then again what did I know of animal instincts. He would curl up close to Ann while she was sleeping and made me want to rethink some of my ideas. Then on the other hand he didn't seem to want anything to do with her while she was awake. That almost seemed human.

The big day arrived and we got set to go. Fred had been getting antsy as the packing and getting ready continued up to today. He was ready also but now seemed to be a bit nervous again. Not the kind he had when the wolves were around but still not very comfortable. I began to feel that in the back of my head again also but different than before. I knew it was a predator but not what kind. It even felt familiar to some extent. Fred ran between my legs and nearly tripped me as the cat-thing came walking into camp. It sat down and licked one paw and looked at me as if to say "OK I'm here we can go now". I couldn't believe my luck.

I keep accumulating companions and didn't know why. I didn't know if the bobcat would be a danger to Fred or Ann but at this point it seemed satisfied just to be in our company. I reached out with my mind to see if I could judge the threat but got nothing in return. I would have to keep an eye on it if indeed it intended to go along with us. Mary watched it carefully and even picked up a spear. I think she had every intention of protecting Ann at all cost but Fred could fend for himself. I tossed a piece of jerky down for Fred and one more for the Bob. That seemed as good a name as any and if it hung around long I would be naming it anyway. So Jed, Mary, Ann, Fred and Bob started out on our next adventure. I sure hope it doesn't turn out to be a miss-adventure.

Chapter seven

The Family

Mary and I had known each other for almost a month now and we had found some words that we could both understand. Maybe she was quicker to pick up the words that I said than I was at picking up hers. Of course the advantage she had was that I did all the talking while she had been really quiet for most of that time. I talked a blue streak during the first two weeks just to let her feel more comfortable with me. Mostly I wanted her to lose any fear of me and let her know I wouldn't hurt her. Once she saw the six men on the other side of the river she had become more vocal. Now I wondered if she would ever stop talking but her voice was so good to hear that I hoped she didn't.

I grabbed the handles of the travois and started after her as she had already taken Ann and headed east. I knew she wouldn't carry the baby very far as she didn't have time to build up her strength yet. I would have to put Ann on the travois but for now the papoose was hanging off Mary's back and she was trudging along at a nice pace. I didn't have to work hard to keep up and felt like we could get to where I had turned around the first time I went this direction. Fred was trying to keep track of everyone including Bob, who was trailing in behind us. That cat was going to need a lot of watching and neither Fred nor I trusted it. You always think that cats are too self assured and can't ever tell what they are thinking. Maybe the lack of food supply brought Bob in to our group but he didn't seem to be interested in a more personnel relationship. If the food got scarce, I wondered how he would react. For now I would try to keep an eye out for any weird behavior on his part, especially around Ann and Fred.

We went a lot further than I thought we would before Mary began showing signs of slowing down. She had a lot of moxie and wasn't going to let me see her as weak but I could see she was limping on that bad leg. I hollered to her to stop for lunch and get something for Ann to eat and she seemed willing to do that. She knew the words stop, Ann, and eat so that would never be a problem but I got the feeling she waited for me to make the first call to stop. We wouldn't be making any fires while traveling unless we came across some wood along the way. I had too much to carry now and we didn't have any wood left back at the trailhead. The sled would have carried a lot more and I was sorry I hadn't gotten it out of the valley before the flood hit. I didn't think of it as wasting my time with it because it kept me busy and was something to concentrate on. Now we ate jerky and drank as little water as we thought we needed. I didn't put out any water for Fred or Bob; they would have to wait till we stopped for the day. As we all shared the bowl, they would get theirs last anyway. If we are able to get down to the river level, I will get more water and we won't have to skimp on it. We did make sure that Ann got her fill.

I took my time getting things off the travois and making sure everyone had something to eat. Rearranging the load to accept the papoose also took some time, giving Mary a chance to rest and get her strength back. When she started to insist that we get going I held back as long as possible and then let her get out ahead. All the time I'm keeping an eye on Bob to make sure he doesn't get in trouble or cause any. He seems to be satisfied just to be in our company. It didn't take long to catch up to Mary as she was moving much slower than she had in the morning and now was using a spear for a cane. It was interesting to see the grasshoppers jumping all over the place and Fred and Bob supplementing their diet with them. I thought about it too but wasn't sure I was that hungry yet. My first experience with them may have been enough, at least for now. I knew we wouldn't starve to death with so many of them around. I then wondered what they would have been like covered in chocolate. I guess I will never know now.

When it became apparent that Mary wouldn't be able to go much farther, I let her make the decision to stop. We would camp for the night and see if she would be ready to continue in the morning. Before we stopped to rest I noticed that Bob had dropped back and then disappeared. I would keep an eye out for him to see if he was interested in staying with us or if he was now on his own. It was that thing about cats again; you're never quite sure what they might do. Everyone got something to eat and drink and I made sure that Mary and Ann would be comfortable for the night. Fred didn't need my help as he managed to get someplace where he could see or hear everything and would cover his nose with his tail. We didn't see Bob for two days and I thought he was gone but he showed up late on the third day out. He seemed to be full of himself as usual. I almost thought he had a Cheshire's grin on his chin. He didn't seem hungry or thirsty so he must have found something out there that we didn't know about.

Each day was slow going after the first one as Mary worked to get her sea legs back under her. She would start out in the morning and set a good pace and gradually slow down during the day. It was now getting warmer with cool to cold nights. The mist from the river was starting to dissipate and we were getting more sunshine. Once we had left the area of the Valley, I couldn't even guess about our location. The river was the only constant and each day the sound from it seemed to get softer or maybe I just thought that. I would look for a way down to it as we went along hoping to get some fire wood and maybe a fish or two. It was the fifth day out that we finally got a break on the canyon wall. I thought it must have been where the water fall was that I had seen many months ago. The river had expanded more in this area and ripped the land away. It looked like the whole area had flooded early on and now there were a lot of flotsam and jetsam everywhere. Some animals had started a path down to the river and now I could see that we had trapped them there as they had no other way out.

We moved past the new trail and decided to camp where the wood items had stacked up. This gave the elk and deer a chance to escape. We had enough meat and hides for now and I didn't think we wanted to spend more time here than necessary. Once the animals had left the river and gone out on the prairie, I went down to get some fresh water. I would check for fish later as we had food but water was getting scarce. Most of the wood that had stacked up here was green and I knew it would smoke but we didn't worry about that. It just made it harder to cook with. We would stay here for a couple days to see if anyone saw our smoke and came to visit or if we saw smoke from someone else's fire. This was a good break for Mary and she would be able to go on without so much pain. We started

[145]

a fire right away after clearing a large area of grasses and other combustibles.

I took a spear and went fishing for our dinner. It was surprising that there would be fish here and even more so that they were really slow to react. I had four big ones in a matter of minutes and would come back later in the day for some more. Mary took the fish, cut off their heads and got them over the fire faster than I could have and I tossed the heads out to Fred and Bob. I didn't think they cared if theirs was cooked or not and this way they didn't have to wait. I knew the fish would be a while cooking, so I went back to the river to get some more. The fish must have had a bad time with the flood and now they seemed to be just resting. I didn't have any trouble getting a half dozen more before the first ones were cooked. We would try to smoke these before leaving the area. There would be no freeze dried food on this trip. I wondered if Mary had any ideas on what to use for the smoke flavor, pine just didn't seem to be what I would pick if I had my druthers.

I was able to build a small smoker chamber that would hold two fish and got that going before nightfall. We could smoke the others two at a time and I could get some more if we decided to stay a day or two longer. I would let Mary make the decision on that as she wanted very badly to find out about her family. I was sure we would find nothing but wouldn't open my mouth about it. Some information is harder to swallow than others and she wasn't interested in hearing the bad news. I tried to pick out some wood pieces that were small enough to add to the pile of stuff I already had. It would be nice to have a fire every night but once we got past this area there may not be any wood for a while again. Mary thought we should make a small travois that she would pull to carry the wood and anything else we could use along the way. I didn't think she should be working that hard as her leg was sore and she was still limping. She was so headstrong about it that I agreed to make one but told her we would have to go much slower than we were.

We had lots of green wood, so we built a big bonfire each morning and tried to keep it going all day. We would then scan the horizon to see if there was smoke someplace else. We saw no smoke other than ours and after three days made the decision to move on. Anyone coming across our trail would probably know we were headed east but I made sure to place a marker of wood sticks aimed in that direction. I thought that when we came back I would pick them up and burn them as they would be dry by then. I had been getting a couple fish each day to smoke and we even put some elk meat in the smoker as the weather was starting to spoil the uncooked pieces we had with us. Fred stayed close to camp but Bob had wandered off again. It looked like he was going to be independent as much as possible and just come in when he was done checking out the surroundings.

The days of travel started to add up and so did the elevation. We had been climbing since the stop by the waterfalls and the terrain changed the higher up we went. I had no idea how far Mary thought she had to go but we must have passed the area where her tribe had been. There of course was nothing in or near the river canyon that would indicate someone had been there. We were able to get down to the river in several more places and would camp there for a couple days or more, but still no one answered our smoke signals. When we started the climb into the mountains, Mary seemed more reserved than before. I guessed that her tribe had not been this far up for some time and she was now losing hope of finding them.

Spring had turned to summer as we slowly gained altitude. The river level had dropped to what seemed like a regular flow but it was still too deep and wide to cross. Several side streams had joined it and we crossed over those without any trouble. When we finally came to the proverbial "fork in the road" we couldn't take it. Two streams met from what must have been verdant mountain valleys but the flood of ice and water had ripped all the dirt out and left high rock walls on both sides. We were at an impasse and I just started to set up camp and would make her turn around in a day or so. I knew she needed to mourn the loss but we needed to start back down before the weather started to change. We had lots of time now to get back but waiting wouldn't make it any easier.

[147]

By the time we had stopped at the two rivers junction, Ann had started to walk. She didn't know we weren't her parents and it may never matter to her. She would learn our names as we called each other and we would leave it at that. Bob the cat had stayed with us off and on and not created any trouble. Fred became more dependent than ever and followed Ann everywhere she went. I think it was because she would drop some food occasionally. Kids tend to do that.

The trip up into the mountains had proved one thing that I was sure I could depend on. Mary was as strong as any one I had ever known. Her arm and leg both healed well and she could go as far and long as I could. If she had cracked or broken ribs from the flood, she never let on and never showed any sign of it. Every time we had stopped to camp she would be busy making things out of the hides and cooking our meals. She had taken really good care of Ann and now was teaching her some words. When I had discovered some clay at one of the stream crossing, she had made some small bowls and plates. It wasn't china ware but good enough to eat off and she made sure they would sit flat. I marveled at her resilience, energy and strong emotions. She had gotten to the place where she could yell and scream at the world for what it had taken and love it for what it gave her. She had no fear of berating me for my ignorance and showing patience with me in what I wanted to do. I had left her these options as I know others never would have. I came into this world without any emotions of my own and now she was giving me some of hers. I couldn't say I loved her yet but my ability to have feelings for her and Ann had increased more than I cared to believe. I had needed companionship from the day I had walked into the river. I now had been gifted with much more than that and I hoped it would be enough to fill the void.

Mary knew that we had reached the end of her search and that some decision needed to be made. She just wasn't ready to do that and she was going to force me to. I would give her a couple days and set up a pyre for her to wish her family good-bye. We would have to represent her family with whatever we could for the burning, but it was going to be the only way to relieve the pain. She made some stick figures and cried over them then tossed them into the fire. I held her and let her finish her release of emotions. She would now be free to continue her life as she saw fit.

We sat by the fire that night and for the first time I told her about my dreams. We sat there for hours and talked while she studied my face and ran her hands over it. She knew I was different than her but now it didn't seem to matter or maybe it never did. She listened intently and made no mention of what she thought I looked like. I could describe her as Native American Asian mix but there was no known description of what I looked like. I too was some kind of mix but almost thousands of years before hers. Maybe it was even longer than that. I was tall, maybe more than anyone she had ever seen. When I stood up straight I towered over her. She barely came up to my shoulder yet she thought she was large for her tribe. The men had all been taller than her but not by much and she thought she wasn't full grown by the time the flood hit. If she grew any taller since I pulled her out of the water, I couldn't tell.

I still couldn't tell her about my previous life. How would you explain airplanes and cars to someone who never even seen a horse? It was like apples and oranges that didn't even exist in this time period. Domesticated animals might be a dog but she never mentioned any. She had been amazed that the fox and bobcat had been accepted in our company. Her tribe would have killed them on sight. She knew I wasn't very good at most of the things she had taken for granted. I couldn't even make my own clothing though some of the things worked for what I wanted. The bow I had made was worse than the toys the little boys in her tribe made. I never got around to making the arrows. We looked for flint stones every time we got near the river. I showed her the ones I had and she quickly made a knife to work the hides with. She showed me what I had done wrong and what a good a job I had done on the spearheads. At first she didn't want to talk about the flood but eventually it started to come out. It was the noise that was so confusing. No one knew what could cause so much noise.

She knew I was big and strong and wanted to know about the bear skin and the hide from the cougar. I tried to explain what had happened and how I had managed to kill them but mostly it got lost in the translation. Some of the words didn't work yet and I had to pantomime a little of it. She thought that was funny. Later she would ask me to retell the bear one so she could get another laugh out of it. When she asked how I got to the river I just shrugged my shoulders. I didn't know and couldn't tell her. She found interest in the fact that I had killed so many wolves. Her whole tribe would need to be there to kill just one of them. When she asked about my family, again I had no answer for her. She found it hard to understand as she had never been without some family around until now.

She cried again for the loss of her tribe and family as she told me what she saw. She had been running away like the rest of the tribe when the water hit. She didn't remember much after that until she saw me. I had scared her badly at the time as she had never seen anyone like me. The only people she had ever seen were from her tribe. She knew about others on the river but never met them. The tribal hunters would talk about trading with them for items that were hard to find. She had been given a talisman to wear around her neck but it must have gotten lost in the flood. At first she thought I had taken it from her and hated me for it. She thought I had done something to her and couldn't understand why she was tied down. The pain was more than she could stand at first and was sure I had caused it.

Then I had talked to her all the time and she didn't understand any of the words. The voice was calm and soothing and after a while it became easy to listen to. It took a couple days to know that she wasn't tied down but her arm and leg must have been broken in the flood. She had never had to have help before in getting up to go relieve herself and was ashamed by it. It was a thing for crippled and very sick people. When she saw the baby she thought I had stolen it from someone. She wanted to hold it and protect it from me. When she saw the fox and then the bobcat, she thought I was a wizard or shaman. When I had built the fires with great billows of smoke she thought I was sending messages to the spirit world. It wasn't until the six men on the other side of the river had tried to contact us that she understood that I had no magic. She wanted to scream at me for lying to her about all that but knew in her heart that I never said those things. It was then that she finally felt safe.

We started back the next morning, with her pulling a small load of firewood. We wouldn't need much as there were several places along the way that had logjams or drift wood. This side of the waterfalls had wood no more than a day or so apart. After the waterfalls we would have to cart more wood or go without. I planned on hunting deer or elk there and we could pack some more meat for the trip west. I had no idea how far it was to where the river ended but that would be where the six men had gone. If it emptied into a lake or ocean, we would have to find a way to cross. The river level kept dropping but still was too wild to cross even at this end. Maybe by early in the fall it would be low enough. I was sure it would freeze over in the winter and then we could cross anywhere. The biggest problem would be getting down to the river level. The canyon was wider now than before the flood and probably deeper.

When we got to the falls, we could see them now as the water cascaded over the rocks. It was hard to see the bottom of them as the mist was rising from the water. The summer weather had gotten quite hot and this place was the coolest we had been since leaving the mountains. The only exception to that was when we crossed the smaller streams and took a quick bath. Now may be the last chance to get wet for a while and we made plans to do just that.

The animal trail down to the river showed signs of heavier use than before and I checked to see if anything was near the water. Whatever was using the trail didn't seem to be down there now so we dropped our gear and took Ann down to test the water. There was a side pool that had been carved out by the flood that now had fresh water cycling through it. While Mary and Ann tested the shallow end I went in a little deeper to see about spearing a couple fish before washing the trail dust off. This time the fish had recovered nicely from the flood and weren't going to be "fish in a barrel" catches. With the two young ladies splashing around in the far end, a couple fish made the mistake of swimming to close to me. As I tossed them up on the bank, Fred and Bob raced down the trail and each grabbed

[151]

one and were off before I could say "boo". Bob was up the trail and gone while Fred had a struggle on his paws with a fish that was almost half his size. I kept fishing for our meal now that the animals were fed.

I got three more trout and then dunked my head in the stream to cool off. Mary had wanted to braid my hair but I had her cut it instead. It had grown to be down to my shoulders and now stopped at my neck line. I thought about having her cut it all off as the insects kept getting in it and biting me. She didn't think she wanted to see it that short. When we got away from the water the insects weren't that bad. We would be leaving the water behind as soon as we left here. Maybe I'll let her braid my hair in the fall but for now I'll just try to wash the bugs out of it.

I was in the process of washing my hair and had gone completely under water to get some sand to scrub with. As I came up for air, I heard this snort behind me. Mr. Moose was standing there trying to guess what we were doing in his waterhole. "Where in the world did you come from" I said. He just snorted again. I had my spear but Mary didn't have any protection at all and I didn't think I could stop this beast with just the one spear. The moose held the high ground and didn't look all that friendly. I motioned for Mary to stay still and I waved the spear over my head to make sure its attention was on me and not her. Ann, however, must have thought the animal was interesting and she started splashing and hollering at it before Mary could stop her. When the moose turned and made one step in their direction, I launched my spear.

I knew the second I threw it that it wasn't a killing blow and I would have to take further action. I had missed the heart and although the spear had gone through and was sticking out the other side, it hardly fazed the brute. It did know where the spear came from and made an immediate charge at me. I knew that I couldn't go to the shallow end where Mary and Ann were, so I dove for the river side of the inlet. The moose came after me with its head down and was only slightly slowed by the water depth. I was at the point where the river was about to take me along for the ride when the moose caught up to me. It tried to return the favor by swinging its antlers at me in an attempt to spear me. Just then the river pulled me

[152]

sideways and I grabbed the antlers to keep from being swept over the falls. The moose didn't recognize the problem and pushed me even further out. When he jerked his head up, I went with it and at the same time pulled it into the current. There was no escape as we were going over the falls and I knew it.

The moose pushed me down with its antlers and I hit bottom. I held on to those antlers with both hands and pushed up from the bottom as hard as I could. I burst to the surface and rolled over the top of the moose, still hanging on. I swallowed as much air as I could and pushed the moose ahead of me as neither of us could touch bottom. I could feel the water grab us and carry us over the edge. The fall was an amazing feeling but the sudden stop at the bottom came as a shock. Unfortunately for the moose I had managed to get on top of it and the rocks at the bottom didn't care who got there first. It seemed as if we were underwater forever but I got lucky again as we popped to the surface at the edge of a whirlpool. I gasped for air and floundered around for a second. I was still hanging on to the antlers and reached out with the other hand and grabbed some of the flotsam to pull us both into the spinning water. When it turned to the shore side I pushed off and dragged the moose with me to the bank. The moose was dead and I was going to be sore for a few days but nothing was broken. I pulled the moose out of the water and looked around. This must have been where the moose came from and now I could see a path by the sidewall. The mist from the waterfall had made it hard to see but there was a way to get from the top to the bottom.

Mary had come to the edge to see if I had survived and I waved to her and pointed to the moose. I thought she was going to come down but I motioned for her to stay up there. The moose wasn't going anywhere and we would have to butcher it where it lay. Even I couldn't have carried it up to the top. I sat there for a while just resting and watched the spinning water as it brought things around and around.

Something shiny had caught my eye but then it was gone. I waited to see if it came back around or not. When the item came back around, I grabbed a branch off the shore and waded out far enough to reach the pile of debris. I was able to hook the branch it was stuck on and dragged it in to the shore. It was a stone of some shining substance and had a rawhide attached. I had never seen anything like it and thought maybe Mary had. I would give it to her when I got up there. It must have been a talisman from someone that didn't make it through the flood. I didn't know if that was bad luck for them or good luck for us.

I sat down again and wondered when I started thinking of us as us. Were we becoming something or had we always been? Was this meant to be or did I have it all wrong? Could I say we were now a family or maybe not. How could you include a fox and bobcat when the next people you meet will try to kill them? I didn't even know if they would try to kill me. I was so much more different then the people I have seen so far. I know that some time it's hard for one group to accept another and I wasn't even a group. Did the nightmares have anything to do with what I was now thinking? Would I have to live with that the rest of my life? I know that I have been accepted by Mary but Ann wouldn't know the difference. Sometimes when bad things happen, people tend to blame it on the unusual, and I was unusual. Would they blame me for the flood and the death of their families? I had lived through the time of the civil rights movement and even fifty years later there was still hatred. Some people just can't get over their biases.

I thought I had some time to work this out in my head but maybe Mary would have a better idea of it. I didn't think I had the words to tell her now so maybe it would wait awhile yet. Then the "why am I here" came up again. What was the purpose of putting me in this position and who could be responsible? Maybe I should scream like Mary did at the unknown and unseen. I could only hope that when the time came, I would do the right thing, whatever it was.

I knew what the right thing was now and that was to get this talisman up to Mary and see what she thought would be the best thing for it. If she would wear it then I would gladly give it to her but if not, then what to do with it. She would be more familiar with the process and the purposes, so I would let her decide. The climb up to the top of the falls was

[154]

enough to make my sides ache. I knew I didn't break any bones but I must have bruised some ribs in the fall. I was glad the moose was under me instead of the other way around.

Mary had taken Ann and gone up to the camp site. I could see her looking down to see if I was coming or not. I gave her a quick wave and went to get the three fish I had speared earlier. I hadn't retrieved the spear from the moose yet as it was laying on part of it. It would have to wait till we butchered it. Mary took two of the fish from me and walked back to the camp site. She would have them ready to cook in a couple minutes and get the third one ready to smoke. I set the fish down and went to look at the smoker. It was still there from when we first went through and seemed to be in good enough shape to use again. It looked like we were the only ones to have used it. There were no indications that anyone had been there since. Even the wood pile and marker arrow were the same except for the little bit of weathering.

I had dropped the talisman where Mary couldn't see it and thought to wait till after we had eaten our dinner. If she got emotional over it I didn't want her burning my food. "Na" I was just kidding. She's a good sport and I just wanted to surprise her with it. After Ann goes to sleep we can sit and talk about the meaning of the thing. Fred and Bob had taken their food where we couldn't see them. I think they didn't want to share it with us. Fred came back first and I think Bob was finishing off what the fox couldn't eat. He had gotten the bigger of the two fish. Now he was going to be a while cleaning the scales off his whiskers. Bob wouldn't be back for a couple days but we were getting use to that. I thought one day he would find a girl friend and stake out his territory and that would be the last we would see of him. Fred, on the other hand, seemed content to hang around us more and more. I don't think you could call him domesticated but he seemed to like our company. His interest in Ann, though, might have more to do with what food she had in her hands. He never tried to take any of it away from her and I wondered if he remembered the time I hit him for stealing my squirrel. He seemed to try to encourage her to drop some and she thought that was funny. I don't think I ever had a dog that was that smart. Then again that's why they are "sly as a fox".

[155]

Ann was getting fussy and as the evening began to cool off, Mary wrapped her in a hide blanket, held her and sang softly to her until she fell asleep. I went and retrieved the talisman and waited till Mary had tucked Ann in for the night. I motioned for her to come and sit by me near the fire and told her that I found something in the river and wanted her opinion of it. When I showed it to her, she screamed in my ear. She grabbed it and jumped up; running around and yelling something I didn't understand. It took several minutes for her to settle down. She grabbed me around the neck and hugged me till I thought she was trying to choke me to death. She couldn't find the words to tell me except that it was a sign. I didn't know what that meant but she seemed to be thrilled with the prospect of having the talisman in her possession. The stone must have been important to her tribe, maybe even precious, but it didn't have anything to do with me. It was like that old story about "all the gold in the world can't help you now". This however may have been more precious than gold to her tribe.

So far this has been the story of my life in this world, wherever it is. Again something unusual happened to bring about something else unusual. Now I was about to find out what that second one was. The first of course, was the moose fight and water drop that led to the finding of the talisman. I couldn't explain why I survived the attack from the moose or the long drop over the falls. How could I have been so lucky to see the talisman in the river flotsam? It seems obvious that something is going on that I have no control over. I am expected to survive each test and given the opportunity to do just that. Is it a test? Am I some kind of guinea pig? Maybe, this is just the way life is here and if I don't try to win each battle, who will ever know? Now I just need to make sure I can help the two little ladies in my charge.

I pried her fingers apart and remove her arms from around my neck. She was still too excited to explain anything and I got up and danced around with her. I thought that if I were to wear her out a little she might come back down to earth. After a while, she began to say that it was an omen from her Shaman. It had been his talisman and now he was giving it to me. I said "don't you mean to you". No, she insisted it was for Jed as it was a man thing and not a woman thing. I didn't know what to say as it had not felt like mine in any way, shape, or form. "How can it be mine, I am not from your tribe". Yes! Yes! When I saved her life it made her my "property" and that can only be for a member of the tribe. I was sure that we didn't have the proper language to communicate the real meaning of what she said. I couldn't have a slave so she didn't have the right words for what it meant. She must have known that I did not control anything she did and wouldn't try to but what would it mean to our family now. We would continue as before until she decided otherwise. I would not take her as my "property".

She hung the talisman around my neck and said we would need the wisdom of the spirits. She thought the dreams I had, come from my past and that I needed to get in touch with the spirit that haunts my dreams. I said that I had no idea how to do that, and she led me to a place overlooking the river. I could see the whirlpool where I found the talisman. She brought me the bear skin and had me hold the talisman. She said that if the Shaman gave me the power to find his amulet then he would help me with everything else. If I were to sleep there, holding the Shamans' talisman, he would come to me and give me instructions. I was skeptical at best but didn't want to upset her by refusing to do this thing. I thought about skinning the moose in the morning and smoking or drying the meat.

I didn't realize how tired I was and fell asleep in the sitting position. I could feel the world changing around me and the dreams came back in a rush. I was looking at the boy again and the things that he had carved on the wall. Slowly the writings took shape and I could understand a very little of it at first. The writings of the fox became clearer and I read that he was sent to warn me of pending danger. He was sorry that he wasn't good at his job and would try harder next time.

The scene changed before I could read anymore and I was looking at the village. It was the same as before with the fire and blood and screaming but this time was different. The little boy was being helped away by an older man and when he turned to leave I saw the talisman hanging from his neck. He led the boy to the cave and hid him there. The old man could not be with the boy all the time but came and went on numerous occasions.

The boy did not seem to notice the old man but still did what he was told to do. He helped him find food and kept him away from those that had chased him. He showed him the stream with the frogs and fish for him to eat. The boy would be alone for long periods of time and he would cry. The old man showed him how to write on the walls of the cave. Then he took him for a walk in the park.

I woke up very confused and not knowing what to think of the dreams. I talked to Mary about them and we both went looking for Fred. He was nowhere to be found. Bob was gone too and we wouldn't go out looking for them. I was sure they would come back when it was time for them to do so. I made the decision to stay there and see if the Shaman would give me any advice or if I had to learn more on my own. The first thing to take care of was the moose and we took turns going down to butcher it. I went first after Mary drew a picture in the dirt on how to cut the hide off to get the most use of it. She knew I had wasted some back at the valley and we might need bigger sections for our living quarters. I was able to turn the moose over to get the spear out despite the pain in my chest and sides from the fall. I cut the head off and skinned it and left the hide there. I took the head up and Mary went next to start cutting the meat. We would use the hide to transfer the meat up to the camp site. I made sure the smoker was going to be ready and then ate the fish that Mary had prepared for me. Ann was having a good time playing in the flotsam and that made it easy to watch her. It was then that I realized that the itch in the back of my head was gone. Fred had drifted far enough away that I couldn't feel his presence. It was almost like a first, since I arrived here. I wondered if he had abandoned me.

The next few days were busy with the moose meat and all the needs of a camp. We built a small shelter to sleep in and waited out the one summer storm that we had. It was unusual as it seemed to hardly ever rain here. The time to leave was fast approaching and still no sign of the fox or bobcat. I had hoped to get more information from the Shaman in my dreams but nothing happened for a long time now. It seemed as if I had been left on my own to find my way. Each day I would hold the talisman and it seemed to have some power over me but it never gave me any help deciding what to do. We started to make plans to leave as the summer was winding down. When everything was packed and ready to go the night before leaving, I went out to the river and sat again hoping for some revelation. I went to sleep there and in the morning I told Mary that we would not return along the river but swing southwest to the hot springs. The Shaman had taken the boy to the Park at the hot springs and I had to go there again to see what I could find. Mary questioned if we left the river, would Fred and Bob be able to find us? I told her that they would and may already be at the Park waiting for us.

I thought it would take a week to get there as Ann had become so interested in her surroundings. She had to see everything and touch or taste them. Keeping her from some of the more dangerous plants had now become a full time job. She insisted on walking with us and her pace was sure to slow us down. The best way to speed her up was for me to put her on my shoulders and let her ride up high where she could see well. I had told Mary about the partridges and that we might see some along the way. She made a sling for herself and we picked some really nice stones from the river for her to toss. She had used a sling before but now needed a little practice. Every day she would fire away at something and after about three days she was getting good at it. I had never used a sling so I didn't think I could get good enough to hit anything in so short a time.

I put Ann on my shoulders and gave Mary our heading and let her lead off. Ann was pushing my head and saying "Go Go Go". We had lots of sunshine and that made it easy to keep a straight line to our target. Mary didn't have to carry anything except the sling and stones as I had attached the second travois to the first and now I had all the stuff with me. We had included as much firewood as the second travois would hold and I thought that if we ran out I would burn the second one.

My hair had grown long enough that Mary was able to pull it into a pony tail. It would be a month or more before she would be able to braid it. Ann found that riding was better than walking, especially after she found the pony tail to hold on to. I knew enough not to mention cowboys and Indians. It was times like that when I would think of the past events in my

[159]

life and knew one day I would have to tell Mary the whole story. For now we were still working on the words to express ourselves. All the common ones had been conquered but the more descriptive ones were taking more time.

We were two days into the trip when the outline of the hills started to take shape. It would be a few more days of hiking but in just seeing them, gave us a feeling of relief. It was certainly different than the first time I went there. This time the sky was clear and you could see forever, as the saying goes. During the trip I had to make sure not to carry Ann all the way as she needed to burn off some energy or she wouldn't want to sleep at night. Then I wondered how many parents in my past would have even thought of that. Mary tried to vary the menu each day so that we didn't get overly tired of one thing. That, of course, only works if you have a variety of things to choose from. We had fish, elk and moose meat, all of it either smoked or dried or as jerky. We only stopped once each day and that would be for lunch. We ate before starting in the morning and again at night when we camped. Then there were times when Ann would cause us to slow way down or even go chase her down as she wandered away from the route we were taking. Once we got away from the river, the problem of insects ended. That is except for the grasshoppers.

It was on the third day out that we saw the first partridge and Mary wasn't ready for it as she was tending to Ann, who had started in the wrong direction again. I warned Mary that the second bird would be close and that she needed to get a stone ready for it. When the second one flew up, Mary let a stone fly after it but missed. It was her first live action since she was a little girl several years earlier. I watched to see where the birds landed and told Mary that they would probably try to run past us when we got near them again. They would try to return to the area they had been in when we spooked them up. We wouldn't be deviating much to get to where they landed and both Mary and I had seen where that was. When Mary had missed the one shot she took, I had split my attention between her and Ann. The little girl was again exploring the reign of grasshoppers. I had Mary put Ann up on my shoulders so she could watch the action from on high. The partridges were getting fat on the grasshoppers and one of them would make a nice change to our diet. As we approached the area we thought they might be in, I had Mary move off to the right a little and I went to the left. I was watching her closely to see if she did better this time as I knew the birds would jump soon. With that, the first one leapt into the air and flew headlong into the stone that Mary hurled. She rearmed the sling and got the other one as it tried to flee just seconds later. "Good shooting" I said as she ran after them. We would be eating well tonight. Ann was pounding on my head the whole time as she cheered for Mary.

I let Ann help me pull the travois for a while and made sure to ask her if she was tired or not. She wouldn't let go and kept helping me, even though her feet never touched the ground. She peddled along as if they were. It was pretty funny to see as she was turned sideways to the direction we were going. We thought it was good training if she wanted to help and we encouraged her to do so. There are some things that children shouldn't do and we would watch to make sure she didn't get into any real trouble. Like most kids, she would push the envelope at times.

Mary had picked some sage to flavor the partridges with and roasted them on a spit over the fire. I had not thought to use any of the wild plants with the ones I had cooked some time ago. The taste of the birds was certainly enhanced with this addition. When I had cooked the duck with the root bulb, it didn't have the same effect. When I told her about it, she wanted to show me other plants that she had seen used but that didn't grow here on the prairie. She promised to look for them when we got back to the river basin.

I sat up late that night, while Mary and Ann slept. Mary had taken Ann and rolled up in an elk blanket, making sure the smoke from the fire wasn't going at them. I had bigger thoughts than I could handle right now and wanted to see if the Shaman would be interested enough to put a light on it. I sat cross legged by the fire and held the talisman tightly in my right hand. It was then that I realized that Mary had not told me the Shamans' name. Did he have a name? What or how should I address him? I needed an answer and didn't know how to ask. It was the big picture and I had been missing it all along and still couldn't get a handle on it. It was the time

[161]

in the cave where I read what the fox had told the boy. That information was written years before or maybe even centuries ago. What could it have possibly been talking about? I thought of the moose attack and the fact that I didn't feel it coming. Fred and Bob were busy with their fish and lost contact with me. I never got the early warning that I should have. Up till then I had always felt something coming my way and now I wondered why. Was Fred really my guardian? Was he supposed to warn me of all impending problems? Then what was Bobs' job? Since they had run off, was I going to have to feel these things on my own? Well, Mr. Shaman, do you have any answers for me? I seem to have more questions again than answers.

I picked up the older moose hide and laid it out across from the sleeping girls. I covered up with the bear hide and went to sleep. I knew before the lights went out that some light would shine through in my head. I could feel the presence of the stone in my hand as it warmed up. It pushed me over the brink of sleep and brought me back to the time of the boy again. "Shaman be with you" I thought, as the dream ship took off. This time the Shaman led me to the cave, pointing out signs along the way. He showed me where the entrance was and then he left. As I tried to look into the cave it moved away from me. Everything was moving away and the landscape got wider and wider. I had asked to see the big picture and now I was getting to see all the lands around the cave as it diminished into the background.

The land was beautiful and pristine with no sign of human activity. Then in rapid succession it changed. First there was one village, then two, then four and then competition for food and land. Then the fighting broke out between villages. Then two of them got together and burned out the other two, killing all the inhabitants that they could find. The last scene showed the two remaining villages fighting each other until no one remained.

Through it all the boy had hid in the cave as his village was the first one to get burned out. I looked on and saw that in each village the people had been different from the others. They were of four distinctly divergent backgrounds and appearances. They didn't share much in common except that they needed the same sources of food and water. Their clothing, habits, cultures and speech had all been different and this had caused great concern among the leaders of each village. They became intolerant of each other and when they started to run out of food, they blamed the others for it. When the fighting broke out, there were no great leaders to step up and quell the violence. I woke up and thought I have to ask a different question next time. Like what about me?

It seemed like a stupid thing to say after what I saw and I rolled over and went back to sleep. Mary woke me in the morning as she was worried that I had slept in. It was not like me and she wanted to know what had happened. I told her about the dream, in between bites of the breakfast that she had fixed for me. I had an answer to the big picture but nothing on why I was here and what the Shaman had planned for me. By the way, what was the Shamans' name anyway? What she called him I couldn't pronounce anyway but it sounded like Sully or Scully maybe even Schally. I didn't know if it would mean anything to him or not but said I would sleep on it and see if he likes any one of those.

It was going to be two days or more before we got to the Park and I wanted to make sure we didn't come up short on wood and hot food before that. We would keep the fires to a minimum at night and start a new one in the mornings. We didn't build any more of the smoky fires as there had never been any answers to the ones we had made. One of the things I missed the most was the morning cup of coffee. I didn't know how you could miss a Walmart until you didn't have one around. Sleeping on the ground had its disadvantages also and you really never get use to it. I tried for the next two nights to get through to the Shaman but his phone must have been busy as he wasn't answering my calls. I guess the good news there was that I slept pretty good those nights. I knew that some dreaming took place but didn't remember any of it or them. I was given the impression that I would have to be in the Park to get any more help or answers.

We were well into the sixth day now as we finally got in to the trees of the Park. We managed to get to the camp site above the lake before it got dark. I had time to get a fire going and set up some sleeping arrangements. I trotted down to the lake and speared a fish for dinner and guess who I saw on the other side of the lake. It may be more like what than who but Fred had become almost a family member. He seemed to be waiting for an invitation and so I called him over. He came around the lake as if to know he wouldn't have to fish for his own meal tonight. Ann would be delighted to see him. I reached into the back of my mind to see if he had actually arrived or not. It felt good to have him back.

We would rest for a couple days while I gathered firewood and Ann and Mary played down by the lake. Well, actually Ann did the playing and Mary kept an eye on her while doing some work with the pelts and some other things she was working on. We had looked for flint stones everywhere we went but hadn't had much luck. We made due with the stones I had but they were getting smaller with use. It's like a lot of other things though first this then that and maybe it will all work out. I built a lean-to like the one in the valley except for the covering was now hides that we had been hauling all over god's green acres. This one was a bit bigger to accommodate the three of us and not feel like we had to climb over each other. There was a deep pine needle bedding to give a soft floor to it. I hoped we didn't need to worry about anything else for a while. I needed to find out why I was there and what to do next. I would try to place that phone call to the Shaman once again.

Chapter eight

The Cave

Before I could even get started on my quest for more information, Mary insisted that I try to find some stones that she could have readily available. We hadn't carried a lot of them from the river as extra weight meant extra slow. I had my throwing stones and she had some for her sling and wanted some more. I remembered stepping on some stones in the lake and headed to the east end to see if I could find any that would work for what she wanted. I would try to spear a few more fish while there and we could smoke them for future use. This time I warned Fred to stay away from my fish as I tossed them up in the bank. He looked dejected and seemed to know what I had said and left them alone.

I waded around in the water and kicked at the bottom to loosen up several of the smaller stones that were imbedded in the mud. When I tossed those up with the fish, Fred took off for higher ground. He must have retained the memory of the stolen squirrel. I guess that he thought it was better safe than sorry if he got out of range. I didn't mean to frighten him but did think of it as pavlovian.

When I got back to camp, Mary had started to put a smoker together and I gave her a hand. It only took a few minutes to get something of a frame up and covered it with a chunk of the elk hide I had almost ruined after the flood. I was in a real hurry then and just got a little ahead of myself. Mary had put some rawhide stitches thru it to hold it together. We just couldn't throw it away and now it would come in handy.

I dug a pit for the fire and set the smoker over it. The front flap would go on after the fish were in there and the fire was going. Mary would use some of the sage she brought from the prairie and some dill type plant from near the lake. She then cut the heads off the fish and tossed one to Fred for being so helpful. I wasn't sure what he helped with but he was glad to get his share.

We still hadn't seen Bob but expected him to show up soon also. This smoker was bigger than the one back at the falls and would hold all four of the fish I managed to spear. I brought some water up to soak the elk hide so it wouldn't burn and I got the fire going. Everything seemed in order until Mary looked at the stones I found in the lake. She insisted that I go get some more and bigger ones if I could find them. It took awhile to find them as the mud had covered them up and I would use my feet to find one and then dig it out with my hands. I had about a dozen of them in all sizes and thought that would be enough. She thanked me for my effort and didn't say another word about it.

I told Mary that I would try to get in touch with Schally the Shaman and see if he had any more advice to give me. The directions to the Cave had not been clear enough, although it seemed that it started here at the fire pit. It was all uphill from there and I would be guessing about which hill it would be. It was late in the evening and Ann was asleep, when I got the bearskin and sat down by the fire. Mary put some plants on the fire to make smoke to let the Shaman know I was ready to hear from him again.

I closed my eyes, held the talisman close and tried to concentrate on communicating with Schally. To my surprise it seemed as if I had been hit in the back of the head. Did someone smack me? I quickly looked around but there wasn't anyone there. Then the word that I had been using as a name for the Shaman seemed to change in my mind. It was pronounced with a silent Sc and sounded like Hhaley. I then pronounced it several times to make sure I got it right. When I didn't get hit in the head again I thought it must be close enough.

It didn't feel good to think that the Shaman was upset with me but knowing I may have got his attention did. If he would now help me get a bearing on the location of the cave, that would be good too. I felt myself drifting off in sleep and released my mind to let it take advantage of that state. I would be disappointed in the morning with the review of the night's dreams. It seemed that the Shaman had gotten more and more involved in the rescue and survival of this boy. The dreams ran through the same sequence again as the last time but added more detail. Why did he want

[166]

me to know exactly what had happened? I had not felt sorry for the boy or the people of the village that he was from. It seemed more like lost history than anything else. It must have happened so long ago that it wouldn't even be noticed in today's environment. I had wanted to know how to get to the cave but no new information was forth coming in that area.

I decided to let it go for a couple days and just think about what the dreams represented. Maybe there was a clue in there somewhere that I was missing. I told Mary about it and she thought it was a good idea to mull over the dreams to see if I could gather more information from them. I then told her that the Shamans name was Hhaley and I got the pronunciation correct. She was thrilled to hear me say it and hugged my neck again.

I suggested a mini vacation, and she asked what that was. I told her a short time away from work and we could go up to the hot springs and relax in the waters there. She thought it would be a good idea and we packed up what we thought we would need and left the lake area behind. We had hung the majority of our possessions up in the trees and used the small travois to carry the items we would need. Mary carefully packed away something she had been working on and acted like she didn't want me to see it. I just assumed it was some female stuff and left it at that.

When we got to the hot springs, I showed her where I had camped and which spring had the best water to soak in. She thought it might be too hot for Ann. I hadn't thought of that as kids are affected more than adults but don't know how to tell. I left Mary and Ann there and went to get some firewood at the far end. It appeared as if no one had been there since I left. I told Mary to keep a spear handy anyway. Fred had come along again and seemed to be taking his job more seriously. I wondered if the Shaman had scolded him for not paying enough attention. Then I wondered why I would even think that way. Is there something wrong with this picture I keep painting around myself? Am I beginning to believe the Shaman controls everything and I'm just his pawn? Isn't he dead?

When I got back with the wood, I set about getting it ready for a fire but didn't light it. It would wait till we were done playing in the water. Mary had taken Ann down a couple more pools from the one I liked so

[167]

much and they were splashing around and having a good time. I went to my goldilocks pool, armed with a spear and some rocks, and proceeded to dunk my body to the max. We had been cold water skinny dipping but now had the opportunity to ease some aches with the warm kind. I checked on Fred one more time before trying to relax and he buzzed the back of my brain to let me know he was there. I started to relax and he buzzed me again to let me know I would have some company. I never felt it coming as I got pushed under and held down. Words popped into my head but I was so busy trying to get to the surface that I missed their meaning. "I can't do what you want if you drown me" I said. I knew there was no one there and I had to now pay attention or he might drown me. "If you are dead, how come you have so much power?" I knew that I wouldn't get an answer to that question.

He was gone and Fred didn't seem to have a clue as to what had happened. I didn't either for that matter. Hhaley wanted me to do something or go somewhere or who knows what and I didn't. The best thing for me to do now was to get washed up and then try to relax. If he was going to haunt me day and night I was going to keep asking dumb questions. I pulled the rawhide tie out of my pony tail and ducked my head in the water. I started to scrub the bugs out of my hair and the words came again. It seemed as if I had to be under the water to get the message. It was then that I realized that I wasn't floating this time. My whole body was sinking to the bottom and the only thing that had changed was that Hhaley wanted to impart some information on me. How did he control these things?

I filled my lungs with air and ducked under the water. I then grabbed the amulet and squeezed it tight. The information started coming and I wasn't going to be happy when it stopped. Hhaley had a limited time to transfer the knowledge that he had and I was wasting his time. He kept me under the water till I thought my lungs would burst. His intent was to inform me of what I would be required to do and not to kill me. Somehow, I wasn't sure about the second part of that as he finally allowed me to come to the surface for air. It's hard to concentrate when you think you're drowning, so the transfer was going on most of the time without me realizing what it was. Twice more I went down for the count and twice more thought I wasn't going to get back up.

He must have known my capacity to survive better than I did. I thought the whole process took a life time as I was finally recovering from the last of it. I looked down to where Mary and Ann were and they seemed to be still having a good time in the water. I laid back and tried to relax. I didn't know if I would ever be in contact with Hhaley again or not. The Shaman had definitely left an impression on me that I would never forget. Our relationship was all business and had nothing to do with friendly interaction. Despite that I thought I would miss him if I didn't ever hear from him again.

I realized that I was still hanging on to the talisman and hadn't finished scrubbing down. I grabbed some sand off the bottom and rubbed it into my hair. I didn't care how many bugs I had to kill to get that clean feeling again. I was just finishing up as the girls came by to say they were hungry and it was time for me to get the fire started. I would wait till later to tell Mary about the meeting I had with the Shaman, that's if you could call it a meeting. It certainly wasn't face to face and I have no idea what he looks like. The images in the dream hadn't given me a good representation and he certainly didn't show up in the water today.

There was something about the connection that I would have to deal with and didn't know how it would turn out. Like when you see someone you should know but can't remember that person's name. I now had lots of things in my head that I couldn't identify. Maybe they would clear up later and maybe not. In this case only time would tell unless the Shaman came back to help me out. I thought it might be a long shot as his time was getting short and his power to help me was on the wane. I would try to get him on the line after we get back to the lake camp site.

I lit the fire and Mary got some food out to warm up for our meal. We never seemed to have three meals a day so calling them by their names didn't always fit. The first meal in the morning could usually be called breakfast but the next time we ate might depend on where and when it was. This meal could be called supper or dinner as it would be the last time

[169]

we would eat for the day. Most days we snacked as we went along or when we would get hungry.

I set about preparing a place for us to sleep by dragging pine needles into a pile and spreading our moose skin out to cover them. This made for a more comfortable bed than just sleeping on the ground. We ate some of the moose meat and got ready to turn in for the night. I told Mary that Hhaley had contacted me while in the pool and would tell her all I could remember about it. It turned out to be not very much but that I would probably remember more later on. I thought he tried to drown me.

When Mary lay down to sleep with Ann, I wrapped up in the bearskin again and sat by the fire. I felt that I needed to shed some light on the encounter in the pool and maybe glean more information from it. I seemed too keep getting lost in the details and still not getting the whole picture. The last thing I thought of before falling asleep was that it wasn't much of a vacation so far.

This time when the dream came back, I had to live through the whole thing from beginning to end. It seemed like it took forever to get through. It started with the peaceful valley with the stream flowing down the middle of it. Then it progressed through the coming of the tribes and then the fighting. There were the fires and deaths and the loss of the beautiful landscape. They left nothing as they fought to the death and destroyed everything. The boy was led away by the Sharman and shown where to hide. He showed him how to get food and what to stay away from. They would eventually leave that area and go to the Park.

My job was to back track their route to the valley and locate the cave. In the cave I would find the information I would require. It was at this point the Hhaley took his final action. His power was fading and being passed on to another. He wouldn't be able to help me anymore but thought that he had given me enough information to succeed. When I woke, I knew that I hadn't been asleep for long but the ordeal had drained me of all my energy. I laid down next to the girls and fell into a deep sleep that had no memorable dreams. I slept well past sunup and for the second time Mary

[170]

felt she had to wake me. She had never seen me sleep so long and motionless.

I told her about the Shaman rerunning the whole thing with the villagers and the boy. Then I explained that Hhaley wouldn't be back as his time was up. I didn't know how or why that happened but only that he let me know it did. Mary cried a little then as she now lost the last contact with her people. She wanted to know if we had to go back to the lake camp. I told her that we could wait a couple days and rest up. I needed that more than she did and Ann would enjoy splashing in the pool some more.

We had been watching Ann carefully to make sure she didn't get in one of the pools by herself. It was then that I noticed that Fred's interest in Ann had seemed to change. He would stay between her and the water holes all the time. She would try to push him out of her way and get him to move. She was bigger than him and he would give ground but as soon as she tried to take advantage of it he would move back to block her path. She would try that once or twice and then look for something else to do.

We spent the next two days just relaxing and enjoying the time away from the normal chores. I had just one thing to worry about and that was how to tell Mary she couldn't go with me. "This is a job for superman" I didn't think that would work. Even the Lone Ranger had Tonto with him. I didn't want to say it was like a rite of passage but in essence that is what it would be. I was being sent on a quest or a mission of discovery. I hadn't asked for this and didn't seem to be allowed to back out of it. The Shaman had made it clear that this was something I had to do and it was for me alone that it was important. I needed to get answers and it would be best if I concentrated just on that and nothing else.

I spent those two days trying not to worry about Mary and Ann but trying doesn't always work. I did get in the pool once each day and that seemed to help with my problem. I had trouble thinking of Mary as a woman who could take care of herself and Ann. I didn't know how old Mary was, I'm not sure she even knew. It colored my opinion of how to treat her and left me with some confusing thoughts. I was sure she would fight to protect herself and Ann but she hadn't had to do that yet. It was like a

[171]

shock to my backside to realize that I had become so emotionally attached to them. The transformation had been gradual and I hadn't noticed it.

I was on the verge of calling Hhaley some pretty nasty words for getting me into this mess. I knew it was his fault but didn't know how. "I ought to call him back from the dead and teach him a lesson". Mary looked at me to see what I was talking about. I just shrugged my shoulders and went off to gather some firewood.

It wasn't long ago that I used to be less attentive, intuitive, or observant but something happened when I got here. Things just seem to be more important and would catch my attention even if I wasn't really looking for it. I now noticed that Mary has been acting differently toward me than before. I'm not sure when it changed or if it was just so subtle that it was hard to see.

She had grown to be a woman and may be seeing me as her only chance to prove it. She was being a good mother to Ann, when she wasn't even related to her as far as we knew. Now she may be getting interested in having her own children. Her commitment to me for having rescued her from the flood might also be coloring her opinion and feelings. The fact that I was the only available man around could also play into it. I knew she was trying to hide something from me and not doing a very good job of it. There just wasn't enough space between us to be secretive. I needed to talk to her about these things before her mind is completely set on doing something on her own.

I started the conversation by asking Mary if she remembered the first time she saw Ann, if she had any idea who the mother was. I knew that the carrier the baby was in would have been made especially for that child and would have some distinct markings on it. Mary couldn't find anything on it that would indicate that Ann came from her tribe and Mary knew all the women that had children. Ann had come from a different tribe. When you looked at her you could see that her appearance had differences that didn't match up with either Mary or me. I then told her that the three of us were different because we came from different tribes.

[172]

If we were to encounter other people, they too could be from a different tribe. It is possible that those people would not like to have us around because we are not the same as them. I told Mary that I didn't think I would want any children of my own until I felt they would be safe around the others we would certainly meet later on. I then explained that I had to find the cave and get the information that was written on the wall there. Once I had that knowledge, we would have to go down the river to see if we could find the six men or any others along the way. While the three of us could be happy, we would still need some more people to make up a tribe of our own.

Mary didn't seem to take the news as hard as I thought she might but I could feel that she was disappointed. She wanted badly to say something but couldn't seem to find the words. I let her think about it for awhile and then asked her to tell me how she felt about my going to the cave alone. She knew that was coming and wanted me to be safe and return to her and Ann. In the morning we packed and headed back to the lake camp. Nothing else was said about the cave or having children.

We spent a couple uneasy days at the lake site while I prepared to leave. I made sure to gather lots of wood for the fire and we made several torches. I told Mary that if she was threatened by any large animals that she should light a torch and hold it in front of her. Most animals will stay away from any kind of fire. She should keep a fire going at night but try to keep from burning it all up. I would take a torch with me to use in the cave for light. Mary kept herself busy around the camp making sure everything had a place and was in place. Ann helped her out by moving the same things around. It added a little comedy to the situation and lightened the mood a bit. Mary had never been left to fend for herself and I could see it wasn't going well. She wanted me to know that she could be self-sufficient and said as much but I knew it was going to be hard for her to see me leave.

In the morning Mary gave me a hug and tried to keep from crying. I picked up my gear and said good-bye with a promise to return as soon as possible. I had the feeling they would be safe while I was gone and noticed that Fred wasn't going with me. I had only gone a short distance when the

[173]

itch in the back of my head changed. I could feel the fading out of Fred's influence and picked up another. This one seemed familiar to some extent but different than I had expected. It got stronger as I walked up hill in the direction that I thought would take me to the valley and cave that the boy had come from.

I knew I wouldn't need to guess where to go as soon as I saw the source of the new feeling in my head. Bob had made his presence known and now wanted me to follow him. He had scouted the trail for me and knew exactly how to get there. I just hoped his concentration didn't get interrupted by some animal or scent. Animals that have a low profile don't always make the best lead dogs. Bob was trying to go in a straight line but tree branches and brambles aren't always accepting of us taller creatures. It wasn't going to be an easy hike if I couldn't get through to Bob that going under those things was causing a real problem.

I stopped and waited to see what Bob would do. At first he kept going and when he realized that I had stopped he backtracked to see why. I talked to him and used hand signals at the same time and got nothing in return. "Think" maybe he needs something else from me. I got down on one knee and grabbed the amulet in my right hand. Then I began the conversation over again. Bob cocked his head to one side as if listening and waited for me to finish. He came all the way back to where I was and walked around me as I stood up. I had the feeling I was being measured and it was what I was looking for. I got the feeling he thought it was a stupid idea but he would try to watch out for those things. He then turned and walked away as if to lead me past any obstacles.

In the space of a few seconds I had talked to a bobcat and realized that a fox was guarding my two girls. This isn't the normal situation that I would have ever considered. I wondered what kind of power the talisman had or if the Shaman was still controlling everything. "Okay, just follow the cat" I said, as we went on our way. I kept reassuring myself that it would all turn out for the best and I would get the answers I was looking for. The strangeness of it just wouldn't leave me.

Bob didn't stop till after dark that day and probably only because he was hungry. He came and sat down in front of me and waited to get something to eat. Sharing my food with a bobcat in what was now a very dark wooded area, I thought it couldn't get much stranger than this. I was right, for the first time in a year or more, it didn't. Sleep, however, was not the easiest thing to come by as I was left alone. Bob had gone off to sleep by himself somewhere and didn't invite me along. I thought that was rude of him.

I had managed to get some sleep and awoke in the predawn hours. I wasn't surprised to see Bob sitting there waiting for some nourishment before leading me off again. I gave him several small pieces of jerky but he just kept waiting for more. I gave him one more and then told him no more till we stop tonight. He was up and going before I could pick up my stuff. He slowed down just enough to let me catch up then we were off again. This day and the next were just repeats of the first one. When we stopped at the end of the third day, I went to get some food and settle down for the night. Bob gave me a fare-thee-well look and walked off into the darkness. I ate my meal alone and went to sleep.

The dream came back again and I saw the whole thing repeated. This time I made a point of watching more closely to see if I could catch the true meaning. Hhaley had wanted me to see something in the dream but I kept missing it. The fact that I had not involved any emotion for the people or the boy could be the clue he was looking for. I realized that I hadn't shed a tear for anyone but myself since my wife died. To become emotionally involved would mean that I had accepted my situation. Up till now, I had fought that all the way. Now I had my two girls to worry about and it seemed to bring everything up to the surface.

"Go over the dream again" and see what you need to feel. Should I feel the pain or the fear that is going on? Should I feel the anger and hatred? Should I feel the heat from the fires? Should I feel the blood on my hands? Should I have sympathy for the dead and dying? Why was the Shaman so interested in the boy, should I have feelings for what he is going through? What is so important about the boy? Can the cave writings be the main reason I needed to look for them or was it the boy? I didn't cry for anyone that night but did want to help in some way.

When I woke in the morning, I felt more like my old self. I had a feeling of comfort in my own skin, and then laughed at the thought of whose skin was I in. Bob wasn't on duty this morning and I did a quick look around. Then I did a search with my mind. He was in the vicinity but his job was done for now. For a few seconds I missed the point and then realized that I had reached the valley. This was the same one that so many lives were lost over. Now I was the only one here. That would be if you didn't count Bob. I was sure he wouldn't be the only animal around but who's counting.

It was a beauty to behold. It spread out before me in a green and healthy looking environment. The stream came out of the mountains in the east and turned south to disappear into the distance. The land appeared to have been unoccupied for a very long time. I had to wonder as to why that would be. Surely some other people would have seen how nice a place this would be to live. I was sorry that I hadn't brought Mary and Ann here to see this. It was then that I felt the talisman warming up on my chest. It had begun to glow, to radiate, and to draw from me the feeling of needing someone. For the first time since I got here I didn't feel like a dead man walking. I felt needed and needing and loved. My journey was not quite over but it was getting very close.

All that emotion came to a quick halt as I remembered the reason I was there. I needed to get to the cave and find out what was written on the walls. It was important to what I would do after that. I sat down to try and visualize the location and how to get to it. It was already clear that Bob wasn't going to help. The pictures in the dream came into view and I tried to see where the Shaman had taken the boy. It would look different now since there were no fires and some trees had grown up in different places. I tried to filter them out and see the bigger landscape. Now I was ready as it showed itself to me.

It seemed to be far away but when I thought about the boy walking to it then surely I could do as much. There was no trail and at times the way was blocked by shrubs and trees and I had to go around them. I didn't waver in my effort and managed to get there as the sun reached its zenith. I did a quick check of the entrance to make sure no animals were using it for a den. I remembered that the boy had encountered a wolf and didn't want to surprise one when I went in.

I then found a level spot just down from the entrance where I could set up my camp. I didn't think I would be there long, but knew if I was to be there overnight, I wasn't sleeping in the bat dung. There was plenty of dead wood around for a fire, so I cleared an area of debris and dug a small pit. I was about to head up to the cave when I remembered the bats. They won't like the fire and smoke and will try to fly out, but in the light they don't do so well. I just might be a victim of my own stupidity if I spook them into flying. I knew that I couldn't see any better during the day than I could at night. I would need the torch in either case.

I decided to go get something fresh for dinner and wait till dark to enter the cave. The boy had been shown where to get something to eat and it wasn't far away. Just down the hill from the new camp site was a stream of fresh running water. I got a drink and then started turning over stones in the stream bed. It wasn't long before I had three nice sized crayfish. These things are sometimes called crabs or crawdads but the tail is good eating and so are the claws if they are big enough. They are like miniature lobsters and taste about the same. I roasted the tails over a small fire and took a nap after eating. I would rest until dark and then chase the remaining bats out of the cave.

I thought it was dark enough that the majority of the bats would have gone out for their nightly romp. I lit my torch and kicked dirt over the remains of the fire, making sure it wouldn't get going again. Getting into the cave opening wasn't easy for someone my size, while trying not to set anything on fire with the torch. Even before I got half way in I could hear the bats starting to take flight. I knew they had another way out and they would stay away from the fire and smoke so I gave them a couple minutes to find the other opening. The cave had at least one chimney like shaft that the bats used for getting in and out. The opening to it was much higher up on the hill. The fire from the torch was drawing fresh air in this entrance and alleviating the bad odor. I could only hope that it would continue to do so. I squeezed the rest of the way in and found that it opened up enough so I could turn around and even sit up.

At first it was hard to tell that someone had been scratching something on the wall. The accumulation of dust and the aging of the wall itself created the allusion that nothing was there. I had to rub my hand over it to see any of the writings. I didn't know where to start as it looked like the scrawl was random and not in nice straight lines. I continued to rub the surface to get a look at the whole area of writing. The air became thick with the dust and I started to have trouble breathing. I anchored the torch further back in the cave to try to get more air to come in the opening but my lungs kept filling up with the residue that was there. I decided to get out and leave the torch to draw fresh air. I knew it would clear in a few minutes but I needed to get out fast. I was able to clear my lungs as soon as I got out of the cave. I was coughing and hacking and spitting up some bad tasting stuff for what seemed like a week to ten days, although I knew it was only a couple minutes before I could breathe easy again. I then went down to the stream and washed my hands and face to remove all the dust and dirt that had accumulated on me. I rinsed my mouth out with clean water to get rid of the foul taste.

I went back in knowing that the torch wouldn't last forever and now I could see some of the writings. Deciphering what the boy had written on the wall was going to be another thing altogether. I put the talisman in my right hand and ran my left over the wall to get a feeling for how it was written. Soon, some of it began to make sense. I now could read what the boy had scratched on the wall about the animals. I read about the bear and the cougar and all the other animals that had to be sacrificed on my behalf.

The fox and bobcat held prominent places in the writings. They were to stay with me for a long time. Their jobs were highlighted by the risks they had to take on my behalf. It was interesting to know that Fred had been required to keep the bear from catching up to me. Now I knew why he risked his life for mine. I just didn't know how that could be or what made it happen. I had to assume that the Shaman did something to cause all this but how was the question still to be answered.

I ran my hand over more of the writings and began to feel the pain that went into it. The boy had named all the people of the village and what they did there. He had been told to run by his parents and they blocked the view of his retreat. He knew that he was the lone survivor and didn't know what to do. The wind came to him and pushed him away from the village. He wanted to go home to his family but the wind wouldn't let him. He tried to fight the wind but it was too strong. It pushed him here and there until he found the cave and got away from it. When he got so hungry he couldn't stay there any more, he went out and the wind pushed him down the hill to the stream. He found things to eat there and water to drink. When he was full he ran back to the cave to get away from the wind. He didn't know how long he was in the cave and he wanted to go home. When he left to see where his parents were, he became frightened. His mind showed him what had happened and how they all died and he ran back to the cave.

The boy had been in the cave for some time and then his stone knife put itself in his hand and started to scratch things on the walls. He had never learned to read or write and so he didn't know what it said. He couldn't stop the knife from doing this thing on the wall. He was afraid that someone would hear the noise of the scratching but no one came. The knife worked for hours and made his hands bleed. When the scratching finally stopped he could see that the walls were covered with these strange markings. Somehow they seemed to bring him a little comfort as he stared at them. Then they faded in the dark and he wondered how he could have seen them in the first place. The cave was always dark and he had no fire to see by. The talisman that his parents had given him at birth had been glowing to light up the cave and he didn't know it. Now the glow was gone and he had to leave the cave for good.

It was then that I released my hand from the talisman and the cave became bright from the light it produced. I didn't need the torch except to drive the bats out. Now I could see the hand print on the wall that the boy had made with his blood. I put my hand over it and wished him peace. He must have been dead for a long time now and the travels of the amulet have come full circle. I wondered who had it in the time before Hhaley or if there was no time between.

Did the boy grow up to be a Shaman and pass it on to the next and the next? What was I suppose to do with it? I wasn't a Shaman and didn't know any live ones. I got some answers but still more questions. I decided to sleep on it and see if I could read more of it in the morning. For now I just needed to get some rest as this had been a great strain on my newly found emotions.

I had started a fire and was now wrapped in the bear hide staring at it. There were things that made lots of sense and things that didn't. The time between the writing on the wall and now seemed to vary with the notion of the talisman. Was I supposed to see how the talisman got to me or assume that I was to find the rightful owner? Did both apply here or is there something I have missed again? Why had Hhaley chosen me or did he? What were the implications of this powerful device that I was entrusted with? I still didn't know how I got from there to here and didn't die a normal death. Maybe I did and didn't know it. When you die what is normal? Why do I have all these questions and who do I blame for what keeps happening to me? Right now I need to get some sleep or I'll go crazy thinking about all this stuff. I didn't even lay down, just dozed off where I sat.

It was the dream again, the same dream with all the terror and pain and fear. It was lying and crying and dying all mixed in to one. It was a war on one side and a holocaust on the other side. It was survival of the fittest and death to the weakest. It was all those things that you hear about on the news. It was the worst experience in the whole world. It was unstoppable. No one came riding in on a white horse to save the day. It was a victory for the black hats in a fight that no one won. "The devil made me do it" wouldn't even be a good answer. It was in the end that even the devil must have missed the mark.

All this seemed to lead to a new opportunity and a new start. The ground had been blackened by the fires that had raged. Now they would produce new growth and maybe a second chance. The meaning of the dream and the writings seemed to be coming together. Something good had to come of it and somehow I was going to be in the middle of it. I had to finish the readings in the cave to get more information. It was becoming an obsession now and I couldn't leave until then.

I woke with a start as I was falling over, something had pushed me. I couldn't see anything around and at first I thought I had imagined it. As I started to get up I got pushed again while stumbling to my feet. I could feel this wind blowing on me as if it were a hurricane. I looked around but nothing else was moving but me. I was being pushed up the hill toward the cave. I yelled at it to stop and it slowed a bit then resumed pushing me. I told it to stop that I could go without all the pushing and shoving. I would have liked to have something to eat and drink before going into the cave but I wasn't getting that opportunity. The thought that the boy had the same thing happen to him made a believer out of me.

I will be glad when this is over and I can see and feel normal again. Somehow I knew that normal wasn't going to happen in this existence and just hoped I could adjust to it.

The wind stopped at the cave entrance and I obligingly crawled in. I held the amulet in front of me and waited for it to warm up. It didn't disappoint me and started to radiate a nice glow that made it easy to see. "I'm glad I don't live in Massachusetts" as they would be setting the bonfire for me by now. I did know they quit burning witches at stakes two hundred years ago. I just didn't know if that was in my old time or my new time. I hoped it wouldn't be anytime soon. I thought to get comfortable before trying to read any more of the hieroglyphics. I sat down and realized that I still had the bear skin hung around me. I didn't think that was a good idea, as I might not be able to get the bat dung and dust out of it. I couldn't send it out to the cleaners. I didn't even have a good brush to work with. I wondered if I would be allowed to take it out and hang it on a tree to air. I let it go, thinking that maybe Mary could get it clean. She was so much better at those things than I was.

I finally calmed down after being manhandled by who knows what. I needed to concentrate on the writings to see if I could learn more and answer some of those questions. I stared at the symbols on the wall and they looked familiar to some extent. Gradually they became more legible and I was beginning to read through the heavy part of the writings. Within a few more minutes I knew that I had seen these symbols before and not in this cave. I continued to go over them and glean all the information I could from them. When I had read through the very last of them I made sure to commit it all to memory.

Somewhere and some time I would need to reference that information and now knew that it was of great importance. I just wasn't sure what it all meant at this time. I knew it was time to go when the talisman dimmed and the light went out and I was left in the dark. Some things were not explained and some I would need a key of some type to access. I knew it was all in there and hoped I could retrieve it when I needed too.

I sat there for a few minutes thinking about what had been a quest for information and seemed as if I didn't get all I wanted out of it. I started to move when the ground began to shake. The walls with all the writing on them began to crumble as I dove for the entrance. I just managed to escape as the whole thing collapsed in on itself.

A cloud of dust flew out of the cave as I crawled away from it. I looked back to see what had happened and the cloud spelled out words in large letters. GO HOME MARY NEEDS YOU. I rushed to pick up my gear and started back for the lake. It took three days to get here and I thought I could get back in two. Bob was there in front of me and moving fast enough to stay there. I was just going to have to duck under the limbs as he wasn't taking the long way around this time.

I didn't think I could run for so long a time and this body wasn't designed for speed. The talisman seemed to supply enough light that we could travel straight through the night. Bob was a cat not a dog and needed to stop for something to eat. I gave him a chunk of moose meat and shared some water with him. I ate jerky and gave Bob a couple minutes to get the

[182]

meat down. I was ready to go as soon as Bob finished eating. We ran through the day and the next night and I began to recognize some of the features of the lake area. Bob was exhausted and I left him to recover as I plowed on ahead.

I went straight to the camp site looking for Mary and Ann but they weren't there. Fred came running up and turned to run away. I knew instantly that he wanted me to follow him. About the same time I heard Ann hollering at someone or something. When I finally saw them, I was in a near panic. A bull moose had Mary trapped and looked like it was trying to kill her. I had to take a second look when I thought Mary was holding the moose hostage. Neither was the case and I was glad of that. Mary had tried to keep the moose away from Ann and lost her spear in the process. Then the moose tried to attack Mary, and she jumped between two trees and didn't get her left arm out of the way in time. The moose rammed the trees but caught Mary's arm between its antlers and the tree and at the same time lodged it antlers in the two trees and couldn't get loose. Mary was on one side of the trees and the moose on the other side. The moose had its head down but could still see what was going on. It must have thought that Mary was holding it there. It had torn the ground up something fierce but still couldn't get loose.

I quickly assessed the situation and went to Ann first. I picked her up and took her to Mary's side of the tree. I asked Mary if she wanted moose for dinner. She said she had seen enough of it and would I please send it away. I took my hammer and broke off the antler that was stuck.

We watched the moose walk off with one antler missing and I began the hard part of this rescue. If the moose couldn't pull the antler loose then I probably couldn't either. I had to calculate the best location to hit the antler to break it and not hurt Mary. Her arm was stuck but did not appear broken or damaged in any way. She may have pulled some muscles and would certainly be sore for a few days. I told her that I would need her help as the weak side of the antler was outside and the inside was pointed at her. If I broke the weak one the rest of the antler might swing into her. She would have to hold it to keep that from happening. She had been there for two days and was very tired but thought she could do that. To help her I tied some rawhide around it and tied the other end to the far tree. I then got a tree limb and forced it between the tree and the antler. If she put her weight against the tree limb it should hold the antler back when it broke.

It was a good guess, as all went as planned and I caught her before she could fall. I picked her up and with Ann and Fred in tow we returned to the camp site. I got Mary some water and a little to eat and made sure she stayed down to rest. She was asleep in no time and I went about getting something for Ann to eat. It wasn't long before they both were catching up on the dreams they missed the last two nights. I hadn't slept in two days either and found it easy to join them.

Mary woke up first as she must have rolled over on her arm. There was enough pain there that she couldn't get back to sleep. Ann and I slept a while longer and Mary didn't want to wake us up. She got a fire going and made a compress of some plants she had found by the lake and tried to wrap her arm with it. She would eventually have to wake me to help her with getting it wrapped up properly.

It reminded us of the splints I had put on her other arm and leg when I pulled her from the flood. We had a laugh about what she thought had happed to her then. She wanted to hear about the trip and if I found the cave. I told her she would have to wait. We could talk about it later as she needed to get some more rest. It was important for her and Ann to get some sleep. She was so tired that she didn't object to that and was asleep in no time. I took the bear hide and hung it on a tree to air. The residue from the cave had not helped with the odor. I hoped we would be able to clean it up some as I was getting to know it real well lately. I had to apologize to Fred for having ignored him since I got back and gave him a nice chunk of meat. I was sure he hadn't gone hungry but he wouldn't ever tell me that. I went down to the lake and washed off the residue that I carried back from the cave. I hadn't taken the time to do that there. It would seem that I would now have time to make some adjustments in my life. They would, of course, affect all of us.

[184]

Bob showed up dragging the half rack of moose antler up to the camp. I think he wanted me to know that I had forgotten about it. I had but wasn't going to tell him that. I did thank him for being such a good guide and getting me out and back. I couldn't tell if that made him happy or not. Cats are hard to read. In any event, he was as tired as the rest of us and walked off to find a quiet place to sleep.

With everyone else asleep, I checked the fire, added some more wood and sat down in front of it to go over the things that had happened. I had only guessed that Mary was trying to protect Ann but she would tell me about it later. The things I had gone through would color the way I looked at all those I would meet and everything I would learn for the rest of my time in this world. I was beginning to wonder what world it really was. Maybe I shouldn't have read so many sci-fi books as a youth.

I found some leek plants down by the lake and made a moose flavored soup. I had it simmering by the fire for an hour or more before the aroma caused Mary to wake up. She could have done better with the flavoring but was so hungry that it didn't matter now. She ate the whole bowl and probably could have eaten more but it would be better if she went slowly. She said her arm didn't hurt as much now but I could see it was black and blue from the bruising. I wanted to know how she managed to trap the moose like that. She said it took her a while to think of such a trick. They had just walked away from the camp and not seen the moose in the water as he had his head down.

Ann had started to the lake as the moose raised his head and saw her. Mary grabbed Ann and started back to the camp but the moose started after them. She had her spear with her but knew she wouldn't get to use it and protect Ann. Fred raced in behind the moose and nipped at his heels and caused him to slow down some. It was just enough so they could get to the twin trees where I found her. She hoped to use the trees to confuse the moose and get away. She put Ann behind the trees and stepped out in front of them. She knew she could get between them but the moose was too big to fit. That's when she made the mistake of using the tree for balance and the moose rammed the tree and trapped her arm.

[185]

When that happened she dropped the spear on the moose side of the tree and couldn't reach it.

That was her story and she was sticking to it, so there. I had to believe her; I didn't think she did it just to get me to come back. It would seem that it worked out and her arm would be better in a few days. I told her I was proud of her for making sure Ann was safe.

When it was my turn to spin a tale, Mary asked that I don't leave out anything. I wasn't sure what anything was so I started with Bob and having to tell him I was tall and he was short. Fortunately he got the idea and walked around the lower hanging things. It was a three day hike to the location of the boy's village and it was beautiful. It was another half day to the cave and then I waited for nightfall to use the torch for light and make the remaining bat leave the cave.

"Okay Okay" she said "just tell me about the writings". I then told her everything that happened up to when the cave started to collapse. The part about the dust coming out of the cave and forming letters in the air about the same time that she got trapped by the moose and Bob and I racing to get back to help seemed unbelievable. Even I would have a problem with that if someone else told this story. It was the way I remembered it and told it like the truth. I know that some things are just in our heads but it is what it is. I told her that the information was now in my head and I couldn't explain it any better. I would be able to use it when the time came. When I told her about the chain of events with the talisman, she looked at me a little strangely. I wasn't sure what to do about the talisman and she just said "it's yours for now". I let it go at that as it was mine for now. There just wasn't anyone else to give it to.

Mary wanted to know if we were going to the place where the boy's village had been and live there. I told her we had to go down river to see what happened to the six men and if there were others that had survived the flood. The three of us did not a village make; we needed some more people to do that.

[186]

Chapter nine

The River

I had to give Mary time to recover from her encounter with the moose and in the mean time I thought I should let her know that I had changed. It was a couple days after my return that I decided to talk to Mary about our relationship. She had stayed away from me, almost like she was afraid for some reason. I knew what it was and as long as her arm was hurting I thought it would be better to wait. Sometimes I think too much and this was one of those times. It would have been better not to let her worry, as in all cases that can only make things worse.

I asked her if she wanted to talk about something and she just shook her head. "I need to say something, will you listen to me"? She nodded that she would. I started by saying that there was an old quote that goes like this. "I know you believe you understand what you think I said, but I don't think you realize that what you heard was not what I meant". She didn't understand the words enough to know what it meant so I tried to explain it better. The fact that I said I wanted to wait to have children had little bearing on the way I felt about her. She knew where children came from and she thought I didn't want to be with her. This was hard for her to accept and the longer I didn't correct it, the worse she felt about it. I then explained that I didn't know the ways of her tribe and how to address the question properly.

If I was her owner and she my property, how do we handle the more intimate relationship? The fact that she thought she belonged to me for saving her life only complicated the feelings I had for her. Then I asked if she would rather be my wife than my property? I knew the answer though she was hesitant while trying to understand what I was asking. I got bowled over by the answer as she literally dove at me. I guessed that we would work out the language problem later.

So far I hadn't explained to Mary who I was and where I came from and all that stuff. Now I wondered if it would ever be worth the effort as I was letting go of more and more of it myself. She seemed to be curious about my tribe and parents and the fact that I kept avoiding the subject. I will continue to delay talking about it unless it becomes a bone of contention between us. I had often thought about how I had lived before and tried to compare it to how I was forced to live now. The camping and fishing I did as a young boy didn't really convert to this life style, when the most modern pieces of equipment I currently have is a flint tipped spear and a bear skin coat.

It is important to get going down the river before the weather starts to change. We have no idea what we will run into but being near the river should supply us with a food source and water. The six men we saw on the other side of the river would have to be so far ahead of us that we will only see them again if they stopped somewhere and set up camp. They may have met others who have had the same troubles. I intended to leave as soon as Mary was able to use her left arm and I checked it every day. She protested that it was doing just fine but I didn't take her word for it. It looked terrible for several days before the coloring started to change to a more yellow appearance.

Once that happened, I knew it would be good enough for her to work with it and we could get going. Ann seemed oblivious to everything that was going on and her faithful sidekick Fred, acted like a lost puppy following her around. I knew that his being there was no accident and that he was watching out for her at every step. Bob, on the other hand, simply didn't seem to care about us at all but never was far away. I would have to keep a close eye on them if we met other people.

It took a week for Mary's arm to change from black to yellow and by then I had gotten most of the stuff ready to travel. I thought we may have cleaned most of the fish out of the lake as we were smoking them as fast as we could. Mary had found a broad leaf plant near the water and used it to wrap the smoked fish in. She thought it had some special power to keep food from spoiling. I had no idea what it was, so kept my mouth shut whenever she did these things. She was still hiding something from me and

[188]

I knew she would have to tell me about it soon. Once the travois was loaded there might not be any room for whatever it was.

The day before we were to leave she came to me and said it was ready and would I like to see what she had done for me. She had done many things for me but for some reason she thought this thing was very special. I would have to act like it was special to me then. She had me turn my back to the camp and got it out. When she was ready with it she called to me to turn around and look. She was holding a beautiful bow and a quiver of six arrows. The bow was taller than she was and I couldn't see how she could have hid it all this time. I took the bow and arrows from her and put them on the ground. She stared in disbelieve until I picked her up and spun us both around and yelled in her ear this time. Ann came to join the party as we hooped and hollered and danced around the fire. The animals had no idea what was going on and almost got underfoot during all the excitement. I sang "Rocky Mountain High" pretending to be John Denver, even to the use of an "air guitar". It was a great night to close down this camp site till the next time we passed this way.

In the morning as we got ready to pull out, I called to Fred and Bob. I held the talisman in my hand and got down on one knee to face them. "I have important information for you two and you must remember it always. We leave today to travel where other people may be and they are not like us. They will want to hurt you and you must remember to stay away from them. I know what you have to do, but in this case it may be my turn to protect you. Listen for my signal as I have listened for yours". I didn't know if what I said made any sense to them or not but they would know to be watchful.

With everything loaded and ready, I put Ann on my shoulders and picked up the handles of the travois and started out. I had found room on the top of the load for my newest pieces of equipment, the bow and arrows. I hadn't had time to practice with them but would make sure to do that with every stop along the way.

Mary took her favorite spear and led the way. Bob was off to one side seeming to have no interest in what was going on and Fred had taken up station next to me. I wondered if they would be able to survive if we were to find someone else to join up with. I wasn't even sure we would be accepted. It didn't matter now as we would find out if and when it happened.

We stopped briefly at the hot springs and left signs that we were headed west. Pulling the travois would leave a trail that our foot prints couldn't. Mary had packed a bag of rocks on the travois and also carried some with her. She had her sling and several stones ready in case we found any more partridges along the way.

It was then that I, Mr. slow to catch on, realized that the arrow heads were made of flint and we had used all the flint before getting to the lake camp. I then recognized the fact that Mary had kept something else from me. Where did she get the flint for the arrowheads? I decided to let her keep that secret for now. It seemed only right since I was hiding something from her. At some point the language barrier would be gone and it would be easier to talk things out.

I gathered some fire wood from up near the mud pot and loaded it on the travois, now stacked high with various items. I knew that getting to the bow would be out of the question now so made sure that my biggest spear would be handy. I had it sticking out the front of the load next to the right handle. I was also carrying the bag of stones that I always kept near.

I was going to have to depend on Fred and Bob for advance notice because I was carrying Ann up high where she could see everything. I wondered if she was trying to pull my hair out or just hanging on for dear life. I told Mary to just follow the trail from the park as there wasn't going to be anything to see on the river for at least two days walk. Mary would look for partridges along the way with the help of Fred. Bob didn't seem to be paying any attention at all as he played drag to this herd.

We didn't expect to see anything of interest or to meet anyone for a while and that went as it should. However, on the fourth day out we began to see signs that a deer herd had passed through the area, going north. Maybe they had found a way to get down to the river. We decided to follow them and if we were lucky, we could be cooking venison for dinner one night.

I motioned for Mary to watch Fred as he seemed to be interested in something just off the path ahead of us. She got her sling ready and bagged a partridge as it jumped into the air. Three more flew before she could reload and we watched to see where they landed. Fred had grabbed the first one and dropped it as I started to scold him. "Boy you've come a long way" I said to Fred. "Now stay here and let Mary do some hunting". Mary went out ahead and circled to the left to chase the birds to go back to our right. That way if they took off, both Mary and I might get a shot at them. "Darn, I forgot my twelve gauge". I fished a stone out of my bag after setting Ann down. I told her to keep an eye on Mary to see what happens.

The birds decided to run instead and Fred just seemed to be waiting for this chance. He ran right into them and grabbed one out of the air. This time Fred kept going with the bird while Mary's next stone hit the trailing one and mine hit the other. Ann was jumping up and down and hollering for us. Bob still didn't seem to be interested in any of this as we picked up our birds and started north. That would be the same direction that Fred had taken. Bob took note of it and loped off ahead of us.

We heard all the hissing and growling as the two of them fought over who was going to get the biggest piece. "Fight nice boys" I hollered, trying to keep them from hurting each other. By the time we caught up to them the outcome had been decided and both seemed to be satisfied with the results. I thought they would be burping up feathers for a couple days. However, we were after bigger game and I told them to get a line on the deer herd so we didn't miss them. Bob just looked at me as if to say "that's not my job". Fred on the other hand took up the lead and started after them. He wasn't in a hurry though, so we didn't have to run to keep up.

It was already late in the day when we crossed the trail of the deer. There wasn't going to be any way that we would make the river before tomorrow night. It might even be later than that as I had no Idea how far it might be. I knew we couldn't miss it in this direction but it could take two days and maybe more. We didn't need to be in a hurry as the deer probably couldn't cross the river.

I had thought we could get there sooner but Ann wanted to do some exploring. Leave it to a kid to teach you something. She kept finding little things along the way that Mary thought would come in handy. Between the two of them they found a plant that looked a little like a carrot or radish but didn't taste like either. Mary thought she could add some to the partridges with more of those dill type plants for flavor.

I thought the partridge tasted pretty good with the carrot type plant and other seasoning in it. Fred and Bob waited for their share, showing the impatience of animals. We sat by the fire chatting some small talk. I did tell Mary that I thought she was the best person I ever saw with the sling. I wasn't lying, as I never saw anyone with a sling before. I didn't tell her that part.

Ann had a busy day and was off to dreamland before the rest of us. She had been running, jumping, crawling and climbing most of the afternoon. Of course the climbing part was all over me. Mary kept chasing her back to me as she pretended to be the great hunter. I guess it was my turn in the box, though I didn't mind the babysitting bit at all. That part would probably be mine for the duration of this journey, since Ann liked the piggy back ride thing. The rest of the way to the river was pretty much the same, without any more birds.

We had seen signs of deer tracks along the way, so Fred was doing a good job in running with the lead. He and Bob trotted out ahead of us as we neared the river. It's funny about water like that. If you have been in a dry place for some time then you can smell water as you get near it. Maybe the moisture level in the air goes up or something. We could even hear the water when the grasshoppers would quiet down.

The deer must have made an abrupt left hand turn at the cliff edge. There wasn't any trail down at this point. We turned west and headed down river after them. Walking the cliff edge gave a good view of the river and we could see it had dropped a little more. From a good half mile away (maybe) we could see the river had a bend in it, going north for a short stretch and then back to the west again. It seemed strange when you can't judge distance that your mind still wants to put a number on it anyway. The bend in the river was a rocky outcropping, much bigger than the one at the valley where I spent last winter. We could see the huge amount of drift wood long before we got there. It must have had a really big whirlpool during the highest part of the flood. The water had eroded a big chunk of the bank at that point and it had caved in to create a slope that was easy access for the deer herd.

I looked across the river and tried to estimate the distance and it would be in the nature of miles and not feet. I thought it had to be two to three miles across and all the flotsam and jetsam would have had a chance to accumulate on this side of the river. Once we reached the top of the trail and got a look at the area below, it was hard to believe. The huge sand bar at the bottom had grown lush with green vegetation and attracted many herbivores. There were at least twenty deer, with ten elk and a moose with one antler. The ducks and geese had found a home here also as did some of the predatory birds.

The log pile was just immense and with a good axe you could have built a dozen log homes with what was there. That would have left enough fire wood to heat all those houses for a year. I had no idea what else was in that pile but hoped it wasn't easy to see.

I checked the trail down and saw that it was on the sandy side and didn't have real good footing. It cut across the hillside at about a forty-five degree angle. The collapsed section was big enough that there weren't any switchbacks needed. The bottom of the trail ended close to the logjam. I knew one thing; the animals down there wouldn't be coming up as long as we were at the trailhead. If we were going to be cooking venison, we would have to go to them. It looked like we would have to set up camp till we could make a good choice for safety reasons. Bob didn't have the resolve to wait and went on down the path to see what was there. Fred was busy watching Ann and trying to keep her from following Bob. I picked Ann up and told her it wasn't safe enough for her to go down just yet.

[193]

I was holding Ann when she grabbed the talisman and said "we can go to the far end and see what's there". I asked her what she said and Mary wanted to know who I was asking as she hadn't said anything. I said Ann talked to me and wants to go to the far end. We both knew that Ann was still having some trouble with getting the words out correctly. Mary came to take Ann from me and saw that she was holding the talisman. "Oh, that's how she's talking to you". That caught me by surprise. "How does it do that"? I knew I wasn't getting an answer so skipped to the next best thing.

I told Mary that we needed to stay here and not let the deer get away. She said she would watch for them. We built a small fire and made sure Mary had her supply of stones. We then put some of the greener grasses on the fire to make smoke. Then Ann and I walked to the other end where the rock outcropping was. Of course I did all the walking while Ann road on my shoulders. It was a long way and when we got to the other end, we waved back at Mary. She was busy with something and didn't seem to notice. I looked at the logjam from here and it seemed even bigger than from where Mary was.

I wanted to check the river after it passed the outcropping and see if the deer could escape downstream. I was sure that if they got in the water they would just have to get past the big turn and would be able to swim easily from there. They just wouldn't have any place to go after that. It seemed pretty rough in the turn area but as soon as it got past the jam it smoothed out and ran straight and calm. It looked as if it were deep but there were no rapids or falls that I could see. It looked like it ran forever as it disappeared into the horizon.

Walking along the river from here would be easy but there didn't look like another place to get down to it for the next week or more. I had been watching for signs of smoke or anything else that was different on either side of the river but saw nothing. If the six men had stopped here they were gone now and it didn't look like anyone had camped down on the sandbar since it was created. Of course, we would check closer when we got down there.

We walked back to the trailhead and watched Bob down on the sandbar. He was dragging a big feathered creature around by one wing. Apparently he had caught a goose that was as big as he was and now he was trying to find a way to kill it. It looked like he was afraid to let go of the wing as it might fly away. He finally rolled it over and grabbed it by the neck. Fred kept looking at the action below and back at us until I told him to go ahead. I felt safe for now and he ran on down to join Bob. It didn't look as if Bob wanted any company just then. I knew they would figure it out. They were partners-in-crime but would never be friends. I wondered if I would ever be able to release them to return to the wild. We set up camp for the night and would take a look at the trail again in the morning. It was a quiet night and Fred came back up to join us. Bob seemed happier to stay down there with all the other animals.

In the morning I told Mary that I would make several trips down and back. I could carry most of the things we would need in about three trips. During the fourth trip, she could carry Ann and I would stay close to support her. We would have to leave the travois and some of our other supplies at the trailhead. We should set up camp close to the bottom of the trail and that should keep the animals from going back up. I wasn't sure what to do about any that might want to come down but that might be their problem. Those that choose the river route may not live long either. There just aren't a lot of places to get out of the river for a real long way. The flood had cut the banks pretty steep on both sides for a long way down. I hoped we could get enough meat before anything drastic happened to the herds.

Everything went like clockwork as the loads I carried were well balanced and didn't present any kind of problem. The path down was soft and I got the feeling that it might slide or collapse at anytime. In some places you could see where one or more animals had a problem and may have tumbled to the bottom. I didn't see any crippled animals in the herds, so those that fell must have not suffered any broken bones. It looked like one of those great places for a motor cycle hill climb but you would have to be a sixteen year old to endure the tumble to the bottom if you didn't make it all the way up. When it came to Mary and Ann, I didn't care to see them go bouncing down.

We were very careful on our decent and managed to get down without any heroics or worse. With every step we took on the way down you could see some loose material break away and slide to the bottom. I always like it when a plan works the way you lay it out. I just didn't tell Mary that I hung onto the talisman the whole time. Fred, of course, being small and light, scrambled down ahead of us and seemed to wonder why we were taking so long. That was his second trip and he hardly moved any sand on either one of them.

Once on the bottom, we began to set up camp. I left Mary with the hard part of getting things separated and I ran off to play in the wood pile. I had to use some muscle to move the dead trees around in order to pull out what I wanted for the camp fires we would need. The first thing I encountered was some kind of vines that had tangled in amongst the other rubble. Mary could see that I was having trouble with them and came over to offer something to help.

She had a flint axe that was better than anything I had been able to make. I didn't ask about the flint as I was still thinking she made the arrow heads from something like it. She would tell me in her own time and I could wait to hear it. The new axe worked really well on the vines and I was able to clear enough to gather firewood for the next couple days. Mary had cleared a big area around a smaller fire pit and got a fire going as soon as I delivered some wood. The herbivores had moved to the far end of the sandbar. They would stay there for awhile as they got use to us being near.

I thought I would wait till morning to go after the deer. By then they may have settled down some and I should be able to separate one or two from the herd. As we settled in for the night I thanked Mary for the axe and commented on how well it worked. She still didn't seem to want to talk about it and I started to drop the subject. I then asked if something was wrong as she was so quiet now. She wanted to tell me about the flint and wasn't sure how I would handle the information. I then told her I thought she did a great job with the arrowheads and now the axe, and that I really liked them a lot. She finally opened up and told how her tribe didn't think girls should know how to do men's work. I put it all together then and said

[196]

to her that we were family and there were no men or women work. It was all the same and we had to work together or some things would not get done. I told her that she was better at some of the jobs than I was and I didn't think that was a problem. It was a benefit to have someone in the family that could do these things. In most cases, it would help if she were to teach me how to do some of these things. I then asked about the flint and where it came from. She seemed to feel better after what I told her and then she told me where the flint came from. The stones I got for her from the lake were almost all flint and she knew I couldn't tell. She didn't know how to explain to me about the stones, so she just did the best she could to use them. I told her that she should show me how to tell one stone from another, and then I could be more helpful to our family. It would be good if she would show Ann some of the things she knew also. Ann might be a little young to do the work but she could watch.

In the morning, I took the bow and arrows and practiced by shooting into the sandy bank. I had never actually used a bow before and it must have looked like it to Mary. She tried to show me the best way to get the arrow to go straight but I would need a lot more time before I could hit a deer, especially if it was moving. I didn't think that any of them would just stand there and let me shoot arrows at them until I hit one. I was pretty good with a spear and my throwing stones and they would have to do today if we were going to cook one tonight. I marched off to combat with my favorite tools and expected to have some success. For a change I got this one right. The deer had converged on the smallest end of the sandbar, leaving them very little room to maneuver. The moose and elk just simply moved out of my way and left the deer to fend for themselves. I picked out a young buck and kept pushing him further toward the water. I cut off his exit route and forced him to make a run for it. The spear did its magic and he went down in a heap. The rest of the animals went back to grazing as I carried my trophy back to camp.

Mary saw me coming and gathered up her tools to skin and butcher it. I would help as she showed me exactly what she was doing. I knew that of the animals I worked on before, I had lost some valuable meat and other parts. We removed the hide and cut away one hind quarter to cook. I put it

[197]

on a spit over the fire and then went back to help Mary with the rest of it. She had learned from her mother how to do these things. She showed me the trick of tanning the hide and how to use most of the deer parts. The things that came so easy to her seemed to confound me. It seemed as if it would be a lifelong learning process for me and I thought Ann would be doing these things before I could.

I knew the principal of how a bow and arrow work and what their purpose was. What I didn't have was the technique of how to use it properly. I could shoot arrows all day but it wouldn't help if I didn't concentrate on where to aim and when to release the arrows. Still targets would be one thing but a moving animal was going to be a work-in-progress. I would have to think about how I got a spear to the intersecting point and relate it to the arrow doing the same thing. I asked Fred if he would like to race across my field of vision so I could practice. He didn't seem to like that idea very much and declined the offer.

The ducks and geese were out of the question as I would lose the arrows in the water. Then I thought of how the geese feed every morning on the sandbar. I could get between them and the river and that way the arrows would land on the ground, unless of course I only wound one of them and they fly away with it. I asked Mary if she could make some arrows without the flint heads. Then I could use them for practice or to shoot at the big beach birds.

That turned out to be the answer for the geese and ducks. It only took a few tries and I was getting the hang of it. Soon we were eating high-on-the-hog so to speak. I stuck with the spear for getting a deer every so often and stayed away from the elk and moose for the time being. Setting the camp at the bottom of the trail had worked as expected and the animals all stayed away from there and couldn't escape. It wasn't like shooting-fish-in-a-barrel but kept enough targets around that we wouldn't go hungry. Speaking of fish, I was able to get a couple of them on every attempt. We had the smoker going almost constantly as we prepared food to use later.

I had made several more trips up and down the trail to retrieve the rest of our gear. I even took the travois apart and brought the whole thing down. We talked about the possibility of staying through the winter or trying to find the six men or someone else down the river. I thought the walk looked like a real challenge and we might get stuck on the high plateau during the winter months.

I began to think about another option, rafting down the river. Maybe I had seen too many movies or something but it began to make more and more sense. It would be much quicker and could lead to the outlet of the river where someone could possibly be. There were plenty of logs to choose from for a raft and the vines that were tangled in the logjam should due for rope. It might be easier to build than actually get it to work. I was sure it would float but how to control it might be a challenge.

I tried to picture it in my head as to what it would look like. I then asked Mary what she thought of the idea and it seemed to make sense to her also. Her tribe had done some boating and floating but nothing on this scale. They didn't do much of it because it was always so hard to get back up the river. In this case, we weren't coming back up the river at least not on the water.

The very earliest signs of the weather changing were starting to show up. The first of several types of salmon started to show up in the river and I knew that more would follow in a few weeks. I didn't know one type from the other but did remember the different times between them. I was sure the fish eagles would be glad to see them and it would be a month or more before they ran out of food. Mary had made a net from the vines to fish with and was showing Ann how to drag them in. Some of the fish were as big as she was and it really looked funny to see her trying to carry one of them. Like all kids, she would always pick up the biggest one. "Anyone for grilled salmon steak tonight" I asked?

The hardest part of getting started on the raft was the vines. They were tangled in amongst the logs and had to be pulled out a little at a time. We needed them to be longer, so couldn't just cut them off. I worked at that for awhile and then would grab hold of a log and get it out in the open. Once we had enough logs, they had to be trimmed of the branches that remained and then rolled over by the river. There wasn't any way to get them all the same size but I planned to put the biggest ones on the outside of the raft. That way we would have some help keeping everything inside that and on the raft. I was hoping this turned out better than the sled I had tried to build.

Working on the logjam wasn't all that pleasant, at times the odor would be overwhelming and I would see some things I would never tell Mary. I did look for any form of trinket or salvageable item that we could use but almost everything was broken or damaged beyond repair. If it looked close to repairable I would take it to Mary and ask her about it. There was no clay on the whole sandbar, so we couldn't fix any of the pottery we found. The pile of logs was so deep that we weren't going to get into the middle of it, where I thought the majority of items would be.

The raft began to take shape after about a week of struggling with the logs and vines. I knew we would need a rudder and support for it and tried to draw it in the sand so Mary could understand what I was talking about. Without it we wouldn't be able to guide the raft and it would just keep running into things or the banks. I found a forked branch for that and just needed to lace some hide between the forks. With it turned so one fork was up and the other down, it would work great for a tiller. The supports for it would be harder to secure but I thought we could manage it.

Mary thought we needed more hides to secure our load and wondered if we should go after something larger than deer. I had to guess that she must have meant the moose as it was the biggest thing around. It might be a little harder to take down than the deer were. I would give it some thought.

I continued to work on the raft and wondered if our two guard dogs would be going with us. I would have to talk to them about that. Fox and cats like drinking water but are not very fond of swimming in it. If being on a raft was going to be a problem I might have to release them from their duties. I wasn't sure that was possible or if they wanted to be released. We would find out soon as the raft was taking shape. The water level had dropped a little more and now I was beginning to worry about the rapids in the turn area. Now it was time to go after that moose.

I had gotten a little better with the bow and arrows but was still a little skeptical of my abilities. I had to get between the moose and the water to keep it from floating away. If I shot it and only wounded it, that's where it would head. With the bow I wouldn't need to get as close as I would with the spear. I had my throwing stick to get some more distance with the spear. I knew I might just need that to get this guy down. There wasn't any way for Mary to help and still keep Ann out of trouble, so I was on my own for this one. It was the same as with the deer; first you make a plan then work it as best you can. The moose and elk saw me coming and moved out of the way. I was using the river side of the sandbar and they just moved up from that. When I moved up a little with them, they again moved away from me. They had gotten used to the deer hunt process and didn't seem too worried about me.

The elk had always put the moose between us and did that again. When I thought I couldn't get them any further from the water, I set my bow and let fly an arrow. It was not a killing shot and the moose bolted for the water. I was ready for that as I had a spear in the throwing stick while running to intersect the moose. I had to get it down before it got in the river. The spear went through its lungs and caused it to turn away from the blow. This gave me enough time to set another arrow and fire it away. This one caught it in the neck and he went down. He was trying to get up when I reached him and hit him in the head with my trusty hammer. I thought that this moose was a lot easier than that first one was but for this one I had a plan. That first one just seemed to be dumb luck on my part or maybe luck had nothing to do with it. I will be debating why I'm here for the rest of this life.

Mary and Ann came running up to help, with Mary carrying her skinning tools. We would do most of the work right where he went down and move the biggest parts over to the camp on the hide. There were two or three days work here and turning some of the meat into jerky would take another two or three. I would get a couple geese and with the fish Mary and Ann caught we should be set for food. Then I hoped the raft would be ready to go and we could test out the river for transportation. I had laid out a couple logs under the raft before starting on it to make sure we could slide it into the river. The sandy bank should give way under the weight of the raft and I tied an anchor vine to a waterlogged stump. If all goes well, we will put the raft in the water the night before we leave and load all the remaining items that next morning. Some things would be left behind to show that we had been there.

Each morning, for those three days before we left, I would go up on the prairie and set a huge smoky fire and watch for a response anywhere on the horizon. We never saw any responding smoke and had to assume that if there were people out there, they were a long way off. Every day that I did that, I would wonder who the people were that had created the one lane trail that led to the hot springs. Like the river, it seemed to go on forever in the direction to the west. Whoever they were, the river must have been their final destination and maybe they still lived somewhere along the route we would take.

The three days just seem to fly by as we were very busy getting it all together. We used some long poles for leverage and forced the raft into the water. Another plan is falling into place as it should. We loaded everything that wasn't essential for the last night here. I then called a meeting of the animal set and informed them of what was going to happen. I gave them the choice of joining us on the river or going back to Mother Nature. I wouldn't know their answer till morning or if they actually had an option.

In the morning as we prepared to leave, I looked out over the sandbar and took note of the remaining inhabitants. We had thinned out the deer herd and removed the moose but the elk got off scot-free this time. Maybe the next time we're by here, we'll bag a couple of those. We celebrated the occasion and wished the remaining animal's farewell.

Fred and Bob were nowhere in sight and we assumed that they had gone. Ann was the first to notice as her constant companion wasn't getting under her feet. I couldn't tell if she was happy about it or not. She just called his name and then forgot about it in the rush to get going. I didn't go up to start another fire on the prairie as it hadn't made any difference so far. We picked up our remaining items and trudged down to the river. I made sure that Ann had something to carry so she would feel like she was helping. When we got to the raft, low and behold, there was the rest of our family. Fred and Bob were sitting on top of the already packed items waiting for us. With that I got one answer but not the other. I didn't know if they had the choice of going wild or not but it sure looked like they were going along.

I had made some tie downs in the middle of the raft for the girls to hang on to if the going got rough. Mary made a harness for Ann so we could keep a hold of her at all times. I warned Mary to hang on to Ann till we got past the logjam and around the turn. We could be bouncing around for the first few minutes. We had two extra poles to help guide with and I used one to get us turned in the right direction as we started out. The tiller was working quite well as I was able to keep the raft oriented in the middle of the river. We didn't lose anything or even anybody in what was an interesting ride for a short run through the narrow part of the canyon.

Once we cleared that, it was smooth sailing for what looked like a long time. Mary and I would try to keep our eyes peeled for any sign of life along the way. The river had been gouged deeper here than anywhere else we had been. The walls were steeper and narrower but the river was running smooth as silk and looked to be like that for days to come. I kept looking for places to stop as we would need to eat and rest. There seemed to be plenty of small sandbars every so often and I felt we could keep going till late in the day. We stopped at one of those for the night and Mary netted a couple fish and we had fresh fish for dinner. It looked like that was going to be the routine for the next few days or longer.

Everyone got their land legs back and we slept on shore. We had brought some fire wood with us but intended to use it wisely. I didn't know if we would find another logjam or any other flotsam for awhile. It felt good to just relax after the build-up of stress while getting ready for this trip. Each of us must have had our own feelings about how this would go. I was worried that I would be risking the lives of the girls, while doing something uncertain. We obviously had a very small party and to lose any one would hit us hard. Now that the tension was gone, we could smile and enjoy each others company.

Each day after that began to look like the last one till we were a week into the trip. Mary was the first to see what looked like a camp site. It was partially hidden and we had floated past it with little chance of going back. I managed to get the raft to that side of the river and stopped at the next sand bar.

I got the raft tied off to a large rock and took a look at the prospects of going up river by foot. It didn't look good but might be doable. I had Mary get a couple deer stomachs ready. We didn't need them for water right now so I had her tie off one end and we blew air in the other and tied it. I then had her tie them together with enough of a gap between them so they might work as water wings. I didn't expect to have to get in the water but better safe than sorry. Reminding myself that I had never been a great swimmer, I made my plans accordingly.

I would only get in the water if I had no other option. I told Mary that and suggested that she keep a sharp eye out for anyone or thing floating down the river. She might have to use her fish net to pull it in but be very careful. I then set out with only my bag of stones, a spear and my ever handy hammer. It was around mid day and I didn't think I would be getting back after dark and told Mary if it got dark I would stay where I was. The risk might be too high along the rock walls of this canyon. If anyone was at that site they would have been there for some time. Since they didn't come out yelling to us I would think they were afraid of whom we might be. What little we saw of the camp wasn't enough to tell if it was in resent use. The fact that we could see it indicated that it was after the flood and maybe more like this summer some time. If someone had found a way to get up and down the cliff face here I would like to know that also.

The travel was treacherous and I had a hard time staying out of the water. I did get my feet wet a couple times but never actually got in past my ankles. I would stop and listen ever so often and tried real hard not to make any noise. If someone was near, they weren't making any noise either. When I got to the place where I knew I was close to the camp site, I stopped and rested. I wanted to listen again just in case I missed something while climbing in the rocks.

[204]

I did hear some kind of noise and it almost sounded like something being dragged along. I waited to see if it continued or stopped and to get a feel for where it might be. I then heard what sounded like slap or smack of a hand to skin followed by a whimper and another slap. This didn't sound good as hurting someone could be for lots of reasons but here on the river with no one around seemed abusive. I knew I was far enough from the camp site that I probably had not been detected. If they saw us go by on the raft then maybe they were afraid that we would come back for them. Of course the question would be, why? What would someone be afraid of in this kind of location? I decided to sit still for a while and try to get a better handle on the situation. So far it seemed like there were two people here but no way to tell the age or anything else about them. They were being very quiet and I would need to get closer to find out more information. I needed to be in stealth mode for this and began moving very slowly with an eye on any movable rock or stick.

When I leaned forward, the talisman swung out and clicked against a rock. I immediately grabbed it and stopped. To me the sound from it was almost like a church bell gong. I thought the whole world would have heard it but there was no reaction in the camp site. I held the amulet to keep it from doing that again and crept forward till I could see more of the camp. There was one small boy close to me but I couldn't see the rest of them or enough of the camp to tell how many there were. I needed to get this boy far enough away from the camp to find out what was going on. Just then the boy started in my direction and going down closer to the river he passed below me and kept going. I followed him till I knew we might not be heard and I asked him to stop. He turned and looked at me but acted like I wasn't there. I asked him to tell me about the camp and how many people were there. He told the whole tale as if in a trance and covered all of it without the minor details. I told him to stay where he was and I would come back for him in a little while.

I went back to the camp site, this time not being so quiet and looked in to see if what he had told me was true. There were two more people, just like the boy had said. I saw an old woman, his grandmother, and another young boy, his older brother. The old woman was busy doing something and I whispered "boy come this way". He walked almost directly at me until I said "go to your brother". He continued on past me to where his brother was and I told them to stay there and I would come for them in a little while. By this time I realized that the talisman was doing this and I had no power of my own to speak of. I just needed to get some more help from it with the old lady. There would be more resistance there and I wasn't sure how to handle that.

I was still holding the talisman as I walked into the camp site. I didn't intend to scare her but I did and she threw a rock at me and started to run away. When I caught the rock with my left hand and held my right one in front of me, she fell to the ground. She felt all over to see where I had hit her but couldn't find any place that hurt. She struggled to her feet and stood staring at me. I held up the amulet and her legs gave way again. This time she knew that I had not thrown something at her, at least not something she could see. I said "gather your things together and I will return to you in a short while". I then went to get the boys and bring them back to the camp site. When we got back, I said to the boys "gather your things, even the ones you hid from your grandmother, and bring them here for me to see". The words were not important as they couldn't understand a thing I said but the information was passed on through the talisman.

The old woman knew this as soon as I said something because her ears told her one thing and her mind told her something else. The boys were still working in the dark because of the way grandma treated them. She would change now out of fear from me and so would the boys but not because of fear but lack of it. The boys took a little longer to collect their things as they had hidden them under rocks and in crevasses where grandma couldn't find them.

I didn't bother to look at what they collected as I looked at the sky and could tell that we had plenty of time to make it back to the raft. The old woman made a small wailing noise when I looked up as if she thought I was calling on my long departed ancestors. She had spent her whole life in fear of something or other and now she expected that I was the one she needed to fear. I felt like I wouldn't be able to change that as it probably was so ingrained in her at her age that she would die that way. It didn't mean that I couldn't try to help her, which of course I would.

With everything gathered up I led the way back along the cliff wall to the sandbar where the raft was located. The return trip seemed so much easier and none of the three had any trouble following me. I made the announcement that we were coming from several hundred yards away. Mary built up the fire and had a moose roast going when we got there.

Ann was thrilled to have company but Fred and Bob not so much. I introduced my family to the new arrivals and vise versa. Grandma's name was Lista and the boys by age were Bakta and Casta. Fred and Bob had heeded my warning and were staying away from the newcomers. The boys were really interested in them but Ann stepped in front of the boys and stopped them from getting close. They were both older and bigger than her but she had something they didn't have yet. She lacked fear of anything and knew that Mary and Jed would protect her. Bakta and Casta would be a while getting to that place. Lista saw the animals that we had and her fear of me grew even greater. I just hoped that her fear didn't stop her from helping out with the knowledge that she had accumulated over the years.

I had let go of the talisman and motioned for the boys sit down. I wanted to see what they had brought with them and indicated to Mary to do the same with Lista and her collection. It was of great interest to me that the items they had collected were so few and common. There was nothing unique about any of the stuff but I was sure it represented something to them. They would be allowed to keep any and all of the items as they wouldn't be taking up much space and I wasn't much for taking things away from anyone else. I had hopes that the boys would soon find other things to hold onto.

We sat down to eat and Mary gave each of them and us a small portion. She then gave some to Fred and Bob, which drew the interest of the boys again. The bigger boy, Bakta, seemed to be the more energetic of the two but Casta may have just been more scared of what might happen to him. There was plenty of food left when we had eaten and I offered some more to Casta. He looked shocked and I could see the fear in his eyes. He glanced over at his brother, who then nodded to him. He then took the piece I had offered and I moved down the line to his brother and then to Lista. The food was then passed to Ann and Mary in that order and I took mine last of the humans. Fred and Bob had to wait this time till we had finished eating. I checked to make sure the boys had enough to eat; I then gave the last of it to the fox and cat.

Fred and Bob had settled on either side of Ann and the boys couldn't keep their eyes off them. They would not be allowed to approach Ann until she indicated it was alright for them to do so.

I indicated that we would sleep on this small spit of land tonight and leave in the morning. I thought that none of our guests had ever been on a raft or boat and it might be of great interest to them. It would have to wait until morning though as it was starting to get hard to see as night had fallen. We supplied some hides for our guests to sleep under and banked the fire to keep it going for a while. Fred and Bob were asked to keep an eye on the raft and our supplies. They weren't exactly guard dogs but would do in a pinch. Bob was better suited for night duty than Fred, but both could hear in their sleep. What you might call them were light sleepers. We slept as well as could be expected there.

When we awoke in the morning and before getting anything to eat, I took Mary on the raft and told her all that had happened and how the troubled trio had come to be where they were. It seems as if grandma was a product of a tribe that treated some women badly and she may have been treated worse than most.

I didn't get the actual relationship between the woman and the boys but they called her grandma and I let it go at that. Somehow they had been out of the river basin during the flood and were on their own for a while. When some hunters were spotted nearby she ushered the boys to the edge of the cliff. The older boy jumped down out of fear and landed in the sandy bank and rolled to the bottom unhurt. When grandma saw that she pushed the other boy down and jumped behind him. They did this to escape from an unknown group that may never have seen them.

They couldn't get back up the cliff and were afraid to go either direction on the river. They were able to get some fish in a small inlet upriver from the camp site and that had been their diet since they got there. All three of them looked thin so they may have been lacking for the proper amount of food. We should keep an eye out for the possibility that one or more of them might try to get into our food supply. I didn't mind feeding them but if they were to over eat now it might make them sick.

Mary went to fix something to eat for breakfast and I stayed onboard to check our supplies. It appeared as if the dynamic duo of Fred and Bob had kept the overly interested away from the goodies. I told them that I did appreciate the job well done and they could now go get something from Mary. As was my habit, I would eat last. The raft had been intended for three people, two animals and our supplies; however, I did make it big so it would be more stable in the water. Now that we where adding three more to our load, I needed to make sure they would not cause us any problems.

After eating, I took the boys aboard first and walked them around. I showed them that by moving from side to side it made the raft lean to the change in weight. They would have to be careful if walking around and it would be better if they did not. I made sure that they understood the last part of that.

Lista wasn't asked to board until we were ready to leave. I then had Mary take her to what could be called the main deck and have her sit there while we were moving on the water. Mary tried to talk to her while Ann tried to talk to the boys. At first neither was successful but after a while Mary started finding words that both she and Lista knew.

Ann didn't have much of a vocabulary yet and seemed to be having some trouble getting the boys to talk. They wanted to know about the bobcat and the fox but as the day dragged on they became more and more open to listening to her. Ann wasn't one for holding back and talked a blue streak for most of the day.

Everyone got their choice of dried fish or jerky for the noon meal and the boys turned up their noses at the fish. I almost laughed out loud as I knew they probably ate nothing but fish for some months. The boys started to pick up some of the words from Ann and began talking between themselves. Ann got angry at them for not talking to her and both Fred and Bob made a point of letting the boys know.

I interrupted just to let all the parties know that it was a language problem and they didn't mean any disrespect. Fred and Bob settled back down on top of the supplies and Ann said she was sorry. It would be several days before the conversation was understandable for some and in many cases it would take much longer. The youngsters would learn from each other much faster than the adults. Lista would be slower than Mary and I but eventually the communications would get better.

The next day I could hear a change in the background noise and asked if anyone knew what it was. The boys pointed to the sky and I looked up in time to see a flock of birds flying overhead. The water running in the canyon wasn't very loud but it was enough to cover some of the outside noises. The birds got closer and I soon recognized the geese and the sound that they were making. They were also on a descending angle and looked to be planning on landing somewhere ahead of us.

We had come a long way but only a day's travel from where we picked up the three lost souls. Now it looked like we were getting to a wider place on the river or maybe something even bigger. We were about two to three hours away yet but this seemed like a reprieve from the monotony of the canyon walls. I thought we had seen enough of them and was looking forward to better scenery.

The walls of the canyon seemed to slide slowly back from the river and drop down in elevation. The waterway opened up before us and almost looked like one of the great lakes. The day was calm and the water was quite still for such a large body of water. I guided the raft toward the right shore line and let it drift along for some time. I was looking for any signs that the six men may have stopped there and set up a camp. Everyone was on their feet looking and I had to remind them that the raft needed to be balanced. We hadn't come all this way to have everything get dumped in the river now.

We didn't see any signs of a camp or where someone may have had a fire or was fishing. I used the tiller to propel us along. We needed to find a location where we could gather fire wood and set up a camp for at least a week. If anyone was on the lake we needed to signal them. I knew the telegraph lines were down so we would have to use smoke to let them know we had arrived. I didn't bother to say that as I knew it would be lost on the rest of my now growing herd.

When the flood came through here it must have raised the lake level up over the banks and that would mean that any flotsam might not be on the current shoreline. We would have to look further out for firewood but the green plants for making smoke where all over the place. I guessed that the river would have pushed most of the trees and plants some distance from the entrance to the lake before it expanded out over the banks. That meant going where the river would have taken all the free floating debris.

It also may have been the reason we hadn't seen any campsites yet. Then there was the possibility that the lake level hadn't gone down yet when the men got here. The river was still in the process of reaching a lower level when we started our rafting trip. If the lake was higher then, they would have had to go out further to get around it or even to camp. I moved the tiller back and forth and we continued on down the lake.

It was starting to get dark when I pushed the raft against a sandy beach and declared our rest stop for the night. Everybody disembarked before I could get the thing tied down. We were all happy to be on dry land that didn't have a cliff overlooking us. Fred and Bob did a quick survey of the area and seemed to be satisfied. There was no wood to be found here so we had to use the small amount that we brought with us. Mary had a fire going in no time and Lista showed that she might want to help. Fear is a tough thing to overcome and she was reticent to get overly involved. I walked away from them and let Mary try to work it out with her.

[211]

I started to think about the coming winter and if we needed to move on or find some place to set up camp for the duration. It had started to get cooler at night and the sun had been moving further to the south. I had worried about getting caught in the canyon when the river froze but now it would be a problem with the open plains.

Then my thoughts turned to the boys and Lista. I had missed something again and now it was coming to me. The three of them must have a real fear of me for just the things they have seen. First and foremost, I must be the biggest person they ever saw and I had all this magic power. I could talk to them and the animals yet I didn't speak their language. Then there was the load of furs on the raft and the raft itself. There had never been anything like it and no way to explain it.

There were moose and elk hides along with a bearskin, a cougar skin and a bunch of wolf skins. There were lots of items made of deer hide and antlers of all sizes. Flint was always hard to come by and we seemed to have lots of it. The bow and arrows would have brought a treasure in most villages. On top of all that, neither Mary nor Ann looked at all like I did.

That night I talked to Mary about the situation and how it might be handled. We agreed that something needed to be done but more importantly, we had to move on in search of the men that we thought should be somewhere near here. She would keep a conversation going with Lista and I should talk to the boys about what I was doing with the raft. Ann would be a great help because she just wanted to keep talking.

Chapter ten

The Lake

Ann was true to her words. Once she learned to talk we never made any effort to quiet her down. She seemed to know that if we were hunting she should not be noisy but otherwise, look out. This morning she was at it again and the boys were still trying to get close to Fred and Bob. She wasn't going to let them and told them so.

We had cleaned up the area we had used as an overnighter and now were on our way further down the lake. The ducks and geese were making quite a racket as we went along but didn't seem all that much afraid of us. They would just move out of the way and holler at us for disturbing their morning. I asked Mary if she would cook some geese for tonight's meal and she thought that would be a nice change from fish and moose meat. We would have to find a wood pile somewhere first, so I asked everyone to keep a lookout for one.

When Bakta indicted to Ann that there might be something off to the north, she climbed up on the supplies and pointed in that direction. It was pretty comical to see her doing that and Mary and I got a laugh out of it. We still had a ways to go though to get even with it, and I suggested that Ann get off the supplies. I gave the two of them the thumbs up sign and kept moving the raft downstream. Ann came back to where I was and started to reprimand me for not stopping.

Everyone was watching to see what I would do and how I would handle this young whippersnapper. I got down on one knee to get close enough that we could see eye to eye. I then took her hand, the one with the pointing finger, and stuck the talisman in it. I thanked her for the effort she had put in and suggested that we not do this again. I then told her why I didn't stop and that soon we would. She was quite proud of herself for having solved this problem and released the talisman and marched back to her chosen place by the supplies. Mary turned to face Ann and started clapping her hands. The others, not knowing what it was all about, clapped their hands also. Ann was very pleased with the response. She had done what she thought was necessary and was willing to take full credit for it. Lista now became more confused than ever as to my status and the power that even Ann might have. She could see that the power might be in the talisman. She would be right, of course, but not in the way she thought of it.

I found a sandy beach area almost straight across from the flotsam pile and guided the raft to shore. I anchored it with the water soaked tree stump and set several things in motion. Mary and I picked a location for a fire and I let her and Lista clear away the grasses and get it ready. I had Ann take Fred and Bob away from the water and let them get some exercise.

I then took Bakta and Casta down the beach in search of some nice throwing stones. I had them pick stones that would fit their hands but Casta kept getting ones that were too big for him. I then set up a target for them to throw at and of course, Casta couldn't hit it because his stones were too big for his hands. That would make them harder to control. I gradually worked him down to smaller ones and his aim started to get better. At first the boys didn't seem to get the idea that it was alright to do this and I joined in to throw a couple myself. It took a few throws for them to get the feeling that they could do this without me getting angry with them and after a while were even beginning to enjoy it. Ann came down to see what we were doing and of course her constant companions came along.

I told them it was time to go hunting and we started down the beach to where a flock of geese and been resting. Most of the birds had flown in from up the river somewhere and would eat and rest before going to their next destination. The geese had little fear of us and that allowed for us to get fairly close. I had the boys ready a stone each and pointed out the goose each should aim for. I knew from what they had done in practice that they would be good at this. They must have been doing the same thing when Lista wasn't watching them. Ann was keeping Fred and Bob back as she could see we were in hunting mode. When the boys seemed to be close enough to their targets I let them take a shot at it. I sent my stone along

[214]

with theirs and we had three good hits. Their birds were not dead so we had to rush forward and catch them before they got in the water. Three big geese would make a good meal for us tonight.

The other birds had flown but seemed to be just circling around and acted as if they would land. One of those made a huge mistake as it came in lower than the others. We got to see the great leaping ability of the bobcat as Bob jumped up and grabbed that goose by the wing and brought it down. I took Ann and the boys along with our geese back to the camp site and dropped the birds off with Mary. I told her that Fred and Bob were working out a deal on which got the best parts of Bob's goose.

I took the boys to get some wood for the fire and Ann wanted to go but I told her that Mary could use her help. She always wanted to help and I knew that Mary would find something for her to do. Pulling feathers from the geese might just be very important for a little girl to learn. More important might be which feathers to keep for bedding and other things.

Bakta and Casta had never seen a logjam before and didn't seem to know what to make of it. It was one of the smaller ones that I had seen but there would be lots of nice pieces in there for all kinds of uses. Mostly we wanted firewood but any other useful item we could find would be great.

I started by going around the outside and checking for any sign that someone else had been there. I located an old fire pit and looked it over very carefully. It had been sometime since it was used so whoever had the fire was long gone. It was also a small fire pit so it wasn't used to signal anyone but to cook on instead. It was the first indication that the men we had seen so long ago may have been here and moved on.

I began pulling chunks of wood off the pile and setting them aside. Anything that the boys could carry or pull went in one pile and the larger ones in another. If it had the possibility of being used for something else I would put it in a third stack. I started them out by giving Casta a branch that was twice his size and aiming him toward camp. He was game for it and I let him go. I was sure he would get it there if it took him the rest of the day. Bakta grabbed some items and started out behind his brother. I pretended not to watch as he stuck out a hand to help Casta with his load. "Good, they have learned to work together and help each other".

I kept working on the pile till I had enough wood for several fires; I was interested in a good sized fire for putting out lots of smoke. We would make a smaller smoke fire from the one we cook the geese on later in the day and use the big one in the morning. The wind was usually calmer in the mornings and evenings so the smoke would go up higher before dispersing. The air currents in the middle of the day cause the opposite effect, making it harder to signal for any distance.

The boys and I made several trips and the girls joined in once the geese were starting to roast. Lista stayed with the fire and food to make sure it wouldn't spread or burn our evening meal. I had Ann sit on top of one of my loads to keep the extra branches from falling off. She was always willing to supply this kind of help. Mary picked through the third pile to see if she could use some of those pieces.

Sometimes you have to trust animal instincts. Fred and Bob were beginning to think of the boys as less than troublesome. However, they seemed to relate to Lista differently. I wasn't sure how I knew that but by some means or other they were giving me that subtle information. They would usually stay as far away from her as possible without leaving Ann by herself. The boys were starting to get the idea that these animals were not pets you could play with and were gradually getting less interested in them.

We were going to be at this site for three or four days so the smoke signal could get a chance to work. Then we would move further down the lake. That is, unless we were to make contact with someone. We knew that by using the raft, we made better time than anyone would have by walking. The six men we had seen so long ago would still have had such a big lead that it was impossible to tell how far they may have gone. We would find out shortly if they were still in the area or not. Then there was the thought of the men that had been looking for Lista and the boys. They would be on the other side of the lake and I was sure it wasn't the same ones.

[216]

I thought I should keep the boys interested in being providers for the future and to see if they had any skills that we could use. I thought from the beginning that they didn't seem to be the normal young males that you would expect in this environment. I started out with the feeling that Lista had created enough fear in them that they just didn't react normally for their ages. That might still be the case but somehow they missed the early training that Mary described to me in her tribe. They almost acted like everything they did had been without supervision. Maybe they had been with Lista longer than she was indicating and they were afraid to say. The longer I could keep them away from her, the easier it may be to get them to talk about it. I could force the answers but thought that might not be good for their mental makeup.

We ate the geese and built up the fire a little, then covered it with green grasses to cause it to produce a large volume of smoke. We kept that going for a while and when it was time to call it a day, we cleared the residue off and put it out. The days were still very nice but the nights were getting quite cool. I made sure the kids were rolled up in warm hides and did the same for myself. Fred's intruder alarm went off in my head and I must have jumped a little. Lista was standing just a few feet away and now pretended to be checking the fire to make sure it was out. She mumbled something and went back to her elk hide blanket. I sent a thank you to Fred and turned over to go to sleep again. It was then that I realized that the dreams were almost all gone. Sometimes they would be just outside the memory area and I would have that vague feeling that I missed one of those moments.

In the morning we started two fires. One to heat food on and one to cause a great smoking cloud. I had spent some time clearing the area for the bon fire and got help from the boys. They needed way too much guidance to do this simple chore. I had talked to Mary about their lack of skills and she found it very odd also. I wasn't sure that I should be the one teaching them as I still needed help from Mary for some of the things I had to do. I guessed that we could learn it all together.

I took Mary's fishing net and pushed the boys up the lake this time to a spot we had passed the other day that looked good for fishing. I gave the net to them and motioned for them to go get some fish. They had no idea what to do with it and looked like they would start crying. I was a novice with the net also but I had seen Mary use it. I thought the weighted end was tossed out first and then pulled back under the non-weighted end. The trick was to hold onto the lines threaded through the top half.

It took us several tries to get the hang of it but by then we had scared the fish away. The boys seemed to get the idea and we moved to another location further up and soon had a little luck. The fish at this site were a little smaller but we caught enough to make a meal for everyone. Especially Bob, when he snuck in and took one of our fish while we weren't watching. He must have left Fred to watch Ann; I might have to talk to him about that.

It was still early in the day and Mary or Lista kept the smoky fire going so I checked the horizon to see if we were getting any return smoke. I didn't see any and thought it might take some time for another group to get a fire going. We would spend some more time here and do the fire thing again and again. With all the fish we needed for today's menu, it was time for a break.

I stripped down and slid into the water. I knew it wasn't deep here and it would feel good to get the smoke and dirt off. I kept an eye on the boys to see their reaction and they couldn't get their duds off fast enough. I had no idea what grandma would have thought about it but us boys were having some fun. I caught Bakta first and scrubbed some sand in his hair then ducked him under to wash it off. It took a couple of tries to get the grease and bugs out but he gave every indication that it felt better. I then did my own while Casta watched. He seemed a little reluctant to try it. Bakta and I worked with him a little to convince him it was safe and didn't hurt any. We finally got him cleaned up and got our stuff together and headed back to camp. I felt that if I was able to get the two of them to feel comfortable around me then they might just tell me what had happened to them. We made a good start with this little swimming lesson and there would be more opportunities in the next couple days.

We handed our fish over to the chief cook and bottle washer when we got there. We then headed back to the logjam to get more firewood for the next day's fires. This time the boys seemed a little more interested in digging into the pile and I gave them some room to work. I had to keep an eye out for the loose logs as I didn't want them to get hurt if the pile collapsed. They were both pulling on a good sized log when something rolled out and landed at their feet. They jumped back and stopped and looked over at me. I couldn't see what it was but thought I better go look as they seemed upset at what had happened.

It turned out to be a human skull and I wondered how the boys would have known enough to be frightened by it. I thought that they would have been more curious than anything else. I would have been at their ages. I use to play in a cemetery as a kid. The people there never tried to stop me from having fun. At that time I didn't believe in ghosts. Now I'm not so sure. Anyway, I set the head aside and looked to see if the rest of the bones were in the pile or not. They were, and it was going to take a little time to get them out. The boys were still nervous but wanting to see what I would do. I dug out the bones a little at a time as I had to move lots of flotsam to get at them. I stuck all the parts in one location and knew that some would be missing. Some of them were broken and only a few were connected to the next one in line. "The head bone, connected to the back bone, the back bone connected to the hip bone". I didn't remember the lyrics or even the way each bone was connected. It hadn't been one of my favorite songs anyway. I had been more into John Denver songs. "Take me home, Country Roads" was a big hit and I could feel that way myself some days.

In this case I thought we should collect the pieces and maybe create a pyre for the deceased. I would have to ask Mary if that was something her tribe would have done. I never mentioned those back at the sandbar site as it seemed too gruesome at the time. I sent the boys back to camp with the wood they already pulled out. I would take care of the skeleton before

[219]

going back myself. I was reaching for what I thought was a leg bone when something flashed off the sunlight at me. "Not again" I thought. Could there be more?

I picked the amulet out of the pile where it had been hiding and took a look at it. It was almost identical to the one I had except for color. The Hhaley talisman was golden in color and the new one was more of a blue tone. Neither one of them was solid but more translucent when you held them up close. I immediately caught the fact that no one was there but me so I wasn't suppose to show this to anyone yet. I didn't just know that on my own, but I knew it anyway. How could these things be finding me? Now who was the Shaman that this talisman belonged to? Were they inter-connected? I should get Mary aside and see what she thought was going on. She might not know as she was not related to the Shaman, Hhaley, but only knew of him in her tribe. I would need more information if I was going to figure out some answers here.

I sat down behind the logjam, out of site of the camp, and held one talisman in each hand. The one from Hhaley was in the right hand and the new blue one in the other. Then the bones that were still in the log pile worked their way out and joined the ones I had already stacked up. A vision of the pyre that was needed passed in front of my eyes with sharp instructions to keep all the bones away from Lista. What did this thing know about Lista?

I got up to look at the bones and felt the need to put the new talisman away, so I slipped it into my stone bag. Just then Bakta came around the logjam with a wolf skin and handed it to me. He asked if this was what I wanted. I indicated to him that it was and took it from him. I would wrap the bones in it and tomorrow morning I would set a pyre for both the bones and the wolf skin. I gave Bakta some more wood to haul back and went about the task of picking up the bones and putting them inside the wolf hide. I aligned them as close as possible but knew that when I wrapped the hide together they would go where they would.

I set the bundle aside and pulled more wood out of the pile. I carried as much as I could back to the camp and checked to see if any food had been served to the boys. I thought they could haul a load to two more of wood so we would have enough for two days. That might be all the time we would be here. Right now I just had no idea what the extra talisman expected me to do. Then I wondered why I would even think that this amulet would expect something. Could I be reading too much into this? I decided not to tell Mary about the talisman or the bones till later. I had never been good at keeping secrets and this time I would just hold off. Maybe things will work out to where I don't feel any worse than not telling Mary about my past life. I don't know if telling her is good for her as she will have to keep it quiet also. I just went out to get some more wood and let it go at that.

I went back to the logjam and retrieved the wolf hide with the bones in it and set it aside for the next day. I told Mary about the bones and asked if she thought a pyre would be expected under these circumstances. She wasn't sure either but said that it seemed like the right thing to do. Before we went to sleep, I put a call in to Bob for his assistance. I didn't want Lista to get near the wolf skin and would he please let me know if she tried to. I got a buzz back from him that I took for a yes.

It wasn't long after we went to sleep that the alarm in my head went off. I rolled over just enough to see someone darting back out of sight. I thought she moved pretty quickly for an old lady. Then I got the feeling that it wasn't Lista at all but one of the boys. I had to think back to the earlier events of the evening and it seemed as if Casta had been hanging around Lista. Did the boy tell her about the head falling out of the wood pile? He might still be having problems separating his feeling from her. She may have been the only adult he knew. Now I would have to be more careful around him and maybe Bakta also.

I must have scared them both enough that nothing else happened to wake me up. I would have to let Bob or Fred or both of them know that I appreciated the help. I was up and going at first light and soon had the pyre wood all stacked up and ready to go. I wanted to make it a ceremony that would impress Lista and make everyone else think about the reason we were doing this.

[221]

I lifted the wolf hide with the bones inside and carried it very carefully to the pyre. I placed the whole thing on top of the wood and watched as it fell open and the bones seemed to take their proper place. I wasn't sure of what to say and thought of all those movies I had seen, where the faithful departed were eulogized and sent on their way. I thought that these people would have worshiped the Sun, Moon and the Stars and so I wished to send this person to the heavens to be a star among his ancestors.

"Oh, most reverent Sun, today we ask your assistance in carrying this most honored among us into the realm of his ancestors. We wish that you would make of him a star to guide us by as we say farewell to his earthly remains". With that we lit the wood on fire. To the surprise of all of us, including me, the flame engulfed the entire pyre and sent up a great cloud of smoke that appeared in the form of a man. The smoke did not go straight up but instead went towards the sun and even blotted it out for a couple minutes. It created a huge shadow over the land before it dissipated.

I had Mary get me some dried fish and the moose bladder to hold water. Then, after filling the bladder, I motioned for the boys to go with me. I took them back to the wood pile and had them look for long sticks that were still flexible. I went looking for shorter straight sticks that were fairly stiff. The bow that Mary made for me was way too big for these tykes and I thought we should work together on making something they could use.

I had brought some sinew for bow string but kept it out of sight for now. I was sure they had no idea what we were doing and I could see that Casta was more afraid of me than usual. He tried to keep his brother between us. That's when I notice his arm was scratched and I knew it wasn't yesterday. I wasn't going to ask him about it now but maybe later he would want to say something. If all went well, we could match war wounds when he got older. Just the thought made my old scars itch. I hoped he wouldn't grow up with mental scars and that he would learn what true loyalty meant. I had no idea how to help Lista get over her mental problems. I had a growing anxiety about what she might do next.

The boys had gathered about a dozen or so sticks and I had found almost as many of the size I was looking for. I checked all of theirs for flex and discarded several that snapped while keeping the ones that sprung back into shape. I picked through the pile of longer ones for one that would suit me for length. I then shortened two of them for what I thought would be better for each of the boys. The one for Bakta was almost a foot longer than the one for Casta.

I then had the boys sit down and I sat across from them. I handed each a flint shard and got one out for myself. I showed them how to clean the bark and smooth the surface of our sticks. Each of the sticks would have a grain that would allow it to bend in one direction without breaking. I was able to show the boys how that would work, but for me it was still an experiment and learning process. Both of the boys worked very slowly as if afraid to do something wrong. I then bent my stick the wrong way and it broke in the middle. I just tossed it aside and got another one to work with and acted as if it was a normal sort of thing that happens every day. The boys seemed to relax a little after that and the pace of work picked up.

When the sticks were clean and ready to go, I started to notch the ends of mine to hold the bowstring. When Bakta saw what I was doing he started to get excited and tried to hurry his along. I let him go, knowing that if he made a mistake it would be a lesson well learned. Well, he did have a problem with it and the end broke off as he had cut the notch too deep. He was looking awful and didn't know what to expect from me. I just pointed to the one I broke and then to the ones we hadn't used yet. He set his broken one next to mine and got a new stick to work with. He cleaned this one off in record time and was much more careful with the notches.

Casta, on the other hand, worked much slower and was more meticulous in what he was doing. He would watch me to see exactly what I did, then try to repeat it on his stick. I don't think he had guessed what the thing was going to be yet even though his brother knew.

[223]

I got the feeling that the younger boy would have been an artist in another time. His concentration on the task at hand seemed to blot out the world around him. For the first time I thought he looked at peace with himself. That should give me ideas to work with in getting him away from the influence of Lista. His ability to focus on one thing might even make him a really good hunter some day.

I set my bow stick in front of Casta so he could see what his should look like and then went to get some of the shorter straight sticks that we would convert to arrows. I set the stack of sticks in front of us and took one to get started with. I handed one to Bakta as he was done with his bow also. We used the flint shards to clean them off. We cleaned all the sticks and got them ready to work. By then Casta was finished with his bow.

I started a small fire and put the end of each potential arrow in the fire just long enough to darken the wood. I wasn't real sure if this was the way it should be done or not but we could learn from this and get more information later. I carried a sandstone over, recovered from the lake, and set it in front of us. I then took one of the short sticks that had been fire treated and started working that end by rubbing it over the stone. As it started to form a point, I would put it back in the fire for a minute or two and then rub it on the stone some more. When the pointed end was done, I took the flint and started to notch the back end to hold the bowstring. This end too, needed to be heat treated and the same process was used for all the sticks.

It wasn't until I got the sinew out to make the bow strings that the light went on for Casta. He finally got excited and wanted to hurry with that part of the construction. I wasn't sure I could master this part and let the boys try it first. Bakta seemed to have an idea of how to do the ends so Casta and I watched to see if he got it right. He made a good loop on one end but was having some trouble with the length. I helped him by holding the bow in a slightly bent fashion and letting him measure it that way. It came out close enough that it would work for now and that was all we needed. I held the other two bows for him and he made the strings. Now we were ready to test them.

[224]

I set a target up and paced back to what I thought would be about right for the shortest bow to have a chance to hit it. We only had six arrows to work with so we had to retrieve them after every second shot. They didn't fly straight but I knew they wouldn't and made sure the boys would know that as well. For now it was just the getting use to the pull of the string and the aiming. The distance we were shooting was relatively short and that gave us a better chance at accuracy. We spent the rest of the day out there making arrows and shooting them all over the place. I had brought along some dried fish and water but later in the day we needed to get in and eat a meal. I pulled some wood off the pile for our fires and had the boys help haul it into camp.

I was following the boys in with a load of wood and I could see Casta trying to get Bakta to take his bow and arrows. He didn't want Lista to see them and probably thought she would do something to him for having them. I managed to catch up to them and offered to take the bow from him. He didn't even trust me yet and was reluctant to give it up. I suggested that he carry mine and I would take his, then we could switch in camp if everything was alright. He couldn't pass up the offer as my bow was so much bigger than his. We must have looked a sight to see as we came into camp.

Mary and Ann started laughing the instant they saw us and Bakta couldn't help but join in. I pretended to be offended by the abuse they were heaping on us and it even got Casta to smile a little. Lista just seemed to be bewildered by the frivolity. She lacked any sense of humor and missed the whole point. When the girls were done with poking fun at me, I told Mary that it would be nice if the boys learned how to put feathers on the arrows we made. Surprisingly, Lista offered to help with that and I had the feeling that I was missing something there. It would be better to include her than not but did she have some ulterior motive for doing so. "Count the arrows" popped into my head and I wasn't sure where that came from but knew exactly how many we had made. I would check on it later to see if the count added up.

I was sure that Lista would know how to use a bow and arrow so took note of the fact that she was interested in the bows the boys had made. She hadn't found the opportunity to make one for herself as she had been restricted to the camp site. I had not asked her to go to the logjam for anything and she hadn't volunteered either. If she had any kind of plan going it probably was to wait for opportunity to knock. I didn't think giving her that opportunity was a good idea.

However, if she were to help out with some things, it would go a long way to accepting her into our family. As of now our tribe was too small to be more than survivalists. We were in dire need of adding to it. I knew that a group this small would be fighting a losing battle if we couldn't expand our numbers. With that in mind, I thought I would give Lista enough rope to hang herself or prove she was worth having around.

I worked with the boys for the next couple days. We went fishing, hunting, swimming and gathering fire wood, which added to our range of knowledge and companionship. The boys were now becoming more interested in what we could do together and what their limits might be. I was being very careful with them and wouldn't let them go exploring by themselves yet. The need to keep the group together was a weighty issue and the prospect of having one or both boys hurt or worse, was always on my mind. They may not have thought about it that way but the leash would have to come off one day and by then I hoped they would be ready for it. It was times like this that the things I had gone through gave me insight to how dangerous this era could be.

I thought that I may have just been run through a training period for what was happening now. The encounters with the cougar, the bear and moose were very physical things. The going hungry and thirsty, eating live things and learning to catch my own food were more mental. Those contributed to the overall survival traits that would be necessary for anyone here in this time period. I must have passed the test, if that was what it was, in order to be of use to the boys and Mary and Ann. I wasn't going to pat myself on the back now as we probably still had a long way to go. I thought about the things I could teach the boys but one of them wasn't

[226]

stealth. They may have learned it from having to deal with Lista on a daily basis. Now the trick was to keep them away from her as much as possible.

The next few days went by quickly and it was time to move on before we knew it. No one had seen smoke from anywhere except our own and now we would try somewhere else. The weather had been extremely calm and pretty hot for fall. We needed to take advantage of it being that way. We planned on seeing if we could reach the lowest part of the lake before setting up another camp. This thing must eventually feed into an ocean or sea of some kind. We could see that the water was continually moving so it had to exit somewhere. We spent the better part of the day loading the indispensable items and some others. The only things left on shore were the sleeping hides and some precautionary tools and weapons. We wouldn't bother with a smoke fire but just a small one to heat a warm broth before we leave.

Everything was quiet in the morning as we got underway. I made no plans to stop for a couple days unless we saw something different than before. I showed the boys how to steer the raft with the tiller and to make it move a little faster by pushing it back and forth. They were a little too short to actually do any of that as I had built it for my height. To get the tiller handle down to where they could reach it would lift the tillers paddle out of the water. I had to do that to show them how it worked and to let them see the paddle end.

I talked to the boys as we went along, trying to keep them occupied during the most boring part of the trip. I asked if they could see things on shore as we passed by and to identify each of them. That didn't turn out to be much fun as mostly we saw birds and most of them were geese and ducks. Even the bird population was thinning out as they had continued their journey south.

This was a big stop over location for the geese and some ducks. I thought we would see other species here but only a handful of different birds came and went. I think that there just wasn't enough swamp type areas on the lake to attract more wildlife. To keep the conversation going, I talked about my time in the valley, especially the part where I went without food and water. When I mentioned that I had to eat grasshoppers, both the boys chimed in saying they had eaten some also.

It was the third day out that we saw what looked like some hills and maybe trees off in the distance. The color of the area we could see was dark and reminded me again of the Black Hills in South Dakota. The distance was real hard to judge but I guessed it to be about a week's walk to get there. It looked like we would need another day or so to get about as close as the lake would take us. I started to make plans to camp when we found an appropriate location. We started to gather the items we would need on shore so that it wouldn't take as long when we did stop. We made sure the boys got their gear bundled up and Mary took care of getting Ann's things ready. We were running close to shore as we looked for some place to set up shop.

It was starting to get dark and we were getting ready to settle down for the night. Everyone was moving around to get their best sleeping areas and covers. It was getting colder on the water and we were looking forward to finding a camp site on land. Then the whole thing came unglued as Bakta went in the water. He either got bumped or pushed but at the time I just assumed that it was an accident and dropped the anchor and dove in after him. I knew he could swim but not sure what might happen if he was left on his own. In the confusion, my head almost split from the reaction of the guard dogs. Fred and Bob were both letting me know that the sky was falling and I needed to get back now. It had to wait as I was making sure that Bakta and I could get to shore or back to the raft. We were being pushed downstream and the raft had stopped.

I guided Bakta to shore and hollered to Mary that we were getting out of the water. I started to get up and something pushed me back down just as an arrow sailed over my head. I had no weapons with me to defend the two of us but knew the dark might give us some cover. I picked up Bakta and sprinted downstream and out into the prairie. I then "hit the dirt" and Bakta and I stayed down for some time. I waited to hear from Fred if it was clear or not. The shrill noise in the back of my head gradually faded but never stopped. It was at that point that I knew we had a big problem on our hands and we raced back to the area the raft had stopped at.

The current had pushed the raft against the bank and allowed Lista to get off without getting in the water. I saw that Mary was down and Ann was trying to help her. Fred was still on the raft but Bob had gotten off. Mary had an arrow through her left side but it looked like it might have missed any vital organs. I was sure it was meant to slow me down and maybe keep me from following Lista and Casta. She had taken the boy and both their bundles of items. I went to Mary and told her to lay still and I would see if I could do anything about the arrow. She said it had to come out and to break off the feathered end and pull it through. I worked as fast as I could to do exactly as she said and she almost passed out from the pain. I had given her the feathered end of the arrow to bite on as I pulled the rest of it out in one quick jerk.

The good news was that the arrow didn't have a flint head on it and the side damage was minimal. The bad news was the same as always, no first aid kit. We would have to wait till morning just to get something for a compress to put on the wound. Bakta wanted to go after his brother and I had to stop him from leaving. I asked Bob if he could track the two of them and let us know where they were going. I got a quick buzz back and he was off like a shot. I wrapped the four of us up in skins in order to keep warm and made sure Mary didn't go into shock. Fred stood guard all night and tried to keep track of where Bob had gone.

In the morning I moved the raft down to where Bakta and I got out of the water. It wasn't the best site for a camp but would do in a pinch. I got some reeds and moss from the lake edge and made a compress and wrapped Mary's side with it. She had done better than I could have expected and was trying to get around on her own.

I set up the camp as best I could and gathered some fire wood along with what we had carried on the raft. I got a fire going and made a fish and leek soup for Mary to eat. She kept trying to tell me to go find Casta and I kept telling her that they wouldn't get all that far away. To keep Bakta busy, I had him gathering fire wood and combing the lake shore for anything that

[229]

we could use. I had him take his bow and arrows and see about getting something to eat. A goose or two would be helpful and he was willing to do that.

We checked Mary's wound twice a day for those first two days and didn't find any infection or pus. I checked the supplies and noticed one thing that was going to make a difference. Lista, in her hurry to leave, had failed to take any water with her. That would mean that she would have to come back to the lake or get very thirsty. You can go without food for sometime but water was indispensable. Without water your chances of survival fall for every day you go without. I had some firsthand experience with that. I was sure she had enough experience herself of surviving in the open or she wouldn't have evaded the hunters looking for her and the boys.

She didn't know that I had a distinct advantage of one wild cat being on her tail. I thought that Casta might want his brother to find him and may just leave a few signs along the way. The next thing to think about was that Lista wanted that talisman very badly and might just plan an ambush instead of running just to get away.

It was the third morning after Mary got shot that it occurred to me that I had something she needed badly and should have remembered it sooner. I had set my bag of stones in with the supplies Bakta and I would be taking. That's where I had put the blue talisman and didn't let anyone know about it. That may have been a good thing as Lista could have easily taken the bag with the other supplies. I fished it out of the bag and tied it around Mary's neck.

She was shocked at the thought and started to take it off. I told her it was for her protection and she had to wear it until there was no more danger. I also told her to not take anything for granted and to look for any sign of trouble. If she listens to the talisman and Fred they will give her all the information she needs. Bakta had brought in five geese over the last two days and caught some fish. Mary would have fresh food for a couple days and I thought we shouldn't be gone for more than a week. I again warned her that Lista didn't take any water so she may have to come back to the lake.

[230]

Bakta and I started out while it was still early and headed straight onto the prairie. Lista would have gone out a ways before looking for alternatives and may have even realized that she forgot the water. I didn't forget it and made sure to carry some extra food also. This time I had my good bow and arrows with the flint tips. I knew if all else failed I would have to insure Lista didn't get a chance to harm anyone. We had come to believe she wasn't totally stable but now I kind of thought "she fell off her rocker". For some people it doesn't take much to "lose it" but I had no idea what caused her to crack. I would have to make sure the end results were in my favor.

Bakta was just interested in getting Casta back unharmed and I would do everything I could to that end. We traveled fast and hard all day long and I knew that Bakta was getting very tired as night fell. We ate and drank while moving and finally stopped after it got too dark to see where to put our feet. I had been getting some indications from Bob that we were headed in the right direction.

When we shut down for the night so did he, I think just to let us sleep. He would be better at night than we were and had me up early to get going. I was sure he had not been detected and that Lista had gone straight out from the lake. She wasn't going to make it to the forested hills in the distance without water. She would have to make a choice of going back or waiting for me to catch up. I think she chose the latter of the two as Bob seemed to indicate that he was holding his position.

The prairie was pretty open and you could see a long way. We had been traveling all morning and as the sun reached its' zenith, we could see some kind of growth out ahead of us. It would be dark before we could reach it and if anyone was there we wouldn't be able to see them. I thought it would be a good place for an ambush. I got most of that feeling from Bob as he must have gotten in behind it and discovered what was planned.

We stopped before it got dark and far enough away that we felt safe for the night. I got Bakta to rest and he fell asleep while sitting up. I put him down and covered him to keep him warm. I built a small fire with the shrubs that were there and some wood that I had brought along. Unless we found some wood along the way, it was the only fire we would be able to make but I hoped it would serve its' purpose. The stuff that was growing out there was just some low brush or bushes but they were up on a knoll. This gave the high ground to anyone that occupied it. The bushes would give enough cover to hide someone in. I made every effort to get some sleep while using the fire as a back light. I knew that if Lista was on that knoll, she wouldn't leave it to sneak out and attack me. She would find the risk was too high and that by waiting she would get me in the open.

I was awake before dawn but continued to rest and let Bakta sleep till it got light enough to see. I got him up and moving around so that Lista could see that we both were still here. I checked in with Bob and he acknowledged me with a light buzz. When we got ready to move in on the knoll, I had Bakta go to one side and I went to the other. I was sure that Lista would ignore Bakta and concentrate on me. That way Bakta could get close enough to see if his brother was alright and maybe even talk him into leaving.

Casta was the real unknown here as he still seemed to have some attachment to Lista. I continued around the side and toward the back of the knoll, forcing Lista to move her position. I made sure to stay out of the range of any arrow. I kept moving slowly along a path that would eventually circle the knoll as I was trying to give Bakta enough time to get in close and find his brother. I knew that they had been able to fool her before while collecting items she didn't know about. It had not been possible on the raft with the lack of personal space.

I had intentionally taken the route to the west as the sun was coming up. I knew that she would see me very well but might not see Bakta. I just needed to know when the boys would be safe as I kept moving at a very deliberate pace. The size of the knoll worked in my favor as it was not possible for Lista to watch the boys and me at the same time. She probably didn't think she needed to worry about them and just had to wait for her shot at me.

When I had attained the far side of the knoll I received a buzz from Bob that indicated something had happened. I held the talisman up and tried to visualize the event. In my mind's eye the two boys were running away. I moved in a little to keep Lista busy and give the boys a little more time. I then resumed the transit of the knoll till I had the morning sun at my back and in her eyes.

It was at this point that she realized what I had done and ran to the side the boys had left from. I was too far away to get a shot at her as she aimed the bow to shoot at Bakta. Before I could close the gap and before she could fire her arrow, a tan and white creature hit her from behind and knocked her down. Bob had attacked her with everything he had and was going to leave some claw marks on a lot of her. I suggested that it was time to go and for him to make a run for it with the boys. I would follow them in and Lista could fend for herself. I thought that leaving her to work out her own survival might be the ultimate insult. She had a bow and some arrows, food and hides and whatever else she had stolen. We would be able to live without those items but I wasn't sure she could live with them. I didn't think we would see her again as I intended to cross the lake.

I caught up to the boys and immediately grabbed Casta and gave him a big hug then hoisted him up on my shoulders and we headed back to the lake. Bob seemed to be exceptionally proud of the job he had done and I remembered to thank him for it. The boys didn't know what had happened to Lista and didn't bother to ask. I would only explain if they felt a need to know. For right now they seemed to be as happy as I had seen them and being together was all they really wanted.

I would try to make it possible from now on as I hoped to put the lake between us and Lista. She would have to wait for the lake to freeze over to cross if she lasted that long. I guess I shouldn't question her survival skill or will power as she had managed it before. I had no idea how she evaded the tribal hunters for as long as she did but under the conditions of this latest one, she failed to recognize all the facts and made some bad judgments. I didn't think that she lost any of the ability to think things out but that the need for haste may have colored her decisions. Her interest in the talisman may have caused her to think of the ambush and she probably knew I would come looking for Casta.

The trip back to the raft took two days but they were a happy two days for the boys. The thought of being separated had been hard on both of them. I let the boys walk together most of the second day. I knew we would be back before dark and they were having so much fun just being boys. It wasn't until we got back that Casta realized that he had lost his most prized possessions, his bow and arrows and other collectables. Lista had taken his bundle of items with hers when she took him off the raft. He would never forgive her for doing that. I didn't tell him that she was going to shot his brother with one of his arrows. Something's are better left unsaid.

Mary was much improved since we left to find Lista and Casta. She was feeling almost as good as new. The compresses had done the work of preventing infection. She listened to the whole story as the three of us tried to fill her in on what had happened. She was glad that I didn't have to kill Lista and that she probably would find her way somewhere. It just wasn't going to be with us. I did notice that Mary continued to wear the talisman I had given her and she never once mentioned it. I had no idea if she thought it had helped her or not. I would wait to pose that question.

Later that night I told her about going to the other side of the lake. We seemed to be in the middle of an "Indian Summer" and the weather would be changing soon. I wanted to be across before then as a raft on rough water only works in the movies. Mary would look at me sometimes for my strange remarks as if I was from another planet and of course I just might be.

In the morning we traveled downstream for a while and didn't see anything that would make me change my mind. I then shifted the direction toward the far bank and started pushing the tiller back and forth. The current would take us downstream and the paddling would take us across so the angle was always forty –five degrees or so. It didn't matter much as we had a long way to go and would have an interest at seeing the lower end of the lake. I didn't want to be close to the end when we started as there was no way to tell how the water left the lake. I wasn't interested in going over a waterfall or even down some rapids.

[234]

The kids hadn't slept much over the last several days and now found an opportunity to do so. I thought that was just as well when Mary came back to point out the lone figure on the receding shore line. Lista had cut across to get head of us for another try. I'm not sure if she even thought about the possibility that we might not stay on that side of the lake. I then began to wonder if she would find a way across further downstream.

I continued to push the tiller back and forth and watched the far side become the near side as we moved in that direction. I still couldn't see the low end of the lake and wondered just how big this thing was. I guess it would have been called Long Lake on a MapQuest site. This side of the lake looked a lot like the other side as the prairie stretched out from the shore.

I was looking for a place to camp overnight as we approached the shore line. I found a sandy beach and guided the raft in. We would spend the night here and in the morning continue on down the lake. We no longer had any wood to burn so would have to wait to start any more signal fires. Mary and I sat up and talked late into the night and wondered how Casta would handle the loss of his items.

Bakta had offered some of his but it looked like that wasn't going to work out. I might have to give Casta the opportunity to rebuild his collection. The boys could wander around the shore line at every place we stop. Maybe they will find something they can value there. We couldn't even make a bow and arrows for him until we find some wood. We will check the next logjam for anything we can use.

Chapter eleven

The Contact

It was the second day on the south side of the lake that we started to see signs of flotsam along the banks. There was nothing big or even enough wood to start a decent fire but you could tell that things were changing. That evening we found a sandbar to anchor off and the boys went scouting for anything that would enhance their stay here.

Without any wood for a fire we would be leaving in the morning but could wait long enough for the boys to feel like they had checked everywhere. They didn't find anything but Mary brought some plants on board that she would add to our food menu. The next day, as we floated downstream, I had the boys looking for anything along the bank that might be of interest. That's when the first pieces of wood started to show up and we had hopes of a warm meal later in the day. That turned out to be more than true as we came across a small bay area with a log pile big enough to handle our needs for a day or two.

I had the boys try netting some fish as soon as I grounded the raft. I got the wood together for a fire and Mary prepared the fish as soon as the boys caught them. Ann and her body guards went for a walk around the bay just to do some scouting on her own. She was starting to get really independent and Mary and I had to keep an eye out for her. Fred and Bob would always let us know if she was headed for trouble. It was too late in the day to start a smoke fire for signaling but I put enough wood together for one in the morning.

The next morning was the first signs of winter coming. There was a mist rising off the lake and a fog hanging over everything. It did clear later in the morning and we started our signal fire. We would do that again the next day and then head downstream on the morning of the third day. With no responding signal, there wasn't any reason to hang around. We needed to get to the end of the lake before winter set in. I was hoping for a good campsite near there. We could wait out the winter there and check to see if the hunters had hung around this area. If no one showed up then we would have a decision to make in the spring.

We headed downstream again after not getting a response from our signal. We only had the one day of fog and now it was clear again. The current in the river was now changing and we could feel the speed picking up. The lake was narrowing at this point and though we couldn't see the end of the lake, we began to hear it.

Gradually we could see the mist rising from the water fall. It was hiding the lakes end but now we knew it was there. I didn't want to get too close to it so we started to look for a place to go ashore. We came across the mouth of a small inlet with a sandbar and I grounded the raft there.

Then for the first time since getting on the river we discovered a stream flowing into the inlet from the prairie. It was a small stream but that could have been because it was the end of the summer. The runoff in the spring may have accounted for the lack of fire wood at this location. Although there was very little fire wood here, some was strewn along the bank of the river.

I thought that there would be much more at the bottom of the waterfall. I would go and check later but for now the boys and I retrieved what we could to get by for the night. While out, we ran into a small flock of geese and bagged two of them. They would make a fine complement to our fish dinner. It seems the boys still preferred something other than fish. I guess I could include Fred and Bob with the boys for the cooked goose meal, although those two could eat just about anything.

We settled down for the night and after the kids had fallen asleep, I asked Mary about the talisman I gave her. She said she wanted to keep it for now and I didn't have any problem with that. However, I did ask her why and she told me that it talked to her. I said "I know the feeling". She went on to say that it would let her know when to give it away but for now it felt safe where it was. I couldn't argue with that and hoped it always was safe there. I went to sleep thinking that I didn't always make the choices but that they were often made for me. That night the dream came back and

[237]

again it was different. It seemed to skip forward to the boy being led away by the Shaman and this time I saw the boy's face and he looked like me. Then as he turned away I saw the talisman hanging around his neck. It was not the same as mine or Mary's. It was a rose color not red or pink but somewhere in between. How many of them are there? The boy then walked through a tunnel of some sort to the other side into daylight. What could it possibly mean? I woke with my hand clenched on the talisman.

I took the boys down the river to see if we could find enough wood to make a signal fire. It seemed as if I never had to worry about them falling in the water or even getting close to it. Lista must have browbeaten them quite a bit to have them not be more curious. They were starting to get that way but Ann would be running circles around them to see what could possibly happen. When we got close to the waterfall we could see a backwash whirlpool that had created a good sized logjam with lots of flotsam. We pulled out enough wood to make a couple smoke fires and still have some for cooking. I sent the boys on ahead with what they could manage and looked real hard at the flotsam to see if the third talisman was here somewhere. I didn't find it and thought maybe I was just dreaming.

Before returning with the pile of wood I took a closer look at the bottom of the falls. It wasn't like the one we saw months ago on the upper part of the river. These falls were steep and if there was a way to get down to the bottom of it, then it would be further down the river. The water had cut the rock back and didn't leave anything like a path or trail down on this side. The gap in the rock canyon looked to be almost twice as wide as the river. I just couldn't imagine how the salmon had managed to get up the river past this waterfall. Even the strongest salmon couldn't swim up these falls. With all that had gone on I was beginning to believe in magic. I took the wood back to camp and pondered the impossible.

We spent the next couple days surveying the area and sending smoke signals. We didn't see any return on those and began to make plans to survey down the river a little way. I wanted to take Bakta and enough supplies for a week. We would look for signs that some tribe or people had been here. I was interested in seeing if there was a way down to the river bed. I was wondering if I missed something about the salmon run. There wasn't some kind of fish ladder that they used or something like that. The only other explanation was that the last flood had created the new waterfall drop and now the fish would stop here. I was intent on finding out as we headed out in the morning.

Casta wanted to go with us but I told him that someone had to stay and protect the girls. I then gave him my shortest spear to work with. I made him promise to take good care of them while I was gone. We had to put on a stern face to keep from laughing as the spear was bigger that he was. He was quite proud to hold that spear and make that promise. Mary gave me a big hug and told me to hurry back with good news. I told her that if there was any good news out there I would find it.

The land started to fall away just as soon as we got past the waterfall. By the middle of the second day it had leveled out again but now we were much closer to the river. A trail cut across our path going directly to the river. I had Bakta look at the foot prints to see if he knew what was using the trail. He had no idea and was afraid to say so but I took my finger and traced around one of the hoof prints. "This looks like the kind of foot that a deer has, so maybe it is deer that are going to the river to drink". "If the print was bigger it might be an elk". He traced another with his finger and looked at me and said "deer".

I took it as progress and we decided to follow the deer to the river. I then wondered if he had ever seen a deer or elk and if he did would he know what it was. I thought back to when I found the boys and wondered how long they had been with Lista. Casta may have been a baby as he didn't seem to know that other people could be nice to him. It was nice to see that they were making progress in a social sense. I hoped they were bright enough to understand more about Mother Nature. She can be a stinker if you're not paying attention.

We followed the deer tracks down to the river and on what turned out to be a nice easy path. The bank had given way at this point and had left a gentle slope down to an open area that some farmer would have loved to plow. The deer were munching on grass and watching us as we approached. They didn't seem much more than a little nervous and just moved away from us as we got closer. Some of them moved upstream and others went the opposite direction. We were intent on going to the falls so the deer that went that way had to keep going or circle back. There was enough room for them to do either and several kept on going while the rest of them went around us and back with the herd. I wasn't interested in them right now, so let them do as they please and we went on up the river.

That night we camped next to the river and built a small fire to keep warm. It was colder down here by the water and the warmth from the fire felt good. The next morning we found our way blocked by a large logjam with no way around it. I looked it over for a while and decided that the upper part of the pile would be the easiest location to break through. We started pulling logs and debris off and kept at it for most of the day. It took some time to get a small enough opening so that Bakta could get through to the other side. With him working on one side and me on the other the opening grew a lot faster.

I was anxious to see the falls from the bottom but we stopped to eat something first. I went back for our gear after eating and handed Bakta his pack. I had just picked up mine and started back through the opening when alarms started going off in my head. I brought my pack up in front of me just as an arrow impacted it. The arrow came partway through the pack I had and I could see it didn't have a flint on the end. I knew exactly who had shot it but from where? I had my bow and arrows with me but I was in the middle of the logjam and unable to get them to a position to use them. With Bakta on that side of the pile I charged through in hopes of getting the time to arm myself.

She wasn't going to give me the time and Bob hadn't gotten down here yet from his perch high on the prairie. Lista had already set an arrow in the bow and was letting it fly as I dove through the opening. I was pulling my bow and arrows away from the pack. This arrow missed by "that much" and I thought "an inch, like a mile". I heard Bakta screaming and could see that Lista was setting another arrow before I could get up. Just as she released the arrow Bakta slammed into her and knocked her backwards.

[240]

This arrow went high and now everything went into slow motion. Bakta had taken Lista straight back into the water and both of them disappeared for a couple seconds.

I hit the water with the most athletic dive I could make and splashed to the surface yards away from the pair as the water was taking them downstream in a hurry. I could see that Lista was fighting to stay afloat and in the process kept pushing Bakta under. I swam as hard as I could, trying to catch up but they disappeared around the logjam and I lost sight of them. When I cleared the logjam I saw Lista being dragged downstream by the current but Bakta was nowhere in sight. I followed Lista, looking for Bakta and the buzzing in my head kept getting louder. I felt like I was going the wrong way.

Something started pushing me toward shore and I realized that I had to go there and helped by swimming in that direction. I looked back to see where Lista was and she couldn't get out of the current. She was being swept downstream in the middle of the river. I exited the water and ran up toward the logjam and then could see that Bakta had grabbed hold of one of the logs that stuck out in the river. He was tired and having trouble hanging on as I dove in to try to reach him. I fought the current and managed to get close enough that I told him to let go and come to me. I think he finally trusted me completely and did what I told him to do. I caught him as he floated by and we worked our way to the shore. I dragged him out of the water and we sat down in the grass next to Bob.

I said "naughty kitten you lost your mitten now you shall have no dinner" "just kidding". Both Bob and Bakta looked at me like I might be a little touched in the head. I did wish I could spit out all the water I swallowed, I know how to swim but I'm not that good at it. On top of that this body has a tendency to sink in most waters.

I lay back on the grass and pulled Bakta to my side and thanked him for saving my life. He returned the favor and thanked me. He then asked about Lista and I told her she had gone downstream and probably would be fine. She was a survivor and I was sure she would get out of the river further down. I was tired but had to have an answer now and got up to go

[241]

look. I told Bakta to stay with Bob and I would be back in a short while. I went through the gap in the logjam and first checked to see the place that Lista had been standing while shooting at me. There on the ground were the things she had taken along with Casta's stuff. The short bow was off to one side where it landed after Bakta slammed into her. The big question was how did she get to this side of the river? I was sure she thought more highly of herself than I did but I was sure she couldn't fly.

I put my limited tracking skills to work as I located her foot prints in the sandy beach. I followed them back to where the water from the falls had erased them. "She came out of the falls". She didn't seem to be all that wet when I saw her at first so she didn't come by water. I stopped where I was and went back for Bakta and Bob, they would have to see this. I told Bakta that all our supplies were safe except for the arrow in my pack and that Casta's things where there also. He showed some real joy for his brother. I told him we needed to get back over there and get our stuff up higher on the bank and then we could start planning to camp for a day or two. The two of them followed me through the gap and over to the other side. We picked our stuff up, along with Casta's and moved them higher on the bank. I then took the two of them over to the waterfall and showed them how Lista got to our side of the river.

Under the falls was a gap as the falls poured past an overhang. It left a trail or path from one side to the other and also had what looked like a fish ladder. The ladder didn't look like it was entirely natural but not manmade either. If the path and ladder had been carved by someone it had to have been a really long time ago. I thought that the local tribes would have known about it and used it a lot. I then wondered if Lista was familiar with the path as she seemed to have gotten there rather fast.

Bakta and I walked under the falls and out the other side. Bob was reluctant to get that close to the water and stayed behind. We were now on the north side of the river and after looking around for a while I found the steps half hidden against the far wall. I cautioned Bakta to watch where he put his feet as the spray from the falls had coated the steps and made them slick. The steps and the fish ladder came out at the same location and were well hidden from view. If you didn't know about them, they would be easy to miss. It now appeared as if the whole thing was a manmade creation and a well designed one at that. However, time and water had taken their toll by eroding parts of it away. I looked across to the other side to see if there had been a staircase on that side also. I could see a vague outline of one but most of it was gone.

We got some wood together and built a fire. I pulled up some green grasses and tossed them over the flames. This created a smoking column that started to rise but the breeze caused it to dissipate before getting high enough to signal anyone. Even Mary wouldn't be able to see it from where she was. I let it go at that and put the fire out. We needed to get back and tell her about it and what had happened to Lista. It was going to be a two day hike and we needed to carry as much wood as possible. We spent the last few hours of the day getting wood into bundles and tying them with the vines that were tangled in the logjam. I got a fire started to warm us up before going to sleep. The arrow had pierced one of the water bags I had in my pack and most of my things were wet. I sat up trying to dry them out before turning in for the night. Bob had done what I thought would be impossible, he waited for Bakta to go to sleep then curled up next to him. I almost laughed at the thought that it wasn't a "two dog night but a one cat instead". They would share body heat in an effort to stay warm.

I was about to call it a night with one last walk around to see that all was well. Something caught my eye as I walked past the logjam. There was a pink glow coming from deep in the pile and seemed to dim and grow bright again. I grabbed my talisman and held it out toward the logjam and the glow got stronger and darker in color. The flotsam just seemed to move out of the way as I walked into the stack. There was the third talisman, just waiting for me. I picked it off the branch that it was hanging on and backtracked out of the pile of logs. The logjam returned to its' original state and I felt completely fatigued. I needed to go to sleep now. Almost like in a trance, I joined the other two and fell into a deep sleep.

I had more of the dream again but still much more was involved in this one. I saw a team of workers chipping away at the rocks under the falls.

There were three Shaman giving orders to the men. One of the Shamans was up on the top of each river bank, and the third one was down at the bottom. Each wore one of the talismans that I had found. The gold one was on the south side, the blue one was on the north side and the rose one was down below the falls. The workers were creating the fish ladders and the stairways. They were working furiously to get the ladders done before the fish came up the river. While I watched, the workers moved aside and two fish swam up the ladders, one to the north and one to the south. Then there was great jubilation as everyone celebrated the arrival of the two fish.

The scene opened up before me in a panorama with the waterfall in the middle. It was vastly different then as the picture showed a great forest of trees and green vegetation. With the job done on the river, the three Shaman lead the workers away to the east. They were walking in single file and creating a path that I could see very clearly. I knew that they were headed home. The path would lead to the hot springs and from there to the big green valley.

In the morning I put the new talisman in the rock bag like I had the one before and didn't mention it to Bakta. We gathered our stuff and bundles of wood and headed back to camp. I was interested in hearing what Mary thought of the Rose Talisman or if she had any ideas on what to do with it. When we passed the deer herd I thought about shooting one of them but with the large load of wood I wouldn't be able to carry it. I decided to come back for the deer later. It turned into a long two day hike with the bundles of wood. I kept thinking that there should be a better way to do this.

Bakta was struggling with his load, especially during the uphill part of the trip and I helped him out as much as possible. He accepted the help even though he never asked for it. Bob made no effort to help but watched those curious humans working so hard. He did mind the store as far as his job was anyway. When we got closer that last day, Ann, Fred and Casta came out to meet us and Casta was thrilled to find out we had his pack and other stuff with us. He didn't ask about Lista, even though he knew she was the one that had it. We were too late to set a signal fire but I put some wood together for a morning one.

That night I told Mary about the dream and how I found the Rose Talisman. I wondered what she thought of it and if I should give it to Ann or not. She wasn't sure so I told her I would sleep on it and see if the Shaman would give me another dream. Maybe they had a plan for it and would let me know. I never believed in this sort of thing before but none of it made any sense in the world that I came from. Now it almost seemed like it made too much sense. I went to sleep while holding two of the amulets in my hands. I expected to dream again and I sort of got my wish.

The dream came slowly at first and gradually got more intense. It was more of a history lesson than an answer to my request. The Gold Talisman held the most power and was to be in the possession of the strongest Shaman. The Blue Talisman was the second strongest, with the Rose Talisman having the least strength. This would be reflected in the abilities of the Shaman that held them. Over time, the Shaman of each talisman became jealous of the others and moved to separate themselves from them. The talisman would be transferred to a new and younger Shaman as the power faded with the separation. The further they got from one another the less helpful they were to the current holder. In the end, the last holders were forced to see the error of this situation and were doomed by it. They would lose the use of any power held by the amulets. With that the dream ended as the little boy that started the dreams walked back through the tunnel and disappeared.

I woke with a start as the dream ended. It was still dark and sometime in the middle of the night. I wanted to scream at the dream maker for causing this problem. I was now the owner of all three of these powerful icons and had no idea what to do with them.

What kind of education is brought about by dreams? Isn't there a school for Shaman that I could attend? Have I been picked, designated, or selected for something? Do they even know what kind of person I was in my old life? Better than that, do they even care? Worse than that, I felt like I now had the body of the boy in the dreams. What happened to him? Did

[245]

they kill him off to put me in his body? This isn't a little boy's body but a body of a fully grown adult. Where are the years that he must have spent growing up? I lay there, beating myself up mentally for a long time. When odd things happen to you, you have a tendency to think it must be your fault. In my old life, I had gotten to the place where I would have accepted death. It wasn't a wish or even a hopeful thought, just acceptance.

That was what I got out of the dream, acceptance. I knew that I would never be given all the answers to the many questions that already have and will arise. I must find the will to set the record straight and make sure during my life time here that whatever happens, I will do the right thing.

My family will keep the talisman amulets and wait for the time that the right one comes along for each of them. I do not believe that we are meant to keep them for the long haul. I refer back to what Mary said about the Blue Talisman, it felt safe where it was. I can only hope that we can keep them safe until they are ready to go to the proper owners.

I had fallen back to sleep and then seemed surprised that something wanted me to get up. It was still a little dark as the mist and fog created by the falls, shrouded the sky. I needed to light a fire but couldn't understand why. I got some wood together and was in the process of starting one when Mary got up and asked me what I wanted. I said I could use a little help with the fire but didn't know why she got up. "You called me" she said. I checked both of the talisman and they were glowing as was the one in the rock bag when I checked it. "Something is happening and we have been called awake for it".

I got the fire going and Mary put a bowl of water near it to heat. She then cut up some of the dried meat and added that and a little bit of a plant she picked earlier. "I need to make a hot soup" but she didn't know why. It was then that both the animals started to let me know that something or someone was coming our way. The message seemed confused as if they didn't know if it was good or bad news.

I took my longest spear, holding it like a staff and stood next to the fire. There didn't seem to be any fear in the messages I was getting. I had to make sure everyone was safe and had Mary get the kids back from the fire and a little out of sight. Bob ran off at an angle to the line of the approach and disappeared into the night. I knew he would be just out of sight and would do his best to avoid any contact. Fred stayed with Mary and the kids but shrank down behind them a little bit. He would be hard to see because of the other furs that were there unless he moved. We could hear the shuffling noise as it was getting nearer. He came bursting into the ring of light and collapsed.

He was face down and close to death. There were three arrows in his back and he is almost as big as I am. Mary got to him about the same time I did as we checked to see if he was still alive. I turned his head to make sure he could breath. We had to get the arrows out and patch him up but neither of us had that kind of experience. Mary held the Blue Talisman over him but got no effect. I pulled the Rose Talisman out and held it over his back and it began to glow. I then took hold of the arrow that seemed to be the least deep and gently pulled. It came out without a lot of tissue attached to it and very little blood. I did the same to the other two arrows with the same results. The skin pulled together in each location but would leave a scar. "Battle Wounds" I commented. I wondered who the fight was with and if they would pursue him here.

Mary wiped the blood off his back and then tried to keep the kids from getting too close. I could see that the wounds would scab over but at least they wouldn't bleed any more. He probably lost way too much blood as it was. I took another look at his face to check for breathing and had instant recognition. He looked like me. While not exactly, but more so than anyone else I had seen so far. The boy in the dream looked a lot like us and I wondered again if it was me. He was unable to move at this point and needed the rest. We covered him with one of our blankets and built up the fire a little more. I shooed the kids to the other side of the fire.

I walked around the camp site a couple times, just checking on everything. Bob had wandered back in and was now sitting just behind the

[247]

kids while Fred had chosen to sit next to Ann. All three of the kids wanted to know what was happening and I thought I should sit with them and tell them all that I could. I didn't know enough to make it a good story but I hoped they would understand.

Just then Ann interrupted my speech with "give me" she said and pointed to the Rose Talisman. I still had it in my hand and felt it would be in a good place if Ann had it. I hung it around her neck and told her that it was a very important amulet and she would have to find the rightful owner some day. She seemed to understand and nodded her head yes. I was thinking that she was three or four years old, not yet five. I was just guessing at that but the talisman had to be somewhere and that would do for now.

I then finished telling them what I knew of the victim and how he must have been running away from someone else. He had been shot in the back with three arrows and we had removed them. He looked like he would be sick for awhile and we would have to help him recover from his wounds.

I watched Bakta and Casta to see their reaction and it was as I expected. They were getting real nervous and jittery. They had been running away from someone for some time while with Lista and maybe didn't even know why that was. We had no intention of running and I let them know. If someone came looking for the wounded person then I would talk to them about it. If he was a bad guy I think the animals would know that. If the others are bad guys then I would deal with them. There would be no more running away. I made sure the boys understood that and made them answer that they did.

Ann of course piped up and said she wouldn't be afraid and run. I gave her an "atta boy", oops girl for that. We went about the normal business of survival while our new guest slept. Mary kept the bowl of soup warm and I had some fresh water handy for when he would wake up. I checked on him several times during the morning and he seemed to be breathing better each time I looked. I was finding this an odd way to create a family, although I wasn't sure he would be part of ours. Fred and Bob had both taken an interest in him and stuck their nose on him from head to foot.

[248]

They must have thought he passed muster as they didn't send me any warnings.

The sun was more than half way across the sky when he finally began to stir. I shooed the kids off again as I didn't want anyone in his field of vision except me when he opened his eyes. He jerked awake and tried to get up but fell back from lack of strength. He focused on me and seemed to be aware that nothing bad could happen in the next few minutes and relaxed. I gave him some water and he tried to speak but couldn't find his voice yet. I gave him another drink and he tried to get up again. I helped him to a sitting position and let him rest for a little bit. I then held the Gold Talisman in my hand and spoke to him. "My name is Jed and you are safe here under my protection". He could see my lips moving but the sound was in his head and not his ears.

He reached up to see what I was holding in my hand. I let him see it and he was overcome and passed out. I didn't know if it was fear or relief at that instant. I would come to realize that it was from the latter and he would come around in a few minutes. The talisman had a strong effect on him when he saw it and I wasn't sure what he knew about these amulets. I think the shock was more because of what had transpired recently in his life and not what just happened in our camp. I wondered what he would think about the rest of my family and hoped it didn't send him into shock again. I decided to start with Mary and work the kids and animals in later. The trouble with that of course would be that Ann was not good at waiting.

I had stepped away from him for a minute and Ann slipped in with her constant companion Fred and introduced herself. He must have really thought it weird that a little girl with a fox was trying to talk to him. I knew I was too late to stop her, so I just let her do her thing. She was a little "jabber monkey" when she got started and it couldn't hurt him to listen to her.

He managed to get into a sitting position again as she kept telling him all about us. He was staring intently at her when I realized she had the Rose Talisman and he seemed to be entranced by it. I walked in behind her so that he could see me and Ann at the same time. Ann said "his name is

[249]

Grotto". He recognized his name but looked about as confused as anyone can get when the fox didn't leave and Bob showed up. I then motioned to Mary to bring the bowl of soup and then he must have really wondered where he was. She handed him the bowl and then stepped back beside me. She had the Blue Talisman hanging around her neck. We must have been a sight for anyone, let alone someone that thought they were going to die just a few hours ago.

I could tell him "it ain't heaven" but he might not believe me. Then the two boys showed up to get a look at him. That was enough, I had everyone leave so he could eat his soup and get some more rest. I had the boys picking up all the wood they could find along the river and stacking it up near the camp. I could get a lot more wood down by the falls but it would take four days each trip. I knew now that I wasn't going to be leaving the camp for any reason. I would have to be here if and when the hunters or warriors showed up. I was sure they would be tracking him to finish what they had started. I held the Gold Talisman up and said "I'm going to need your help with this one". I don't know what made me think I hadn't been getting it all along.

I could see that Grotto wanted to get up and just didn't have the strength to do it. I was always one to let people do what they want to do and wait to see if they are successful. If they were to ask for help I would jump right in and do my best to assist them. This was no different as I waited for him to figure out that he would need some help. He didn't have to ask as I could see it in his face. I wrapped his arm around my neck and put my shoulder under his and hoisted him up. We walked a little ways from camp and I let him lean against me. When he finished, I helped him back and Mary had a hide for him to sit on and blanket to cover up with. He would be getting cold as a consequence of losing all that blood. She offered him some fish to eat and more of the soup. He seemed to perk up for a little then and looked around at the different people here in our camp.

The only two, beside him and me that looked even slightly alike were the two boys. The age difference on those two made them not quite a perfect match although if you looked close you could tell they were brothers. Like the boys, he was very interested in the two animals in our company. They knew he was curious about them and each paraded across in front of him and then returned to sit next to Ann. The boys had learned to ignore them and that made life a bit easier on everybody. The fire wood pile had gotten big enough to last several days and the boys were really tired from all that work. They were ready for bed as soon as they had eaten.

Mary made sure they had enough covers as it would be cold again tonight. Ann didn't seem to be the least bit sleepy and wanted to keep bothering Grotto. I had to remind her that he needed to rest if he was to recover from his injuries. Then I told her I had to borrow Bob for the night as I had a special mission for him. She wanted to know what he would be doing and I told her that we would have to ask Bob if he was interested in spying on the enemy. She was sure he would volunteer as he looked so disinterested. You just can't tell what a cat is thinking. He walked off into the night. I sent him a thank you and wished him well. There was an old phrase "god speed" but I never understood it.

Mary and I sat by the fire and talked about the odd situation here. Of all the times we sent up smoke signals and never got a response, how is it that someone just runs into our camp? We can now expect to have more people show up that may find us to be a problem for them.

If they try to eliminate us I will have to fight them somehow. How good are the talismans at stopping a war party? If they show up I guess I will find out. Bob hadn't come back yet so they couldn't be very close. We decided that they would find us and it would be best if it was on our terms. They probably wouldn't be traveling at night so I went to sleep with the hope that we would have time to get ready for them in the morning.

I had a dream that didn't seem to apply to this situation and wondered what it was all about. It came from the Bible and was Moses and the Exodus. He was standing at the Red Sea and raised his staff to cause the water to part. Then another scene showed the fight with the Amalekites. Moses held up the staff and the Israelites would be winning. What did the talisman and Shaman know about the Bible? It was a strange dream and I would have to think about it before it made any sense. I wasn't any Moses that could make my staff into a snake or change water into wine. I didn't have four hundred years of people to lead out of bondage. I couldn't even get across the river without lots of help. On top of all that I didn't even have a staff.

I woke in the morning with Bob sitting on my chest and I could have sworn he was smiling, the "Cheshire Cat" thing. What did he want from me this early in the day? I took the talisman in hand and said "give me the news Mr. Cat". I then got the feeling that our approaching war party would be here about midday. That should give me some time to think about the response I would have to make.

"Ok ok, I'll get you something to eat if you get off my chest". He seemed to be about as proud of what he did as you would expect from a cat. Of course they never seem to be ashamed of anything regardless. He wandered over to see if Grotto was up yet and made sure to give him a wider berth than the one he gave me.

Everyone was still asleep as I started a fire and put a couple bowls of water close to heat. At times like this I really miss the Starbucks from down the street. It was such a simple life back then. I got a dried fish out to share with Bob and walked off down by the river to think. I would have to meet the incoming group out away from the camp to keep the kids safe from any accidental or incidental arrows or spears. It seemed funny, as in strange, that I didn't feel in any danger at all. I felt that everything would be taken care of without any bloodshed. I bent down to get some water to splash on my face, just to get the sleep out of my eyes. The reflection in the water was startling. The water was rippling and changing the expression of what I saw. The Golden Talisman had dipped into the water and made it seem as if I was aging in that reflection. It kept changing until it showed an old man with white hair grinning back at me. I took it to mean that I would live a long time in this world. The image defused and became a spear.

I finished washing my face and returned to camp. Mary and Ann had already gotten up and they were busy getting things together. They would fix something to eat for the boys and our guest. Whatever Mary had

[252]

put in the soup for Grotto had done its' job as he had slept all night and seemed to be in a lot less pain this morning. He could now manage to get up and down by himself and smiled at the thought of something more to eat. I talked to Mary about the timing of the arriving troop and suggested that she make sure the kids stayed back and out of sight till I could get things handled. She nodded her head as if to say yes but gave me the impression that she would do as she pleased, regardless.

I started a signal fire to let the incoming warriors know where we were. They wouldn't have to guess and wonder about it, except to think it might be a trap. The prairie land was hard to hide in for us bigger creatures and I wouldn't waste any time trying to. The morning went by fairly quickly as we busied ourselves with camp activities.

I took the time to look at the arrows that we pulled from Grotto and notice that they had a dark flint for the heads. The flint that Mary had used for my arrows was lighter in color. These arrows were a little shorter than mine which probably meant that they had shorter bows. That would mean less distance of travel for the arrows. Not that it would make much difference as I intended to get fairly close to them when they got here. I started to get the early warning signals from the animals and made the announcement that I was going out to meet the incoming troop.

Bob led the way to where I was to stand and then beat a hasty retreat. I could see them coming and waited to make sure they saw me and would keep coming. From a distance they wouldn't know it wasn't Grotto and might not know even when they got closer. I had gone out to meet them with a limited supply of arms. That would be just the long spear and my ever present hammer. I didn't even bring my bag of rocks that I usually carried. When they reached archery range, they stopped and fired a volley of arrows at me. I raised my spear, holding it parallel to the ground and in front of me and all the arrows fell short of their intended target. At that time I could feel the presence of someone behind me and knew without looking that Mary had come out to join me. When the warriors saw that their arrows landed short, they moved up closer and fired again. There were ten of them in the group and ten arrows again fell short.

[253]

When Ann showed up with Fred, I had her go out and gather up the twenty arrows. Ann was loaded down with arrows as twenty of them were a lot for a little girl. Fred had followed her out and back and the warriors had now become animated in their anger at what had just happened. The leader coaxed them forward and sent another batch of arrows on the way. When these all came up short, several of the group tried to fall back but the leader hollered at them and they stopped. Ann couldn't hold any more arrows so I waved the spear over the last ones and sent them back to the original archer. I made sure that they landed just in front of them. I then put the Golden Talisman in my right hand and spoke in a booming voice "pick up your arrows". By this time the boys and Grotto had joined in our company and were watching everything.

The now panicking tribesmen were trying to move back and get away from what was happening. Something was holding them in place as they struggled with the fear inside. I had the boys go and collect all the bows and arrows and walk around behind them. I turned everybody toward camp and we marched the band in front of us.

In camp I had the ten soldiers of misfortune sit on one side of the fire and put Grotto and my group on the other. I asked Fred to locate the one that was most afraid of what was going to happen. The ten became extremely nervous as Fred walked in behind them. He stopped at one of those that were trying to hide in the back and I walked over had physically lifted him up and brought him around to the side of the fire. All of these men were much smaller than me and about the height of Mary. I asked him to point out the leader of this troop. I had him sit down and asked the leader to come and join me. Then I told the others to stay where they were and we would be back in a little bit.

I asked Mary to prepare some food for all the men and to make sure they were comfortable. They were not allowed to leave. She should hold up her Blue Talisman if they tried to. The leader and I walked away to get some distance from the rest, and hold a meeting that wouldn't seem so intimidating.

[254]

I asked his name before starting the conversation and he responded with "Cantu". I then asked him to explain why he was so determined to kill Grotto. He was reluctant at first to talk at all but the Gold Talisman started to have an effect on him and he soon opened up about the differences between his tribe and the one that Grotto came from. I let him talk for some time to get as many words out of him as I could. The longer he talked the more obvious it was that it was more than a bias between tribes but something that went back a very long time. I was sure he didn't even know how it started. The four tribes had been fighting for so long that two of them had been eliminated and now these two had a dwindling population. He had assembled the ten fighters to hunt down and kill the remaining ones of Grottos' tribe. He thought they might have the same number of fighters left. Then he admitted that chasing one for such a long distance would have left his tribe in danger of being wiped out. They had not expected Grotto to keep going for so long. Each time they thought they had him; he would escape and continue to run. Cantu began to believe that Grotto was trained for this purpose. He was to draw the fighters as far away as possible and then the remaining members of Grottos' tribe could attack his.

That sounded quite plausible to me except for the reading we got of Grotto when he first arrived at our camp. If it turned out to be true there would be nothing we could do about it. I urged Cantu to keep talking to see if there was a way out of this without more killing. He admitted to being the defacto leader of the tribe as all the leaders before him had been killed in the fighting. Now he worried that as the leader he had condemned his tribe to extinction. He had finally run out of things to say and sat sullenly staring at the water. I told him to stay there and I would return shortly.

I walked back to camp and asked Grotto to join me and Cantu down by the river and reminded the nine fighters to stay where they were. When we got back I then asked Grottos' view of what was going on between the two tribes. He essentially told me the same story with few exceptions. Cantu nodded with each piece of the story as it was retold. Grotto had only the difference of why he was running and that his tribe was not in a position to attack Cantus' tribe.

He had been selected to be the leader but because of the heavy loss of life they had sustained in the ongoing war, could not get enough fighters together to continue to fight. He suggested that they send a peace envoy to stop the killing. It would mean that they would have to move further away and relinquish their rights to the forbidden lands.

That would leave Cantus' tribe with the sole possession of it, even if they couldn't use it. That enraged the remaining fighters and they drove him out. He ran into Cantu and his fighters by accident and since he couldn't go back to his tribe he just kept running to stay alive. His hope, of course was the same, to keep Cantu from attacking his people.

I then asked them both what they knew about the talisman amulets. Neither one could give me a good answer as they both had heard about them but never saw any of them before now. Then I asked about the other tribes again to see if they knew for sure how many tribes there had been and are now. Both answered the same way with four original tribes and now just the two. I knew the math didn't add up so I tried to phrase it several different ways but got the same answer.

Next I wanted to know about the forbidden lands and if they knew why they were forbidden? How could any tribe own rights to a land that was forbidden? Did someone hold some kind of document to that effect? They, of course, could not answer these questions as it was tradition and not a given right by some deity as far as they knew.

I was going to need more information if I was going to get the kind of answers I would need. I was guessing about what the forbidden land was and if the four tribes all lived there at one time. If there were four tribes but only three talisman amulets, that didn't make sense. Next I needed to find a way to get everyone to cooperate if this was going to work.

None of these people knew why they were fighting or how they would possess the forbidden land if they won the fight with the other tribe. They just didn't want the other tribe to have it even though they couldn't. You can't lose something you don't have to someone else if neither of you have a way to use it. There didn't seem to be any intelligent way to explain what happened or who was to blame for it.

I took both of them back to camp and had them sit off to one side while I talked to the other nine fighters. They would be allowed to listen but not say anything. I then told the nine that Cantu could no longer be their leader and for them to chose another. They seemed dumbfounded and none of them would volunteer. They were mostly hunters and not trained warriors. They didn't want to point at another fighter for fear that someone would point at them.

I gave them a few minutes to think about it and had the boys set their bows and arrows out by the fire. I looked carefully at the arrows from Grottos' back and at the ones that had been collected. I knew that the arrows would be marked in some way to identify the owner. This is especially true with hunters as they wouldn't want someone else to claim their kill. After a short wait and no new leader was selected, I had each fighter pick his bow and arrows out of the pile. I then noted which ones took arrows that were a match for the three I had. With one bow and arrows left that matched one of the arrows I had, only two of the nine had been able to hit Grotto. I had the seven sit back down and took the two aside and explained to them that they had been the ones to shoot Grotto and I wasn't very happy about it. I asked them if there was something they would like to do to make amends for having shot him. Now they were even more confused than they had been when asked to select a new leader.

Their old leader was sitting next to the guy they had been trying to kill for at least a week and now what were they suppose to do? The answer was not easy for anybody so I told them what I wanted and they would have to live with it. "I want you to remember who he is and that you are not to try to kill him ever again". I said that with great authority so that all would hear it and understand.

I then told the nine that as soon as they could replenish our wood supply they could go home. It would also help if they were to bring in some food like the deer or elk that frequent the river area near here. I gave them instructions on where to go for the wood and meat and how far it was.

They were familiar with traveling light but we supplied them with some food and water bladders. It was now late in the afternoon and they left thinking that they could make the round trip in three days instead of the four it took Bakta and me.

The next thing on the agenda was what to do with the ex-chieftains? I had to get them to understand what really happened to the other tribes and was happening to theirs. First and foremost they would have to learn to work together on something. Then we would see what the prospects of cooperation would be for their tribes. I had no idea how much influence each would now have with their tribe.

If I was to get involved, would the tribes listen to me long enough to make a difference? Had they been at war with each other so long that it was ingrained in their genes? What would it take to make them want to work together? Could their populations be so depleted that they would not recover now? Was I brought into this world just for this purpose? Was I to be the mediator for all the tribes?

I knew that I had a limited time to get these two men working together so I started them right away. I would have to figure out the rest of it as we went along. For now they would do as I asked because they feared the power I had. I had commanded animals to do my bidding and stopped arrows in flight. There were other things they would notice but eventually they would recognize that I was as human as they were. I knew that Grotto would still be weak but he could do a little work as long as I monitored it.

I had them start to disassemble the raft as we could no longer use it and the wood could come in handy for other things. Cantus' bow and arrows remained by the fire and I picked them up and put them in with mine for now. They both knew who shot the third arrow into Grottos' back. I would watch them to see if there was any animosity left in them for war.

I had forgotten about the vines we had packed along from where we had built the raft. They just might come in handy for something else. I now hoped to get everything packed up and head up to the hot springs before winter set in. I still didn't know where the two tribes were and would need Grotto and Cantu to show me that.

I informed the two of them that they would be watched constantly until I felt they could be trusted not to kill each other. Then I asked Bob to sit in for me while the two deposed leaders worked on the raft. I then warned them that Bob was in constant communications with me. I would come for them in a little while and they were to set the vines off to the side.

I was on my way back to the camp when I saw smoke rising from down the river. I didn't think the nine hunters could have gotten that far yet nor could I tell which side of the river it was on. Mary helped me to set up a signal fire and get it lit. It was late enough in the day that the wind was calm and the smoke would rise a long way up.

I took a hide and wet it down to keep it from burning and sent up my three two three signal so that anyone seeing it would know it wasn't just a wild fire. No one here would know a S.O.S. if it bit them in the butt. I sent the same signal three times and then waited to see if we got a response. It must have taken them time to get a hide to make the signal with but it finally came. They didn't bother with the three two three but that was fine at least we knew they got our signal and were returning one to us.

Cantu and Grotto had taken a lot less time to break the raft down than it took me to put it together. Bob let me know that they were done and ready to return to camp. I went down to get them and the vines and told them I would explain the smoke later that night. First we had to get back and eat, and then I needed to have the vines braided into a long rope. After we ate I sat the two of them down and explained what I wanted with the rope. It had to be about five times my height with hand and foot loops every so often on opposite sides. In essence a rope ladder made from the vines.

While they were working on it, I had the family assembled in front of them and then asked if they knew what was wrong with the picture of us as they saw it. I tried to present this as just a family and not a scare tactic but both men showed fear of answering in a truthful manner. I then asked

Grotto his opinion, to which he replied that only the two boys come from the same tribe. The rest are of different tribes and should not be together. This must have been ingrained into the social fabric of the different tribes as Grotto had been treated nicely by all here and yet he had trouble seeing it for what it was. I then asked Cantu if what was said meant the same to him and he just nodded his head. I then pointed out to them that they were sitting side by side while working on the rope and doing what I had asked them to do. I did not force them or threaten them or coerce them in any way. I had them working on the raft and left a bobcat to watch over them but they did such good work that I no longer needed to do that.

I thought I would start with myself and simplify the story as much as possible, and then I could move on to the others in the family. I stated that I was an orphan and that my parents had been killed in a raid and I was left on my own for a long time. It seems that I am from the same tribe as Grotto but we had never met and I do not know where he lives. Then there is Mary, whose real name I do not know, she had lived on the river and lost her tribe to the flood. Ann also lost her tribe the same way but neither Mary nor I knew her before or what tribe she came from. Bakta and Casta come from yet another tribe and were probably kidnapped at a young age and do not remember their real parents or what tribe they came from.

Now, as you can see there are four different looking people in this family. None of us knew the other ones before the great flood of this past year. It is my belief that we have been brought together by the previous wearers of the talisman that we currently have. It is also my belief that there was one talisman for each tribe, so one has yet to be found. I hope that when it is located we will be able to unite all the tribes into one. It seems as if the two missing tribes were not wiped out but left of their own accord in order to keep from fighting to survive. It may have been unfortunate that they chose this river to settle on and then were lost in the flood.

I then let our two visitors continue to work on the rope and chew on the information I gave them. At some point I would have to make a decision on exactly what to do with them. They would be needed to interface with their tribes and me. I would need to know that they had bought into the unity thing or it wasn't going to work. I talked to Mary about how her tribe would have reacted to her and me getting together. She wasn't sure, as it had never happened that she knew of. Her parents had not been strict and let her enjoy the freedom of her own decisions. It was hard for her to talk about her family so I let it go at that. We might talk some more about them but only if she started the conversation. She knew I was just looking for some kind of reference to work with. With that we called it a day and left the animals to do the night shift.

The next day was busy for everyone as we started making plans to move out. I wanted the boys to go fishing so we could smoke enough for everyone for the winter. Grotto and Cantu were back on the rope ladder and I was putting a second smoker together. I set another signal fire to let the group down river know that we were still here and waiting for them. Ann was making everyone pay attention to her as she kept trying to get into some kind of trouble or other. She seemed to be growing up awful fast and I could see that Fred was getting frustrated with her but hanging in there none the less.

I thought the nine hunters would be down by the falls later in the day. I started a hole to put in an anchor post for the ladder. I used one of the logs from the raft for that and two smaller ones to brace it in place. I thought that if we tilted the anchor log back by a few degrees that it would hold the weight of anyone on the ladder. I kept a watch on Grotto to see how he was doing. For a guy that could have been dead two days ago, he seemed to be having a rapid recovery. The boys would bring in a couple fish and go out for some more. Mary was filleting them and getting them in the smokers. Bob had taken the position of watch cat over the two rope builders. I hadn't asked him to do that but I think he wasn't interested in following Ann all over god's half acre. He left that to the frustrated fox.

Chapter twelve

The Unification

It was getting late in the day and I walked down by the falls to see if the hunters had made it there yet. They had been traveling day and night and they were just arriving as I watched from the bluff overlooking the falls. They saw me and waved to indicate so. I let them know I could see them and that they should rest and start on the pile of wood in the morning. I notice that there were only six of them and asked about the other three hunters.

It seemed that they ran into the deer herd and shot several of them. The men were on their way back to camp with the deer. We would need the wood to convert the deer into jerky. I checked on the rope builders and they were almost done with it. It looked like everyone would get some needed sleep tonight except for the three deer hunters. I would make sure they got some sleep when they got in.

I checked on Grotto to make sure his wounds hadn't become infected and to see if he was feeling better. He seemed to have regained some strength. I then ask him about his tribe as he had stated that they were in no shape to attack Cantus' tribe. He then told me that there were only four or five healthy hunters and four or five that could fight but not travel. The tribe consisted of maybe thirty adults and only six children, most of which were girls.

I then asked Cantu the same question and got a very similar answer. The ten hunters were all those available to fight with two left behind that could not travel. He thought they had about twenty or so women and only two boys among the children. It sounded like these two tribes were on the verge of extinction due to war and low reproduction rates. I had to take all this into consideration as I tried to formulate a plan to unite the tribes.

I went to sleep thinking about the two known tribes and how to integrate them with our party. Of course it had to be a formula for another dream. It started out with the boy again and his village getting raided and burned out. The picture was bigger now and showed the village to extend further along the stream and more than half of it was untouched. The fighters from the rest of the tribe were able to drive off the intruders but at a terrible loss. The boy had been forced to flee and didn't see the surviving tribe members. He only knew that his family had been killed and thought he was on his own. The tribe moved to another location to put some distance between themselves and the attackers. The other two tribes had already left and established villages on the river. They had made sure to keep a safe distance between each other.

The flood then decimated the two river tribes leaving just a few survivors. The last remaining tribe tried to claim all the land but found that nothing would grow and no animals could live there. It was suspected of being cursed and though their Shaman tried to remove it, he was unable to. It then became the forbidden lands where no one could live. They moved to a more remote area and continued their war like ways. They would attack any of the other tribesmen that they met and that left them quite isolated.

There were many attempts to remove the curse over the years and a lot of pitched battles between the two remaining tribes. Some of their hunting and fishing territories would overlap and cause ongoing skirmishes. The Shaman of each tribe would find the talisman to be useless and attempt to discard it, only to have it show up again with someone else in the tribe. None of the people that found the talisman could wear it. It would not stay around their neck. Only the Shaman could keep it on and it held sway over the tribe but had no power to alter their circumstance.

I woke up thinking that the remaining talisman was green and I had a clearer picture of what each tribe member should look like if I were to see them. I again found that I had more questions than answers after the dream. How could Mary and Ann have the talisman and still know that it would have to go to someone else? The Shaman had always been male, and women would not be allowed to even touch it.

I was still pondering these things when the alarm in my head went off again. This time Bob indicated that we were to have company this morning and I should get ready to meet them. They would be coming from

[263]

the south along the small stream. It was an armed hunting party and they were looking for someone. I knew the smoke signal had been to the west, so this was a new group. They had not returned the smoke signal so I was sure they had wanted to surprise us. I wasn't sure who they could be looking for but had to guess it was Lista and the boys. If they had been looking for anyone else they would have been along the river and not off to the south somewhere.

I made sure everyone was up and moving around before having to greet the incoming group. I told them what was happening and that we would all go out together. Then I let them know the three hunters with the deer would be coming in about the same time. Busy, busy, busy as the six men getting the wood together would need to be informed not to start back with any of it yet. If it worked out right I could have a small army standing here when the hunters arrive. Hopefully none of them would get overly excited and launch an arrow.

I had Mary and Ann start heating some food and getting the smokers ready for the deer. Grotto, Cantu and I went to get the ladder set up and the boys needed to catch a few more fish. The six men down by the falls were already collecting wood to bring back when I called down to them to gather their hunting gear and wait by the cliff. Up on top I showed Grotto and Cantu how I wanted the rope looped over the main pole and the other two poles to support the first one. Then we dropped the end of the rope over the cliff. We needed one of the men at the bottom to hold the rope taut while I had Cantu climb down and send up the men one at a time. They were to bring their personal stuff and any wood that they could carry.

I needed to start another signal fire for the tribe members coming from the west and to let the group from the south know we hadn't gone anywhere yet. I sent the first three wood collectors to go meet the deer hunters and help them. The other three were to set up the signal fire and get it burning. I sent Grotto down to help Cantu anchor the rope by tying it to the heaviest log they could find. Then they were to climb back up and get something to eat. I wanted everyone to get something to eat before either of the new groups could get here. I grabbed a quick bite while I was at it.

I had the three fire builders put up a rack to hang the deer when they got here. I wasn't sure when we would have the time to skin and quarter them. The whole time Bob was keeping me informed as to where the new group was and about how long before they got here. The smoke from the fire was rising straight up for all to see and I thanked the powers that be for that.

The six men with the deer arrived and hung the deer up to fully drain. Then I made sure they got something to eat. The three that had been carrying the deer hadn't sleep in two days. I told them they would have to wait for a couple more hours, and then they could sleep as long as they wanted to. After everyone had eaten, I checked on all the other things that had to be ready. I made sure everyone was armed except for Ann. She was in charge of the fox and I made sure she knew that. Fred didn't seem amused by that but again he was willing to put up with the sarcasm. I lined everyone up and we marched out to meet the new arrivals.

Mary, Ann and I led off with me in the middle. Grotto was off to one side and Cantu off the other. The boys were right behind me as I didn't want them to be seen right away. The nine hunters were spread out with five on one side and four on the other. Everyone held a weapon so it could be easily seen. The incoming group could see us as we walked toward them and they stopped. I was sure they had no idea what to expect.

We continued until we were in archery range and then stopped. I asked to speak to their leader and to have him come forward. They could see that the element of surprise was gone and that we were expecting them and well prepared.

One man stepped toward me and stopped to ask if I was the Shaman for this group. I said that I was without any hesitation so that he would feel like I knew what I was doing. I stepped forward to meet him half way and told him my name. His name was Oakta and the five of them were looking for someone. I told him that if he was looking for Lista, she had taken a swim in the river and would be downstream somewhere. He could see that I was holding an amulet of some kind and that I must have some strange power to talk to him and know what he wanted. I looked at his

[265]

features and could see that this man came from the same tribe as Bakta and Casta.

I said "I have your two boys in my protection and would like for you to join us in our camp where you and I can talk about what to do with them". I then called the boys forward so that he could see them. I told him to have his men put up their weapons and we could all go into camp. We would be willing to supply them with food and help them in any way that we could, if they would be willing to help us.

He seemed to understand that I was holding all the cards and his cooperation would be more of a benefit for his group than mine. At his command, the hunters of his group displayed some great courage and hung their bows over their shoulder. I then lead the whole group back to camp and made plans to signal the others if they arrived before we finished with these. Food was supplied to all that were hungry and the three really tired hunters went off to get some sleep. I had Cantu send two of his men to the river to watch for the other group coming from the west. The introductions were made and a quick summery of events to fill in the new men.

They were already aware of the fact that their village was gone. They had spent some time looking for survivors but managed to miss my family somehow. They had lost Lista's trail and followed a false one off to the south. She had managed to elude them and they were ashamed of it. They had seen our smoke signal and thought it might be her.

I asked Oakta to wait for a little while to get some of his questions answered. I told him that another group was coming up the river and we needed to go and meet them. They too had lost their families and now were looking for the same kind of answers he was. I then asked him to help us in collecting fire wood and if any of them was really good with deer pelts and meat. They had seen the three deer hanging there when they came into the camp. One of his men volunteered to help with the deer and hides. Mary would work on the deer and Ann would help by keeping the fire going. She would separate the smaller wood pieces for use in the smokers.

[266]

I took everyone else down to the falls and showed them what I wanted done. I kept the two group leaders and Grotto up on top to help with the men climbing the ladder with the wood. The wood collection was going really well and some animal parts were being discovered in the pile. I told the men it would be alright if they kept the antlers and bear claws that they might find. If they found any human remains, we would have to set them on a pyre. There were quite a few of those but none that could be identified.

The sun was half way down the sky when the other group arrived. All work was stopped and we waved a greeting to them. I motioned for them to stay put and we would come to them. I was sure they thought I was crazy but they didn't have much choice or thought they didn't anyway.

I sent the two group leaders and Grotto down the ladder and followed them. I then led them to the falls and showed them the path to the other side. We went over as a group and climbed the stairway on the far side to the surprise of the waiting group. It must have looked like we came out of the water to them and they almost ran. They had seen us disappear under the waterfall and then we reappeared in front of them. It made for a grand entrance and worked well for my persona. The three I brought with me were impressed also but for a different reason of course. They had not seen the walkway or the stairs and wondered how I could know about them. Some questions should never be answered.

I asked who the leader was and introduced myself and the other three. His name was Runde and he had stepped forward to be recognized. With two of us, myself and Grotto, it must have appeared as if we were the dominate members and were treated as such. I was sure that Grotto felt less secure about that than I did. I could tell from the overall appearance that these were indeed members of Mary's' tribe.

I explained that there was a stairway down from this side and a walkway under the falls. We now had the ability to go from one side to the other. I told Runde that we needed to get into camp and I would have more information for him. The other leaders would need this information also. I led the way with Cantu and Oakta, and asked that Grotto follow the Runde tribe members. As soon as they stood at the top of the stairway they could see the steps and understood how we had gotten over to them.

The men working on the wood pile had been watching the ongoing activity and waited for us to come out from under the falls. All of them had stayed back from the falls as if it was a magic trick of some kind. I informed them that it was just a path and that they could try it if they would like. They looked around at each other to see who would be that brave. No one wanted to be the first but none wanted to be the last either. I had Grotto lead them through it and then it became a game as they ran back and forth from side to side. They were having so much fun splashing water on each other that they didn't seem to notice that they were from four different tribes. It was a nice break from the constant working and tension.

I asked Runde to have his men help with the wood and have then come up to eat if they were hungry. I then had the leaders join me in camp to explain all that was going on. I asked Runde to tell us how they managed to get out of the flood as Mary thought they were on the river fishing. He stated that they had seen some deer down by the river and followed them up to higher ground. When the flood came they lost all their fishing gear and saw their village get washed away. I then introduced Runde to Mary and for the first time we had someone that was recognized. They weren't sure how to explain their relationship but I took it to mean that they were cousins. That might have been the case in all members of any of the tribes.

The size of the populations of each tribe had been declining for some time and the inbreeding was beginning to take its toll. I would now have to convince these men that what I had to say may be the only thing that would save them all. The fighting constantly had cost them the biggest and strongest men. This supplied me with the best opportunity to alter their behavior.

Before we could get a conversation going, Ann came up holding her Rose Talisman and told me that it wanted something. I looked at both mine and the one Mary had and all three were glowing. I looked over at Runde and asked if he knew anything about a Green Talisman. He said he did and dumped it out of his bag. I then asked him to tell me how he came by it. He said that one of his men found it in a logjam on the river and tried to put it on. It wouldn't stay on but kept falling off even though the rawhide cord didn't seem to be broke.

He tried it himself and so did everyone in the group. They all had the same results and he got angry with it and tried to throw it away but it just came back and landed at his feet. He could pick it up and hold it but it would burn his hand if he held it too long. When he put it in his bag, it stayed there and didn't cause any harm, so he left it there. I thanked him for the information and the fact that he brought it to us. Now we just had to find out who it was suppose to go too. I asked Ann if she knew who was going to wear it and she pointed at the boys. I called them over and had Ann pick up the talisman and put it on Bakta. It wouldn't stay on him either and fell to the ground. Ann then picked it up and put it on Casta where it stayed. "I think it has found the rightful owner". I told Casta that it might not be a permanent thing and he may have to give it away some day. Until then he should take very good care of it.

Runde wanted to know if we were the ones he saw from the other side of the river so long ago. It looked like the same smoke signal that he had seen then. I told him it was and that Mary wanted to see for herself what had happened to their village. I then gave him a quick summation of what I told the others about Mary and me and how the kids came into our family. The fox and bobcat were harder to explain but seemed to have some relationship to the talisman. I checked with Oakta to make sure he understood about Lista and the boys. He could not take them home because there was no home. They would be given the opportunity to decide what was best for them. That question would probably be answered by the Green Talisman or the combination of all of them.

With the introductions, the resent history lesson, and the talisman all taken care of, it was now time to get to the meat of the problem. I started out by making sure each knew that someone in my family was somehow related to them and that all of us where related by the presence of the talismans. I then pointed out the fact that two of the tribes had been wiped out by the flood except for the few remaining hunters. The other two tribes were on the verge of decimation if the fighting didn't stop and maybe even that wouldn't matter. Their reproduction rate and declining population would eventually make it impossible to survive. It appeared as if their children were growing up faster than should be normal. Not that it mattered much from that stand point but that they probably had a shorter life expectancy because of it. This too could lead to lower reproduction and falling birth rates.

I knew that most of this was going over their heads but it is hard to get the big picture on something like this. They had been living it and I was an outsider looking in. I then proposed that we all go to the hot springs and spend the winter there. I would mediate between the two remaining tribes and help the hunters to settle in. It would be a huge change for most of them but we needed to stop the fighting before any progress could be made to sustain the populations. I wasn't going to give them a choice on doing this as the situation was at a critical stage. They could agree to it willingly or I would force them to do what I knew had to be done. I had already proved to Cantu that I could stop his tribe from attacking me and those I protected. I made it clear to all that I could also use my power to inflict some pain if need be.

It was a lot of information for them to process and I knew they would need time to get a handle on it. The three leaders with men here would have to talk to them about what was said and make sure that they understood the consequences. I would be willing to talk to anyone about the chances that some problems might arise or if they had any questions. If someone needed to be shown the light, I could do that to. I didn't have the Wisdom of Solomon but I did have the Gold Talisman and hoped that would be enough.

I then sent them off to talk with their men and took Grotto aside and asked if he would need my help with his tribe. I was sure I knew the answer before he said anything but I felt required to ask. They had driven him out and he would be a pariah in their midst if he went back alone.

The next two days were filled with arguments and questions and smoking of deer meat. Everyone was getting plenty of rest but that can lead

[270]

to restlessness and we had some of that too. Hunters tend to be independent thinkers and don't always want to be told the truth. They usually get around to it but have to do all the gyrations first. In the end those that didn't like the idea had to admit that they didn't have a better one. They weren't anxious to go against me and knew that I spoke the truth about their tribes.

It was now up to Cantu and his men to get their tribe moved to the hot springs before winter. The two tribes with family members would need to have the choice spots because of the children and I made sure everyone understood that. I was going with Grotto to make sure we could get his tribe moved. Mary and the kids would go to the hot springs with the two members of the Cantu group and the men from Oakta and Runde groups. Cantu would take seven men with him to help move his tribe. Everyone would have to hunt along the way to insure we had enough food for the winter.

The night before we broke camp, we had a ceremony for the departed. We set a pyre with all the bones that had been found in the logjam and collected by the men. There was no way for us to tell one from the other as far as tribe members went. We could only tell by size if they were adult or children. Most of them were adults. I was sure that members from all the tribes had been on the river during the flood as all the talisman were found in the flotsam. How Ann got there along with all four Shaman we would never know. It was possible that Ann's parents where there to fish. The Shaman could have had a meeting or coven or whatever it would be called, that would have put them on the river at that time. Otherwise, to have the four of them there doesn't make sense. They weren't exactly from tribes that got along but maybe they got the same call I did. I don't think these colored stones are going to tell us.

In the morning Cantu and his seven got an early start, while Grotto and I were held up by a few last minute instructions and plans. Bob was going with us and Fred would stay with Ann and Mary. Several travois were put together along with more backpacks. Everyone that could carry something would be doing so. Even Ann had a small pack and a bow with arrows. Casta had given her the bow he had as he had now outgrown it. Oakta and his men had helped Bakta make a new bow and he gave his old one to Casta. You could almost see the kids grow from day to day. Bakta was almost full grown now and I wondered how long they would live. Maybe the aging process slowed as they got older.

Two of the Runde group offered to stay and finish drying some more fish before starting out. That would help with the food supply. They thought about two days would be all they needed.

Grotto and I started out with the main group, following the now obvious path east. We left them in the evening and turned more southerly. They were stopping for the night and checking on everyone to make sure it was going well. Grotto and I kept going and would do so for the next several days with brief stops for food and water and some rest. I would not have thought to travel at night but Bob had that cat's ability to see in the dark. We let him lead and I kept a mental contact with him.

I talked with Grotto a little while traveling as I wanted as much information as possible before getting there. I asked if we needed to talk to an individual or a group of hunters before addressing the whole village. He wasn't sure now that they ran him off, so I thought that the hunters would be better for the first contact. We would have to challenge them to come out to meet us and take it from there. I then asked Grotto how he managed to find our camp. He stated that the Cantu tribe lived to the east or up river, that going away from their village seemed to be a logical move. He stumbled into our camp and didn't even realize where he was. By then he had exhausted all his energy and will power. He saw the light from the fire and just stumbled into it. He was sure he was going to die and no longer had any fight left in him.

When we got to his village and saw how poorly they were living, I didn't think it would take much to have them move. I used the talisman voice to let the tribe know we were there and that we wanted to talk to the hunters. Several of them came out and voiced a condemnation of Grotto. They wanted to know who I was and why had I come there. When I informed them that I was their Shaman and they needed to listen to me,

[272]

they laughed and said that their Shaman was dead and they would pick the next one.

Bob had let me know that one of their tribe had used the ongoing communications to slip around behind us. He was going to shoot Grotto and me in the back. I warned the hunters that if there was an attack on myself or Grotto that I would cause some amount of pain on the attacker. When he didn't heed my warning and released an arrow intended for Grotto, I interrupted its flight and with a wave of my spear sent the hunter hurling into the middle of the group. He landed awkwardly and broke his collar bone. He wouldn't be able to pull a bow string again for some time unless we could get him to the hot springs for medical care. I then told the rest of them that if they would like to follow in his wingless flight I could oblige them also. I had made my point and now they seemed less aggressive and more inclined to listen.

The one with the broken collar bone had been acting as their leader but now seemed less likely to want to lead anyone anywhere. I then sent the hunters a strong message stating the Grotto was their leader and they needed to do as he says. I would advise him on all matters of importance and council anyone that found that to be a problem. The word "council" in this case had a really rough edge to it and they got the meaning.

If we had more time, I wouldn't have used force or that much pressure to get the results that I wanted. I didn't want to spend even a couple days arguing and explaining the whys and where for's. Winter was on its way and we needed to get moving quickly.

I accompanied Grotto to the center of the village and the hunters assembled all that were in need of this information. When Grotto explained that the tribe was to move to the hot springs for the winter and that the other tribes would be there, a chorus of boos and hisses rose from the crowd. With a wave of my spear the people that were making the loud noises, suddenly lost their voice. I then informed them that they would be allowed to speak after Grotto was done. He then finished with the informational part and proceeded with the physical needs for the move. People were appointed tasks to do and everyone else was expected to pack and be ready to leave at the earliest possible time. Everyone was excused to begin the packing and getting ready. Those that had questions could stay and ask but no one would be permitted to stay behind. Those that could not travel should be placed on travois with whatever support they would need. The only real question to be asked was what if the other tribes were to attack us? When I informed them that I could take care of that just as I had the hunter here, it seemed to be enough to quell that fear. Their fear of me, however, was strengthened when Bob showed up and seemed to be leading me around as if he knew exactly where I wanted to go. I left the actual running of things to Grotto and took an only advisory position. I could settle any arguments or discussions simply by being there. The packing and preparing didn't go smoothly but it still got done and two days after we arrived, everything was ready. The trek out to the hot springs began and ended without any more controversy.

Mary had taken to the leadership role as if she were born to it. She had organized the camp site locations and sent help out to the two tribes that were not yet there. The three men that were sent to help us were immediately assigned to those that were having the most trouble. Other men were given orders to gather fire wood for all the sites and set up shelters at those sites. The fact that Mary held the Blue Talisman may have had something to do with the control she now had over the group of workers. The fact that everyone was busy helped to keep the thoughts of fighting from getting too much play. That was likely to change after the work load diminished and people were sitting around waiting for the winter weather to break. I hoped we would be able to keep the disruptions to a minimum.

It took a little time to get everyone settled as to where they could and couldn't go. There was to be no crossing of tribal lines without first seeking permission. None of the hot springs was restricted to any one tribe and sharing would have to be worked out on a case to case basis. The men had the biggest problem accepting other tribe members in the same pool with them and I had to mediate in an ongoing basis for awhile. The women didn't seem to have the same problem, especially those with children. Most of them were proud to be mothers and wanted the other women to see their kids. It was important for the expectant mothers and for smaller children to be further down the chain of pools where the water was a lot cooler. The men tried to be macho and get in the hottest water that they could stand. After we had to rescue a couple from overheating, I suggested that they be more careful. It did have one very good effect, in that the competition would put two or more men in the same pool.

Everyone knew that I was the Shaman for the Grotto tribe and the overall leader. Each of the other tribes had an acting Shaman and could go to them for help in most things. Ann had the Rose Talisman and it was instrumental in healing. She was in high demand for the first few days and weeks that we were at the hot springs. One of her first healing jobs was to repair the damage that I caused to the hunter in Grottos village. I assisted her in the process by guiding the bones back together while she applied the talisman to the injured area. It couldn't have happened before with the fear of each other and not having someone to supervise.

The talismans were not all powerful and couldn't fix everything but acted in a manner that helped solve most problems. Each of them had a specialty that made them unique. They all had some of the same power but were most useful in their particular field. Whenever a dispute between tribes occurred, then it was best to have all four talismans present to help settle it. The major power of each of them is as follows: Gold Talisman = power and strength, Blue Talisman = cooperation and understanding, Rose Talisman = healing of mind and body, Green Talisman = advice and prophecy.

The first couple weeks were spent just ironing out the basic problems of health and survival. Everyone was willing to pitch in to do their share and get their tribe ready for the coming winter weather. The problems started to show up after that as the two tribes with more women than men had to deal with the two tribes with no women. The demand for Casta and the Green Talisman started slowly but rapidly expanded as soon as the women found out about its powers. It was a tough position to put Casta in as some of the questions were beyond his knowledge to answer. It became essential for Mary to accompany him and make the explanation of the advice to the prospective woman. When it became apparent that some women were willing to cross tribal lines then I had to be involved for their protection. Since everyone in each tribe was related to the rest of their members in some way or other, it was important that they understand that this was going to happen. The tribe should accept this as a good thing and not try to stop it. I would sit down with each tribe and explain the genetics to them in words that they could understand. If they continued restricting their tribe to contact with only their own, they would stop being a tribe in the next several generations. Those alive might never see their grandchildren born and there probably wouldn't be any great grandchildren. The conversation about this had to take place over more than one occasion and required much work with all four of the Talisman holders being involved. Mary, with her use of common sense and ability to get cooperation, helped to some extent. Ann, with her mental healing, would make most of the tribe feel better about what was going on. I could always physically enforce it but that shouldn't be the best way and was only used in the worst cases.

There were about twenty women that either lost their mate or never had one. Now they were getting interested in the real chance to have one and raise a family. It would take most of the winter to iron out the biggest of the problems. Those would be customs and appearances. The women from the Grotto tribe were the most willing to change but also the least likely to be picked. They were as big as or bigger than most of the men and had an enlarged brow or forehead. This made them look more formidable or even angry. I couldn't say much since I had a similar look to my face. In the end most of that would be overlooked in the process of need verses want. There were plenty of arguments and fights but no one got killed and I was happy to intervene in the ones that might have gone that way. We progressed to the place that even the hunting parties would consist of men from different tribes. It did promote competition as to who were the better hunters and it was good that they should shoot some game rather than each other. When the hunters came back with something to show, it made for a party atmosphere. All those that could help render the meat into food and clothing did so.

The winter set in like it had for many years now with a skiff c
and lots of clouds. No one in any of the tribes had recalled it any differ
The odd thing about that was that there were no old people in any o
tribes that could recall any of the things I asked about. They didn't thin
terms of birthdays or years of age so it was hard to tell if any of them ha
lived long enough to see the real change take place. I talked to the leaders
of the four tribes and they would tell me the same story. Things had been
different in the past but because of the way things had gone, many of the
traditions were lost. I asked about the trees not having lower limbs and no
one could remember how that came about. Maybe someone cut them for
fire wood. None of them remembered the prairie being covered with trees
all the way to the river. The birds and animals had been getting less
abundant each year as the dry spell seemed to last longer and longer. That
would make sense if you looked at the tribes. Their life process was
speeding up to compensate for the dwindling food supply. The nutritional
value was dropping and they died younger. The hunters got the first crack
at the food and were in better health than the rest of the tribe. The
Talismans needed an influx of new blood and may have gotten it with the
current holders. Mary, Ann, Casta and I had all been living on the river
recently and maybe the food from there was better or just more nutritious.
On the other hand, it may have had nothing to do with it.

I had been watching the weather and wishing I could do something
about it. We needed the snow this winter and rain in the spring. If the
drought continued, all our on-going efforts would be for naught. We need
some spiritual help to get the weather to cooperate. The thing we need
most is a drum and to see if we could come together for a rain dance. It
would have to be for a snow dance instead because of the time of year. It
could work also for a good communal get together and help bring some of
the interested singles into the open.

I called the tribe leaders together and asked if anyone in their
groups would know how to make a drum. They had never seen a drum and
didn't know who might have that kind of knowledge. I explained the
purpose of one and the most logical way to build it. It would require a
rawhide for the drum surface and a base unit for amplification. We would

eed a hollow log and Mary should have a skin to stretch over it. The size of the log and the thickness of the rawhide would make a difference in the sound that it would produce. Each of the tribes decided to make their own drum and would see who had the best one. I reminded them that the amount of rawhide was limited so they needed to keep the size of the hollow log down to something reasonable. All the bark would have to be removed and holes in the sides would reduce the sound it made.

The tribes took on this task with much enthusiasm. There were no hollow trees around so the next best thing was to use a log that had been burn down to a stump. Those were much easier to get or create and soon we had teams of men and women working on several at each tribe site. The ones that had holes or bad spots in them were turned back into firewood. I knew that pine wood wasn't the best tone carrier but we didn't have any other type of wood to work with yet. The shorter ones could be hollowed out faster than the long ones, so all the tribes spent more time with those. They could work on longer ones some other time. The tools each tribe had to work with dictated the time it would take to hollow out each log. I kept thinking that the Stone Age wasn't the greatest time to be alive but when you're the big dog it can't be all bad.

While the hunters and some women were working on the drums, I had the younger children picking up pine cones. They could be used as fire wood but I wanted them brought to me in a whole condition. I then had a couple other kids breaking them open and getting the seeds out. Some were already open and the seed just fell out and others had to be heated to get them to open up. I had no idea how many seeds would be good for replanting but the more we got the better the chances would be. The seeds were also edible as anyone who ever watched a squirrel would know. Replanting would only work if we got some snow and rain but the combinations of keep busy and opportunity goes hand in hand. The children from the two tribes didn't seem to notice that they looked different and could work and play together. With the adults busy on the drums and other work, they didn't have time to stop the kids from their involvement. Those that would think about it might just find me standing in their way.

I had been dragging pelts around for a long time now and to see some of them get used to make the drum heads was well worth it. Most of them were collected during the big flood and Mary helped me rework them later. I never got good at handling the skins but they didn't get ruined either. Now as the tribes put the drums together, those skins could be used to make some unique sounds. With each log being a different size and the skins a different thickness, they would produce a variety of sounds. I then demonstrated the two ways to create sound with either a drumstick or by hand. The kind of drumstick used would cause a sound that could be different also. Everyone in the tribes got to try their hand at it until they could decide who was best at it. We didn't want to waste any hides so each tribe was given only one and had to make that one work for their drum. If we get good at it, we may have more drums made later.

I talked to the tribe leaders to make sure all the hunters would be back before we had our winter snow dance. I also informed them that everyone was required to be there or have a note from their mother. In order to get an appropriate response from the spirit world, we needed to have complete participations. The process of making everyone understand that the old ways of fighting for territory was over. Everything needed to be shared in order to have a chance for long term survival. We would need each and everyone to believe that it would snow if we asked for it as a whole group and not as individuals. I told them that the Shamans could do many things on their own but the things that affect all the tribes needed all their participation. The lack of unity among the tribes was the cause of the current problems. This would be an ongoing situation for most of the winter, as all the tribes had been ingrained with the thought of "us first" philosophy. I continued to harp on the fact that we all had to work together. Some individual competition would be allowed but nothing that might bring about the feelings of isolation for any one or their tribe. I then told them that I would talk to each tribe in turn and give them the same speech. I would start with the smallest tribe and work up to the largest. I then sent the leaders off to tell their members what I said and that I would be talking to all of them. If anyone had questions they could ask at that time and I would be glad to answer. What we planned to do might not be pretty but it was important.

I had been working on a special project since getting to the hot springs. I wanted to make a really big show of my power and the connection to the spirit world. I knew from a historical point that many spiritual leaders used sleight of hand and other tricks to influence the general public. I would take a few minutes each evening to get the four talismans together and concentrate on black magic. Actually, it was black powder instead. I knew that sulfur was one of the ingredients along with charcoal and needed help with the rest of the formula. When the picture of the cave that the boy and writings were in kept coming back to me, I couldn't see the connection. It would sometimes show the movement of the bats as they went in and out of the cave. I would wake up in the middle of the night with the smell of the cave in my nostrils. It took about a week or so of that to get it into my thick skull.

It was the bat guano or droppings that contained the special ingredient to complete the formula. It didn't work directly but needed to be treated first and mixed in the proper amounts. The yellow cake sulfur was the easiest to collect at the hot mud pool and the charcoal was scrapped off the burnt wood in the fire pit. It took a little longer to find another location of the bats as their cave had collapsed and they moved. Bakta was most helpful with the collecting of the guano once we located the new cave. I couldn't leave the springs area long enough to gather the material, so I sent Bakta as he was nearing adulthood and wanted to prove he could be trusted. I experimented with very small amounts of it until I thought it would work for my purpose. I then made enough to do the job and put it in a pouch to hang on my belt. I had thoughts of making a rocket with it but changed my mind. It would be a disaster if it blew up and hurt someone. I might think about that for sometime later with a lot more practice.

I waited until the weather seemed to be getting heavier as if the clouds held more moisture. It was the kind of day that you would expect it to snow because it just felt like it. We had spent a few days getting a site ready by removing the vegetation and creating a large fire pit. It was surrounded by an area where everyone could gather and it was out on the prairie. I didn't want the trees to interfere with the smoke or to have them catch fire. As soon as it got dark, the drummers were called out to start the procession with a steady beat on their newly acquired percussion instruments. Each tribal leader followed the drummers with a lit torch, in front of their tribe.

There were about a hundred total members, of which were sixty percent female, and of those about 15 were children. That would mean that less than forty percent were male and 5 of those were children. If you discounted the older members and those that were already paired up, you would have about an even match between the men and women available. I did the math and wondered how the Shaman managed to get it so close.

The mating thing was a secondary consideration for now as we needed some form of precipitation to get the moisture back in the ground. If that failed, matching up people wouldn't make any difference to the overall picture. We would all be forced to move to another part of the world to get the mix of proper diet and better gene mix.

The firewood was stacked in such a way that it had a very clear four corner look to it. Beforehand, I had placed small amounts of black powder in each corner. I then instructed the leaders to represent their tribe by standing next to one of the four corners with their torch. I would let them know when to light the wood as I would be giving a short speech before we started.

The speech

"In the beginning, this land was fertile and the Flora and Fauna were abundant. It was a time before man came and the land was beautiful and green. It welcomed our forefathers with open arms and allowed them to live in peace and harmony. It supplied them with all of their needs and cradled them in its luxury. In time man forgot how important it was to have these things and sought to control it all. In doing so, most of the plants and animals were destroyed. It has now fallen on us to regenerate the land and make it whole again. We are in need of guidance from our ancestors and wish to have them participate in this ceremony with us. If it pleases them in what we do here then they will send us the required moisture to renew the land."

[281]

I then told the four tribal leaders to light the ceremonial fire. At the same time I cued the drummers to "hit it". It was a fantastic opening and caught some of the tribe members by surprise. I needed them to be excited and get their emotions up and this did the trick. I then started the dance by waving my hands and stomping my feet. I then coaxed others to join me and pulled Mary in to the circle. Ann took her cue from that and pulled Casta in and we spun each other around and grabbed others as we went. There was no formality to any of this, just the need to get as many participants as possible. Before long, we had everyone stomping and waving and hollering to the beat of the four drummers. I would toss some black powder on the fire every once in a while to keep the excitement going.

I sent up requests to our ancestors to send down snow to replenish the ground and make it green again. We continued this activity until the fire had burned itself out. It appeared as if everyone had been involved and now they were tired. I sent them back to camp and stayed a little longer to make sure our request was heard. I held the talisman in my hand and looked up at the sky as the first snowflake came down and landed on my all too big nose. I said a thank you to the powers that be and called it a day.

I was now confident that we would not only survive, but prosper. I knew in that instant that I would be a father to our son.

There are many more hurdles to get over before we can be a single people but the beginnings are now in place and I will do the best I can to propagate it.